the BINGE WATCHER'S guide to The Twilight Zone

AN UNOFFICIAL JOURNEY

Jacob Trussell

The Binge Watcher's Guide to The Twilight Zon: An Unofficial Journey ©Jacob Trussell 2021

All Rights Reserved. No part of this book may be reproduced or transmitted in any form or by any means, electronic or mechanical, including photocopying, without permission in writing from the publisher.

The Binge Watcher's Guide is a Trademark of Riverdale Avenue Books

For more information contact:
Riverdale Avenue Books
5676 Riverdale Avenue
Riverdale, NY 10471.

www.riverdaleavebooks.com
Design by www.formatting4U.com
Cover by Scott Carpenter

Digital ISBN: 9781626015838

Trade Paperback ISBN: 9781626015845

First Edition, May 2021

*To my wife, my family,
and Rod Serling*

Table of Contents

INTRODUCTION 1
ZEITGEIST 5
   "You Are About to Enter Another Dimension" 5
   As a Child 6
   Rod Serling's War 7
   Radio Days 8
   Getting in The Zone 10
   The Fifth Dimension 15
   It's Twilight Time 17
Before You Watch 21
   "There's a Signpost Up Ahead" 22
   "The Time Element" 23
   Mini Binges 25
      The Scariest Binge 26
      The Funniest Binge 27
      The Cerebral Binge 27
      The Romantic Binge 28
      The Sweetest Binge 28
      The Socially Relevant Binge 28
      The War Binge 29
      The Atomic Fear Binge 29
      The Best of Serling Binge 29
      The Best of Matheson Binge 30
      The Best of Beaumont Binge 30
      The Unsung Binge 31
      The Unequivocally Best Remembered 31
   Where to Binge 32
If You Watch Only One Episode 355
AFTER YOU WATCH 361
   Welcome to the Night Gallery 361
   Entering The New Twilight Zone 364
   The Lost Classics 368
   Twilight Zone in the New Millennium 369
   Twilight Zone Returns 371
   Films from the Fifth Dimension 373
Appendix 381
About the Author 383

INTRODUCTION

"You Unlock This Door with the Key of Imagination"

You know *The Twilight Zone*. Maybe you haven't seen a single episode, but you still know *The Twilight Zone*. You can probably hum Marius Constant's iconic theme music, or recall famous scenes like when a bookworm's glasses break on the steps of a bombed-out library. You know these things because *The Twilight Zone* is ingrained in our culture. If you don't believe me, just look into the bewildered eyes of someone who feels "like they're in *The Twilight Zone*," or in the bright faces of recognition when you mention the show to a group of friends. The series has endured because it offers new perspectives on life by letting audiences indulge in the fun mysteries of the universe.

More simply though, *The Twilight Zone* has remained popular decades after it first aired for two reasons: binge watching and holiday marathons.

The Twilight Zone saw its first resurgence in the immediate years following its cancellation in 1964. The series was sold into syndication to local television stations around the country, where it cultivated a growing fanbase of "Zoners" who may have missed it during its original broadcast. While late night reruns brought the show to prominence in collegiate circles, it was a series of annual holiday marathons that turned *The Twilight Zone* from a simple television show into a cherished family tradition.

There is some debate over when the marathons officially began, but you can narrow it down to two separate stations: KTLA in California and WPIX in New York. In 1991, KTLA's program director Mark Sonnenberg told the L.A. *Times* that the first *Twilight Zone* marathon at his station was on Thanksgiving Day, 1980. The 12-hour block of episodes was a hit, so they followed that up three years later with an Independence Day marathon, and soon other stations joined in and gave other holidays, from Memorial Day to New Years, the *Twilight Zone* treatment.

These local holiday marathons helped popularize the series in two of the biggest television markets in the country, but it wouldn't be until The Sci-Fi Channel (prior to their rebranding as SyFy) took over duties in 1995 that the local tradition became a national one. Now anyone with a cable package, from anywhere in the country, could watch the series with a pristine quality that they wouldn't get from their local rabbit ear channels. Cable TV also expanded the marathon into multiple days' worth of hand-curated classics, so you could now kick back on the morning of New Year's Eve and enjoy *The Twilight Zone* well through the early hours of January 2nd. If that's not the ultimate binge watch, I don't know what is.

Before streaming put every episode in the palm of our hand, these marathons were how millennials like me were exposed to the series. Every holiday break from school we could post up on the couch, catch a mix of classic and "forgotten" episodes, and get a real feel for what the show—and by extension its creator Rod Serling—was all about.

The first marathon I remember watching was on a local Central Texas station in the early 1990s. What episodes I watched are blurry, but the show was impactful enough to make a lifelong fan out of a five-year-old. After that, I found myself gravitating towards anything related to the series, especially eye-catching oddities like the *Twilight Zone* pinball machine. I have a distinct memory of being transfixed by a curio shop displayed in the backglass art teeming with *Zone* iconography where an imposing figure, clad in a black suit, stood on the threshold of a doorway to the unimaginable. It's the kind of image children live to get lost in.

My parents later bought me a beat-up copy of *More Stories from The Twilight Zone* where I got my first taste of classic episodes like "The Odyssey of Flight 33." Sure, I didn't *really* understand what I was reading, but it didn't matter. The world that was opened to me was unbelievably alluring. I remember staring at the cover portrait of Serling, bronze moons gradually eclipsing his face, and wondering "Who *is* this guy?"

My story isn't unique. Ask any number of fans and they'll tell you these marathons are how they fell in love with *The Twilight Zone* too. It's just how the series was able to sustain its popularity with every generation. What *is* unique is that audiences fell in love with the show by binge watching, decades before binging became the new normal.

The Twilight Zone makes for such a great holiday binge because the series is like comfort food. It's pop entertainment with a message that can connect with both kids and adults, because it follows a tried-and-true formula filled with surprises. You start with an opening narration that frames a character-driven supernatural mystery that waits until the very last moment to pull the rug out from under you. The twist endings, akin to magic tricks, kept us tuned in episode after episode, delighting us through unexpected reveals like an alien short order cook or the beautiful face of an "ugly" woman. These energizing endings were all the motivation we needed to rewatch episodes over and over again, looking for clues and discussing theories with friends about what it all meant.

In 2013, when binge watching was just becoming the norm, cultural anthropologist Grant McCracken told CNN that binging is "...not reckless or indulgent. It's a smart and an even contemplative way to watch certain kinds of TV. Good TV especially." This is why *The Twilight Zone* was made to be binged. The marathon model is how the show got its hooks into the nation's soul, because watching multiple episodes, back to back, allowed us to view the series as more than just a fun look into the "dimension beyond that which is known to man."

And now we don't have to wait for the holidays to get a chance to revisit our favorite stories, we can just click over an app on our TV and have all 156 episodes at our fingertips.

Rod Serling maybe made an inauspicious decision selling the series' syndication rights to CBS, but if it wasn't for this choice—and how brazen the network was in peddling the show to local stations—we may not have seen the proliferation of *The Twilight Zone* into modern Americana. Now it's not only a holiday and pop culture staple, but a common ground that can connect people from all walks of life. In no insignificant way, *The Twilight Zone* has become like great American folklore, touchstones that every generation can use to learn about life and what might come next.

Jacob Trussell

* * *

There are a lot of compendiums on *The Twilight Zone* out there. Some delve into the show's striking visuals, while others look at it from a philosophical perspective, but most just offer a backstage peek at the ins and outs of producing the pivotal series. None of these are more popular, or exhaustive, than Marc Scott Zicree's *The Twilight Zone Companion*. First published in 1982, and now in its third edition, the companion is the be-all-end-all tome that every fan of the series should read if they want firsthand accounts of what it was like creating the series, being on set, and experiencing Serling's humble genius.

But what I aim to do in *The Binge Watcher's Guide to The Twilight Zone* is offer you something the *Companion* does not: a microscopic look into the themes and ideas that Serling posed to give you deeper insight into why the show still resonates today. I'll look at how the socio-political turmoil of the early 1960s influenced Serling's life and work, and how he used *The Twilight Zone* as a bully pulpit to push back against everything from racism and censorship to McCarthyism and totalitarians. By taking a modern perspective, I will illustrate why the show is as relevant now as it was 60 years ago and shed light on what I think Serling may have fought against in the 21st century. Whether this is your first trip to the *Zone* or you're an old fan returning for one more round, this retrospective is an opportunity to engage with the timeless classic in a way that can help you make sense of our here and now.

In 2021, our reality is overflowing with uncertainty and nothing feels right anymore, like we've looked into a mirror and seen a face that wasn't our own. We're living through a time when the world is on the precipice of raising a midnight sun, authoritarians are attempting to label cultural institutions as obsolete, and our individuality is slipping through our fingers. Are these ripped from the headlines, or are they stories from the mind of Rod Serling? If you are looking to make better sense of our future, you don't have to keep your eyes peeled for a signpost up ahead. We've already crossed over into *The Twilight Zone*.

ZEITGEIST

"You Are About to Enter Another Dimension"

If you binge *The Twilight Zone* on Netflix, you'll be met with the amusing parental guidelines TV-14 for "fear and smoking." Fear we get; the show is famously known for chilling plots and bleak twist endings that can prove too intense for younger viewers, but smoking? That can only be attributed to the cigarette clenched between the fingers of the show's creator Rod Serling as he voices *The Twilight Zone*'s iconic narration.

In the final episode of Season One, before an audience consisting of producer Buck Houghton, director Ralph Nelson, and the watchful eye of cinematographer George T. Clemens, Rod Serling—with thin wisps of smoke spiraling up from a cigarette anxiously gripped in his hand—entered the living rooms of countless homes for the very first time. Serling has said that "Every writer is a frustrated actor who recites his lines in the hidden auditorium of his skull," but you wouldn't know that by watching him in the final moments of "A World of His Own." His narration is spoken through clenched teeth with an unusual staccato, yet he's perfectly at ease, unaware that he was on the precipice of global celebrity with a show that would spawn theme park rides and board games.

The success of *The Twilight Zone* came from his dark fantasia's powerful storytelling, but it was Serling himself—black tied with a cigarette by his side—that elevated it to a pillar of pop culture. He's the criterion of science and superstition that would inspire generations of writers to create strange new worlds that entertained and enlightened us through their individual convictions on truth and justice. Serling introduced audiences to a new way of looking at the world, and the people within it, in a manner they maybe hadn't considered before.

But who *was* Rod Serling? That really depends on who you ask. The entertainment industry described him as television's golden boy and angry young man, an enfant terrible of live TV who had no qualms pushing the limits of what could and couldn't be said on broadcast. That title is counter to the loving—if not often distant—husband and father he was to Carol Serling and their two daughters, Jodi and Anne.

He was also a man whose thoughts were frequently spirited back to his formative years in Binghamton, New York, with its vibrant main street spotted with gazebos and Victorian era architecture. These would become the central locale for the nostalgia-driven, world-weary proxies he'd write like Martin Sloan in "Walking Distance" or Gart Williams in "A Stop at Willoughby." These stories were portkeys for Serling, giving him a way to return home whenever he needed, even when he was a continent away in *The Twilight Zone*'s Culver City studios. Escaping to a quieter life where he didn't have to be the angry young man trying to save the world is how he recharged, filling him with the energy that allowed him to write like he was running out of time.

No one could have known how little time he had left. No one, except Rod Serling.

As a Child

Serling's birth, in a way, was a miracle. In the first instance of a *Zone* affecting the Serling's lives, his father Samuel worked as a cleric for General George Goethals in the Panama Canal Zone. It was there that Samuel's wife Esther contracted Yellow Fever and was told she would be unable to conceive another child. And yet, against all odds she proved them wrong and Rodman Edward was born on Christmas Day, 1924.

Growing up, Rod was a rambunctious, motor mouth of a kid who loved pulling pranks and cracking jokes. After catching matinees and double features with his brother Robert (who was seven years his senior), Rod would act out the entire film to his bemused parents. They recognized his knack for performance and built Rod a small stage in their basement to put on comedies and musicals for his primary school friends.

An Unofficial Journey Into The Twilight Zone

As Rod matured, so did his charisma. By all accounts, he was Binghamton's resident womanizer, never in short supply of a Friday night date. This would be an attitude he'd carry through his life and career. He may have been a shrewd, creative businessman, but he made professional strides with his talent *and* effervescent charm. Serling had a way of making impressions—on women and executives—that would prove pivotal in an entertainment industry on the verge of booming.

The one thing Serling couldn't achieve with his charm however, was a spot on his high school football team. While he had the courage and drive of a quarterback, Serling was too small to be effective on the field. His self-consciousness over his height would stick with him throughout his life, from *The Twilight Zone* to his time in the army.

Rod Serling's War

Counter to the peace activist he'd mature into, young Rod Serling wanted to join the fight against the Nazis in World War II. He originally had his sights set on a dangerous career as a tail gunner, but after watching military newsreels detailing allied efforts, Serling decided he'd rather hunt down Hitler as a paratrooper. As such, he was prepared to drop out of high school and enlist immediately, but a civics professor persuaded him into finishing his degree because, as he pointed out, Serling needed to plan for his life *after* the war.

Serling's virulent urgency to combat the Axis Alliance and their anti-Semitic ilk was likely born out of his Jewish heritage as much as his American patriotism. His Judaism would be an aspect of Serling's identity he'd examine throughout his writing career, even after he converted to Unitarianism in college.

Though his dreams of becoming a paratrooper were almost crushed by his slight frame and short stature, he proved himself capable to his commanding officers during training through his sheer will and determination. Unfortunately however, his dreams of directly fighting the Nazi's were stymied when he was ordered far from the European front to the Pacific Theatre facing Japanese forces.

Serling's entire body of work would be shaped by his time in the Pacific—specifically the Philippines—but none more so than *The Twilight Zone*. Surrounded by death and despair, the otherworldly detachment of war would be one of the essential building blocks of the series. Serling was given a front row seat to the traumatic psychological effects of combat, both to his fellow soldiers and himself.

In an early short story he penned, called "First Squad, First Platoon," he recounts a true event about a cut-up soldier screaming praises for crates of rations as they're being air-dropped. The supply containers pushed from the cargo planes were meant to land safely in their camp, but the chutes didn't pull in time and the crates came thundering down around scrambling soldiers. As the rest of the squad took cover, this one soldier proudly kept his head raised towards the sky, delirious with relief. As they called for him, Serling watched as the man was decapitated by one of the containers. Through all the tough leathery exterior of these G.I.'s, watching something like that doubtlessly changes you for life.

It was one of the many grim realities that Serling and the rest of his company would face, including his own near fatal encounter. During the Battle of Leyte, a Japanese soldier stepped mere feet in front of Serling, catching him in his crosshairs. Serling froze, death staring him in the face, but luckily someone from his regiment saw the soldier and fired off a shot first, saving his life. Serling never publicly discussed his brushes with death, but it's a demon he exorcised in many scripts of *The Twilight Zone*, like "The Purple Testament" and "A Quality of Mercy."

That latter episode ends in almost the same way Serling's own stint in the army did, with word that the atomic bomb had been dropped on Japan. An entire generation was redefined by the war, but the whole world changed after the destruction of Hiroshima. On September 2nd, 1945 the Japanese forces would formally surrender, but Rod Serling's life would be altered for a different reason; his father had passed away from a heart attack at only 55.

Radio Days

Serling was deeply affected by the death of his father, magnified by the fact that the Army refused to give him emergency leave to attend the funeral, as his company was occupying post-war Japan. After being discharged and disillusioned with the military, Serling attended Antioch College in Yellow Springs, Ohio, where his interest in professional writing for radio blossomed. His first experience with the medium had been during the war when he wrote a propaganda skit for Jack Benny's *Amphitheatre in the Jungle* program on the shortwave "mosquito network" radio. Serling was humbly shocked when Benny recalled the skit decades later as a guest on the comedian's television show.

It's hard to really comprehend just how monumental radio entertainment was during this golden age. Radio wasn't like podcasts, or what we know of satellite stations today. It was an entirely new kind of entertainment producing everything we take for granted, such as the superhero antics of *The Shadow,* the skin crawling horror stories in Arch Oboler's *Lights Out,* or the socially relevant dramas of Norman Corwin, who would directly inspire Serling's own work. There was a voracious appetite for radio, and new writers were ready to feed it.

The radio was how the entertainment industry got its first "viral sensation" with the infamous broadcast of H.G. Wells' *War of the Worlds*. Creator Orson Welles unintentionally sent the tri-state area into a panic as he duped Grover's Bend, New Jersey into believing Martians had landed in their own backyard. Just narrowly escaping legal blame for the mass hysteria he ignited, Welles made people buy in wholesale to what he was selling, and it's a lesson that Serling likely learned from.

After an internship at WNYC radio in New York—and following his marriage to Carol Kramer—Serling was looking for economic stability that didn't require him to test parachutes, and he found it managing the Antioch Broadcasting System, his campus radio station. From November 1948 through February 1949, Serling wrote, produced, and frequently starred in his own Corwin-esque radio anthology series—a sort of predecessor to a predecessor of *The Twilight Zone* that employed themes and ideas he would cement in his seminal show's most famous episodes.

A turning point came for Serling when Carol persuaded him to submit a script to *The Dr. Christian Show*, a light medical melodrama that held an annual writing competition, featuring Serling-idol Arch Oboler as one of the judges. To his delight—and surprise—Serling won third prize, which included a check for $500 and an all-expense paid trip to New York City to accept the award on-air. There he would meet fellow competition winner Earl Hamner, Jr. who he would later collaborate with on *The Twilight Zone*. Serling had gotten his foot in the door, and he wasn't about to remove it for the world.

After graduating from Antioch, Serling found a place to expand his professional writing career at WLW-AM in Cincinnati, and eventually their sister station WLW-T for the emerging television market. The writer found solace in his new job because he could now work on both radio *and* television scripts, but he wasn't anticipating the ennui he'd experience churning out multiple scripts a week for asinine sitcoms and variety shows.

Still, at WLW he was able to stretch the muscles he'd need for his future in television through *The Storm, a* dramatic local anthology series that would be the true precursor to the work he'd revolutionize over a decade later. But Serling could see the writing on the wall of what awaited him if he kept plunking out radio scripts in Cincinnati. It was either acquiesce to a life of boring commercial copy or take a personal and professional risk by diving headlong into live, televised drama.

And that's exactly what he did.

Getting in The Zone

Before Serling left WLW he was able to get representation in New York from literary agent Blanche Gaines, who facilitated the sale of his initial teleplays to the major networks at the time—CBS, NBC, ABC and DuMont. Serling's television debut came on April 29th, 1952 on NBC's *Armstrong Circle Theatre,* and was followed quickly by teleplays on *Lux Video Theatre, Hallmark Hall of Fame* and *Kraft Television Theatre*.

Through 1953, Serling had a modicum of success with scripts like "The Strike" (1954), which was a play about a military general forced to make a fatal decision in war-torn Korea. "The Strike" and its thorny anti-war sentiments were seen as provocative at the time, giving Serling his first taste of controversy.

My personal favorite early teleplay of his is a haunting episode of *Suspense* called "Nightmare at Ground Zero" (1953), about a sculptor who replaces a bombsite test dummy with his bedeviling wife on the eve of a nuclear blast. It's bizarre, expressionistic and sickly evocative of a drive-in horror movie, except Serling fills his world with husbands and wives rather than killers and lunatics. These are everyday, average people who become trapped in a frightening downward spiral against the backdrop of a looming atomic threat. But none of these stories could match the phenomenon that would be "Patterns" (1955), the teleplay that would give him his name, his star, and a one-way ticket to *The Twilight Zone*.

Part of the anthology program *The United States Steel Hour*, "Patterns" was a scathing look into the modern corporate world through the eyes of Fred Staples (Richard Kiley), a young executive hired to work for the imposing Walter Ramsie (Everett Sloan). Ramsie is a sociopath who lords over his company like an unchecked dictator, gaslighting and chiding his Vice President Andy Sloan (Ed Begley) until he suffers a fatal heart attack. In a complicated, if not entirely realistic twist Staples blames Ramsie for Sloan's death, but decides to stay on as Vice President for the sole purpose of challenging and eventually usurping his boss. Besides, as he tells his wife, he really *does* want the job.

The teleplay was a runaway hit, best represented by an immediate reaction that the Serlings were not anticipating. So much so they didn't even tune in to the live broadcast, instead going for a night out to celebrate Rod's belated birthday. As Carol Serling told *Twilight Zone Magazine*, "We had just moved to the east coast. We went out the night the show aired, and we'd told the babysitter that no one would call because we had just moved to town. And the phone just started ringing and didn't stop for years!" When they returned home, their babysitter was frazzled after screening the non-stop carousel of congratulations.

The *New York Times* Jack Gould would say of the teleplay, "The enthusiasm is justified. In writing, acting and direction, 'Patterns' will stand as one of the high points in the TV medium's evolution... For sheer power of narrative, forcefulness of characterization and brilliant climax, Mr. Serling's work is a creative triumph that can stand on its own." Needless to say, the Serlings *did* tune into the unprecedented second airing of "Patterns" a month later; it was the first time a teleplay had ever been restaged and rebroadcast.

Serling followed "Patterns" with a series of less-than-successful teleplays like "The Rack" (1955), about a Korean War veteran facing charges of cowardice and treason, whose tepid response still warranted a film adaptation starring Paul Newman. "The Arena" (1956), for *Studio One in Hollywood,* saw a newly elected Congressman go toe-to-toe with a senior Representative who disparaged his father years before. Armed with the knowledge that the senior Rep was involved with a Ku Klux Klan-style group during the Great Depression, the young man looks to kneecap the Representative before ultimately taking the moral high ground. What knocked the wind out of this interesting setup, however, was *Studio One*'s sponsors. The political issues his characters were debating in the extended scenes on the House floor had to be neutered and vague, straying from any content that could alienate current or potential consumers. Despite pushback, Serling lost the fight, and "The Arena" was sidelined as an ambitious, if ambiguous, peek into American politics.

In the same month "The Arena" premiered, Serling was dealt his first major sponsor controversy with "Noon on Doomsday" (1956). Serling drew inspiration for the teleplay directly from the 1955 case of Emmett Till, a young Black teenager lynched by a group of white men who were subsequently found not guilty by a local jury of peers. The sponsors didn't want to anger viewers with a story about racial prejudice, so they forced Serling to change the plot to such a degree that it didn't resemble the point he wanted to make about hate in an insulated community.

Deeply attuned to the injustices in the world, Serling's clashes with program sponsors over the content of his teleplays can often be tantamount to civil disobedience. He wanted to make the voiceless heard by giving a platform to stories that needed to be told. "Noon on Doomsday" may have been one of the first teleplays that would mire Serling in contention with studio executives, but it was also one of the first times he took a stand for a social issue he felt deeply about. As the Civil Rights movement began in the mid-1950s, Rod Serling wasn't afraid to say the name Emmett Till. It was incredibly important that a white man used his privilege to try and get the nation to understand the evils of prejudice, especially in 1956. This was only the beginning of Serling's friction with corporate sponsors, a fight that would start in America, and end in *The Twilight Zone*.

An Unofficial Journey Into The Twilight Zone

During the time immediately following "Patterns," Serling was wracked with the anxiety of replicating his gargantuan success. "The Arena" and "Noon on Doomsday" weren't connecting with audiences in the way he wanted—likely because of meddling sponsors—and it caused television critics to believe they spoke too soon in saying that Serling was the Arthur Miller of live TV. In reality, their reassessment of Serling's prodigious talents were premature themselves, because a year after "Patterns" he went all 12 rounds with "Requiem for a Heavyweight" (1956).

When he had first enlisted in the Army as a paratrooper, Serling's unit was sequestered for two years waiting for orders to actually join the fight. During this time, his unit held boxing tournaments where Serling was a flyweight. Even with his slight frame, he was able to go 16 bouts, advancing to the division finals before his 17th—and career ending—final fight left him with a shattered nose. While Serling wouldn't box again, the mentality he learned in the ring would stay with him and become paramount to the lived-in feel of "Requiem."

The teleplay premiered on October 11th, 1956 on *Playhouse 90*. The story follows Harlan "Mountain" McClintock (Jack Palance), an almost-heavyweight champion of the world, who is forced into retirement after receiving one too many right hooks to the head. Unsure of what to do with the rest of his life in a world with no need for his unique talents, his cut-man Army (Ed Wynn) brings him to a social worker (Kim Hunter) who, being touched by his brusque gentleness, proposes he become a boxing instructor for a boys camp in the Adirondacks. Mountain is enthusiastic about this change, but his manager Maish (Keenan Wynn) is pushing him into professional wrestling so he can weasel out of a debt to the mob. Torn by loyalty to his manager, but unwilling to tarnish his reputation as a fighter who doesn't take dives, Mountain stands up for himself and turns his back on Maish to start a new life, with a new purpose.

The teleplay was a resounding success, garnering multiple awards and was restaged across the world, most notably on the BBC with a then unknown Sean Connery in the role of Mountain. The film version was also a remarkable achievement, with the unprecedented acting talents of Julie Harris, Mickey Rooney, and career best work from both Anthony Quinn as Mountain and Jackie Gleason as Maish.

Jacob Trussell

Muhammad Ali—then Cassius Clay—even has a small cameo in the opening scenes as the final boxer to face Mountain! The film would restore Serling's original ending where Mountain coalesces and becomes a wrestler and saves Maish's life, but dooms his own. It's a bleak and powerful portrait of the inner struggle of a fighter on his last legs, decades before Martin Scorsese and Robert De Niro would have their own crack at it with *Raging Bull* (1980).

Serling would follow up the success of "Requiem" with a trio of *Playhouse 90* teleplays: "The Comedian" (1957), "A Town Has Turned to Dust" (1958), and "The Velvet Alley" (1959). About an amoral comic, "The Comedian" was the first instance of Serling working with Mickey Rooney who would later star in the film version of *Requiem* and *The Twilight Zone* episode "The Last Night of the Jockey." Rooney's temperament on set would prove perfectly suited to entertainer Sammy Hogarth who shamelessly terrorized his writing staff and belittled his older brother Lester (Mel Tormé). Lester is crushed when he learns that Sammy made a pass at his wife Julie (Kim Hunter) on their wedding night, but there's nothing he can do about it as he's wholly dependent on Sammy. And in the final devastating moment, he turns his back on his wife to stay with his brother, resigning himself to life as a punching bag. It's a blistering look at ego and power in the entertainment industry, anchored by a virtuosic performance from Rooney who earned an Emmy nomination alongside wins for Outstanding Program, and Serling's teleplay.

With "A Town Has Turned to Dust" Serling revisited the Emmett Till case, but while "Noon on Doomsday" focused on the trial that acquitted the murderers, "Dust" shifted its view to the inciting incident: the lynching. In a harrowing opening act, Sheriff Harvey Denton (Rod Steiger) vainly attempts to protect Pancho Rivera (Eugene Iglesias), a Latino man that shopkeep Jerry Paul (William Shatner) claims robbed his store and made a pass at his wife Annamay (Fay Spain). Jerry has riled up the town against Pancho and, despite protestations from Denton, they cart him away and hang him in the town square. Jerry remains indignant at his actions and doubles down on his prejudice, even as the rest of the town becomes disenchanted to what happened.

The following day, after a group of local Mexican families refuse to enter his store, Jerry goads one of them into a fight. The sheriff can sense what is happening and shoots Jerry dead before he can incite another mob. Weary and filled with guilt, he confesses that a decade before *he* had been like Jerry, using his prejudices to also lynch an unconvicted man. It's a chilling snapshot of the worlds that can exist in small parochial communities across the country. Serling wanted to show that these people *knew* what they were doing was wrong, they just didn't care. Capturing the horror at the heart of racism, "Dust" is easily Serling's most powerful, and dark, teleplay from this period.

Serling ended this run of successes with "The Velvet Alley," his personal diatribe against the television industry. The teleplay details the skyrocketing success of Ernie Pandish (Art Carney), a writer supported by his wife Pat (Katharine Bard) and his manager Max Salter (Jack Klugman). Following a similar trajectory of Serling's own ascent into Hollywood, Ernie's view on life and his place in it begins to change, leaving no room for either his wife or his manager, whom he fires as his fame exceeds him.

Despite his success, and surrounded by friends, Ernie is sunk with loneliness when he receives word that Max has suffered a fatal heart attack. In despair, he returns to New York looking to reconcile with his father, only to be greeted with scorn for forgetting where he came from. You can see Serling's own pain for the decisions he had made in his past mirrored in the script, specifically his own experience of letting go long-time manager Blanche Gaines after moving to the west coast. He may be contemptuous about how the industry chews you up and spits you out, but just like Fred Staples at the end of "Patterns," Serling *wanted* the job he had in television. And later that same year, his future in the medium would be set in stone.

The Fifth Dimension

In the midst of these post-"Requiem" successes was "The Time Element" (1958). A teleplay for the *Westinghouse Desilu Playhouse*—an anthology show from Lucille Ball and Desi Arnaz—it was about an everyman who reluctantly visits a psychiatrist for a recurring nightmare. "The Time Element" served as a backdoor pilot for *The Twilight Zone,* incorporating the fundamental themes that the series would embody over the following year (learn more about this episode in the chapter *Before You Watch!*)

Before *The Twilight Zone* premiered in 1959, Rod Serling was interviewed by Mike Wallace (*60 Minutes*) where he was asked, "You're going to be obviously working so hard on *The Twilight Zone* that in essence, for the time being and for the foreseeable future, you've given up on writing anything important for television, right?" Like any good boxer Serling countered with a bluff replying, "If by important you mean I'm not going to try to delve into current social problems dramatically, you're quite right. I'm not."

What Serling didn't want the world—but more specifically the network executives—to know is how false that statement was. He wasn't done talking about the things that mattered the most to him, he had just figured out a way to do it under the nose of his sponsors and censors in an alternate reality called *The Twilight Zone*. As he said, "I found that it was all right to have Martians saying things Democrats and Republicans could never say." And for five critically acclaimed seasons that's exactly what he did.

Of the 156 episodes of *The Twilight Zone*, Serling wrote a remarkable 92 of them. This was auteurism on television at a time when that didn't exist. His unwavering hand supplied the series with a tone, look, and feel that was consistently engaging and thought provoking. Not only did Serling have his creative fingers in every single episode, but his vision of what the show was trying to say overshadowed any monster-of-the-week stories that peppered less than stellar trips into the *Zone*. These facts stand alone as to why the series has flourished over 60 years later—and why attempts at reviving it fall short. To effectively replicate what he did on television would require a showrunner to dedicate the same amount of time, involvement, and dedication to the craft of insightful genre storytelling that Serling gave the original series. It's a tall order not many can fill, even Academy Award winners.

The Twilight Zone, and Serling himself, would be bountifully awarded from critic's circles through the series run. In the first two seasons alone, it would win three Emmy Awards, one for George T. Clemens cinematography, and the others for Serling's writing. It would go on to be nominated for four more Emmys, including Outstanding Achievement in Art Direction for Philip Barber, two more cinematography nominations for Clemens and, for Season Three, a final writing achievement for Serling. That same season would also award Serling his sole Golden Globe for Best TV Producer and Director. The series would go on to be nominated for, and win various other awards beyond the major shows, including multiple Hugo Awards and Writers Guild of America and Directors Guild of America nominations. These awards and nominations are in addition to the tidal wave of honors Serling would receive total in his career, including the first Peabody Award for television writing with "Requiem for a Heavyweight," an Edgar Award for *Night Gallery*, and inevitably—in a gesture that surely would have tickled Serling the most—a posthumous star on the Hollywood Walk of Fame in 1988.

It's Twilight Time

After the fifth season of *The Twilight Zone*, Serling was understandably exhausted with fantasy television, and the industry as a whole. After the series was cancelled—a decision he was in agreement with—Serling recharged in his comfortable home in upstate New York while teaching classes at Ithaca College. He still pursued creative projects during these periods of gestation like John Frankenheimer's *Seven Days in May* (1964), about an attempted coup d'état in the US government that Serling adapted from the novel of the same name.

There was also *The Loner* (1965), an "existential western" starring Lloyd Bridges as an ex-soldier wandering a post-Civil War-ravaged America. Serling wanted his protagonist William Colton to be more philosopher than gunslinger, but CBS had other ideas and the series was cancelled after one season. In 1966, Serling penned the TV film *The Doomsday Flight* about an airplane with a bomb on board that would detonate if the aircraft dropped below a set altitude, a plot device that would be retooled for the smash 1994 action movie *Speed*. The film would haunt Serling in the weeks following the broadcast, as the Federal Aviation Administration reported copycat bomb threats had been called in to various airports across the country. On learning of this, Serling would say, "I wish to Christ I had written a stagecoach drama starring John Wayne instead. I wish I'd never been born."

Most famously of all, Serling co-wrote *Planet of the Apes*

(1968), even if most of his elaborate story was heavily altered. In his original, the film took place on a modernized planet populated by the titular apes. They go to work, wear business suits, have nuclear families—just like us! It would have proven too costly however, so the modern world became a primitive one. It was that alteration that the ending Serling wrote works so well, however. As George Taylor (Charlton Heston) escapes to the beach, he drops to his knees screaming, "They finally really did it" as we see before him the rubble of the Statue of Liberty. "You maniacs! You blew it up!" Serling may not have achieved the success in Hollywood he so wished for, but it's proof to his talent that this moment would go on to be one of the most iconic, lasting images in all of cinema.

Even though the series ended in 1964, *The Twilight Zone* was far from dead, and while neither a sixth season nor a Rod Serling helmed *Twilight Zone* movie ever came to fruition, he did shop a new genre anthology show around, catching the interest of NBC. Serling had edited an omnibus of scary stories called *Rod Serling's Triple W: Witches, Warlocks, and Werewolves* that the network wanted to adapt into a series. While they wanted a more conventional suspense show, Serling wished to approach themes of occultism maturely. The resulting series, *Night Gallery*, offered a similar setup to what Serling did with *The Twilight Zone*—he introduced each story, while writing a majority of the early scripts—but he relinquished any creative control so he wouldn't find himself in the same draining position he held on *The Twilight Zone*. This, unfortunately, would prove to be a mistake as his stories were re-edited to the point of becoming unrecognizable, with series producer Jack Laird writing out much of Serling's intelligent intentions. *Night Gallery* wasn't free of great episodes (for more go to *After You Watch*), but it failed to have the spark that made *The Twilight Zone* timeless.

The teleplay that cemented his meteoric rise, "Requiem for a Heavyweight," in many ways proved prophetic in what shaped his latter career. He found himself taking any job that came his way from small walk-on television guest star roles to, most mortifying of all, a shill for the kinds of sponsors he castigated a decade before. He became something of a cult spokesperson for anything and everything that needed his indelible touch from hocking floor wax and toothpaste, to purring over Radio Shack's electronics.

He did have highlights, like narrating the docuseries *The Undersea World* from famed explorer and conservationist Jacques Cousteau, to the pulpier *Encounter with the Unknown* and *UFOs: Past, Present, and Future*. He even had a six-month stint as host for the game show *Liars Club* where a panel of celebrities offered humorous descriptions of strange objects and contestants then had to guess who was telling the truth. Serling becoming a commercial spokesman isn't exactly Mountain McClintock donning a Native American headdress and chanting around the ring in the devastating original ending of *Requiem*, but it surely was an irony that did not elude him.

Between these jobs he admittedly did "for a buck," Serling focused his time on public speaking, extolling his virtues to graduating college classes or local chapters of the National Academy of Television Arts and Sciences, where he was president from 1965 to 1966. It was at one of these engagements that Serling first began to have health issues related to his unrelenting pace, not to mention the copious packs of cigarettes he smoked every day. The memory of his father's premature death from cardiac arrest at 55 was like a phantom throughout his life, and he explored this fatalism in his writing. In May 1975, like his father, Serling suffered his first heart attack, quickly followed by a second. On June 28th, in the middle of open-heart surgery, he suffered his third—and fatal. He was only 50.

It's cosmically frustrating that we never had the opportunity to see what Rod Serling would have created throughout the 1980s, especially as *The Twilight Zone* was having its first major resurgence. What would Serling have done with the ill-fated 1983 film, or the subsequent 1985 revival? What new, socially relevant films, novels or plays would he have written? Most heartbreaking of all is that Serling never got to see the gargantuan success *The Twilight Zone* has had, from the holiday marathons and postage stamps, to the action figures and video games. As a creator who put social and civil rights at the core of his work, imagine how thrilled he would have been to see a writer like Jordan Peele get the chance to pick up the torch he passed on.

What we can do is keep a promise that Serling hoped for in his final 1975 interview with Linda Brevelle for *Writer's Digest Magazine:* "I just want them to remember me 100 years from now. I don't care that they're not able to quote any single line that I've written. But just that they can say, 'Oh, he was a writer.' That's sufficiently an honored position for me."

Rod Serling will be remembered as a writer; his stories are carved into our collective consciousness like Martin Sloan's initials etched into his hometown gazebo in "Walking Distance." But he'll also be remembered as a cultural icon who affected societal change through the allegories he wove into his "land of both shadow and substance, of things and ideas." Rod Serling won't just be remembered 100 years from now—he'll be remembered forever. In this world, and the next.

Before You Watch

If there is one question you should keep in mind before you start your binge watch, it's this: where is *The Twilight Zone*? Is it a location, some hamlet that only exists in the creases of a map of the universe? Is it a feeling, that queasy sensation you get in the pit of your stomach when you know something isn't right? Or is it actually a state of mind, a proxy for the psychological issues we all struggle with?

We take for granted how open we are about our mental health in the 21st century. It's a collective issue that bonds us together by giving people an innate way to relate to one another. Finding someone who understands what you're living with is like finding a beacon in the middle of a storm you thought raged only against you. But when *The Twilight Zone* premiered in 1959, people were reticent to talk about their emotional problems. The stigma was that if you experienced something like bi-polar depression, you would be labeled "crazy." Even worse for soldiers returning from war was how little was known of Post-Traumatic Stress Disorder. Young men were coming back shadows of their former selves, and families and physicians had no way to adequately understand what they were going through.

Rod Serling had an acute awareness for the emotional needs of his fellow veterans because he also suffered from his own post-traumatic stress following his experiences during World War II. He intrinsically understood the reluctance these strong men had in discussing wounds invisible to the naked eye, so Serling produced stories that featured tough everymen dealing directly with their mental health as a way to dispel the toxic masculine myth that you are weak for openly talking about your feelings. There was still skepticism, slight distrust, and a whole lot of stereotypes, but for the first time on television we had people talking about their emotional well-being in a way that was free of judgment. Where is *The Twilight Zone*? It's in our mind's eye looking towards the vast unknowns of consciousness, full of the horrifying realities and dazzling fantasies that help us understand who we are.

"There's a Signpost Up Ahead"

When I jump into binging a new series, I want to go in as blind as possible. I'll cover my eyes when trailers pop up, avoid spoilers like the plague, and generally try to know as little about the show as possible. I want to get swept up in the story, surprised by the twists and turns that may have been forecast to me if I'd read reviews or paid attention to ads. But that's not exactly a luxury you get with *The Twilight Zone*.

The original series has grown into a TV version of *Aesop's Fables*, perennial parables that have been passed down for generations to the point that you likely already know "It's a cookbook," even if you've never seen "To Serve Man" (S3E24). Knowing these key elements won't ruin any fun of discovering (or rediscovering) the series, and they can even allow you to be more analytical throughout your binge. Use it as an opportunity to look below the surface at the writer's intention and ask yourself introspective questions like "What would I have done on Maple Street?"

As you prepare for your long journey into *The Twilight Zone*, also consider the social consciousness of the series, a quality I feel is routinely—but not unexpectedly—lost on both new and old fans, especially during a time in pop culture where people balk at politics in entertainment. On the surface, *The Twilight Zone* is remembered as a horror and science-fiction show, but Serling used genre tropes only so he could talk about relevant social issues without advertisers and executives calling his ideas too political. Rather than writing in frank terms about mental health, intolerance, fear of technology, and individuality, he masked these topics in fantastical—if unsubtle—allegories about robots and aliens, so that his liberal stories were practically censor-proof.

The fact is *The Twilight Zone* is nothing if not political, full of fury and ferocity from a man whose moral compass was perfectly attuned to the compassionate people we should all aspire to be. That's why, now more than ever, we need the dark fables of Rod Serling. The series provided the perfect soapbox for him to get his point of view across to a worldwide audience, but this wasn't just one man writing like he was running out of time, it was a collective of brilliant storytellers concocting narratives that begged you to reflect on your own values.

"The Time Element"

None of this is meant to make you feel overwhelmed at the onset of this television journey, but you still may want a primer before jumping into the zone of the unknown. There's no better place to start your voyage than "The Time Element," a 1958 teleplay that premiered on the *Westinghouse Desilu Playhouse*. This episode served as the backdoor pilot for *The Twilight Zone* and helps introduce key aspects we'd come to recognize in the series. "The Time Element" blends psychological realism with supernatural fantasy as told through a salt of the earth voice audiences could relate to, all tied together with a haunting twist ending that leaves the viewer exhilarated and contemplative. Everything Serling would tackle in his monumental series is right here in under 60 brief minutes.

Serling doesn't personally inform us that we're travelling through another dimension in "The Time Element," but the play still opens with a narration that is straight out of the *Zone*.

> *"Once upon a time there was a psychiatrist named Arnold Gillespie and a patient whose name was Peter Jenson. Mr. Jenson walked into the office nine minutes ago. It is 11 o'clock, Saturday morning, October 4th, 1958. It is perhaps chronologically trite to be so specific about an hour and a date but involved in this story is a time element."*

It's ham-fisted compared to what the writer would give in the series proper, but it still has that conversational tone we'd become accustomed to, as if we're being told an unbelievable tale from an old friend. The narration carries us into one of the most important locales of a Serling story: a psychiatrist office. The patient is Peter Jenson (William Bendix) who jokes to Dr. Arnold Gillespie (Martin Balsam) on arriving, "The only time I saw a psychiatrist before was in a cartoon!" This is a perfect summation of how therapy was perceived by the general TV viewing public in the late 1950s—something so foreign it's comical.

More than just countering stigmas around mental health, Serling looked to normalize therapy and psychiatry as something that should be as routine as seeing your general practitioner. Remember, we were still 20 to 30 years away from the introduction of TV therapists like Bob Hartley in *The Bob Newhart Show,* or Frasier Crane on *Cheers* who helped further break down barriers between the public perception of psychiatry and the actual good it can do.

One way Serling tried to change the stigma was by having addiction—specifically alcohol dependency—frequently factor into his scripts. Alcoholism was a mental disorder people could understand and relate to, so it wouldn't seem like such a strange concept to visit a psychiatrist for treatment. Serling would use alcoholism at length in *The Twilight Zone*, but it's only subtly introduced in "The Time Element." Even though Dr. Gillespie never asks about it, Jenson's prophetic dream starts with a blistering hangover that bleeds into constant day drinking. He never admits he has a problem, but we are made acutely aware of it by how the other clubgoers interact with him. Alcoholism is interwoven into the tapestry of Serling's stories as a way to make the need for mental health counseling feel legitimate.

Serling always described *The Twilight Zone* as fantasy mixed with science fiction, but horror is a major reason why the show continues to resonate with new generations. The terror Serling describes doesn't always come from obvious totems like a killer doll or an evil kid, but sometimes comes from the traumatic effects of global strife. The tension of "The Time Element" isn't sprung from why Jenson is in the past or how he traveled through time, it comes from the looming threat of war and the panic so many felt in Honolulu on the morning of December 7th, 1941. He would continue this fascination with the moral ambiguities of war throughout his career, always forcing you to consider the innocent lives caught in the crossfire.

It's not all heavy though! Serling's natural humor is ever present in "The Time Element," especially with Bendix's nervous, jittery performance. After trying to warn the police of the coming Japanese armada, the cops become suspicious of how Jenson knows things that haven't happened, but can't seem to remember who the sitting Vice President is. Feeling cornered and crazy, he slowly backs out of the office offering platitudes for why he made it up before flashing a peace sign and randomly yelling "Buy war bonds!" a common invitation from radio entertainers during World War II. Silly moments of levity like this would be peppered throughout *The Twilight Zone*, and they help make the show feel accessible.

Nothing defines *The Twilight Zone* more than its twist endings though, and "The Time Element" has a doozy of one. After Jenson describes his fear at what will happen if he doesn't wake up, Gillespie finds himself jolting awake and suddenly alone. When he checks his day planner, his schedule is completely clear. "What's going on?" he quietly thinks. Shaking off the strange feeling, he goes to his corner bar and orders a double whiskey—the same drink Jenson ordered throughout his dream. Gillespie notices a picture behind the bar of an old bartender that's the spitting image of Jenson. When he asks about it, he's told the man died during the attack on Pearl Harbor. Instantly sobered, we're left to sit there with Gillespie as he succumbs to perplexed sadness. Is there a rational explanation? Was Jenson real, or did Gillespie just imagine all of this in a fit of exhaustion? Serling's twist endings were shocking, and often fun, but overall they were disconcerting, forcing you to reconsider a world you thought you understood 60 minutes earlier. Rod Serling was blowing mid-century minds left and right, and years later the twists still haven't lost an ounce of their power.

These puzzle pieces are what make up *The Twilight Zone*, and they should be at the forefront of your mind as you make your way through the series. Let these following chapters guide your inquisitive journey into the vast imagination of Rod Serling.

Mini Binges

Before streaming, or even DVD, I remember classic television shows like *The Twilight Zone* being released in best-of volumes on VHS. There were typically two episodes per tape, and usually were all out of order. Sometimes you'd be lucky and find one that had two all-time classic episodes that featured some of the best monsters or cameos. These were wonderful opportunities to get to know the show better without having to wade through all 156 episodes. Trust me, I know it's *a lot* of content. As I made my way through this series, it took me well over a month religiously watching a few episodes every day to make my way through. If you stack it up, that's just over three full days of streaming, 100% commercial free without a single bathroom break.

I know what you're thinking, "I don't have the time to binge *all of that* at once!" Well you're in luck! Since this is an anthology show, none of these episodes need to be watched concurrently. That means you can skip around, or jump backwards and forwards in seasons, and still get a full picture of *The Twilight Zone*.

In the spirit of those best-of tapes, and to help you navigate the hills and valleys of *The Twilight Zone*, I've devised a series of mini-marathons based on whatever mood you might be in. Looking to get scared? Laugh out loud? Go on a head trip? All of that is represented here, from the cerebral to the tender hearted. These shortlists can be used as a personal starting point, or a way to turn your friends into fans of the show. You can even use these mini binges to concoct your own *Twilight Zone* holiday marathons! These succinct binges will guarantee you'll never waste time Googling "What are the best episodes of *The Twilight Zone*?" ever again!

The Scariest Binge

Perhaps the most asked question about the series, these episodes will show you how deep under the skin Serling goes with his tales of horror.

- *And When The Sky Was Opened* (S1, E11)
- *I Shot an Arrow into the Air* (S1, E15)
- *The Monsters are Due on Maple Street* (S1, E22)
- *After Hours* (S1, E34)
- *Long Distance Call* (S2, E22)
- *It's A Good Life* (S3, E8)
- *The Dummy* (S3, E33)
- *Living Doll* (S5, E6)

An Unofficial Journey Into The Twilight Zone

The Funniest Binge

Frequently hilarious, these episodes will challenge the perception of The Twilight Zone as being just a show about aliens and communists.

- *A Nice Place to Visit* (S1, E28)
- *Mr. Bevis* (S1, E33)
- *Mr. Dingle the Strong* (S2, E19)
- *Once Upon a Time* (S3, E13)
- *Showdown with Rance McGrew* (S3, E22)
- *To Serve Man* (S3, E24)
- *Hocus-Pocus and Frisby* (S3, E30)
- *Cavender is Coming* (S3, E36)
- *The Printer's Devil* (S4, E9)
- *The Bard* (S4, E18)
- *Mr. Garrity and the Graves* (S5, E32)

The Cerebral Binge

Remember when you unlocked that door with the key of imagination? These are the episodes directly behind it.

- *Where is Everybody?* (S1, E1)
- *Perchance to Dream* (S1, E9)
- *The Fever* (S1, E17)
- *Mirror Image* (S1, E21)
- *Shadow Play* (S2, E26)
- *The Arrival* (S3, E2)
- *One More Pallbearer* (S3, E17)
- *Little Girl Lost* (S3, E26)
- *Person, or Persons Unknown* (S3, E27)
- *The Parallel* (S4, E11)
- *Nightmare at 20,000 Feet* (S5, E3)
- *Ring-a-ding Girl* (S5, E13)

Jacob Trussell

The Romantic Binge

Yes, that's right, Twilight Zone Holiday Marathons can extend to Valentine's Day!

- *The Lonely* (S1, E7)
- *A Penny for Your Thoughts* (S2, E16)
- *Two* (S3, E1)
- *The Last Rites of Jeff Myrtlebank* (S3, E23)
- *The Trade-ins* (S3, E31)
- *Jess-Belle* (S4, E7)
- *The Long Morrow* (S5, E15)
- *Black Leather Jackets* (S5, E18)
- *From Agnes - With Love* (S5, E20)

The Sweetest Binge

The Twilight Zone wasn't always saccharine, but when it was, it made your teeth hurt in the best of ways!

- *Night of the Meek* (S2, E11)
- *Nothing in the Dark* (S3, E16)
- *The Hunt* (S3, E19)
- *Kick the Can* (S3, E21)
- *I Sing the Body Electric* (S3, E35)
- *The Bewitchin' Pool* (S5, E36)

The Socially Relevant Binge

These episodes have the heart and spirit of how Serling felt about the world.

- *Third from the Sun* (S1, E14)
- *The Shelter* (S3, E3)
- *Four O'Clock* (S3, E29)
- *The Gift* (S3, E32)
- *He's Alive* (S4, E4)

An Unofficial Journey Into The Twilight Zone

- *No Time Like the Past* (S4, E10)
- *The Masks* (S5, E25)
- *I Am the Night - Color Me Black* (S5, E26)
- *The Encounter* (S5, E31)
- *The Brain Center at Mr. Whipple's* (S5, E33)

The War Binge

Rod Serling was absolutely defined by his experiences in World War II, and he wrote that into the very essence of the series

- *Judgment Night* (S1, E10)
- *The Last Flight* (S1, E18)
- *The Purple Testament* (S1, E19)
- *Deaths-Head Revisited* (S3, E9)
- *A Quality of Mercy* (S3, E15)
- *The Thirty-Fathom Grave* (S4, E2)

The Atomic Fear Binge

If Rod Serling was defined by the Second World War, the power and fear of the Atomic Bomb defined the next half century.

- *Time Enough at Last* (S1, E8)
- *Third from the Sun* (S1, E14)
- *The Shelter* (S3, E3)
- *It's a Good Life* (S3, E8)
- *One More Pallbearer* (S3, E17)
- *The Old Man in the Cave* (S5, E7)

The Best of Serling Binge

The man himself wrote 92 episodes of the original series, and this is a smattering of his very best.

- *Walking Distance* (S1, E5)
- *The Purple Testament* (S1, E19)

Jacob Trussell

- *The Big Tall Wish* (S1, E27)
- *A Stop at Willoughby* (S1, E30)
- *The Silence* (S2, E25)
- *In Praise of Pip* (S5, E1)
- *Last Night of the Jockey* (S5, E5)
- *The Jeopardy Room* (S5, E29)

The Best of Matheson Binge

Richard Matheson is a name that is as synonymous with the series as Serling's own.

- *A World of Difference* (S1, E23)
- *A World of His Own* (S1, E36)
- *Nick of Time* (S2, E7)
- *The Invaders* (S2, E15)
- *Little Girl Lost* (S3, E26)
- *Once Upon a Time* (S3, E13)
- *Steel* (S5, E2)
- *Night Call* (S5, E19)

The Best of Beaumont Binge

The absolute very best from the most remarkable and forgotten writer of the series Charles Beaumont.

- *Elegy* (S1, E20)
- *The Howling Man* (S2, E5)
- *Long Distance Call* (S2, E22)
- *Shadow Play* (S2, E26)
- *The Jungle* (S3, E12)
- *Person, or Persons Unknown* (S3, E27)
- *In His Image* (S4, E1)
- *Miniature* (S4, E8)
- *Number 12 Looks Just Like You* (S5, E17)

An Unofficial Journey Into The Twilight Zone

The Unsung Binge

These are the greatest episodes of the series you may have not heard of.

- *Elegy* (S1, E20)
- *People Are Alike All Over* (S1, E25)
- *The Big Tall Wish* (S1, E27)
- *Long Distance Call* (S2, E22)
- *The Silence* (S2, E25)
- *The Arrival* (S3, E2)
- *The Jungle* (S3, E12)
- *Printer's Devil* (S4, E9)
- *Uncle Simon* (S5, E8)
- *Ring-a-Ding Girl* (S5, E13)
- *You Drive* (S5, E14)
- *Night Call* (S5, E19)
- *An Occurrence at Owl Creek Bridge* (S5, E22)
- *I Am the Night - Color Me Black* (S5, E26)
- *Mr. Garrity and the Graves* (S5, E32)

The Unequivocally Best Remembered

These episodes will give you every story every TZ fan should know by heart.

- *Time Enough at Last* (S1, E8)
- *Walking Distance* (S1, E5)
- *And When the Sky Was Opened* (S1, E11)
- *The Hitch-Hiker* (S1, E16)
- *The Monsters are Due on Maple Street* (S1, E22)
- *The After Hours* (S1, E34)
- *The Howling Man* (S2, E5)
- *Eye of the Beholder* (S2, E6)
- *Nick of Time* (S2, E7)
- *The Night of the Meek* (S2, E11)
- *The Invaders* (S2, E15)

- *Odyssey of Flight 33* (S2, E18)
- *Will the Real Martian Please Stand Up?* (S2, E28)
- *The Obsolete Man* (S2, E29)
- *It's a Good Life* (S3, E8)
- *Five Characters in Search of an Exit* (S3, E14)
- *To Serve Man* (S3, E24)
- *Little Girl Lost* (S3, E26)
- *The Little People* (S3, E28)
- *The Dummy* (S3, E33)
- *On Thursday We Leave for Home* (S4, E16)
- *Nightmare at 20,000 Feet* (S5, E3)
- *A Kind of Stopwatch* (S5, E4)
- *Living Doll* (S5, E6)
- *The Masks* (S5, E25)

Where to Binge

Stream
- *Netflix (Seasons 1-3, 5)*
- *Hulu (Seasons 1-5)*
- *Paramount+ (Season 1-5)*

Buy
- *Amazon (Seasons 1-5)*
- *Apple iTunes (Seasons 1-5)*
- *Vudu (Seasons 1-5)*

> # The Twilight Zone

SEASON ONE

OCTOBER 2, 1959 – JULY 1, 1960

"Where Is Everybody?"
Episode 1
Original Airdate: October 2, 1959

Directed by Robert Stevens
Written by Rod Serling

> *"The barrier of loneliness: The palpable, desperate need of the human animal to be with his fellow man. Up there, up there in the vastness of space, in the void that is sky, up there is an enemy known as isolation. It sits there in the stars waiting, waiting with the patience of eons, forever waiting... in The Twilight Zone."*

Mike Ferris (Earl Holliman), dressed in an Air Force flight suit with no recollection of where he is and how he got there, wanders lost into a small idyllic community looking for help. Instead, he finds a ghost town, stores left open but empty, as if everyone just vanished, leaving nothing behind but mannequins and an eerie quiet. Attempting to jump start his memory, he speaks to himself aloud, trying to find reason in the unreasonable as he begins suffocating under an oppressive feeling of claustrophobia. Phone booths and jail cells seem to be closing in on him, as if attempting to trap him in the town. Is this the portrait of a paranoid mind, or is Mike Ferris slowly losing his grip on reality?

Five years before *The Twilight Zone* premiered, series regular Richard Matheson wrote the prototype for the modern American apocalypse story, *I Am Legend*. This episode doesn't outwardly express anxiety over nuclear energy post Hiroshima—a theme felt in Matheson's story—but there are major similarities between this and his original novella. Both center on men who appear to be the last people on Earth and, through internal dialogues with themselves, we watch them grapple to make sense of their new world.

I would have preferred if Serling had peppered in a few post-apocalyptic vampires, but one of the most intrinsically scary things about this episode is the absence of a villain. There is no enemy for Mike to overcome, so we have nothing to root against to ease the tension. All we can do is stew in anticipation and watch him spiral with stress, unsure of exactly how he'll escape from his waking nightmare. In a theme that permeates the entire series, the dread in this episode is one of our own unconscious making. It's why the answer to the titular question is far more chilling than any supernatural force. In the end, no matter your strength or mettle, the unseen pressures of the human mind can emotionally destroy you.

What "Where is Everybody?" establishes so well for *The Twilight Zone* is that the series is an open door into the unknown. That unknown could be the alien feeling of waking up in a town with no soul in sight but your own, or it could be the uncharted vastness of the human mind. We can easily perceive fears and horrors that come from far-off planets, but what about those from the people we pass on the street, or the reflection we see in a mirror? They are the cast of characters that will make up *The Twilight Zone*.

Zone Fact

The original pilot was called "The Happy Place,, about a society that euthanized its citizens when they turned 60.

"One for the Angels"
Episode 2
Original Airdate: October 9, 1959

Directed by Robert Parrish
Written by Rod Serling

"Street scene: Summer. The present. Man on a sidewalk named Lew Bookman, age 60ish. Occupation: pitchman. Lew Bookman, a fixture of the summer, a rather minor component to a hot July, a nondescript, commonplace little man whose life is a treadmill built out of sidewalks. And in just a moment, Lew Bookman will have to concern himself with survival—because as of three o'clock this hot July afternoon, he'll be stalked by Mr. Death."

Aging hawker Lew Bookman (Ed Wynn) fixes toys and sells his wares, while holding court over the neighborhood children. That is until Bookman is visited by Mr. Death (Murray Hamilton), an unsuitable—but well-suited—Grim Reaper who informs Lew that he will die at midnight. Gripped by the anxiety of his looming demise, Bookman naturally looks for a way to prolong his life the only way he knows how: peddling. But as you should know, Death doesn't like to play games. And this Mister shows he's not screwing around when he sets his sights on replacing Bookman's soul with a young girl from the neighborhood. That is unless Bookman can actually make that one great pitch "for the angels."

In this two-hander from Rod Serling, Ed Wynn's charisma and joie de vivre are the perfect foil to the buttoned-up Murray Hamilton. Bookman only has a few short hours to save the young girl's life, so Serling keeps the pace tight to match the urgency of the episode's soul collecting pact.

Bargaining for your soul is a story archetype that goes back multiple centuries, being best represented in Christopher Marlowe and Johann Wolfgang von Goethe's *Faust*. While Mr. Death is no Mephistopheles, there is a similarity in the impish glee he brings to soul collecting that calls to mind the classic character. That, of course, and how Mister almost sounds like Mephisto.

In contrast to the moral and psychological complexities of later

Jacob Trussell

episodes, I marvel at the sheer simplicity of early stories like this one. It's just about a guy doing the most relatable thing imaginable: trying to stay alive. Who's to say what you or I would do if Death did us the kindness of telling us when we're about to die? Would you go willingly? Would you try to save your own hide? Or would you, like Bookman, consider giving your own second chance to someone who actually needs it?

"One for the Angels" is a story that encourages us to be selfless and consider how precious life is, especially for those who have yet to fully experience it. It's simple, succinct, and ultimately quite sweet. Only in *The Twilight Zone* does Death have a heart.

Zone Fact

Mr. Death is none other than the money-grubbing Mayor in Steven Spielberg's Jaws. That famed director would later go on to direct the pilot episode of Rod Serling's Night Gallery.

"Mr. Denton on Doomsday"
Episode 3
Original Airdate: October 16, 1959

Directed by Allen Reisner
Written by Rod Serling

"Portrait of a town drunk named Al Denton. This is a man who's begun his dying early—a long, agonizing route through a maze of bottles. Al Denton, who would probably give an arm or a leg or a part of his soul to have another chance, to be able to rise up and shake the dirt from his body and the bad dreams that infest his consciousness. In the parlance of the times, this is a peddler, a rather fanciful-looking little man in a black frock coat. And this is the third principal character of our story. Its function: perhaps to give Mr. Al Denton his second chance."

Al Denton (Dan Duryea) is a town drunk with a torrid past. At one point he was the fastest gun in the west, but after a series of duels that left him feeling the weight of the pistol on his hip, he drowned his trauma deep at the bottom of a bottle. It was only when he was passed out blind that the visions of all those gunslingers he shot down—one as young as 15—would vanish. But when the local town tormenter Dan Hotaling (Martin Landau) sets his sights on humiliating Denton further, a traveling salesman named Mr. Fate (Malcolm Atterbury) brings Denton not only a little bit of his old courage, but a lotta bit of magic. Leave it to the impartiality of fate—and a little trip into *The Twilight Zone*—for Denton to begin his long road to recovery.

The popularity of westerns throughout the early 20th century allowed writers to speak to modern themes by leaning into archetypes that audiences were already familiar with. For Serling, he smartly uses the stock character of the town drunk to make a point that society has always been impacted by mental health issues, even if we were reticent to discuss it publically.

In the wake of World War II, the United States began to talk more openly about mental health, and Serling wanted to point out that this is something we've struggled with for centuries, even if we only began discussing it openly in the 1950s. Denton didn't become a drunk because he was a louse, but because he had residual trauma

Jacob Trussell

from the deaths he caused. That's something that many Americans could directly relate to after World War II and the Korean War—a time when men were taught to bottle up their emotions, both literally and figuratively. Audiences may not have been able to wrap their head around something as complex as mood disorders, but they could definitely understand the reality of alcoholism and the impact it causes on so many lives.

Zone Fact

Mr. Denton on Doomsday is contemplative and melancholy, but one person was able to mine humor out of its core emotional crux: Mel Brooks. Denton's sad reason for drinking is hilariously lampooned in Brooks' 1974 comedy Blazing Saddles in Gene Wilder's Jim, also a gunslinger with a crippling alcohol addiction and a hand so shaky you think he's drying it.

"The Sixteen-Millimeter Shrine"
Episode 4
Original Airdate: October 23, 1959

Directed by Mitchell Leisen
Written by Rod Serling

"Picture of a woman looking at a picture. Movie great of another time, once-brilliant star in a firmament no longer a part of the sky, eclipsed by the movement of earth and time. Barbara Jean Trenton, whose world is a projection room, whose dreams are made out of celluloid. Barbara Jean Trenton, struck down by hit-and-run years and lying on the unhappy pavement, trying desperately to get the license number of fleeting fame."

Barbara Jean Trenton (Ida Lupino) is stuck in a celluloid dream, longing for her heyday when she was a glamorous star of the silver screen. But the older she gets, the more she attempts to hang tight to her fading youth, much to the concern of her agent Danny Weiss (Martin Balsam). In order to give Barbara some perspective on aging, Danny invites an old co-star to help her come to terms with her twilight years, only to cause her to revert deeper into herself. As the lines between reality and her films begin to blur, Barbara will soon pass through that point of no return called *The Twilight Zone*.

The themes at the heart of Billy Wilder's *Sunset Boulevard* have been copied and referenced for years after its release in 1950, but it only took less than a decade for that influence to be found on television in this episode about a fading Hollywood star. Ida Lupino's Barbara Jean Trenton is a far cry from Norma Desmond, with none of the latter's Grey Gardens-esque disconnect from reality, but there is still a palpable yearning for days gone by. What's even more heartbreaking is how this portrait of beauty standards and aging in Hollywood is still relevant today. The characters speak about Barbara as if she's 90, when in reality Lupino was only 41. She's had this perception about what age means forced upon her by a misogynistic society. It's no wonder she toils her time watching movies from an in-home projector. Hollywood insiders suck!

Barbara's longing for the past is endlessly relatable, especially in our nostalgia-loving modern world. We relish in the things that connect us to our youth, because there is a lot to gain from taking the time to reflect on your life. However, you don't have to be a yogi to interpret that Serling's central message is about the power of staying in the present moment. Think about what good it really does to fixate on a time you'll never get back. Doesn't it obscure your view of the future, or even what's in front of you right now?

The Twilight Zone gives Barbara a way to exist forever as her younger self, but only at the cost of her own life. In a way, the ending to this episode is a metaphor for suicide. She wanted to revel in the past so much that she became consumed by it. I don't see the end as optimistic. I see it just like Barbara's maid did: a nightmare.

Zone Fact

Star Ida Lupino would go on to be the sole-female director of an original series episode!

"Walking Distance"
Episode 5
Original Airdate: October 30, 1959

Directed by Robert Stevens
Written by: Rod Serling

> *"Martin Sloan, age 36. Occupation: vice-president, ad agency, in charge of media. This is not just a Sunday drive for Martin Sloan. He perhaps doesn't know it at the time, but it's an exodus. Somewhere up the road he's looking for sanity. And somewhere up the road, he'll find something else."*

Martin Sloan (Gig Young), an advertising executive from New York takes a trip out of the city, stopping for an oil change and a lube job. Noticing his hometown is in—wait for it—walking distance of the gas station, he strolls into town and visits the old drug store where he used to spend his days drinking chocolate sodas. Opining how they used to cost a dime, an odd sense grips him as he realizes that everything is remarkably still the same, 30 years later. The feeling continues as he learns his old house is still in his name, even though his family moved away years ago. He really begins to panic upon meeting a young boy who looks just like him, with parents the spitting image of his own. Sloan has traveled into the past, and the only way he may get out is by confronting the one thing that's keeping him there: himself.

    In "The Sixteen Millimeter Shrine," we see how nostalgia can be used as a way to tether us to the past to forgo our future. Taking a different perspective on a similar theme, Serling takes Martin on a literal trip down memory lane in "Walking Distance" to show how cloudy memories of the past can subsequently blind us to the realities of our present.

    Martin is enraptured by his return to Homewood, especially how it hadn't changed a bit since he left. But once the realization dawns on him as to where he is, he refuses to reckon with it. Rather than embrace or shun what's happened, he chooses to keep one foot in reality and the other in his subconscious mind. It's why he runs around town looking for himself, but remains incredulous as to why

Jacob Trussell

his young parents don't recognize their adult son. He knows that he can't stay in this version of Homewood, but he doesn't want to do anything about it either. As he says, Homewood is where he belongs, but in *The Twilight Zone*, Homewood isn't a place, it's an idea. The faded memory of a time before he became shackled with the responsibilities of adulthood.

The way we remember the past doesn't always align with what actually happened.

Call it rose-colored glasses or nostalgia goggles, but fond memories do not mean the good ol' days were everything they were cracked up to be. Sure, we all miss not having to pay bills, but does anyone really want to go back to high school? It's why the message Martin's father gives him at the end is so vital. He truly has no place in the past. Hindsight can make us appreciate what we've experienced, but we only threaten our future by becoming preoccupied with days gone by.

Zone Fact

This is one of Rod Serling's most personal, and favorite, episodes

"Escape Clause"
Episode 6
Original Airdate: November 6, 1959

Directed by Mitchell Leisen
Written by Rod Serling

"You're about to meet a hypochondriac. Witness Mr. Walter Bedeker age 44. Afraid of the following: death, disease, other people, germs, draft, and everything else. He has one interest in life and that's Walter Bedeker. One preoccupation, the life and well-being of Walter Bedeker. One abiding concern about society, that if Walter Bedeker should die how will it survive without him?"

Hypochondriac Walter Bedeker (David Wayne) believes he is on death's door, regardless of what his quack doctor or busybody wife says. Walter's even sure that they are conspiring to murder him! Afraid for his life, he strikes a deal with the mysterious Mr. Cadwallader (Thomas Gomez), where he'll get immortality all for the measly price of his soul. Walter begins to immediately exploit his newfound lease on life, getting his rocks off with near death experiences and cashing in on insurance money, but soon finds out you really can have too much of a good thing. Soon Walter will understand that staying alive can easily become a fate worse than death.

If you've ever made the mistake of Googling symptoms when you feel sick, then you'll know that we all have the capacity for hypochondria, especially during a global pandemic where getting sick can become a death sentence. Our will to live is one of the things that makes us human, so we can't help but relate to Walter, even if his fear of death is holding him back from enjoying the life he so desperately wants to keep.

But becoming immortal overshoots his ambitions. He wants to live, but without the fear of death, the perilous feats he throws himself into ring hollow the moment they are done. Who hasn't patiently waited for something—a present in the mail, an important date—only to feel deflated the moment it arrives, realizing the anticipation was the motivating factor, not the gift itself? He lived by

Jacob Trussell

fearing death, but the moment death was no longer a factor, he realized how much it brought to his life.

I do wish we could have seen what would happen if Walter had chosen to stay in prison for the rest of his life. What would his jailersgaolers have done once they realized he's not aged in decades? It reminds me of the television series *Castle Rock*, where a young man is freed from prison having not aged. Walter isn't some long dormant evil that's come home to roost like in Stephen King's show, but it's the power of *The Twilight Zone* that we're always inspired to ask, "What if?"

Zone Fact

Appeared in Stories from the Twilight Zone, a collection of first season episode adaptations for Bantam Books

"The Lonely"
Episode 7
Original Airdate: November 13, 1959

Directed by Jack Smight
Written by Rod Serling

"On a microscopic piece of sand that floats through space is a fragment of a man's life. Left to rust is the place he lived in and the machines he used. Without use, they will disintegrate from the wind and the sand and the years that act upon them. All of Mr. Corry's machines, including the one made in his image, kept alive by love, but now obsolete—in The Twilight Zone."

Exiled on a far distant, barren planet in the near future, Joseph A. Corry (Jack Warden) spends his time restoring an old car while waiting for the quarterly supply runs from Captain Allenby (John Dehner) and his crew. But Corry isn't a sequestered research scientist, or some recluse squirreled away in a shack, he's a convicted murderer. It may have been in self-defense, but Corry is still sentenced to a life of solitude with his singular loneliness being his only friend.

That is until Allenby presents Corry with a gift: a robot in the image of a young woman named Alicia (Jean Marsh).

Initially Corry rebuffs the robot, disgusted and disturbed by how realistic she is, as if mocking the very nature of humanity. Upon seeing her reaction to his rage however, he comes to realize that she is more than a machine—she has the capacity for deep emotions and feelings. Alicia brings a spark of joy to Corry's life that he thought he had lost. When he learns that he is being returned to Earth, he's faced with a decision: go back to his old life, or stay secluded with his new love?

With a strong ensemble cast featuring Jack Warden (a recurring *Twilight Zone* player) and an early role for Ted Knight (best remembered as simple-minded Ted Baxter on *The Mary Tyler Moore Show*) "The Lonely" confronts two interwoven themes: justice and humanity.

The first theme is born from our world. In this uncompromising society where crime is black and white, there's no room for justifiable homicide. It doesn't matter that what Corry did was in self-defense, murder is murder. But is this resolute interpretation of the law extended to soldiers and law enforcement, people whose job it is to use deadly force if necessary? If not, then what kind of justice is served by exiling Corry? There are better ways to atone. After a spate of riots in the 1950s brought attention to the need for prison reform, you can see the subtle critique of the prison industrial complex in Serling's measured writing.

The second theme is born from *The Twilight Zone*, asking "what makes a person?" Is it the blood and guts that make up the systems of the human body? Is it the presence of a personality, or the ability to express emotions like love and happiness and pain and sorrow? If that doesn't make us human, then what does? Serling doesn't outright answer these questions for the audience, but you can make plenty of presumptions based on his brutal finale.

Corry attempts to persuade Allenby to bring her on board, much to the amusement of his crew. With time running out, and the window for them to safely take off slowly closing, the captain shoots Alicia in the face. Allenby tells Corry that the only thing he is leaving behind is his loneliness. This snaps Corry out of his reverie, and they head to the spaceship, leaving Alicia's lifeless body behind.

Serling is warning us that we shouldn't get too attached to our machines. They may make us happy, temporarily, but they'll never cure loneliness.

Zone Fact

This is the first episode to be filmed in Death Valley, a favorite location for the series.

"Time Enough at Last"
Episode 8
Original Airdate: November 20, 1959

Directed by John Brahm
Written by Rod Serling (based on a short story by Lynn Venable)

"The best laid plans of mice and men... and Henry Bemis... the small man in the glasses who wanted nothing but time. Henry Bemis, now just a part of a smashed landscape, just a piece of the rubble, just a fragment of what man has deeded to himself. Mr. Henry Bemis...
in The Twilight Zone."

Henry Bemis (Burgess Meredith) has a singular passion: books. He loves them because he can fall into worlds apart from his own, transporting him far away from the constraints of his humdrum life. Not only is he constantly berated by a young, upstart boss (Vaughn Taylor) at the bank where he works, but he then must go home to a shrewish wife (Jacqueline deWitt) who couldn't care less about him. To Mr. Bemis, their greatest sin is a singular distaste for literature.

On his usual lunch break, lazily reading in the bank's steel vault, the unthinkable happens. An atomic bomb is dropped, decimating his city, but sparing him thanks to the vault's imperviousness. Saved from the immediate impact of the blast, Mr. Bemis wanders through the fallout finding his old neighborhood reduced to nothingness. In his despair, Mr. Bemis realizes there is a silver lining to his newfound solitude. But for every silver lining, a dark cloud is always looming on the edge.

It took only eight half-hour episodes for *The Twilight Zone* to tell a story that would stand the test of time, and it's only fitting that it's titled "Time Enough at Last." It also took only eight episodes for *The Twilight Zone* to first touch upon a major theme of the series: anxiety over nuclear power. This episode isn't tangibly connected with the Second World War, but the specter of Hiroshima lingered over society long after that bomb was deployed. Nuclear anxiety would be addressed more directly in future stories, but here it's a powerful presence to represent how all-encompassing the fear of this new energy was. The end of the world could happen anywhere, at any time, all with the press of a button.

Jacob Trussell

The final moment of this episode is one of the most famous twists in the series, but the monumental image that stands out to me is watching as Mr. Bemis silently wanders through a never-ending wasteland, his coke-bottle glasses fogged up by the mists of the fallout. This beautifully composed sequence was shot by series cinematographer George T. Clemens and is evocative of the apocalyptic images we would have seen coming out of war-torn Europe.

Whether intentional or not, it's hard not to look at the scope of this vast wasteland and not draw correlations to the quiet vistas of film director Akira Kurowsawa's Japan, shot by his longtime director of photography Asakazu Nakai. After all, Kurowsawa and Nakai would have had first-hand experience knowing the devastation atomic energy can wreak. More than Serling himself would ever know.

Zone Fact

The steps where Mr. Bemis breaks his glasses also appears in "A Nice Place to Visit" (S1E28)

"Perchance to Dream"
Episode 9
Original Airdate: November 27, 1959

Directed by Robert Florey
Written by Charles Beaumont (based on his short story of the same name)

"They say a dream takes only a second or so, and yet in that second a man can live a lifetime. He can suffer and die, and who's to say which is the greater reality: the one we know or the one in dreams, between heaven, the sky, the earth—in The Twilight Zone."

Edward Hall (Richard Conte) is suffering from a weak heart and a fear that penetrates his every waking moment. He's positive that if he falls asleep, he will die. Edward visits a psychiatrist in hopes of unlocking exactly why he's paralyzed by fear, because his heart condition will only be exacerbated if he can't sleep. In his dreams, he can't escape a macabre carnival and a threatening woman who beckon him onto a roller coaster. As the lines between our world and his fantasies begin to mesh together, Edward suddenly realizes that you do not have to dream to experience a nightmare.

Anyone who has ever had problems falling asleep because anxiety compels them to dwell on past decisions and mistakes can sympathize with what Edward is going through in "Perchance to Dream." While you can identify narrative threads that speak to the series underlying emphasis on psychiatry and psychology, this is the first episode that directly addresses these themes in the plot of the story.

This episode acts like a mission statement from Rod Serling. His way of saying, "This isn't your garden variety spooky suspense show! We're here to change some misconceptions on mental health!" Serling and his writers were limited to what was known about psychology compared with today, but the message is still meaningful. We have to approach mental health issues like anxiety and depression from a place of understanding and compassion, rather than dismissal.

This is also the first episode written by Charles Beaumont who—while not having as recognizable of a name as Rod Serling or

Jacob Trussell

Richard Matheson—is responsible for some of the most brutal episodes of the series. There is a fatalistic foreboding that pulses through each of his stories that is unlike anything else in the series.

The dread in this episode, the idea that if Edward rests he'll die, is unmistakably similar to the premise of Wes Craven's *A Nightmare on Elm Street*. And while the only Freddy Krueger that Hall has to deal with is a carnival woman and the unknowns of his own mind, the 1984 film and this episode do share a commonality in imagery. The episode is steeped in dreamy visuals that call to mind the 1920's German expressionism film movement and is a valiant attempt to give a visual representation to what our subconscious minds sees.

Zone Fact

Beaumont's short story that served as the basis for this episode was first published in Playboy, once an authority on fresh new voices in literature from Stephen King and James Baldwin to Joyce Carol Oates and fellow Twilight Zone scribe Ray Bradbury.

An Unofficial Journey Into The Twilight Zone

"Judgment Night"
Episode 10
Original Airdate: December 4, 1959

Directed by John Brahm
Written by Rod Serling

> *"For the year is 1942, and this particular ship has lost its convoy. It travels alone like an aged blind thing groping through the unfriendly dark, stalked by unseen periscopes of steel killers. Yes, the Queen of Glasgow is a frightened ship, and she carries with her a premonition of death."*

Carl Lanser (Nehemiah Persoff) stands aboard the deck of a large ship, unsure of how he got there. He speaks with a heavy German accent, but he doesn't appear to know where he is from. Still, he is gripped with an unmistakable sense of doom, like he must avert a tragedy before it is too late. His memories begin to slowly flood back to him, like an intimate understanding of German naval tactics, but how he came to be on the ship alludes to him even as he recognizes the faces of the other passengers. Soon, those faces become as blank as slate as Lanser has the epiphany the ship will sink at exactly 1:15AM. His sense of dread is the key to unlocking his past, but often the answers we search for are best left unearthed.

Don't bother trying to look up and see if there really was a S.S. Queen of Glasgow. There was an HMS Glasgow that did routinely travel from the British Isles to New York, but none that were sunk by a German ship in the height of World War II. There was definitely no Carl Lanser, which feels like a result you would get from a Nazi Officer Online Name Generator.

Rod Serling always used *The Twilight Zone* as a way to grapple with his own experiences during the Second World War, so you don't have to read too far between the lines to surmise what he wanted to say with this episode about a Nazi hiding in plain sight. What happens to Carl Lanser is none other than poetic justice. Serling sticks his Nazi officer in a timeloop, submitting him to a Sisyphean nightmare where he'll kill himself forevermore. It's cosmic retribution to force a war criminal to face the destruction he caused, firsthand, for the rest of his death.

Jacob Trussell

Another thing that stood out in this episode—aside from George T. Clemens lush cinematography playing with shadow like a film noir—was the idea of a German officer seemingly forgetting that he was a Nazi. It struck me as veiled reference to Operation Paperclip, a controversial government program that saw the United States bring over German officers during the 1940s to keep developing technologies out of the hands of the Nazi Party. Not every scientist in Operation Paperclip was a Nazi, but some were, and I feel like this is what Serling is getting at. They may be here, they may walk among us, but we can't let them forget who they are.

Zone Fact

This was the first episode where Serling was censored. A character originally ordered a cup of tea, but since the episode's coffee sponsor didn't want to promote the competition, the cuppa was cut.

"And When the Sky Was Opened"
Episode 11
Original Airdate: December 11, 1959

Directed by Douglas Heyes
Written by Rod Serling (Based on a short story by Richard Matheson)

"Her name: X-20. Her type: an experimental interceptor. Recent history: a crash landing in the Mojave Desert after a 31-hour flight 900 miles into space. Incidental data: the ship, with the men who flew her, disappeared from the radar screen for 24 hours... But the shrouds that cover mysteries are not always made out of a tarpaulin, as this man will soon find out on the other side of a hospital door."

Lieutenant Colonel Clegg Forbes (Rod Taylor), Colonel Ed Harrington (Charles Aidman), and Major William Gart (Jim Hutton) have all returned from a test flight of an experimental aircraft that can reach far beyond the Earth's atmosphere. During their flight, they lose consciousness only to regain it having safely crashed back on Earth. Their survival marks them as minor heroes, but to the horror of Forbes, Harrington suddenly vanishes and worse, no one seems to remember him. As he attempts to maintain his sanity, Forbes feels his grip on reality slowly slipping as he risks becoming nothing more than a faded memory in a world that will move on, with or without him.

I have never been a fan of in media res—starting a story in the middle, only to flashback to the proper beginning for added effect—but in "And When The Sky Was Opened" the gimmick intentionally lets the audience embody the confusion and existential horror that the characters are experiencing on screen.

From the opening moments we are as lost as the pilots are afraid, which feels apt for an episode that patently is a metaphor for Post-Traumatic Stress Disorder (PTSD). These pilots have come back after a catastrophic accident that has physically and mentally wounded them, and because of this they are literally disappearing one by one. For those suffering from PTSD, the fear is that you are losing control of what is real and what is not. This is chillingly represented when

Forbes, attempting to find proof that his co-pilots existed, remembers that he wrote down their names on a note to his girlfriend. He's shocked to discover that the note isn't what he remembered writing. He can't trust the world around him, and now he can't even trust himself.

It's not just PTSD that you can read in this episode, but survivor's guilt as well. Each pilot, as the others disappear and are forgotten, are left wondering why they weren't taken. Like the never-ending grind of war, they know that if they were spared this time, it's unlikely they will be spared again. I'm even reminded of the treatment of veterans of Vietnam, a war that *The Twilight Zone* would only briefly touch upon with "In Praise of Pip" (S5E1). While our pilots here haven't returned from a war, it's the idea that they are being slowly forgotten, eaten by time, like all of the veterans who felt abandoned by the system, and country, that made them.

Zone fact

Charles Aidman would later go on to provide narration for the first two seasons of the 1985 revival of the series.

An Unofficial Journey Into The Twilight Zone

"What You Need"
Episode 12
Original Airdate: December 25, 1959

Directed by Alvin Ganzer
Written by Rod Serling (based on a story by Henry Kuttner & C.L. Moore (as Lewis Padgett))

"You're looking at Mr. Fred Renard, who carries on his shoulder a chip the size of the national debt. This is a sour man, a friendless man, a lonely man, a grasping, compulsive, nervous man. This is a man who has lived 36 undistinguished, meaningless, pointless, failure-laden years and who at this moment looks for an escape—any escape, any way, anything, anybody—to get out of the rut. And this little old man is just what Mr. Renard is waiting for."

Traveling salesman Pedott (Ernest Truex) peddles wares out of a beaten-up suitcase, but these aren't just slightly used curios. Pedott's trinkets are imbued with magical powers that he can give to a specific person, at exactly the moment they need it. When he offers a bus ticket to out-of-work baseball player Lefty (Read Morgan) he miraculously receives an interview for a minor league team in the town the ticket is to. Hard-nosed asshole Fred Renard (Steve Cochran) realizes he can exploit these powers for his own personal gain, despite Pedott's warnings about what happens to those who feel entitled to anything in life. Because of his selfishness, Renard will be forced to confront what fate does to those who desperately need a kick in the pants.

When Pedott tells the out-of-work ball player that he has a ticket for him to Scranton, Pennsylvania, Pedott is tight lipped about what's there. He's playing coy for effect, but if you're a notorious binge watcher like myself, you know exactly what's in Scranton! It's the home of Dunder Mifflin, the little paper supply company at the center of the U.S. sitcom *The Office*. At least if the guy doesn't get to pitch in the minors, he can always make lifelong friends working at a soul-sucking corporation! Who knows, maybe the true genesis of everyone's favorite *Office* weirdo Creed Bratton is that he's straight out of *The Twilight Zone*! As Pedott tells Lefty, "You just never know!"

What we do know at the end of this episode is that nothing in life is free. Renard lives his life only to take, never to give. To him, Pedott and his items are nothing more than a vending machine, dispensing whatever he wants, whenever he wants. Which is funny, because Pedott only acts like a machine because his character was originally written as one!

Seven years before *The Twilight Zone*, Lewis Padgett's short story was faithfully adapted for the series *Tales of Tomorrow*. In it, Pedott is replaced by a fortune-telling machine that predicts the future, not unlike the malevolent bobble-headed devil that prophesied disaster for William Shatner in "Nick of Time" (S2E7). Pedott isn't malicious, but he does serve his own brand of vigilante justice. To pull a quote from Clive Barker's *The Hellbound Heart*, he is demon to some, and angel to others. Pedott can be a kindly stranger, offering a helping hand when he's needed the most or for the abusive ne'er do wells in the world, he can raise a stiff middle finger and pronounce "Gotcha!" the moment their lights go out.

Zone Fact

Arline Sax, who is the girl in the bar, would appear again as the ominous night nurse in "Twenty-Two" (S2E17)

"The Four of Us Are Dying"
Episode 13
Original Airdate: January 1, 1960

Directed by John Brahm
Written by Rod Serling (based on a short story by George Clayton Johnson)

"He was Arch Hammer, a cheap little man who just checked in. He was Johnny Foster, who played a trumpet and was loved beyond words. He was Virgil Sterig, with money in his pocket. He was Andy Marshak, who got some of his agony back on a sidewalk in front of a cheap hotel. Hammer, Foster, Sterig, Marshak—and all four of them were dying."

Arch Hammer (Harry Townes) is a man with an extraordinary gift to shapeshift into anyone he sets his eyes on. He becomes attracted to the ex-girlfriend of a recently deceased jazz trumpeter, Johnny Foster (Ross Martin), so he adopts his identity just to steal his girl. Boring easily, Arch shape shifts again into Virgil Sterig (Phillip Pine), a gangster whose face he uses to extort a quick buck. As the mob grows wise to Arch's con, he morphs again into a boxer on a bill poster. Unfortunately for Arch, the boxer's father has an axe to grind with his son after he violently left his wife and family. It's only then that Arch realizes that by donning a man's face, he must also carry that man's burdens. And in *The Twilight Zone*, those burdens can lead you six feet straight underground.

We are told in the opening narration that Arch Hammer has been able to shapeshift his appearance since he was young, but we aren't left with much in the way of answers to how he makes these changes. Is it just some kind of superhuman trick? Was he touched by angels, or aliens? The way that he changes his face reminds me so much of the shapeshifting bounty hunters in the 1986 horror-comedy classic *Critters*, so an outer space influence is in the realm of possibility.

We don't even know if the face we see when we're introduced to him is his real face. We learn his name in Serling's narration, but we don't have any way of knowing that this is his original face. Arch Hammer could just be one more persona on top of yet another persona. It raises the question, where does our central character really begin and the faces he becomes end? Does he ever age? Is shapeshifting his only power? The show may not be interested in answering any of these questions, but I find the mere thought of them revitalizes this episode's thin plot.

The biggest unanswered question though is, if he's been given this gift, why the hell is he using it to do so much damage? In its own twisted way the episode is a cautionary tale, Serling's way of saying not only that absolute power will corrupt, but that corruption always has a way of eating its own tail. But like Arch's changing face, there is never any way to tell who is corrupted or not. It's the same unnerving thought that the series pummels into you. We can never know what's going on in the minds of the people we pass on the street. It may look like you are walking by a boxer, or a trumpeter, but you may very well be passing someone with something sinister to hide. An ugly secret that they will protect with every fiber of their being.

Zone Fact

This is the first story from George Clayton Johnson, writer of Logan's Run, Oceans 11, and Star Trek!

An Unofficial Journey Into The Twilight Zone

"Third from the Sun"
Episode 14
Original Airdate: January 8, 1960

Directed by Richard L. Bare
Written by Rod Serling (based on a story by Richard Matheson)

"Quitting time at the plant. Time for supper now. Time for families. Time for a cool drink on a porch. Time for the quiet rustle of leaf-laden trees that screen out the moon, and underneath it all, behind the eyes of the men, hanging invisible over the summer night, is a horror without words. For this is the stillness before the storm. This is the eve of the end."

William Sturka (Fritz Weaver), a military scientist and friend of test pilot Jerry Riden (Joe Maross), learns from his colleague Carling (Edward Andrews) that the world is on the brink of a nuclear holocaust. With Riden and their families, Sturka has 48 hours to plan a daring escape in an experimental spacecraft before the bombs are set to detonate. Believing in unquestioning allegiance to a global superpower, as well as the saving grace of fire and brimstone, Carling will stop at nothing to thwart their plans. But humanity has a way of thriving, even in places where no humans have yet to exist.

This is the first episode of *The Twilight Zone* that stars Fritz Weaver, who would later appear in one of the most celebrated episodes of the series, "The Obsolete Man" teaming him with another stalwart of the show, Burgess Meredith. Here, Weaver takes a more amiable role as the hero father trapped in an unsubtle metaphor for the Red Scare and McCarthyism, a still fresh wound in the United States in the late 1950s when the episode was written. Edward Andrews' Carling, a prejudiced man who salivates for a violent end to that which he despises, embodies everything that Serling found wrong in the world at the time. Carling is the personification of an evil in the world that we've never been able to defeat, a bloodlust that is nothing more than fear disguised as hate.

Rod Serling populates his worlds with characters who push back against those who believe hate and war are the answers to strife, but he never makes his heroes morally black and white. Our protagonists are the very architects of the looming war they look to escape from, but do they deserve our forgiveness for the part they played in their world's coming holocaust? That idea gets to a major question that always surrounds war. Can you forgive crimes that were committed by someone strictly following orders? Are those men behind the development of the Atomic Bomb responsible for every lost life in Hiroshima and Nagasaki? The answer is both no, and yes, which is an idea that Serling forces us to confront.

This important question is quickly sidelined in the episode's final moments as we languish in the first of many "they were aliens after all!" twist endings. Are Sturka and Riden the ancient astronauts that conspiracy theorists love to refer to? Are they the one's that crash landed at Roswell? Are we actually the aliens? There's no wrong answer to these existential questions! We'd see the influence of this twist in future episodes of *The Twilight Zone*, most notably "The Invaders," but if you were a '90s kid like me, you'll recognize this twist-archetype in *Welcome to Camp Nightmare*, an early entry in R. L. Stine's highly successful *Goosebumps* series.

Zone Fact

Matheson's short story appeared in the first issue of Galaxy Science Fiction, the magazine that also debuted Ray Bradbury's story that would become Fahrenheit 451.

An Unofficial Journey Into The Twilight Zone

"I Shot an Arrow into the Air"
Episode 15
Original Airdate: January 15, 1960

Directed by Stuart Rosenberg
Written by Rod Serling (based on a story by Madelon Champion)

"Her name is the Arrow 1. She represents four and a half years of planning, preparation, and training, and a thousand years of science, mathematics, and the projected dreams and hopes of not only a nation, but a world. She is the first manned aircraft into space and this is the countdown. The last five seconds before man shot an arrow into the air."

A plane that is able to reach space crashes on a distant, desolate asteroid. With most of the eight man crew dead, the three survivors Colonel Donlin (Edward Binns), Corey (Dewey Martin), and Pierson (Ted Otis) attempt to salvage their supplies to endure their new environment. They hike for miles on end, finding nothing other than more barren dunes in every direction. As water runs dry, tensions begin to flare and paranoia sets in as the men square off against each other, with one of them harboring a deadly secret. Just as their situation quickly turns violent, it becomes painfully clear that maybe they aren't as far from home as they originally thought.

"I Shot an Arrow into the Sky" has arguably the greatest twist ending of the series. Some of those twists are meant to surprise or trick you, but here it does nothing other than sink you with heavy sadness. It's a gut punch because the character that we've reviled the whole episode is the man we find ourselves identifying with and pitying in the very bleak ending. We're forced to ask ourselves, "What would we have done differently?"

What happened isn't exactly Corey's fault. The crewmen were disoriented, lost, and thought they were on some other planet. Corey did what he had to do to survive. But they landed somewhere in Death Valley, not on a space rock. If they had just hiked a few more miles as a crew they would have found those highways to salvation.

Instead the elements bested Corey, both physically and mentally.

This whole incident would likely have been swept under the rug by the government, but Corey is condemned to live the rest of his life

Jacob Trussell

knowing what he did to men who depended on him. Every time he closes his eyes, he will see their lifeless bodies, face down in the dust. The grisly image of the two dead astronauts in the episode's final moments is evocative of war photography, and even made me think of the footage of lifeless bodies that came out of the Kent State shooting a decade later.

"I Shot an Arrow Into The Sky" is a bleak horror story about a man losing his mind that Serling made slightly more palatable to a wider audience, but also to CBS executives, by channeling it through the lens of science fiction. I'd love to have been a fly on the wall when the CBS executives got their first glimpse of that twist!

Zone Fact

Serling gave Madelon Champion credit for this story after she pitched it to him at a cocktail party!

An Unofficial Journey Into The Twilight Zone

"The Hitch-Hiker"
Episode 16
Original Airdate: January 22, 1960

Directed by Alvin Ganzer
Written by Rod Serling (based on a story by Lucille Fletcher)

"Her name is Nan Adams. She's 27 years old. Her occupation: buyer at a New York department store. At present on vacation, driving cross-country to Los Angeles, California, from Manhattan...Minor incident on Highway 11 in Pennsylvania. Perhaps, to be filed away under "accidents you walk away from." But from this moment on, Nan Adams' companion on a trip to California will be terror. Her route: fear. Her destination: quite unknown."

Nan Adams (Inger Stevens) is road tripping across America, traveling from Manhattan to Los Angeles. During her trip she gets a flat, causing her to momentarily lose control of her car before safely skidding to the side of the road. She's able to get her car fixed and back on the road, but she becomes increasingly disturbed by the presence of a hitchhiker who is always supernaturally one step ahead of her, despite always looking for a ride. Paralyzed with fear that the hitchhiker is stalking her, Nan slowly realizes that maybe she is going his way.

"The Hitch-Hiker" is based on a Lucille Fletcher 1941 radio play of the same name, but I think its genesis can be tracked even further back than that. In 1906, E.F. Benson wrote the short story "The Bus-Conductor" about a man's premonition of a fatal bus crash when a hearse driver beckons to him with the famous line, "Room for one more!" The most faithful adaptation of this story was in the 1945 Ealing studios anthology film *Dead of Night*, while *The Twilight Zone* would properly tackle the tale in "Twenty-Two" (S2E17). "The Bus-Conductor" features so many properties of "The Hitch-Hiker" that it's difficult to overlook, like its unique inclusion of automobiles, and how the protagonist learns that death isn't just around every corner, but could be actively pursuing you. Hell, even the catchphrase, "Going my way?" has a similar cadence to "Room for one more!" But Fletcher's story would go on to become influential all on its own,

Jacob Trussell

spawning not only this episode, but a section of the E.C. Comics inspired film *Creepshow 2* as well as the dreamy, expressionistic horrors of Herk Harvey's *Carnival of Souls*.

Fletcher's play was originally written for Orson Welles and his radio show. There, it was a—pardon the pun—vehicle for Welles, and Serling smartly adopts it to the paranoia of a woman traveling alone. This plays into a reality for women, that is as true now as I'm sure it was then, that they must carry with them the constant threat of harassment, especially in desolate locations like the side of the road or walking alone at night. This sad fact is made slightly more bearable through its supernatural element, even if Nan ultimately cannot escape death. The titular hitcher becomes an albatross, an omen, not only for the character but the actress herself. A decade later, Inger Stevens tragically died from a drug overdose that was eventually ruled a suicide. Nan was frightened that something pursuing her would eventually catch up. For the character, it was the hitchhiker, but for the actress, it was her own struggles with mental health.

Zone Fact

The story is based on Lucille Fletcher's own experience seeing a strange man while traveling across the country with her then husband, Psycho composer Bernard Herrman.

An Unofficial Journey Into The Twilight Zone

"The Fever"
Episode 17
Original Airdate: January 29, 1960

Directed by Robert Florey
Written by Rod Serling

> *"Mr. and Mrs. Franklin Gibbs, three days and two nights all expenses paid at a Las Vegas hotel, won by virtue of Mrs. Gibbs's knack with a phrase. But unbeknownst to either Mr. and Mrs. Gibbs is the fact that there's a prize in their package, neither expected nor bargained for. In just a moment, one of them will succumb to an illness worse than any virus can produce. A most inoperative, deadly life-shattering affliction known as the Fever."*

Flora Gibbs (Vivi Janiss) is thrilled to have won an all-expenses paid vacation to Las Vegas after winning a caption contest. She is tantalized and dazzled by the electric lights of the Vegas strip, but her husband Franklin's (Everett Sloane) mood sours at the idea of the city's main attraction: casinos. He detests gambling, believing it immoral and a guaranteed scam designed to take your money. Mr. Gibbs temperament won't spoil Mrs. Gibbs' excitement as she decides to play just one nickel. Much to the smug delight of Mr. Gibbs, she loses, but while the Missus can easily walk away from the machine, the Mister can't after trying his hand at the slots.

One nickel soon turns into a dime, which turns into a dollar, that then turns into cashing check after check until Mr. Gibbs has become a slave to gambling. Is this the beginning of a man's downward spiral into addiction, losing himself and his marriage to the possibility of "just one more?" Or is there something more supernaturally sinister happening with this one-armed bandit?

Frenzied and freaky, "The Fever" is perhaps the first "Are you fucking kidding me?" episode of the series, as the core villain—if you can even call it that—is a demented slot machine. The anxiety that Mr. Gibbs feels is acutely specific, because Rod Serling had a similar incident with his own wife. Following the plot of the episode almost to the T, Serling reluctantly put a coin in a slot machine on a Vegas vacation after *The Twilight Zone* was picked up by CBS. After one draw

67

Jacob Trussell

of the arm, Serling was hooked and just like in the episode, proceeded to spend most of his vacation testing his luck again and again.

At face value it may be hard to really buy a story about a killer slot machine, but that completely minimizes the episode's true horror. It was never from the machine itself, but from watching Gibbs lose control, and his life, through the nightmares conjured from the addicted mind. The core message is powerful—no matter how much you think it won't happen to you, addiction is nondiscriminatory. It'll get you when you least expect it. Serling made a point to show how miserly Mr. Gibbs is in the beginning, so that the contrast of the end can be blisteringly stark. He's lost himself to an expensive thrill that doesn't fill the hole he's found in his appetite, no matter how many times he wants to spin again.

Addiction doesn't care if you're a great parent, have an important job, or lead your community, it can still insidiously sneak into your life through one innocent slip. "The Fever" captures the angst and anger of a compulsive disorder that no one should have to endure.

Zone Fact

Everett Sloane first worked with Rod Serling as the sociopathic Mr. Ramsey in his monumental teleplay Patterns.

"The Last Flight"
Episode 18
Original Airdate: February 5, 1960

Directed by William F. Claxton
Written by Richard Matheson

> *"Witness Flight Lieutenant William Terrance Decker, Royal Flying Corps, returning from a patrol somewhere over France. The year is 1917. The problem is that the Lieutenant is hopelessly lost. Lieutenant Decker will soon discover that a man can be lost not only in terms of maps and miles, but also in time—and time in this case can be measured in eternities."*

In 1917, World War I pilot William Terrance "Terry" Decker (Kenneth Haigh), Flight Lieutenant of the 56 Squadron Royal Flying Corps, finds himself lost in a mysterious cloud amidst an aerial battle with German fighter planes. He lands at a modern United States air base in France where, to his amazement, he's traveled forward in time. The commanding officers, Major Wilson (Simon Scott) and General Harper (Alexander Scourby), are unsure of what to believe, especially as Decker tells them that he saw his friend and co-pilot Alexander Mackaye (Robert Warwick) die in battle. Except Mackaye is still alive, a celebrated war hero, and coincidentally visiting the base that very day. If he didn't die in battle, then who saved him once his plane went down? Looking to redeem himself from his perceived cowardice, Terry's second chance may be found in that space where the sky meets *The Twilight Zone*.

Season One of *The Twilight Zone* features two stories based on short works by Richard Matheson that Rod Serling adapted ("And When The Sky Was Opened" and "Third from the Sun"), but "The Last Flight" is the first episode that the master of the genre strictly wrote himself. The set-up of an airplane that can travel through some mysterious fissure in space time would also be revisited later in the series in "The Odyssey of Flight 33" (S2E18).

That episode hinged on the horror and fantasy of time travel, but Matheson squarely grounds "The Last Flight" in a deep-seated fear that men—and especially soldiers—would have held: the shame of being called a coward. Matheson goes a step further, positing that his pilot's conflict comes from the complex guilt he carries from abandoning his friend during battle. Matheson is impressing on any soldier watching that they can't hold on to the guilt of being a human and trying to survive. That's not a weakness, it's hardwired into our factory settings.

What Decker is really feeling is the sense of regret that comes from hindsight. Free from danger, he can reflect on his actions, and along with the twisty time motif, it becomes the catalyst for the satisfying resolution. Not everyone gets to have a second chance. But not everyone is from *The Twilight Zone*.

Zone Fact

Richard Matheson's first episode as the sole writer.

"The Purple Testament"
Episode 19
Original Airdate: February 12, 1960

Directed by Richard L. Bare
Written by: Rod Serling

"Infantry platoon, U.S. Army, Philippine Islands, 1945. These are the faces of the young men who fight, as if some omniscient painter had mixed a tube of oils that were at one time earth brown, dust gray, blood red, beard black, and fear—yellow white, and these men were the models. For this is the province of combat, and these are the faces of war."

At the height of the Second World War in the Pacific Theatre, a rumor is circulating through a platoon of soldiers that Lt. Fitzgerald (William Reynolds) has a unique gift: he can accurately predict a soldier's death. He reveals his powers to Captain Phil Riker (Dick York) and explains that he sees a purple shimmer envelop a man's face as a harbinger of his death. Fitzgerald feels cursed, but Riker believes the Lieutenant is simply unraveling under the pressures of war. Time waits for no man, and neither does the purple glow of death, something they'll both soon learn first-hand.

Rod Serling was stationed in the Pacific Theatre during World War II, so many of *The Twilight Zone's* war stories take place in the Philippines. Maybe it's because of the circumstances of war, but I find taking a soldier's perspective—in and out of *The Twilight Zone*—allows for more complex masculine emotions to be expressed, which is especially surprising during a time in media history that idealized traditional masculinity.

Men were expected to be rock solid and stoic—show no emotions or else you'll be deemed a weak coward. While toxic masculinity is unquestioningly pervasive throughout the military, Rod Serling had firsthand experience seeing traditional masculinity grapple with the mental health issues that sprout during wartime. Here we don't just see soldiers with rugged, emotionless exteriors, we get to watch without judgment a man falling apart with shameless sorrow. It's heartbreaking, especially when you contrast it with the impenetrable troops of allied propaganda films of the 1940s.

Jacob Trussell

    This powerful episode is made better through an insanely stacked cast featuring the aforementioned Reynolds and York (best known for playing the first Darrin in *Bewitched*), but also cameos from Paul Mazursky (director of *Bob & Carol & Ted & Alice*) and Warren Oates (*The Wild Bunch*). The only drawback is that we can't see the purple shimmer, since the series was shot in black and white. I wonder what Serling would have done if he was allowed to be more extreme, replacing the shimmer with more realistic images of death. The horrors of war were surely burned into Serling's mind, and he frequently used the series to impress those horrors on the viewer.

Zone Fact

Influenced heavily by Serling's time in the Pacific Theatre during World War II.

"Elegy"
Episode 20
Original Airdate: February 19, 1960

Directed by Douglas Heyes
Written by Charles Beaumont

> *"The time is the day after tomorrow. The place: a far corner of the universe. A cast of characters: three men lost amongst the stars. Three men sharing the common urgency of all men lost. They're looking for home. And in a moment, they'll find home; not a home that is a place to be seen, but a strange unexplainable experience to be felt."*

Astronauts Captain James Webber (Kevin Hagen), Kurt Meyers (Jeff Morrow), and Peter Kirby (Don Dubbins) are forced to make an emergency landing on a far distant asteroid when their spacecraft runs low on fuel. Exiting their ship, they are shocked to discover not only a breathable atmosphere, but an entire town that looks just like any on Earth. Except the world appears to be frozen in time, with vibrant parties and parades made unnervingly static. As they theorize why this could be, like time moving slower on the planet, they discover someone who can move—the cyborg Mr. Wickwire (Cecil Kellaway).

He explains that they landed at Happy Glades, a kind of mortuary built into an asteroid so those interned can relive their happiest days. Wickwire is awakened whenever he is needed, keeping Happy Glades clean and tidy even 200 years after its initial use. Desiring to find a way to return home, Mr. Wickwire is happy to oblige the astronauts. But in a future pock-marked by nuclear war and famine, the home they seek will only come on Wickwire's terms.

Any other genre anthology show that came after *The Twilight Zone* will invariably be likened to the series, even if the similarities really just stop at the "sci fi anthology" descriptor. For instance, Charlie Brooker's *Black Mirror* is the modern equivalent of Serling's show, but *The Twilight Zone* rarely dipped into the deeply sad and disturbing stories that *Black Mirror* has made its name on.

This episode takes a uniquely strange, borderline uplifting idea—an asteroid retrofitted as a makeshift funeral parlor so the dead can forever experience the happiest days of their lives—and rips the rug out from under you with the frightening unknown dangers of artificial intelligence. We're all a little afraid of the potential of a robot uprising, and here it is, over 20 years before James Cameron sent his *Terminator* back in time.

Mr. Wickwire is no T-800, but he is very similar to our modern-day digital assistants like Alexa and Siri; his operations are based solely on the needs of a human. But the question Cameron was wondering is the same that Beaumont asks, "What would happen if a robot achieved sentience?" Would they recognize that man is a scourge to the universe, destined for war, avarice, and destruction despite their best intentions? And if they came to that conclusion, what else would they do but annihilate us?

Elegy's deadly ending has a morose message: war is a disease that's caused by man, and as long as there are men who believe in it, we'll never find the peace we so desperately crave. We'll be destined to relive the same cycle of violence year after year, lifetime after lifetime.

Zone Fact

The large motionless crowd scenes were achieved without the use of dummies or special effects; those are all real actors!

An Unofficial Journey Into The Twilight Zone

"Mirror Image"
Episode 21
Original Airdate: February 26, 1960

Directed by John Brahm
Written by Rod Serling

> *"Obscure and metaphysical explanation to cover a phenomenon. Reasons dredged out of the shadows to explain away that which cannot be explained. Call it 'parallel planes' or just 'insanity'. Whatever it is, you'll find it in the Twilight Zone."*

Millicent Barnes (Vera Miles) is waiting for a bus at her local depot, on her way to a new job in Cortland, New York. When she asks the ticket teller when the bus will arrive, she's told that this is the third time she's approached his booth, even though she knows she only just arrived. Soon she notices more odd things, like her bags disappearing and others at the bus station swearing they saw her somewhere she knew she wasn't. With the help of Paul (Martin Milner)—another man waiting for a bus—she begins suspecting there is a universe directly next to this one that is slowly merging with our own. The only way to save herself, and possibly the world, is by killing her double. Believing she is having a nervous breakdown, Paul attempts to get Millicent help before she hurts herself, but when he sees his own mirror image, he realizes there is more out there than just three dimensions.

    Despite the intimation that we are seeing two Vera Miles because of the multiverse theory, "Mirror Image" is more thematically aligned with stories of doppelgängers. This concept is steeped in folklore and still used in metaphors today, from the cheesiest Troma films to modern horror like Stephen King's *The Outsider* and Denis Villeneuve's *Enemy*.

    Writers revisit the themes of doppelgängers frequently, because if you think metaphorically facing yourself is terrifying, consider how worse it would be if you had to physically. Doppelgängers are the actualization of our own self-consciousness, a way for us to embody our fears of inadequacy in an external way. What would we do if we encountered our double and they were better than us in every way? If my double has its shit together, why can't I?

Whether intentionally or not, this episode also speaks to our treatment of the mentally ill. At the episode's end, when Paul finally gets Millicent the help he believes she needs, she is silently scooped up by a pair of unannounced cops who throw her in the back of their car before speeding away. No questions, no compassion—she is treated like any common criminal and not as someone that needs professional help. This is Serling once again saying if we don't approach those in need from a place of merciful understanding, it will only perpetuate a cycle of violence and misconception about those with mental health issues; something we should continue to practice today.

Zone Fact

This episode inspired Us, the sophomore feature from Jordan Peele, creative force behind the 2019 revival of the series.

"The Monsters Are Due on Maple Street"
Episode 22
Original Airdate: March 4, 1960

Directed by Ronald Winston
Written by Rod Serling

"Maple Street, U.S.A., late summer. A tree-lined little world of front porch gliders, barbecues, the laughter of children, and the bell of an ice cream vendor. At the sound of the roar and the flash of light, it will be precisely 6:43 P.M. on Maple Street... This is Maple Street on a late Saturday afternoon. Maple Street in the last calm and reflective moment—before the monsters came."

Something strange is happening on Maple Street. First the residents—including Steve Brand (Claude Akins) and Charlie Farnsworth (Jack Weston)—watch a looming shadow pass overhead, accompanied by deafening thunder. Soon their appliances go on the fritz, electricity shorts out, and the neighborhood is plunged into darkness. Amidst the confusion, a young boy points to his comic books for answers, that the phenomena they're experiencing is the prelude to an alien invasion. As the neighborhood devolves into an angry mob, fingers are pointed, accusations fly, and blood will be drawn before the evening is through. Who are the real monsters? Those amongst the stars, or the flesh and blood neighbors hiding in the house across the street?

Not only is "The Monsters Are Due on Maple Street" one of the most beloved episodes of the original series, but it manages to capture practically everything you want from an episode of *The Twilight Zone*. On the surface there is a compelling quasi-supernatural mystery, but it's made relevant by its parable on persecution and prejudice in the wake of the Red Scare. It's Rod Serling taking a note from Arthur Miller who used the Salem Witch Trials to draw comparisons to McCarthyism in *The Crucible*.

In many ways, this is the original "Monsters of Men" story we see in practically every modern apocalypse movie. It's the idea that when the structures of the world break down, people will revert to their most animalistic tendencies, unafraid to use deadly force no matter what. It's clear that Maple Street would have been a haven for human marauders and psychopaths if the living dead, instead of aliens, visited their neighborhood.

Perhaps what's most terrifying about this episode is how nothing has changed. The fears of the white middle class are still rooted directly in prejudice of "the other," a faux-enemy that's used to perpetuate hate mongering. The day I rewatched this episode was the first day we learned about the murder of Ahmaud Arbery, a Black man who was pursued and fatally shot by two white men while out jogging. Their excuse for shooting an unarmed man was because they thought he was a criminal, but he wasn't. He was just out for a jog. Their inherent fear of someone who did not look like themselves made them perceive any action as a threat of violence. So, they murdered him.

While it is not beat for beat what happens at the end of this episode, it's hard not to discern the same implications of the finale. The residents of Maple Street will say that it was just an accident, that they didn't know he wasn't a monster. They were just scared and felt the need to protect themselves, even if that need supersedes another's right to life. I wonder how Rod Serling would feel if he knew that the monsters never left the neighborhood.

Zone Fact

Steven Spielberg intended to adapt this episode for the 1983 feature film.

An Unofficial Journey Into The Twilight Zone

"A World of Difference"
Episode 23
Original Airdate: March 11, 1960

Directed by Ted Post
Written by Richard Matheson

"The modus operandi for the departure from life is usually a pine box of such and such dimensions, and this is the ultimate in reality. But there are other ways for a man to exit from life."

Arthur Curtis (Howard Duff) is your regular everyday '60s kind of guy. He's got a good job, a friendly secretary, and a wife to plan a vacation for. But today's different, because the moment he steps out of his office, he hears someone yell cut. Others begin approaching him, addressing him by a name that is not his own. Why does everyone think he's an actor, and how did his office suddenly become a film set? But above all else, who is Gerry Reagan, and why does everyone think that's who he is? Is he really an actor having an identity crisis, or a businessman plunged into a nightmare?

Actors relish in disappearing into their roles. It's not an ego trip though, it's about escaping. There's a real comfort in not having to worry about your real-world problems, if for just a few hours. Some actors, like Daniel Day-Lewis, take it a step beyond, and it becomes not about escaping for a few hours, but days and weeks. Throughout the 1950s a new style of acting was becoming prevalent that focused on realism. The approach sprung up from the Neighborhood Playhouse and The Actors Studio in New York City, focusing on different interpretations of Stanislavski's Method, and this trend produced the glut of popular actors throughout the era, many of which were featured on *The Twilight Zone*, from Robert Redford to Robert Duvall. I'm not saying that Gerry Regan is method acting Arthur Curtis, but I am positive Day-Lewis would be envious of his level of commitment.

No doubt aware of this shift in acting styles, writer Richard Matheson looked at the method through the lens of psychology to ask the question "What would happen if an actor went so deep into a role that he couldn't find his way back out?" The answer to that question is what we see in the episode, but we're compelled to probe further. Why is this happening to him? Why is he losing control of who he is? Is he retreating into his fantasies to escape the realities of a terrible divorce, his drinking problems, and his career slowly imploding? Or is the real reason something more supernatural than we can conceive?

The supernatural final beat is meant to inspire optimism for Gerry Reagan-cum-Arthur Curtis, but is it really a happy ending? He gives himself fully to his fantasies, so much so that he physically disappears into the film set, but isn't submitting to your delusions just the easy way out? Or would the truly optimistic ending show Gerry confront his mounting problems so he can finally breathe after years of suffocation? Happy endings are only what you make of them in *The Twilight Zone*.

Zone Fact

Was lampooned in The Beaver Papers, a 1983 satirical examination of the supposed lost season of Leave It to Beaver.

"Long Live Walter Jameson"
Episode 24
Original Airdate: March 18, 1960

Directed by Anton Leader
Written by Charles Beaumont

> *"You're looking at Act One, Scene One, of a nightmare, one not restricted to witching hours of dark, rainswept nights. Professor Walter Jameson, popular beyond words, who talks of the past as if it were a present, who conjures up the dead as if they were alive.*

Walter Jameson (Kevin McCarthy) has a secret, and his soon to be father-in-law Professor Samuel Kittridge (Edgar Stehli) has his suspicions of what that might be. Samuel has realized that Jameson has a keen mind for facts that he couldn't possibly have found in a textbook, not to mention being the spitting image of a soldier he found in a Civil War photograph. Is this the clue that Samuel has been searching for all these years, as he's watched himself grow older, while Jameson has remained the same age? But before Jameson marries his daughter, the father must know the secret of his everlasting life. Because someone else wants to drink from the fountain of youth: Samuel himself.

Jim Jarmusch directed a film in 2013 called *Only Lovers Left Alive*. The film follows two vampires, played by Tom Hiddleston and Tilda Swinton, who slowly become disillusioned with their immortality. It's a meditation on the repetitiveness of life and the dark truths of our lofty wishes. So many of us long to live forever, *Highlander*-style, without thinking about the implications of what comes with it. Living forever means you'll eventually experience everything that there is to experience. And because you'll never die, those experiences will grow just as tired as the boring routines we all on occasion find ourselves in.

In many ways this is exactly what Walter Jameson is feeling. He recognizes the true curse that comes with eternal life and that fuels the sinister undertones in his performance. I was constantly expecting him to secretly be some supernatural Jack the Ripper or otherworldly Lovecraftian abomination, like Charles Dexter Ward. But to emphasize the unremarkableness of his immortality, Jameson is actually none of these things. He's just a lousy husband from the Classical Period of Plato with nothing but time on his hands to continue being, you guessed it, a lousy husband. This all makes his demise even more fitting. No matter how old you are, bad behavior always has a way of catching up to you. And in Jameson's case, his consequences come from the muzzle of a pistol-packing ex-wife turned granny.

Zone Fact

Designer William Tuttle would be the first make-up artist to win an Academy Award for the film The Seven Faces of Dr. Lao, also written by Charles Beaumont.

"People Are Alike All Over"
Episode 25
Original Airdate: March 25, 1960

Directed by Mitchell Leisen
Written by Rod Serling (from a short story by Paul Fairman)

"They're taking a highway into space, Man unshackling himself and sending his tiny, groping fingers up into the unknown."

Two astronauts with very different views of alien life are on a mission to Mars. Sam Conrad (Roddy McDowell) is wary of meeting extraterrestrials, unsure of how we'd be able to discern their intentions, while Warren Marcusson (Paul Comi) has hope that those they meet will be like us: compassionate and welcoming. When attempting to land, their ship malfunctions, killing Marcusson in front of a helpless, scared Conrad. After he gathers his courage and exits the ship, he's greeted by Martians who, to his relief, do in fact look just like us. They offer food and shelter, with all of the comforts of Conrad's life at home. But something doesn't sit right, especially once Conrad realizes there are no windows or doors to his new home. That's because what Marcusson didn't account for is that the uncaring and compassionless are alike all over too.

Based on the short story "Brothers Beyond The Void" by Paul W. Fairman, Rod Serling really gives away every single twist in the episode title, but he hides it all in a double meaning. After Conrad discovers that the Martians look just like Earthlings, we think, "OH! That's what they meant. People may physically look alike all across the galaxy!" But as creeping dread permeates through the episode once he exits the ship, you realize there is a more psychological reading of the title. Our desire for greed, deception, and enslavement travels far beyond our atmosphere than we may ever know. The idea of "human zoos" is one of Season One's most unnerving twists that begs the question: how many people became members of PETA after having their mind blown by this shocker of an ending?

I also find this satirical episode to be an indictment of post-war American exceptionalism and the pitfalls that come with it. During the Space Race we had this expectation of conquering the galaxy (and beating the Soviet Union and China) by following an interstellar manifest destiny. But we're not invincible just because we invent machines of destruction. Serling seems to say with the downbeat final moment, "Damn our egos! We are nothing but specks in a vast galaxy and we would do best to not forget that." Otherwise, it would only be fitting that the first lifeforms we find would throw us in a public exhibit that's charging admission. That's intergalactic capitalism, baby! It's cosmic karma for a man from a world filled with war to be treated like nothing but an animal to those alien eyes looking from the outside in.

Zone Fact

Human zoos sound too terrifying to be real? Think again. In 1906, the Bronx Zoo displayed an Mbuti man, Ota Benga, in an exhibit. It would take 114 years for the zoo to publicly apologize for this unconscionable act.

An Unofficial Journey Into The Twilight Zone

"Execution"
Episode 26
Original Airdate: April 1, 1960

Directed by David McDearmon
Written by Rod Serling (from a short story by George Clayton Johnson)

"This is November 1880, the aftermath of a necktie party."

Joe Caswell (Albert Salmi) is a thief and a murderer of the worst kind, dangerous and unrepentant to the very end. The moment he was expecting his neck to snap at the end of a rope, he's suddenly transported 100 years in the future by Professor Manion (Russell Johnson) who's successfully made Caswell the very first time traveler. What the Professor doesn't realize is that his invention had plucked someone straight from the gallows, and this dead man walking has no intention of playing nice with the stranger who brought him into an alien world where TV's and jukeboxes are practically black magic. But for Caswell, death has a sick sense of humor, and always finds a way of catching up with us, no matter where we are in time.

If "People are Alike All Over" is meant to tell us that even on far distant planets you'll find aliens that are just as terrible as people are here, then this episode is impressing on the viewer that the evils that plague us today have been plaguing us for centuries. It's why Caswell's death is framed rather tragically—a victim of not only his circumstances, but a kind of twisted comic fate. A murderer and a thief killed—extremely casually might I add—by another murderer and thief.

This is also Serling's way of saying that we should be careful what we wish for, especially when inventing new technology. The Professor hadn't considered the ramifications that come from transporting someone from the past into the present day. He's actually dangerously underprepared for it! His own hubris for inventing the impossible got in the way of taking into consideration the shock that his time traveler would feel. Without sounding completely heartless, Manion gets what he deserves at the episode's end, because do we really want the keys to time in the hands of someone who cannot properly care for it?

Zone Fact

Russell Johnson must love playing a professor as he would don the white coat once more as The Professor in Gilligan's Island!

An Unofficial Journey Into The Twilight Zone

"The Big Tall Wish"
Episode 27
Original Airdate: April 8, 1960

Directed by Ronald Winston
Written by Rod Serling

"In this corner of the universe, a prizefighter named Bolie Jackson, 183 pounds and an hour and a half away from a comeback at St. Nick's Arena. Mr. Bolie Jackson, who, by the standards of his profession is an aging, over-the-hill relic of what was, and who now sees a reflection of a man who has left too many pieces of his youth in too many stadiums for too many years before too many screaming people. Mr. Bolie Jackson, who might do well to look for some gentle magic in the hard-surfaced glass that stares back at him."

Bolie Jackson (Ivan Dixon) is a prizefighting boxer on the last legs of a floundering career. But while he may have lost all faith in his own abilities, there is one person who still believes in him: Henry (Stephen Perry), the son of his girlfriend Frances (Kim Hamilton). When Henry tells Bolie that all of his wishes come true, his mother remarks that he has a preternatural ability to turn his dreams into reality. Bolie will have his faithlessness in magic tested when Henry's desire for him to win his next match comes true. But are a child's wishes strong enough to change Henry's future? Or is it something that should have stayed buried in his past?

It speaks volumes that Rod Serling was able to get CBS to air an episode told from the perspective of a Black man in the very first season of *The Twilight Zone*. I can imagine that this door was partially opened when Nat King Cole became the first Black entertainer with his own variety show in 1956, but this was during a time when *Amos 'n' Andy* and *Beulah* were the most prevalent representations of Black people on screen, both mired in racially offensive stereotypes. Even popular anthology programs like *Playhouse 90*—which Serling wrote for—didn't give leading roles to Black actors. Which means this episode is not only good, but it's historically significant.

What I find striking, and perhaps most important, about the

episode is that it's not only focused on a Black family, but it's not intrinsically a commentary on race, even though it's impossible to ignore as the episode aired during the beginnings of the Civil Rights Movement. It could have been easy to revolve his story around prejudice and racism, but instead Bolie becomes the proxy for Serling himself who had a short stint as a boxer during the Second World War. More than anything else, "The Big Tall Wish" is autobiographical.

It's also a meditation on the melancholy of losing the wonderments of life as we grow older. It's heartbreaking to hear Henry give up wishing for magic. Bolie tries to reassure him after he loses, but the damage is already done. But growing up doesn't mean letting go of the mysteries of life. While the magic we believe in as children may not actually exist, perhaps the true secret of staying young is never forgetting that it still just might. All we have to do is remember to believe.

Zone Fact

This episode's diversity and inclusion would garner it the 1961 Unity Award for Outstanding Contributions to Better Race Relations.

An Unofficial Journey Into The Twilight Zone

"A Nice Place to Visit"
Episode 28
Original Airdate: April 15, 1960

Directed by John Brahm
Written by Charles Beaumont

"A scared, angry little man who never got a break. Now he has everything he's ever wanted—and he's going to have to live with it for eternity—in The Twilight Zone."

Henry Francis "Rocky" Valentine (Larry Blyden) is a stick-up man who catches a bullet from a cop during a pawnshop robbery gone awry. When Rocky wakes up, he's shocked to find that not only is he still alive, but he's being waited on hand and foot by Pip (Sebastian Cabot). It dawns on Rocky that he died, but since Pip is more Guardian Angel than Satan's Little Helper, he realizes that he's gone to The Good Place and not The Bad Place! After all, Hell wouldn't reward with him a never-ending supply of broads, booze and blackjack, would it?

I find it hilarious that hell can look a lot like heaven when you are a scumbag! Because at the episode's beginning, that's exactly where Rocky thinks he is. And can you blame him? Look at what he's got! Cheap thrills and dolls soaked in free booze and as much gambling as he wants. These are the golden age stereotypes of immorality spelled with a capital S-I-N.

The title of the episode is derived from the popular phrase, "It's a nice place to visit, but I wouldn't want to live there," which I imagine was once a slogan for Las Vegas. It's the kind of place that would make a fine vacation where you can experience the lights and thrills of a place where dreams are made of. Invariably, those thrills can't maintain their highs forever and they will lose the luster they may have once had. That's what happens to Rocky. He got everything he could ever dream of only to realize everything he ever dreamed of isn't something that can sustain you forever. It's why I find this episode to be thematically similar to "Long Live Walter Jameson" (S1E24). In it, Jameson is immortal and has grown weary of the same pattern of life where his friends and colleagues grow old and die, leaving him behind to try and start anew every half century. There really can be too much of a good thing, be it everlasting life or having the same kind of fun for all eternity.

Zone Fact

Beaumont asked Rod Serling if he'd consider starring in this episode, originally titled "The Other Place"

"Nightmare as a Child"
Episode 29
Original Airdate: April 29, 1960

Directed by Alvin Ganzer
Written by Rod Serling

> *"Month of November, hot chocolate, and a small cameo of a child's face, imperfect only in its solemnity. And these are the improbable ingredients to a human emotion, an emotion, say, like—fear. But in a moment this woman, Helen Foley, will realize fear. She will understand what are the properties of terror. A little girl will lead her by the hand and walk with her into a nightmare."*

Helen Foley (Janice Rule) lives in an apartment building where she meets a young girl named Markie (Terry Burnham). Helen has never seen Markie before, but the girl seems to know her. Even more troubling, Markie knows that Helen witnessed her mother be violently murdered as a child, but repressed the identity of the killer. Distressed by the young girl's ominous presence, Helen is visited by a man named Peter Selden (Shepperd Strudwick) who worked for her mother. He reveals to Helen that Markie was actually her childhood nickname, and the girl she met bears more than a passing resemblance to her. Is Markie's arrival meant to help Helen heal an old wound, or is she there to provide warning for an even greater danger?

    Something Serling was trying to get across throughout the entire first season of the series is that it's scary how little we really know about the human mind. Our brains have the power to manifest things that are beyond our control and imagination, like the concept of a subliminal, supernatural albatross for impending danger.

    Because society had not warmed to the idea of psychiatry in the 1950s—let alone the 1930s when the murder took place—Helen never sought help for the trauma she experienced as a child. As her subconscious memory has been holding on to what happened, it's unintentionally come to define her whole life and bleeds into her everyday interactions and distrust of strangers. The appearance of Markie then becomes Helen's way of finally processing the trauma from her past. Serling implies that the secret to unlocking the root of a mental health problem starts by looking back at our childhoods, and the traumas we may have experienced. Once you can make that realization for yourself, like Helen, you can begin your road to recovery.

Zone Fact

Rod Serling named his lead character after a teacher he had in high school.

"A Stop at Willoughby"
Episode 30
Original Airdate: May 6, 1960

Directed by Robert Parrish
Written by Rod Serling

"This is Gart Williams, age 38, a man protected by a suit of armor all held together by one bolt. Just a moment ago, someone removed the bolt, and Mr. Williams' protection fell away from him, and left him a naked target. He's been cannonaded this afternoon by all the enemies of his life. His insecurity has shelled him, his sensitivity has straddled him with humiliation, his deep-rooted disquiet about his own worth has zeroed in on him, landed on target, and blown him apart. Mr. Gart Williams, ad agency exec, who in just a moment, will move into the Twilight Zon—in a desperate search for survival."

Between his taxing job and vexing wife, New York City executive Gary Williams (James Daly) begins to feel trapped by the never-ending stresses of his life. That is, until he accidentally dozes off on his nightly commuter train home and finds himself stopped at a little hamlet called Willoughby. What he finds so enticing about this strange little town is that it seems to be in a time when life was slower—simpler even. But is Willoughby just a figment of his imagination, a dream of a more peaceful life? Or is Willoughby something else, something that won't become apparent to Gart until it's too late?

While "Willoughby" may be light on thrills, it more than makes up for it in a wildly unexpected twist that feels more like the bummer endings of Charles Beaumont than the episode's writer Rod Serling. Willoughby is less of a town and more of an idea for Gart. The grind of life has ground him down and the escape he needs is in a little town down the line about 60 years out of time. Is the proper way to escape the troubles of life by completely eschewing your world though? Something Gart learns the hard way is that the grass isn't always greener. It's a similar problem that follows other versions of Serling's burnt out businessmen, like Martin Sloan in "Walking Distance" (S1E5) or Gerry Reagan in "A World of Difference"

(S1E23). Fantasizing about starting a new life may be what we think we want, but rarely does it give us the sense of contentment that we actually need.

There was never a Willoughby, it was just the name of the funeral parlor that inevitably would carry Gart's body away. Once you learn the truth behind the town, you'll want to revisit the episode to see if there were any clues leading up to this eventual discovery. Serling leaves the door wide open for interpretation of this twist. Has the town been nothing but the personification of Gart's desire for normalcy in his sea of mental troubles or is it something darker? Did he just sleepwalk and accidentally fall off the train, or did he purposefully leap? Mental illness doesn't wax and wane, they remain pervasive, even if the person always puts on a happy face.

Zone Fact

First episode to feature the series name in the opening narration, which would become the standard for the subsequent revivals of the series.

An Unofficial Journey Into The Twilight Zone

"The Chaser"
Episode 31
Original Airdate: May 13, 1960

Directed by Douglas Heyes
Written by Robert Presnell Jr. (from a short story by John Collier)

"Mr. Roger Shackelforth. Age: youthful twenties. Occupation: being in love. Not just in love, but madly, passionately, illogically, miserably, all-consumingly in love with a young woman named Leila, who has a vague recollection of his face and even less than a passing interest. In a moment, you'll see a switch, because Mr. Roger Shackelforth, the young gentleman so much in love, will take a short but very meaningful journey into The Twilight Zone."

Roger (George Grizzard) is head over heels for Leila (Patricia Barry), a flirt who won't give him the time of day. Feeling spurned by this one-sided love affair, Roger looks for some assistance in matters of the heart from an old man named Professor A. Daemon (John McIntire). Surprisingly, the Professor's name raises zero alarm bells for Roger, so he eagerly buys a love potion for the low price of one dollar, disregarding the warnings Daemon lays out for him. Leila falls instantly in love with Roger who soon realizes why Daemon originally hesitated in selling him the potion. Leila's love becomes too devoted and eternal, quickly getting under Roger's skin as he pines for the days when she challenged his every beck and call. Will he live stagnantly with a woman who does not have a will of her own, or return to Daemon for one more potion with graver implications?

In modern slang, a "fuckboy" is a guy who will say or do anything to get into bed with a girl. This bit of slang was invented long after 1960, but there is no doubt in my mind that Roger is the perfect midcentury representation of one. He can't seem to get it into his mind that if a girl calls him a "silly, stupid, sophomoric clod" that maybe she isn't interested in bedding him. It's completely valid to really hate this creepy guy, especially now that men are (finally) being held accountable for not listening when a woman says no.

On the surface, "The Chaser" is meant to be a lighthearted story about a man not being careful with what he's wished for, but I also find a darker streak when you look at the well-worn cliché of the love potion in a modern context. After Roger has purchased the potion to give to Leila, we see them having drinks together. With her back turned, we watch Roger slyly dose her drink before swirling it around and serving it back to her none the wiser. We know it's a love potion, but it sure as hell looks like he is slipping her a roofie. It's the same move we've seen time and again from skeevy guys in movies and TV shows about this, like Michaela Coel's *I May Destroy You*. Was that always the vile undercurrent in these love potion stories, from *Love Potion No. 9* or Screamin' Jay Hawkins "I Put a Spell On You"?

Regardless of how you view the uncomfortable implications that come with forcing someone to fall in love with you through alchemical means, the episode's twist ending is one *The Twilight Zone* loves to engage in—you really can have too much of a good thing. For Roger, he reaped what he sowed for being a sexual predator, even if he does deserve a fate far worse than having someone who loves you to a fault.

Zone Fact

Only episode in the first season to not be written by Rod Serling, Charles Beaumont, or Richard Matheson.

"A Passage for Trumpet"
Episode 32
Original Airdate: May 20, 1960

Directed by Don Melford
Written by Rod Serling

> *"Take what you get and live with it, sometimes its sweet frosting, nice gravy. Sometimes it's sour and goes down hard, but you live with it, Joey. That's a nice talent you go, making music, moving people, making them want to laugh, make them want to cry, tap their feet, make them want to dance. That's an exceptional talent, Joey. Don't waste it. "*

Joey (Jack Klugman) is a Jazz musician with a trumpet that could rival Gabriel's own horn, if not for his crippling depression and wallet-draining alcohol addiction. When he's drunk, he doesn't see his ruined life or his dingy apartment, just the warm embrace that comes with being soused. In order to get another drink, Joey resorts to selling his trumpet, but it's in this act of desperation that he realizes he has nothing left to live for. Rather than continuing to fight and scrap, he attempts suicide by throwing himself in front of a delivery truck. Rather than killing himself however, Joey wakes up to a world where no one can see or hear him. That is, no one but a mysterious jazz musician (John Anderson) who seems to know not only a lot about Joey and his situation, but the mystery of his new reality. Is he dead, or is this the second chance he didn't know he's been craving?

After the Second World War, mental health issues were prevalent, but not fully understood or discussed. Joey is clearly suffering from severe depression, but Serling had to find a way to frame his health issues in a way that the viewing public could understand and ultimately sympathize with. "A Passage for the Trumpet" isn't about war or a veteran, so the best way to give reason to his condition was through alcoholism. People can understand the tortured mind of an alcoholic far easier than the tortured mind of someone struggling with clinical depression, especially in 1960. Furthermore, an alcoholic watching the episode can acutely understand the abuse Joey lumps on himself when he believes that his talent and the bottle are interlaced, rather than being tangled together in knots.

Gabe, our mysterious jazz musician who happens to be the spitting image of Abe Lincoln, then becomes his psychiatrist, prodding Joey to remind him that he has a lot to appreciate in his world, and he himself has a lot to offer. People may have been reluctant to visit a shrink in the late 1950s, but Serling impresses on his audience that visiting a psychiatrist is like talking to your local Rabbi or Priest, or in this case the archangel Gabriel. Therapy is just a way to get perspective on life, to better understand that the world is bigger than you, and there is plenty out there to still appreciate.

Zone Fact

Jack Klugman's first of four appearances on the series!

"Mr. Bevis"
Episode 33
Original Airdate: June 3, 1960

Directed by William Asher
Written by Rod Serling

"Mr. James B. W. Bevis, who believes in a magic all his own. The magic of a child's smile, the magic of liking and being liked, the strange and wondrous mysticism that is the simple act of living. Mr. James B. W. Bevis, species of 20th century male, who has his own private and special Twilight Zone."

Mr. Bevis (Orson Bean) is a man with a joi de vivre unlike anyone else he knows. He loves and cherishes life's many frivolities, like new styles of music and old models of cars, the loudest colors of suits and the littlest trinkets and souvenirs from trips taken long ago. Bevis' world is rocked though when he has a streak of bad luck losing his job, his car and his apartment all in the same afternoon. After getting loaded at a local bar, he meets a friendly gentleman, J. Hardy Hempstead (Henry Jones), who says he is his guardian angel and has come to solve all of his problems. But problems are like weeds—for every one solved, a new one will inevitably rise up. Which begs the question, are you really living life, if the life you're living isn't your own?

Is Mr. Bevis the most relatable character in *The Twilight Zone*? Maybe! He lives by his own rules in a society dictated by structure. He has a youthful spirit, the heart of a child, loves bright clothes, zither music (which has a tonal similarity to early electronic music), and garish tchotchkes. Bevis is the kind of fixture every community needs. The world gives Mr. Bevis lemons, he doesn't just make lemonade, he shares it with the entire neighborhood. In the 21st century, we aspire to have the self-assurance of a James B.W. Bevis. This is the struggle of growing up. That pull between acting your age and asking why being older means losing a joy for life?

Serling puts his beliefs in individuality front and center in "Mr. Bevis" by posing the question, "Is life worth living if you can't live by your own rules?" The short answer is no. For centuries, older generations have forced youth to adhere to an unwritten set of strict guidelines and passed down expectations of what being an adult means. It's a sobering thought to imagine all of the brilliant artists and minds we never learned from because someone, somewhere in their life, forced them to conform. Shape up or ship out, as the old saying goes. But they didn't ship out immaturity, they shipped out creativity. Luckily for us "Mr. Bevis" has a happy ending, as he comes to understand that it's not him that needs to change, it's society. And right about now, we could use a lot more people like Mr. Bevis helping to make our world a better place.

Zone Fact

The episode was intended to be a backdoor pilot for a show starring Burgess Meredith.

An Unofficial Journey Into The Twilight Zone

"The After Hours"
Episode 34
Original Airdate: June 10, 1960

Directed by Douglas Heyes
Written by Rod Serling

"Marsha White, in her normal and natural state, a wooden lady with a painted face who, one month out of the year, takes on the characteristics of someone as normal and as flesh and blood as you and I. But it makes you wonder, doesn't it, just how normal are we? Just who are the people we nod our hellos to as we pass on the street?"

Marsha White (Anne Francis) is shopping in a department store when an express elevator operator takes her directly to the ninth floor, an abandoned department where she's told she'll find a gold thimble. After purchasing one from a mysterious saleswoman (Elizabeth Allen), she discovers the thimble is damaged and attempts to return it, but no one seems to know who this woman was that she spoke with. Even worse, she's told there isn't a ninth floor. After accidentally dozing off in a manager's office, she finds herself trapped in the department store at night, discovering to her horror that the mannequins of the ninth floor are alive, and desperate to make Marsha one of their own, or so she thinks.

If you grew up wandering the aisles of department stores and malls as a kid, your imagination most likely ran wild when looking at a mannequin. If you were like me, you had more than a healthy sense of skepticism when it came to the dangers of these inanimate objects. What did they do when we weren't looking? Do they move? Can they talk? Why does it always feel like they are on the verge of reaching out and grabbing you?

I mean, I definitely thought about it as a kid, and clearly so did Rod Serling (and Andrew McCarthy for all my fellow fans of the 1987 comedy classic *Mannequin*). Even virtuosic composer Stephen Sondheim, five years after this episode aired, would do his own riff on the idea with Anthony Perkins (of *Psycho* fame) in the TV musical "Evening Primrose," part of *ABC Stage 67*.

I am glad that I wasn't a child in the 1960s, because the

mannequins at the center of "The After Hours" are super spooky, especially the ones with the old-school ski masks. I mean, yikes right?! Why are they scarier than modern ones? Maybe that's why 21st century mannequins don't look as much like humans, because when they did 60 years ago they freaked everyone out!

Needless to say, this is by far one of *The Twilight Zone*'s most frightening episodes. The moment when Marsha first hears the mannequin's disembodied voices, leading up to the elevator jump scare before the commercial break is perhaps the most palpably terrifying scene in the whole series. Just when you thought the episode couldn't get even spookier (or sadder), Rod Serling has one last melancholy twist up his sleeve. The episode leaves us to consider the strangers we pass every day. Could they be dealing with their own mental health issues? Yes. Could they also be mannequins on a month-long vacation? Also, yes.

Zone Fact

In a process he'd become known for, William Tuttle made a mold of Anne Francis' face to create the life-like mannequin head in the episode.

"The Mighty Casey"
Episode 35
Original Airdate: June 17, 1960

Directed by Alvin Ganzer and Robert Parrish
Written by Rod Serling

"What you're looking at is a ghost, once alive but now deceased. Once upon a time, it was a baseball stadium that housed a major league ball club known as the Hoboken Zephyrs. Now it houses nothing but memories and a wind that stirs in the high grass of what was once an outfield, a wind that sometimes bears a faint, ghostly resemblance to the roar of a crowd that once sat here. We're back in time now, when the Hoboken Zephyrs were still a part of the National League, and this mausoleum of memories was an honest-to-Pete stadium. But since this is strictly a story of make believe, it has to start this way: once upon a time, in Hoboken, New Jersey, it was tryout day. And though he's not yet on the field, you're about to meet a most unusual fella, a left-handed pitcher named Casey."

The Hoboken Zephyrs are the worst of the worst in professional baseball, even if they are confidently coached by Mouth McGarry (Jack Warden). As the Zephyrs hobble through the season, they are tossed a lifeline when a Doctor (Abraham Sofaer) introduces the team to a monumental pitcher named Casey (Robert Sorrells). Except something is different about Casey. He seems to be unfeeling, both emotionally and physically as he shrugs off taking a foul ball square between the eyes. He's able to do that because Casey's secret is that he's a robot. The only problem with a robot pitcher on the Zephyrs is that league rules stipulate every player must be human, and humans have hearts. So the Doctor and McGarry give Casey a heart, not realizing everything that will come with it, namely a trait that humans always forget about: compassion.

Baseball, America's favorite pastime, always seems to be used by writers like Stephen King as a metaphor for American values, a personification of a simpler time. For Serling, he uses the sport as the conduit to illustrate how emerging technologies will ultimately change the very things we love, a theme that is similarly touched on in Richard Matheson's "Steel" (S5E2).

Jacob Trussell

Season One of *The Twilight Zone* needed a healthy dose of levity, especially after such nerve-wrackers like "The After Hours." (S1E34) This cutesy episode about a robot baseball player with a beating heart, that finds he doesn't have the heart to strike out the other batter, is Serling's strategically deployed antecedent to the series' more sinister episodes about sentient robots like Charles Beaumont's "Elegy" (S1E20). Unlike Mr. Wickwire in that episode, Casey doesn't have it in his electric heart to hurt another person, even if he's only hurting their feelings. Rather than reacting coldly to his human counterpoints, Casey recognizes the fallibility inside every man and greets it with empathy. Casey, with circuits and wires, is better at being a human than those with flesh and blood.

The episode doesn't outwardly allude to racism in sports, but I can't help feeling that it was on Serling's mind when writing. Here, the league says only humans can play baseball, and as Casey has no heart, he is not human. Dehumanization is a tactic that white supremacists still use to diminish the humanity of people of color. In 1947, Jackie Robinson would become the first African American baseball player to join the Major Leagues. This was during a time when Jim Crow laws were still being enforced and years before the Supreme Court's decision on Brown vs. The Board of Education deemed public school segregation unconstitutional. Undoubtedly the famous player had to deal with dehumanizing language, but luckily Robinson would have the last laugh. No one remembers the racists, but no one will forget Jackie Robinson. Casey didn't break down any barriers like this, but by juxtaposing baseball with what makes us human, Serling subtly puts into perspective the importance of Jackie Robinson's legacy.

Zone Fact

It's quite morbid, but wickedly ironic, that Robert Sorrells plays a robot with a heart of gold considering, later in life, he would drunkenly murder someone before dying in prison.

"A World of His Own"
Episode 36
Original Airdate: July 1, 1960

Directed by Ralph Nelson
Written by Richard Matheson

"The home of Mr. Gregory West, one of America's most noted playwrights. The office of Mr. Gregory West. Mr. Gregory West—shy, quiet, and at the moment, very happy. Mary—warm, affectionate... And the final ingredient: Mrs. Gregory West."

Playwright Gregory West (Keenan Wynn) is a serial philanderer, much to the disappointment of his remissive wife Victoria (Phyllis Kirk). Gregory denies any allegations, explaining to his wife that the younger woman she saw him with isn't a woman at all, but rather a creation of his own writing—a character that's walked off of his page and into real life. More so, he has complete control over these characters, making them disappear the moment he burns the dictation tape that brings them to life. Victoria, refusing to believe it and wanting to have Gregory committed, is shocked at the revelation that she may be a creation of Gregory's too, but the only way to know for certain is to destroy the tape on which Gregory says Victoria was invented. Is she a figment of his imagination, or is Gregory losing his marbles?

Like "The Mighty Casey," this story is meant to be a lighthearted riff on what writer Richard Matheson saw as a uniquely masculine trait—the egotistical writer—and gives it in a fantastical device. But what I can't get over is how terrible this playwright is at writing women. He'd be right at home on hilarious sub-reddits that highlight the profound lack of understanding male authors have when writing the opposite sex.

When speaking about Victoria, Gregory says, "I had forgotten to put in a little human frailty." I can understand Matheson's intention to be that Gregory wrote a character with immobile emotions, but in a modern context it smacks of thinly veiled misogyny. As if the playwright is saying that a woman who is strong and confident and doesn't take this dude's shtick is a shrew. Again, I don't think this is

Jacob Trussell

what Matheson had in mind, but it is a good example of how much progress we've made in talking about female characters, and how far we still have to go in showing equality between sexes on screen.

Shortcomings aside, the episode shines in a closing narration that is as meta as it is silly. We see Serling, in his first on screen appearance saying "...we want you to realize that it was, of course, purely fictional. In real life, such ridiculous nonsense could never—" before being abruptly cut off. Rather than being an omniscient figure in the periphery, Serling is noticed by the playwright who offers him a warning: "Rod, you shouldn't! I mean, you shouldn't say such things as 'nonsense' and 'ridiculous'!" before throwing the dictation tape into the fire. With a shrug Serling says "Well, that's the way it goes," before flickering out and vanishing. This is a perfect, forgotten cap on the first season of this seminal TV show.

Zone Fact

This is the first on-screen narration from Rod Serling!

The Twilight Zone

SEASON TWO

SEPTEMBER 30, 1960 – JUNE 2, 1961

"King Nine Will Not Return"
Episode 1
Original Airdate: September 30, 1960

Directed by Buzz Kulik
Written by Rod Serling

> *"Odd how the real consorts with the shadows,*
> *how the present fuses with the past.*
> *How does it happen? The question is on file in the*
> *silent desert, and the answer?*
> *The answer is waiting for us—in the Twilight Zone."*

A B-25 Bomber has been shot down over an African desert, leaving only one man alive—Captain James Embry (Bob Cummings). Embry can't remember what happened to his plane, and worse, the bodies of his squadron have gone missing. His confusion deepens as he watches fighter jets fly overhead, decades before jet engines would be the industry standard. Is he just hallucinating the specters of his lost battalion, or is there something worse haunting him? The key may be hidden further in his mind than he ever dared go.

"King Nine Will Not Return" is a one-man horror show attempting to convey the hopeless anxiety of being lost, alone, with no help in sight and what that would do to a man's mind. Serling peppers this feeling of crawling death with some truly unnerving images, especially the moment where we see one of Embry's copilots—whom we know to be dead—silently laughing at him. The unease doesn't come from the visuals, but rather the lack of sound, as if the only voice Embry remembers is that of his own. And with delirium like that, it slowly dawns on the viewer that the more Embry talks to himself, the more he becomes an unreliable narrator.

The true meat of this episode is how it directly addresses PTSD, which would have been called Combat Stress Reaction in the late 1950s. Embry blames himself for the death of his crew, and that guilt has tortured him for the better part of two decades, resulting in this never-ending nightmare. To him, the desert is punishment for failing his men, even though their deaths weren't his fault.

Like Serling is wont to do, the supernatural element of "King

Jacob Trussell

Nine" offers a modicum of levity in the twist ending. Once Embry is in the hospital, we understand that everything we've just seen has been a delusion. But in the episode's final moments, the audience—and the characters—watch as sand is poured from the man's shoes. Sand that shouldn't be there. Maybe it is all in Embry's head, the product of years of bereavement, or maybe it's something that truly cannot be explained. Something that can exist only in *The Twilight Zone*.

Zone Fact

Partly inspired by the mystery surrounding the Lady Be Good, a US aircraft that disappeared in 1943 and was finally discovered in 1958, missing it's crew but remarkably intact.

An Unofficial Journey Into The Twilight Zone

"The Man in the Bottle"
Episode 2
Original Airdate: October 7, 1960

Directed by Don Medford
Written by Rod Serling

"A word to the wise, now, to the garbage collectors of the world, to the curio seekers, to the antique buffs, to everyone who would try to coax out a miracle from unlikely places. Check that bottle you're taking back for a two-cent deposit. The genie you save might be your own. Case in point, Mr. and Mrs. Arthur Castle, fresh from the briefest of trips into The Twilight Zone."

Arthur (Luther Adler) and Edna Castle (Vivi Janiss) own a small antique shop that's on its last legs. Bills are piling up and unless they get a sudden influx of money, they fear they'll lose the store for good. After a woman brings in a mysterious bottle she found in the trash, the Castle's accidentally summon a Genie (Joseph Ruskin) who will grant them four wishes. The first wish fixes a broken display case, while the second wish brings them a great fortune. As they continue wanting more, the Castles slowly realize that wishes from Genies come with unexpected consequences, and they find themselves plunged into a nightmare darker than they thought possible.

Let's face it, there's only two things you can count on in this world: death and taxes. This episode isn't necessarily concerned with death, or even taxes, but the themes of economic hardship in "The Man in the Bottle" gives you a stiff reminder about the latter. Even if a Genie in a bottle grants you a large lump of money, fair and square and tax free, the IRS will always have a way of finding out! That being said, in hindsight, Serling's joke about taxes may be the most unbelievable aspect of this episode. As history has sadly proven, millionaires and billionaires never have a problem getting out of paying taxes. The Castle's maybe should have just hired a more unscrupulous accountant!

The black comedy of a genie that you'd never want to make a wish with would be riffed on to an even greater degree in "Je Souhaite," a seventh season episode of *The X-Files*. After discovering a genie in a rolled up rug—rather than a dusty old lamp—Mulder (David Duchovney) attempts to wish for world peace, but because of the trickster nature of this Genie, he's forced to write a multipage, highly specified wish that looks more like a dissertation than the whims of a lucky man.

Even if you did find a Genie and made a wish that was incorruptible, it would likely still be in vain because nothing in life is free. Something, however minor, always has to give. Maybe the give shouldn't be as ruthless as forcing a Jewish shopkeeper to cos-play as Adolph Hitler for a hot second, but I suppose that is one way to get this malevolent Genie's point across: absolute power is always destined to corrupt absolutely. Still, Serling manages to end on an optimistic, but realistic, note. Life is cruel, but it is also short, so rather than being consumed by your anxieties, you might as well try and laugh. What else are you going to do?

Zone Fact

Luther Adler played Adolph Hitler twice before in 1951's The Magic Face and The Desert Fox: The Story of Rommel

"Nervous Man in a Four Dollar Room"
Episode 3
Original Airdate: October 14, 1960

Directed by Douglas Heyes
Written by Rod Serling

"Exit Mr. John Rhoades, formerly a reflection in a mirror, a fragment of someone else's conscience, a wishful thinker made out of glass, but now made out of flesh, and on his way to join the company of men. Mr. John Rhoades, with one foot through the door and one foot out of the Twilight Zone."

Two-bit gangster Jackie (Joe Mantell) is pushed around by his commanding boss, George (William D. Gordon). George gives Jackie an opportunity to redeem himself by killing a barkeep making trouble for their gang. Jackie's not a murderer though—he's just a thief and a conman. But if he goes through with the hit, his life—or what was left of it—would be gone. He would be thrown into jail, a grave, or at the very least trapped by unbearable guilt. Thinking aloud to come up with a plan to save his life by sparing another, Jackie hears a familiar voice speak back to him. It's his own, coming from the mirror in his cheap hotel room. If Jackie can't conjure up the courage to leave behind the life he's chosen, could his mirror image have the confidence he needs to become a better man?

"Nervous Man in a Four Dollar Room" is best described as a bottle episode—a term for a television show that sets their entire story within the confines of one room. Bottle episodes are limited in scope and have a tight economy of words, which allows the writers to flex their creativity. Rod Serling puts into flesh something we've all done before, talking to ourselves, by making his two-hander into a one-man show with Joe Mantell essentially acting with himself. This gimmick is similarly used in the 1945 anthology film *Dead of Night* that served as inspiration for other episodes of *The Twilight Zone*. In one segment, a man continues to see himself in a mirror, but the room he sees in the reflection isn't his own and, much like Jackie's double, his other wants out.

Serling uses this supernatural mirror as a way to embody how we speak to ourselves. We all have the capacity to build ourselves up with personal pep-talks, but we also are our own worst critic, tearing ourselves down with ease. Would we actually listen to our reflection if it finally talked back, or would we just further bury our heads in the sand and ignore it? We don't talk about low confidence and self-esteem in the same way as we do anxiety and depression, but it's still a psychological problem that is at the core of Jackie's dilemma and this episode. If your mirror image can believe in you, why shouldn't you be able to believe in yourself?

Zone Fact
Serling would revisit this monologue-conversation gimmick in "Last Night of the Jockey" where Mickey Rooney acts opposite himself. (S5E5)

"A Thing About Machines"
Episode 4
Original Airdate: October 28, 1960

Directed by David Orrick McDearmon
Written by Rod Serling

"Mr. Bartlett Finchley is a malcontent, born either too late or too early in the century, and who, in just a moment, will enter a realm where muscles and the will to fight back are not limited to human beings."

Bartlett Finchley (Richard Haydn) is an old-fashioned kind of guy. While he has all of the cutting-edge appliances every modern house needs, he doesn't really care for them. That's probably because he revels in being a misanthrope, even if beneath his thick skin you can see him craving social interaction. With building anxiety over the omniscient technology around him, Finchley lashes out, pushing friends away while putting boots through television sets. What he doesn't know is the TVs, electric razors, and radios are tired of his abuse, and they plan to do something about it.

It may just be basic household appliances rising up against Bartlett Finchley, but this is still proto-techno horror at its finest! The niche subgenre would really take off in the early 1990s with the boom of personal computers and how it affected us socially. In the extremes, techno-horror spawned films like 1999's *Virus* featuring Jamie Lee Curtis, Donald Sutherland, and one of the many Baldwin Boys aboard a ghost ship filled with Cronenbergian robot-monsters. For more subtle techno-horror, look towards Kiyoshi Kurosawa's *Pulse*, which begged the question, when our life is spent entirely online, will the social isolation make us cease to exist?

This early example of the subgenre speaks to how we've always been cautious around emerging tech. However subconsciously, we fear that it will pull us further away from what makes us human or, in Finchley's case, it will exacerbate our inherent anxiety over feeling inadequate. In the 50s, when these appliances were literally becoming household items, things that people were accustomed to doing with their own two hands were now being done in a flash—and better. This is what makes Finchley believe the devices are telling him to

Jacob Trussell

"Get out!" He's become useless in his own home, and it drives him crazy. His only defense is to use the machines as a patsy for his own failures. Finchley saying "it wasn't my fault, it was the machines!' is essentially a modern riff on "the devil made me do it!"

Analytical readings aside, I find this episode to be blithely silly, especially since the new tech we are seeing in the 21st century is far and away more frightening than anything here. The machinery terror in this episode amounts to electric razors descending staircases but it's ridiculously amusing, and I can't help but marvel at it.

Zone Fact

A likely source of inspiration for Stephen King's killer car novel Christine.

"The Howling Man"
Episode 5
Original Airdate: November 4, 1960

Directed by Douglas Heyes
Written by Charles Beaumont

"Ancient folk saying: "You can catch the Devil, but you can't hold him long."

David Ellington (H.M. Wynant) recounts his journey to a mysterious European monastery in the wake of the First World War. On the brink of complete exhaustion, Ellington stumbles across a brotherhood who refuses him aid, before he collapses at their feet. He's awakened by a chilling howl somewhere in the castle. Investigating, he discovers a man (Robin Hughes) imprisoned and begging for help. One of the Brother's, Jerome (John Carradine), explains that he is not a man at all, rather Satan himself. Since imprisoning the howling man at the end of the war, the Brothers believe they've brought peace to the world. If they release him, who knows what new atrocities—or world wars—may befall humanity. Have the Brother's lost their minds or have they imprisoned the harbinger of another hundred years of hell?

You have to marvel at the craft in this episode, from cinematographer George T. Clemens' liberal usage of Dutch angles—a term that means the frame of the image is tilted at a 45 degree angle—to the in media res structure that brings to mind the opening passages to so many H.P. Lovecraft stories. That Lovecraftian sensibility extends into our lead character David Ellington, anxiety-riddled and panicked, directly addressing the audience as if he is dictating a letter to a close colleague, like many of Lovecraft's tortured narrators.

Even though this episode takes place over a century ago, the themes that are discussed between Ellington and Brother Jerome are still so relevant today. Faith is still tested, regardless of creed, and we still have fear and anger at the way religion is used as a tool for the corrupted, like how Adolf Hitler weaponized "positive Christianity" to persecute people of Jewish faith. World War II offered the world a deeper understanding of evil; if only the answer to why Hitler rose to power was as simple as the Devil being accidentally released.

Jacob Trussell

But is the man imprisoned actually the Devil? Or are his jailers zealots? Have their actions actually made the world better? Much is left to interpretation at the episode's end, but the biggest moral of the story is one we've been taught since childhood: never open a door that someone expressly tells you not to open.

Zone Fact

Robin Hughes transformation into the devil was made possible through red/green lighting gels that corresponded with different colored makeup, a camera trick masterfully used in the 1937 horror comedy Sh! The Octopus.

"Eye of the Beholder"
Episode 6
Original Airdate: November 11, 1960

Directed by Douglas Heyes
Written by Rod Serling

> *"'Where is this place and when is it?' 'What kind of world where ugliness is the norm and beauty the deviation from that norm?' You want an answer? The answer is it doesn't make any difference, because the old saying happens to be true. Beauty is in the eye of the beholder, in this year or a hundred years hence."*

Janet Tyler (Maxine Stuart when bandaged, Donna Douglas when unmasked) has undergone extensive surgery to correct a disfigured face that has blighted her entire life. Resting in a hospital after multiple cosmetic surgeries, she is eager to see if the operation was successful to fix her "pitiful twisted lump of flesh," even as the attending surgeons warn her that she may not get the results she desperately craves. After convincing her doctors to remove the bandages early, she is horrified to discover that the operation was a failure. But what is repulsive to some, may be considered gorgeous to others.

    The iconic episodes of *The Twilight Zone*, like "Eye of the Beholder," are defined by their big twists. It's the sharp left turns of episodes like "To Serve Man" or "The Invaders" that have made them timeless, but detrimentally they overshadow the core emotional weight of the stories. Just through cultural osmosis, we know what's going to happen in this episode, even if the entire twist is literally foreshadowed with lighting and cinematography. It can be argued that the visual metaphor of not showing the doctor's faces mimics the obscured vision of Janet Tyler, but from an audience perspective, you can connect the dots that there is a greater reason why we're not seeing everyone clearly. And that reason is the twist that's been burned into our minds for the last 60 years.

    Even though we know that the other shoe is going to drop, it doesn't suppress the powerful themes of self-loathing and beauty standards coursing through the episode. Serling even manages to touch upon themes of Maoism and segregation as the doctors discuss in hushed terms the potential consequences for their compassion with Janet and her ilk. This speaks to the thinly veiled metaphor for the nation's culture of prejudice that directly led to Japanese Internment camps during World War II. The doctors mention sending Janet to a community where others who look like her live and thrive, ostensibly an optimistic ending for her, but also a convenient solution for society. We don't want them near us, so just ship them off to camps where we never have to hear from them again. Segregation doesn't fix problems, it just further drives a wedge between us. The allusions here aren't subtle, but subtly never had a home in *The Twilight Zone*.

Zone Fact

This episode is called "The Private World of Darkness" in syndication due to a naming dispute with a General Electric Theatre episode from 1954 called "The Eye of the Beholder"

"Nick of Time"
Episode 7
Original Airdate: November 18, 1960

Directed by Richard L. Bare
Written by Richard Matheson

> *"Counterbalance in the little town of Ridgeview, Ohio. Two people permanently enslaved by the tyranny of fear and superstition, facing the future with a kind of helpless dread. Two others facing the future with confidence—having escaped one of the darker places of*
> *The Twilight Zone."*

Don (William Shatner) and Pat Carter (Patricia Breslin) are a young married couple road tripping across the States to New York City, where Don is set to start a new job. That is, if he gets it. Unfortunately, their car breaks down in a small Ohio town, but fortunately the diner they drop in features a Mystic Seer—a penny fortune teller with a devil bobblehead affixed to the top. After consulting the psychic machine, Don discovers he got the job as an office manager, which he then verifies with his new employer. Enthusiastically, Don begins to ask more questions, but his curiosity turns into desperation when he realizes the machine isn't just telling the future but predicting their untimely fates.

Is a sense of superstition harmless, or not? Is saying bread and butter when you're holding hands with someone actually going to avert bad luck, or is it just simply a force of habit instilled from childhood fantasies? When the going is good and superstition is in our favor, it's as if we have a mystic eye like the one at the center of this episode watching our back. But when our good luck runs out, superstition can become binding, making you question the very fabric of your reality.

Thematically this episode is drenched in American paranoia, especially as the Cold War escalated during McCarthyism, but it's also about anxiety for the future. World War II left people in a constant state of uncertainty with the looming possibility of a nuclear Armageddon wiping out life as we know it. That's why Don grabs tightly to the prophecies of the fortune teller after it makes one correct prediction, even though Pat points out that the answers are vague on purpose so you can conclude whatever you want. He needs something to tell him that tomorrow, and the next day, will be ok. He doesn't want to be responsible for his own fate. It's the existential crisis every young person goes through as they realize their place in the quote-unquote real world.

In Don's desire to gain control, he doesn't realize that he completely loses it, making the fortune teller also an apt metaphor for the insidious crawl of addiction, ensnaring you before you even know you're caught in its web. The final beat of the episode visualizes that sobering reality. We see two people that could have been the Carter's future, stuck under the thumb of a fate they bought for a penny. This ending is a mirror for the audience to look into and perhaps see their own future. What they do with that knowledge though is up to them.

Zone Fact

Patricia Breslin was originally approached to reprise her role as William Shatner's wife in another Richard Matheson penned episode "Nightmare at 20,000 Feet"

"The Lateness of the Hour"
Episode 8
Original Airdate: December 2, 1960

Directed by Jack Smight
Written by Rod Serling

"The residence of Dr. William Loren, which is in reality a menagerie for machines. We're about to discover that sometimes the product of man's talent and genius can walk amongst us untouched by the normal ravages of time. These are Dr. Loren's robots, built to functional as well as artistic perfection. But in a moment Dr. William Loren, wife and daughter will discover that perfection is relative, that even robots have to be paid for, and very shortly will be shown exactly what is the bill."

Dr. William Loren (John Hoyt) is an inventor and a damn good one. He's made five perfectly humanoid robots that serve his house, caring for his wife and their young adult daughter Jana. The Lorens' insistence on using these robot maids and butlers to do their bidding is slowly getting under Jana's skin, and she craves to break free from the repetitive cycle of their lives. But there is a good reason that the Lorens have relied on their servants for everything, and it's a secret that will change Jana's life forever.

The second episode after "The Hitch-Hiker" (S1E16) to feature the late Inger Stevens is also the first of six episodes that were shot completely on videotape. It gives the striking appearance of being filmed live, despite it just being a different kind of production. That's not the most jarring thing in this episode though. That belongs to the strange pronunciation of the word robot, like rabbit with a hard "ih" sound. It's not like it was a new word, either. Robot was first used in *R.U.R.*, a 1920s Czechoslovakian science fiction play by Karel Čapek, adapted from the Czech word Robota which means forced labor. It's a fitting definition too when you consider some of the themes of this episode, like what we aim to lose by living life complacent to the amenities of the modern world.

The Lorens have a group of robot servants who maintain not only their house, but their lavish relaxed lifestyle. They don't even need to move if they don't want to as they can rely on their robots for their every whim, not unlike the society at the end of Pixar's *Wall-E*. Are you really living if you have everything done for you? We gain so much so quickly with advanced technology that we never take the time to consider what we may also be losing. Jana wants to go out for dinner, but the father lists everything inconvenient that could come with it, like getting soaked in the rain on the way there. Even if there are minor inconveniences, tactile experiences make you feel more alive and when it's shared with someone, can bring you closer together.

The episode's somber note is one that I think plays well with "A World of His Own" (S1E36), where a character realizes that they weren't who they thought they were. Here the note is even more dour. Sure, the Lorens desperately wanted a child when they couldn't conceive, but do they deserve one, considering how easy it was for them to erase their "daughter's" memory and turn her into a maid? If they couldn't find the courage to be honest with their robot daughter, how could they have ever done so with a human one?

Zone Fact

This was the first episode shot on videotape.

An Unofficial Journey Into The Twilight Zone

"The Trouble with Templeton"
Episode 9
Original Airdate: December 9, 1960

Directed by Buzz Kulik
Written by E. Jack Neuman

"Mr. Booth Templeton, who shared with most human beings the hunger to recapture the past moments, the ones that soften with the years. But in his case, the characters of his past blocked him out and sent him back to his own time, which is where we find him now."

Renowned actor Booth Templeton (Brian Aherne) is sunk with depression in the twilight of his career. The joys of the stage cannot eclipse the sorrow he feels for his wife's premature death decades before. Compounding his mental stress, the Broadway play he is starring in has hired an egotistical director who, in no uncertain terms, goes out of his way to belittle the respected actor. Templeton erupts into a panic attack, retreating from the theatre only to find himself amongst a throng of fans, celebrating the success of a play he starred in three decades before. If he's traveled to the past, that must mean his wife is still alive, and if so, he may have a chance to reclaim a part of him he lost long ago. It may be what Templeton wants, but is it what he needs?

We all enjoy relishing in the past. It's why nostalgia is so present in modern pop-culture. It's comfortable getting lost in old memories, but it isn't exactly a healthy thing to do. For someone with anxiety, it's easy to replay miscommunications or dwell on an unfortunate mistake that can sink you into depression. This is exactly where Templeton finds himself as he's jettisoned to a past he wants back, but what does he gain from eschewing his present? He's so focused on who he was, because deep down he doesn't want to face what he's become. If he wants to overcome the intolerable feeling of losing control, he must snuff out the fantasy he's made of his past.

This is a great example of *The Twilight Zone* being a metaphor for the human mind. We've all been in arguments that sparked intense, vibrant memories, we're just usually not sent decades back in time. What looks like Templeton being transported through the fourth dimension to revisit his lost lover in a speakeasy, is really just him becoming quite literally lost in thought. It's why the club stops and stares silently at Templeton as he leaves. If this is his mind, and he's learned his lesson, then he has no more need for the other bar goers and they cease to function.

I must say I love the continued appreciation *Twilight Zone* has for metafiction, sprung from the fourth wall breaking season one finale, "A World of His Own" (S1E36). It's peppered throughout Serling's book-ended monologues, but it's exemplified in the idea that everything Templeton went through generated a piece of literature. It's almost a representation of Serling himself, despite the episode being written by E. Jack Neuman. Serling takes life experiences, and by churning them through his mind, creates stunning works of fiction.

Zone Fact

The new director of Templeton's Broadway play is none other than future Academy Award winner Sydney Pollack (Out of Africa).

"A Most Unusual Camera"
Episode 10
Original Airdate: December 16, 1960

Directed by John Rich
Written by Rod Serling

"Object known as a camera, vintage uncertain, origin unknown. But for the greedy, the avaricious, the fleet of foot, who can run a four-minute mile so long as they're chasing a fast buck, it makes believe that it's an ally, but it isn't at all. It's a beckoning come-on for a quick walk around the block—in The Twilight Zone."

Chester (Fred Clark) and Paula Diedrich (Jean Carson) are a couple of happily married crooks who've come away with a strange looking camera. To their surprise, the camera develops photographs that predict the future, like showing Paula's brother Woodward (Adam Williams) returning home unannounced after breaking out of jail. Looking to get rich quick, Chester has the million-dollar idea to go down to the local racetrack, snap a shot of the winners, and reap the rewards. However, as they earn more and more money, their greed turns into distrust, and soon the camera that brought so much wealth to their lives will unceremoniously rip it all away.

Since the invention of cameras, we've been intrigued by the cross section of the captured image and the supernatural, from the oft-cited cultural myth of photographs stealing your soul to early 20th century spirit photography, to even the prevalence of spooky photographs in films like *Shutter* (2008), *Insidious* (2010) and *Polaroid* (2016). For my fellow monster kids of 1995, I don't think we can watch or read a haunted killer camera story without being transported back to our first experience reading R.L. Stine's *Say Cheese and Die*, the fourth book in the original *Goosebumps* series. It would even be adapted for television in 1996, starring a very young Ryan Gosling!

But the supernatural element of the camera is secondary to the true horror of the episode, greed. People will do anything for money—gamble, fight, kill—but it won't fill you up no matter how much cash you collect. Just ask all those billionaires in the world!

Jacob Trussell

The trio at the center of the episode have more money than they know what to do with, but it's still not enough. It's why they ultimately turn on each other. They realize that their cut of the profits will grow exponentially if they knock off one or two of their co-conspirators. As the saying goes, there's no honor among thieves.

The appeal and power that comes with wealth is all consuming, but it solves none of our problems. Money doesn't make the lives of jerks better. It just makes them rich jerks. And rich jerks always get their comeuppance, especially in *The Twilight Zone*.

Zone Fact

Adam Williams appeared previously in "The Hitch Hiker" as a sailor Inger Stevens meets on her trek cross country.

"The Night of the Meek"
Episode 11
Original Airdate: December 23, 1960

Directed by Jack Smight
Written by Rod Serling

"A word to the wise to all the children of the twentieth century, whether their concern be pediatrics or geriatrics, whether they crawl on hands and knees and wear diapers or walk with a cane and comb their beards. There's a wondrous magic to Christmas and there's a special power reserved for little people. In short, there's nothing mightier than the meek."

Henry Corwin (Art Carney) is a department store Santa with a crippling alcohol dependency and luck that is running out faster than the dollars in his pocket. He drinks because it helps him cope with not being able to live up to the character he plays, unable to bring joy to the poor children he sees every day on the streets. Out of a job and on his last leg, he stumbles across a bag that seems to be teeming with presents. Moreso, whenever he gives someone a gift, it happens to be exactly what they wanted. Is this Santa's bag? Has his wish that the meek shall inherit become a self-fulfilling prophecy? And if so, will Henry put the real Santa out of a job?

"Night of the Meek" is far more melancholic and touching than a movie like *Bad Santa,* even if the episode's set-up feels like a punchline to a borderline-offensive joke. What does a down-on-his-luck, alcoholic, department store Santa ask Ol' Saint Nick for Christmas? To Henry Corwin, it's a request straight out of the book of Matthew: that the meek shall inherit. To me the phrase is more synonymous to a song from the musical *Little Shop of Horrors* than it does the Bible, but both use it to say in a deific way that those who have seen the worst of life will get the best in the end. At least that's what a guy like Corwin is hoping for with this magical gift from the North Pole. Even if he doesn't get to keep it, tonight he has inherited the world.

It's an optimistic read on Rod Serling's riff on what happens when the angry young man turns into the sorrowful old man. The ones that look back on life and think "What if?" What if I hadn't picked up the bottle, what if I had made a different choice? But life is nothing but unanswered questions when we focus on what we've done, rather than what we can become. For some looking into the future could mean staying sober another day, or finally getting off the couch and going outside, and for others like Henry Corwin, it could mean becoming the happiest fella, either real or imaginary.

Season Two of *The Twilight Zone* was also the season that experimented with a new cost-cutting filming method. Instead of their normal stock, they'd shoot on videotape, and then transfer it to 16 mm film with a method called kinescope. It gives each episode the quality that veers closer to a soap opera than the cinematic style we come to expect from *The Twilight Zone*.

Zone Fact

An ordinary man with an extraordinary bag of toys would be a trope used in more upbeat stand-in Santa films like Ernest Saves Christmas or The Santa Clause.

"Dust"
Episode 12
Original Airdate: January 6, 1961

Directed by Douglas Heyes
Written by Rod Serling

> *"This village had a virus, shared by its people. It was the germ of squalor, of hopelessness, of a loss of faith. With the faithless, the hopeless, the misery-laden, there is time, ample time, to engage in one of the other pursuits of men. They began to destroy themselves."*

In a desolate, isolated town, an alcoholic named Luis (John Alonzo) stands convicted of the accidental murder of a young boy. He sits patiently awaiting his execution, at peace with his demise, knowing he must pay for what he has done. His father Gallegos (Vladimir Sokoloff) wishes to save his son's life, even if that means buying a bit of magic off of Sykes (Thomas Gomez), the same man who sold the town's sheriff (John Larch) the rope his son will be hanged with. Will magic save the life of his son, or is it something more mysterious and uncertain like the depths of the human heart?

The Twilight Zone swings back and forth on providing veiled metaphors on alcoholism to being very on-the-nose about its commentary on the matter. This episode doesn't blame alcoholism for why the man got drunk and killed the child, even though it should. The young boy's death was due to Luis' uncontrollable drinking, but the sorrow he feels isn't that of a sloppy drunk, but a sober man filled with remorse. Not only for the death of the child, but for the decisions he made that got him there. You can't say for certain that Luis will never drink again, but you can see in his eyes a man who will never forget the consequences that come with his addiction. Much like "Mr. Denton on Doomsday" (S1E3), Serling sets this episode in the past as a way to frame mental health as something that's always been hidden under the surface of society. It may have taken until the late 1950s for people to start feeling comfortable speaking about it openly, but that doesn't mean it hasn't existed for centuries.

As this is a story about a hanging, it's impossible not to discern commentary on capital punishment. Is it an effective deterrent on crime, or does it just feed a collective bloodlust that flows from the murderer to the judges to the court of public opinion? The episode's conclusion, the family showing mercy to the man after the rope supernaturally snaps, gives credence to the public perception of the death penalty in the 1950s. In part due to the allied nations abolishing the death penalty following the Second World War, execution rates dramatically began falling in the United States when *The Twilight Zone* began airing.

Zone Fact

Douglas Heyes Jr., son of this episode's director who has a minor cameo, would later write for a different kind of sci-fi television series, Farscape.

"Back There"
Episode 13
Original Airdate: January 13, 1961

Directed by David Orrick McDearmon
Written by Rod Serling

"...a journey into time with highly questionable results, proving on one hand that the threads of history are woven tightly, and the skein of events cannot be undone, but on the other hand, there are small fragments of tapestry that can be altered."

Peter Corrigan (Russell Johnson) is debating with his fellow social club colleagues what would happen if they could go back in time and avert the Stock Market Crash of 1929. No sooner had he raised the question than Corrigan found himself almost 100 years in the past, on the eve of the assassination of President Abraham Lincoln. With strange clothes and raving about the president's looming death, Corrigan is thrown in jail only to be subsequently plucked out by a mysterious proto-psychiatrist who believes he may be suffering from trauma in the wake of the Civil War. Is the psychiatrist here to help him avert a tragedy, or has Corrigan put into motion the very thing he intends to stop?

With the amount of political assassination attempts we've had since 1964, it's wild to think that when this episode premiered, the last presidential assassination had been Abraham Lincoln. It's not necessarily prescient by any means, but three years prior to the assassination of John F. Kennedy, there's a queasy shroud cast over an otherwise action-packed story and its revisionist take on John Wilkes Booth.

"Back There" is a riff on the butterfly effect, a concept that first appeared in Ray Bradbury's novella *The Sound of Thunder* that has gone on to be the standard conflict in time-travel stories. Essentially the butterfly effect is what would happen to our future if we made the slightest change to the past, or as the terms inventor Edward Norton Lorenz would describe in his article, "Does the Flap of a Butterfly's Wings in Brazil Set Off a Tornado in Texas?"

Peter Corrigan didn't try to make a slight change to the past either. If he had saved Lincoln's life, he would have made irreparable

Jacob Trussell

changes to the world, despite his best intentions. He even inadvertently caused what he intended to stop, a twist that is elaborated on in the iconic short film *La Jetée* (1962), which would be adapted by Terry Gilliam in 1*2 Monkeys* (1995). We only see one small change, the club's attendant now being a member himself, but who knows what the world has in store for him after the episode ends.

A trend I love in *The Twilight Zone* is how characters like Corrigan don't purposefully enter the realm of the supernatural like some H.G. Wellesian protagonist, rather they are unceremoniously thrust into it. It's darkly hilarious that Serling often dumps his leads, without reason or warning, back in time whether they like it or not. Corrigan merely discusses what would happen if you changed the past, he didn't expressly want to do that! He was thinking out loud, bumped into an attendant, and then boom! It's 1865, he sounds crazy, and a late 19th century psychiatrist who just so happens to be a political assassin in disguise is shrinking his head. Rod Serling doesn't care about your dinner plans: it's *Twilight Zone* time, baby!

Zone Fact

Russell Johnson also appeared in another Ray Bradbury related sci-fi story: the 1956 film It Came from Outer Space.

"The Whole Truth"
Episode 14
Original Airdate: January 20, 1961

Directed by James Sheldon
Written by Rod Serling

> *"This, as the banner already has proclaimed, is Mr. Harvey Hunnicut, an expert on commerce and con jobs, a brash, bright, and larceny-loaded wheeler and dealer who, when the good Lord passed out a conscience, must have gone for a beer and missed out."*

Harvey Hunnicut (Jack Carson) is a used car salesman of the greasiest kind. He's got a lot filled with lemons, and he plans to squeeze dry the wallets of anyone unlucky enough to look under the hood. All of that is set to change for Hunnicut when he inadvertently buys a haunted car that curses him to tell nothing but the truth to everyone from his coworkers, wife, and even potential customers. Will this change Hunnicut's life, or will he find a way to pawn the possessed Pontiac onto a fella who could really use it?

If only Rod Serling had written this episode after Stephen King's *Christine* or even *Maximum Overdrive,* then maybe this story would have the injection of energy it so desperately needs. I'm all here for a tale about someone who's forced to tell the truth, but to make it because he accidentally buys a possessed car is just straight up silliness that squanders the clever concept. The focus should be on the car, not the greasy salesman who says things like "Getting more money out of me is as likely as pouring hot butter into a wild cat's ear." A phrase I'm sure *none of us* have ever heard before.

Each episode of *The Twilight Zone* has meaning, but Serling's message in "The Whole Truth" feels muddy. I'm not too sure what he wants me to take from this strangely redemptive arc for someone I should find despicable, especially in a series that has hammered home the evils of greed, which Hunnicut clearly represents. I suppose it's to show that every person has the capacity for compassion, but will Hunnicut only be compelled to do good when the stakes are high, like selling a truth serum car to Nikita Khrushchev to bring down a totalitarian regime? That's not what it should take to force someone to do the right thing.

Jacob Trussell

Maybe the silliness of the haunted car setup should have been our clue in how serious to take this episode. This could just be Serling's way of exorcising his own bad experiences dealing with used car salesmen, writing one into *The Twilight Zone* so he can needle and torture him. What can I say, writing has always been a healthy way to vent emotions!

Zone Fact

The supernatural angle of this episode would be elaborated on in the Jim Carrey vehicle Liar, Liar

"The Invaders"
Episode 15
Original Airdate: January 27, 1961

Directed by Douglas Heyes
Written by Richard Matheson

"The invaders... who found out that a one-way ticket to the stars beyond has the ultimate price tag... and we have just seen it entered in a ledger that covers all the transactions in the universe... a bill stamped "Paid in Full"

An elderly mute woman (Agnes Moorhead) lives in a small, run down cabin in the middle of nowhere. After being shocked by a loud noise, she begins to be besieged by diminutive invaders who leave her with radiation burns and slashed ankles. As she hunts down the creatures, she discovers a large spaceship, showing that these aliens may be anything but. That is, at least to us.

If there is one thing that Rod Serling and Richard Matheson never want you to forget, it's this: aliens may look a lot like us, and we may look a lot like aliens to them. It's the central crux of the series overarching examination of injustices and prejudices that come from fearing "the other."

"The other" is an idea that someone far away could be colluding to do us harm, so we develop a distrust for anyone who doesn't look and sound like us. In the 1960s, this fear was in part sparked by the global anxiety following World War II that would only be exacerbated by America's ingrained prejudices against immigrants and people of color. But a fear of "the other" is just a fear of the unknown, not someone else. The old woman is more afraid of what might be outside her door, not what actually is.

As we are reminded every day, these unfounded fears have only gotten worse through time. You'd think in an advanced world where we can interact with people from across the globe, the fear of "the other" would be dampened. Instead, frightened bigots have given themselves more to hate. By revealing that the one human in the episode that we've been identifying with is actually the alien, the audience is wordlessly asked to reconsider their own held fears by giving us a simple reminder that we are "the other" too.

Jacob Trussell

The one giveaway to the episode's big reveal is in the tenacity of the adorable little astronauts. Their persistence is so uniquely American! This woman is minding her own business, on her own property, when in swoops a little spacecraft like they own the place. Considering this, "The Invaders" is also a metaphor for American globalization and the reminder that maybe manifest destiny isn't good for everybody.

Zone Fact

Despite being a classic image of the series, writer Richard Matheson famously hated the look of the titular aliens.

"A Penny for Your Thoughts"
Episode 16
Original Airdate: February 3, 1961

Directed by James Sheldon
Written by George Clayton Johnson

"Mr. Hector B. Poole, resident of the Twilight Zone. Flip a coin and keep flipping it. What are the odds? Half the time it will come up heads, half the time tails. But in one freakish chance in a million, it'll land on its edge. Mr. Hector B. Poole, a bright human coin—on his way to the bank."

Hector B. Poole (Dick York) may not have lucked out in the confidence and charisma department, but what he lacks in charm he more than makes up for in luck, and today may be his luckiest day of all. Not only did he land a flipped coin perfectly on its edge, but he also saved the bank he works at a large sum of money when he stops a potential loan from reaching a con artist. He could do this because he's been magically endowed with the gift of telepathy. But just because he can hear thoughts doesn't mean he can discern their meaning. The ability could come back to bite him, however it also may be the thing he needs to boost his confidence and finally ask out his crush, bank teller Helen Turner (June Dayton).

Much like the recurring cast of actors we see in Ryan Murphy's television universe *American Horror Story*, I love that Rod Serling put together a stock of actors that he could return to throughout the series run. Here, we see the second episode featuring Dick York (*Bewitched*) after his appearance in "The Purple Testament" (S1E19) as well as the series debut of Cyril Delevanti who would appear in three future episodes!

Here we have another episode of the series that revolves around a character who is unceremoniously thrust into *The Twilight Zone*. The used car salesman in "The Whole Truth" didn't want to own a truth-telling demonic Dodge, Peter Corrigan didn't ask to be sent into the past to save Lincoln in "Back There," and Hector B. Poole definitely didn't ask to hear other people's thoughts. Poole may lack confidence, but he doesn't need the comeuppance that generally accompanies other trips to *The Twilight Zone*. His ability to read

Jacob Trussell

minds is indicative of the randomness of life. All he did was flip a very lucky coin. It's a good reminder, for better or worse, how our world can change at a moment's notice.

But that doesn't make this episode dark! On the contrary, it's probably one of the sweetest and genuinely romantic episodes of the series. The chemistry between Dick York and June Dayton is cute and feels real, an authenticity you don't always get in the early days of television but feels at home on *The Twilight Zone*.

Zone Fact

The odds of a coin actually landing on its edge are 1 in 6000!

"Twenty-Two"
Episode 17
Original Airdate: February 10, 1961

Directed by Jack Smight
Written by Rod Serling (from an anecdote by Bennett Cerf)

"Miss Elizabeth Powell, professional dancer. Hospital diagnosis: acute anxiety brought on by overwork and fatigue. Prognosis: with rest and care, she'll probably recover. But the cure to some nightmares is not to be found in known medical journals. You look for it under 'potions for bad dreams—to be found in the Twilight Zone."

Liz Powell (Barbara Nichols) is a dancer plagued by the same recurring nightmare, where she's beckoned into a morgue by a sullen nurse (Arline Sax). She swears that the nightmare is more than a dream, but her doctor chalks it up to simple exhaustion. He attempts to manipulate Liz's subconscious by guiding her through a lucid dream meant to conquer her fears, but it's no use. No matter what Liz does, the nurse is there telling her, "Room for one more, honey." Is this the nightmare of an anxious mind, or is it foreshadowing something very grave in Liz's future?

E.F. Benson's "The Hearse Driver" served as inspiration for "The Hitch-Hiker" (S1E16), but "Twenty-Two" would be *The Twilight Zone*'s direct adaptation of the short story. This stunning retelling replaces the hearse driver with a stone-faced nurse in a hospital, but it retains the original story's dread-inducing tone, perfectly set up in the opening moments.

We watch Liz Powell's nightmare happen in real time as she follows a nurse down shadowy corridors until finding herself in a morgue. The doors swing open, and in a classic jump scare, we see the nurse in full frame. This reveal isn't just great because we get a face to the shadow we were following; it's the never-ending corridor stretching infinitely behind her, brought to life in a gorgeous matte painting. It's a great little spooky representation of the interminable unknowns of the mind, especially since Liz is hospitalized for "exhaustion," '60s code for a nervous breakdown.

But let's talk about that ending for a second. As Liz readies herself to board a plane, she's greeted by the nurse, now dressed as a stewardess. She refuses to board and goes back to the terminal where, shocked, she watches the plane explode on take off. Liz's nightmares weren't dreams after all. They were omens of a looming danger.

The ending is a complete surprise, but even more surprising is how it's incredibly similar to the opening moments of *Final Destination* (2000), co-written by Glen Morgan, who would go on to write for the 2019 *Twilight Zone* revival. The horror film is about a group of teens pursued by death after a vision forces them off of an international flight minutes before it explodes. Just like in *The Twilight Zone*, sometimes it really pays to trust your gut.

Zone Fact

Arlene Sax, who plays the sinister nurse, was known as The Chameleon for her ability to seamlessly get lost in her characters.

"The Odyssey of Flight 33"
Episode 18
Original Airdate: February 24, 1961

Directed by Jus Addiss
Written by Rod Serling

"Unbeknownst to passenger and crew, this airplane is heading into an uncharted region well off the beaten track of commercial travelers—it's moving into The Twilight Zone. What you're about to see we call "The Odyssey of Flight 33.""

On a transatlantic trip from London to New York City, the crew of Flight 33 find themselves hurtling through the sky by an errant jet stream. As they regain control of the plane and calm the passengers, they face an even bigger problem: they've traveled almost 65 million years into the past. Not wanting to panic the passengers, but unsure of what to do, they fly into the current again hoping it will send them back to their own time. Even if Flight 33 does manage to travel through time again, will their return journey be far enough, or will they become forever lost searching for a way home?

Does every episode of *The Twilight Zone* need to be a sociopolitical parable? No. Sometimes it's just about going beyond the limits of possibility and experiencing the inconceivable. In "The Odyssey of Flight 33," the unthinkable is a jetliner that accidentally breaks the sound barrier, sending the airplane through time like it was 1985 Delorean hitting 88 mph. Just, rather than the time machine being caused by nuclear energy, here it's a supernatural jetstream that sends them between centuries.

I grew up reading Serling's novelization of this episode in *More Stories from the Twilight Zone*, but what resonated with my seven-year old self the most was the gobsmacking image of a modern plane flying over all those claymation dinosaurs. Could the crew see other dinosaurs? Were they afraid of pterodactyls flying next to the wing? My imagination was quick to answer these questions, but that preoccupation also caused me to overlook the dark, fatalistic ending for so long.

Once Flight 33 realizes they have not gone forward enough in time, Captain "Skipper" Farver (John Anderson) veers the plane back into the jet stream, refusing to land until they are back in their own time. You can feel the weight of this decision as they wonder if this is all in vain. Will it work, or are they lost in time forever? Rod Serling leaves their fate up to the audience, as he intimates in his closing narration, "But you and I know where she is. You and I know what's happened. So if some moment, any moment, you hear the sound of jet engines flying atop the overcast—engines that sound searching, lost, and desperate—shoot up a flare or do something. That would be Global 33 trying to get home—from *The Twilight Zone*."

Zone Fact

Stephen King's The Langoliers also deals with an airplane that goes through a vortex, displacing them in time.

An Unofficial Journey Into The Twilight Zone

"Mr. Dingle, the Strong"
Episode 19
Original Airdate: March 3, 1961

Directed by John Brahm
Written by Rod Serling

> *"In just a moment, a sad-faced perennial punching bag, who missed even the caboose of life's gravy train, will take a short constitutional into that most unpredictable region that we refer to as The Twilight Zone."*

Luther Dingle (Burgess Meredith) is a mild-mannered vacuum salesman who doesn't have much gumption when it comes to standing up for himself. Case in point, after he is roped into an argument by bookie Joseph J. Callahan (Don Rickles), Dingle takes a fist square on the jaw just for giving an answer Callahan didn't like. All that changes once Dingle is endowed with the strength of 300 men from a bi-headed Martian with an eye for experimentation. What will Mr. Dingle do with his newfound strength? Will he stand up for himself and prove his worth, or will he practice the time-honored American tradition of making a quick buck?

The Twilight Zone is incredibly important in the history of genre television as one of the first shows to masterfully interweave social commentary into horror and science fiction stories. That doesn't mean that every episode is mired in metaphor and allegory, though. You can file "Mr. Dingle, The Strong" under F for Fun because it has a silly narrative device that acts as the much-needed dose of levity every season of the show requires. You may find deeper, analytical meaning in an episode like this, but that doesn't mean you can't just take it strictly at face value. The episode's humor is most apparent in its cast pitting *Twilight Zone* stalwart Burgess Meredith against the godfather of insult comedy Don Rickles, which fittingly plays a scurrilous man.

If casting wasn't a dead giveaway to the episode's comedic tone, then the two-headed Martians that give Dingle his powers definitely are. Could they be any more ridiculous looking? They have satellite dishes and antennae protruding from their heads like some proto portrait of trans humanism, decades before we ever heard the words

Jacob Trussell

Google Glass. The Martians' appearances are only topped by the mustachioed little Venusians we meet in the finale. That's definitely not what we expected when we learned that men were from Mars and women were from Venus!

"Mr. Dingle, the Strong" ultimately is about self-worth, asking us to consider where our true strength lies. Is it something we gain from outside of ourselves like a magical problem-solving elixir? Or do you find confidence deep within where you've yet to look? Maybe it's something simpler though. Maybe for Mr. Dingle, the confidence he lacks could easily be gained by, at the very least, getting himself a better last name.

Zone Fact

The reporter with the camera crew at the end of the episode is also featured in Season One's "The After Hours" as the snooty department store attendant!

"Static"
Episode 20
Original Airdate: March 10, 1961

Directed by Buzz Kulik
Written by Charles Beaumont (from a story by OCee Ritch)

"No one ever saw one quite like that, because that's a very special sort of radio."

Aging bachelor Ed Lindsay (Dean Jagger) has been living in the same boarding house for over two decades, growing colder and more unpleasant with every passing year. He couldn't care less about the wonders of the modern world, their vacuous radio shows, and ear-splitting rock and roll music—he just misses the classics like Tommy Dorsey and Edward Bowes. When his radio begins playing these old shows again, he becomes entranced as the quality is better than recordings. The broadcast sounds live. Every time Ed attempts to get his neighbors—including Vinnie (Carmen Mathews) who he planned to marry years before—to believe him, all they hear is static. Is Ed's desire for the past blurring the line between reality and fantasy, or did he actually dial in to an errant signal from *The Twilight Zone*?

Charles Beaumont stories are as dark as pitch, but when adapting someone else's story (in this case from Oliver Rich), it doesn't quite pack the same punch. Continuing the series' interest in nostalgia, what Beaumont does bring to "Static" is a pulsating streak of melancholy. It's the sense of loss that comes from reflecting on the past, that innate feeling that the choices you made caused you to miss out on something, even if you don't know what that something is. It's what Ed is forced to confront when memories of his past come flooding back to him. Memories he wants to hang on to forever, even though rationally he knows he can't. By hanging on tight to those memories, he threatens to strangle the life out of them.

We want to recapture the feeling that something like a song gave us, but if we aren't receptive to change, we risk losing why the music mattered in the first place. From the shows that play on his phantom radio to the life he squandered with Vinnie, Ed's unflinching craving to revert to a past self will only further alienate him from those in his present life.

Which is exactly what happens.

After his friends sold the radio in hopes he'd snap out of his delusions, Ed takes it home and—to his relief—it still works. As if slipping through a crack in time, the radio transforms him into the golden age he desperately misses. Vinnie joins him, looking just as she did all of those years ago, completing the life they never had together. The radio, and his nostalgia, have physically transported him back.

Is this really a happy ending? Ed may have gotten what he wanted, but it's not going to help him. In a way he dies in this final scene, because he's given up on his life in pursuit of something that won't make up for all the years he wasted. Our memories can't do that, but our future can. For Ed Lindsay, he has no future if he is comfortable staying in the past.

Zone Fact

This is the fourth of six episodes filmed on videotape in efforts to cut costs!

"The Prime Mover"
Episode 21
Original Airdate: March 24, 1961

Directed by Richard L. Bare
Written by Charles Beaumont (based on an uncredited and unpublished story by George Clayton Johnson)

"Portrait of a man who thinks and thereby gets things done. Mr. Jimbo Cobb might be called a prime mover, a talent which has to be seen to be believed. In just a moment he'll show his friends, and you, how he keeps both feet on the ground, and his head in the Twilight Zone."

Jimbo Cobb (Buddy Ebsen) has a talent for making things happen with just his mind. Sure, he can lift a broom directly into his hands and right a flipped car, but he can also control the dice in a crap game. Once his buddy Ace (Dane Clark) discovers this particular subset of his talents, it's off to the casinos with the both of them. Cobb though isn't the kind of guy who likes to flaunt his talents, and he's even less the type to use his god-given gifts for purely selfish reasons, unlike Ace who wants to exploit his kindly friends' abilities. Deciding he needs to learn a hard lesson, Cobb plans to teach his friend why great power comes with great responsibility.

From a story by George Clayton Johnson, "The Prime Mover" is more appealing to a broader audience than Charles Beaumont's usual cerebral stories as it lacks the typical fatalism and dourness that accompany his scripts. This episode is more for those *Twilight Zone* fans who aren't craving food for thought to go with their evening TV dinners.

What makes this episode memorable is the earnestness of Buddy Ebsen's impeccably named Jimbo Cobb. He's a salt of the earth type that audiences could relate to, with a supernatural power simple enough for them to wrap their heads around. Jimbo reminds you of those family friends and favorite Uncles that wielded a timeless, old school code of ethics that's still admirable today. He's the kind of guy who can be friendly with the assholes of the world, but still have the self-awareness to know when they need to get a taste of their own medicine.

Jacob Trussell

We shouldn't read Jimbo using his psychic powers on Ace as vindictive, or so he can wield some sense of moral superiority over him. Jimbo just knows what the substance of a good person is, and he wants to impress that on his friend. It's simple: don't be selfish, don't be egomaniacal, and above all else, don't be a horse's ass.

Zone Fact

One year after this episode, star Buddy Ebsen would climb to new heights of fame with his role as Jed Clampett in The Beverly Hillbillies.

"Long Distance Call"
Episode 22
Original Airdate: March 31, 1961

Directed by James Sheldon
Written by Charles Beaumont and William Idelson

"A toy telephone, an act of faith, a set of improbable circumstances, all combine to probe a mystery, to fathom a depth, to send a facet of light into a dark after-region, to be believed or disbelieved, depending on your frame of reference. A fact or a fantasy, a substance or a shadow—but all of it very much a part of The Twilight Zone."

Billy Bayles (Bill Mumy) isn't a mama's boy, he's a grandmama's boy who's thrilled to get a telephone for his birthday just to call up Granny Bayles (Lili Darvas) whenever he wants. But after Billy watches his grandmother die, he begins receiving mysterious calls on the toy phone. The voice on the other end of the line says that it's his grandmother, and she wants him to come visit. How? By killing himself. Is there a psychological answer as to why a five-year-old is being driven to suicide, or is there something much more sinister making this long distance call?

The episode is credited to Charles Beaumont and William Idler, from a story by Idler, but the authorship of the episode has been disputed throughout the years. The writer Maxwell Sanford has been purported as the real author, but that may just be the nom-de-plume for another *Twilight Zone* scribe, Richard Matheson, that assisted Idler at the time. But the episode still feels incredibly Beaumontian, because this episode isn't just dark, it's black as night. If you are looking for arguably the most fucked up episode of the series, congratulations! You found it.

Some of the darkness comes from "Long Distance Call" being the first episode to really tackle childhood psychology. "Nightmare of a Child" (S1E29) touches upon it, but more to show how our childhood traumas can still affect us today. Here it's being used to give meaning to what a young boy can go through when confronted with death at such a young age. It's traumatizing for an adult to watch someone slowly pass away, but imagine being a child and literally

Jacob Trussell

witnessing your most beloved family member die. No wonder he reverts into fantasy, playing that his grandmother is calling him from beyond a grave. It's a coping mechanism. One that may or may not be real.

The central conceit—a dead woman pushing her grandson to commit suicide—is as bleak as they come on *The Twilight Zone*, but the relationship between Sylvia Bayles (Patricia Smith) and her mother-in-law are the episode's core tragedy. Their strained relationship is because the grandmother felt that her son Chris (Philip Abbott) was stolen from her when he married Sylvia. In a way to reclaim Chris, she dotes on her grandson Billy, stopping just short of spitting poison in his ear about his mother. Grandma Bayles may have been an angel to Billy in life, but in death, she is nothing but the wraith her grandson never saw.

Zone Fact

The babysitter, Jennifer Maxwell, was tragically murdered less than 20 years later. She was shot in a suspected robbery gone wrong.

"A Hundred Yards Over the Rim"
Episode 23
Original Airdate: April 7, 1961

Directed by Buzz Kulik
Written by Rod Serling

"This man's name is Christian Horn. He has a dying eight-year-old son and a heartsick wife, and he's the only one remaining who has even a fragment of the dream left."

A wagon train in the mid-1800s limps across the vast midwest, dangerously low on food and supplies with a sick child in tow. The child's father, Chris Horn (Cliff Robertson), refuses to turn the train around and head back to their home in Ohio, because he knows a better life awaits them in California. Chris decides to scout the area for any kind of lifeline and is surprised to see, over the rim of a hill, a small store with supplies that will save his son's life. He's taken aback by the shop-keeps odd clothing and new medicines, but strangest of all he's told that it's 1961. If Chris is in the future, then what happened to his family in the past?

I'm not a religious person, so prayer in my book is nothing more than the power of intention. What that idea means is that if you put your mind to something, however improbable of a task, you can still accomplish it through sheer will—and a hearty dose of persistence. That to me isn't a supernatural ability. If anything, our unending doggedness is one of humanity's most natural traits.

Optimistic persistence, even when faced with insurmountable odds, is perhaps best actualized in the late 1800s on the backs of wagon trains heading west looking not just for gold, but new beginnings. These are the reasons why Chris Horn doesn't turn the wagon train around and head home once his son falls ill. Because despite their current situation, their potential future is worth the struggle. Horn leans on his prayer, because he has literally nothing left to hang his hope on than the supernatural.

I'll be honest, this episode isn't one that will stick with you long after. Cliff Robertson turns in a fine performance and we do have a fun little cameo from Gomez Addams himself John Astin, but

Jacob Trussell

otherwise it's about as dry as the desert they are stuck in. More than anything this episode feels like a discarded concept—people travel through time on location in Death Valley—that would be recycled into the following episode, "The Rip Van Winkle Caper."

Zone Fact

Cliff Robertson would appear in a future episode of The Twilight Zone as the star of the series favorite "The Dummy."

"The Rip Van Winkle Caper"
Episode 24
Original Airdate: April 21, 1961

Directed by Jus Addiss
Written by Rod Serling

"Introducing four experts in the questionable art of crime. In just a moment, these four men will utilize the services of a truck placed in cosmoline, loaded with a hot heist cooled off by a century of sleep, and then take a drive into The Twilight Zone."

Four men—DeCruz (Simon Oakland), Farwell (Oscar Beregi, Jr.), Brooks (Lew Gallo), and Erbie (John Mitchum)—have developed a foolproof plan to pull off a train robbery, evade the cops, and live to tell the tale, all while still being young enough to enjoy the cool million they've lifted. All they have to do is hide out in a cave, put themselves into a hyperbaric chamber, and fall asleep for over 100 years. When they wake up, no one will be the wiser and they'll be able to unload all of the gold bars without raising any suspicion. The thieves think the hard part is already over, but it's not. When they wake in the new world, they'll have more to contend with than cops and jail—they'll have their paranoia and rapacity.

Greed baby, it doesn't do anybody any good! What Serling is really trying to impress in "The Rip Van Winkle Caper" is that avarice doesn't just infect lowlifes and corrupt politicians. Even the most brilliant, educated minds are capable of eschewing their morals in the hopes of making a quick buck. Or not so quick buck since the four men have to wait 100 years in suspended animation before they can enjoy their earnings.

The Rip Van Winkle of the title is from a Washington Irving short story about a Dutch colonist who falls asleep in the mountains, only to wake up 20 years later completely missing the American Revolution. In this episode, the men go into suspended animation and miss their own kind of revolution, except this one wasn't about freeing ourselves from physical tyranny, but the more metaphysical evil that comes from being drunk on wealth.

We consider so much when we fantasize about the future, but we

Jacob Trussell

never think that the power of money and wealth will ever go away. We don't get to really see the nature of society at the end of this episode, so we can only theorize what other problems have been solved by making gold worthless. Does greed still exist or has it been replaced by something worse? Do people still have to pay rent? Taxes? Do they at least get universal healthcare? We'll just have to wait and see, because after all, we're only 40 short years away from living the future these Rip Van Winkle's awoke to.

Zone Fact

Rod Serling would revisit the idea of suspended animation in Season Five's "The Long Morrow."

"The Silence"
Episode 25
Original Airdate: April 28, 1961

Directed by Boris Sagal
Written by Rod Serling

> *"Mr. Jamie Tennyson, who almost won a bet, but who discovered somewhat belatedly that gambling can be a most unproductive pursuit, even with loaded dice, marked cards, or, as in his case, some severed vocal cords."*

Archie Taylor (Franchot Tone) really has it out for Jamie Tennyson (Liam Sullivan), a young man in his social club. Taylor has an idea that will not only shut Tennyson up for the better part of a year, but potentially get him booted out of the club all together! He wagers him a bet that he can't stay silent for one full year. If he can, he will be rewarded $500,000—the equivalent of over $4 million today. He'll just have to submit to being kept in a glassed-in apartment where he can be carefully monitored by Taylor. As Tennyson appears to acquiesce well to his new silent world, Taylor becomes enraged and fearful that he will have to pay up. Will it be the bet, or the psychological warfare that he's raged on Tennyson, that will spell Taylor's demise?

    Addiction and man's stubbornness go hand in hand. When you're addicted to something, you will not only stop at nothing to feed your craving, but you are also assaulted with constant thoughts about what you are addicted to. For the alcoholic, that could mean the gnawing voice that yells at you from morning till night about when your next drink will be. For the smoker it could be the carousel of thoughts that send anxious jitters into your arms until you break down and light up. "The Silence" attempts to frame how gambling is a habit worse than smoking and more addictive than alcohol because of how it can catastrophically destroy more than just the addicted man's life. It can bring down an entire community.

    In the finale of this no-win episode, we discover that everyone is a loser, none more than Archie Taylor who, through sheer stubborn determination, can't let himself forfeit despite knowing he can't pay up. This is made even more tragic when, in an O. Henry-esque twist, we discover that Tennyson also felt compelled to cheat in order to win. Just for him, he lost more than his stature in a social club, he lost his oratorical talents. It's why you can't bluff your way through life. Eventually it'll be called, and all you'll have to show for yourself is your own ass.

I don't know about you, but this episode makes me viscerally angry in a way that *The Twilight Zone* rarely does. You really want to reach through the screen, pull out the characters, and shake some sense into them. This is in part due to the strength of Serling's writing and how the story unfolds, but it's really the performances from our two leads, Franchot Tone and Liam Sullivan. The series has never had two better faces that you'd simply love to punch!

Zone Fact

This is the first episode to feature Liam Sullivan, who would appear in Season Three's "Changing of the Guard!"

An Unofficial Journey Into The Twilight Zone

"Shadow Play"
Episode 26
Original Airdate: May 5, 1961

Directed by John Brahm
Written by Charles Beaumont

"We know that a dream can be real, but who ever thought that reality could be a dream? We exist, of course, but how, in what way? As we believe, as flesh-and-blood human beings, or are we simply parts of someone's feverish, complicated nightmare?"

Adam Grant (Dennis Weaver) has been sentenced to death by electric chair at midnight. But as he hears the verdict, he begins to laugh, proclaiming that reality is nothing but a dream and the people of the courtroom are mere figments of his imagination. He knows this, because he's already been tried, convicted and put to death time and again. Sometimes his lawyer is the bailiff, while other times he's the judge or a court reporter.

Grant is led out of court, but his outburst sticks in the mind of District Attorney Henry Ritchie (Harry Townes), especially once he notices implausibilities in his own life that could give credence to Grant's belief. As the clock ticks further to midnight, Ritchie must decide whether he believes Grant or not. If he does, what will that revelation mean not just to his life, but to his mind?

The Twilight Zone is a way to take us to the very edge of human imagination, dazzling us with the infinite possibilities of our universe. But it also serves as an opportunity to put ourselves in another person's shoes, even if it's a dead man's. Adam Grant isn't just any dead man walking either—he already knows the cold touch of the electric chair and the smell of the death shroud that will be placed over his face.

There are plenty of horror tales about men getting sent to the electric chair just to come back as some kind of abomination—I'm looking at you *Shocker* (1989) and *House III: The Horror Show* (1989)—but this episode's more meditative approach veers closer to Stephen King's problematic tome *The Green Mile*, especially since both can be viewed as indictments on capital punishment. Beaumont's point is that putting someone to death will not fix the root of the world's problems. Violence will beget more violence, and we'll continue to be caught in the same sick time loop that Grant has found himself in.

"Shadow Play" is philosophical and heady, but I love that, through inventive editing, they give us a beat of levity. In the opening scene, there is a moment where Grant tells another inmate what he remembers feeling the last time he was sent to the electric chair. The tense description of the moment before the switch is pulled is then juxtaposed by a quick cut to a close up of sizzling pork chops. It's rare to see these kinds of visual punchlines in an episode as serious as this, but it's done so well that you can't help but admire the injection of black comedy.

Zone Fact

The narrative device of a character reliving the same day over and over would be mined for comedic effect in Harold Ramis' Groundhog's Day, the slasher-comedy Happy Death Day, and serve as inspiration for Vince Gilligan's episode of The X-Files "Monday"

"The Mind and the Matter"
Episode 27
Original Airdate: May 12, 1961

Directed by Buzz Kulik
Written by Rod Serling

"A brief if frenetic introduction to Mr. Archibald Beechcroft. A child of the 20th century, a product of the population explosion, and one of the inheritors of the legacy of progress. Mr. Beechcroft again, this time Act Two of his daily battle for survival, and in just a moment our hero will begin his personal one-man rebellion against the mechanics of his age, and to do so he will enlist certain aides available only in
The Twilight Zone."

Archibald Beechcroft (Shelley Berman) is a modern man beset by the anxieties and stresses of the 20th century. He commutes daily on a crowded train, just to pack himself into a busy office with nary a moment of peace and quiet. When he is given a book on the power of the psyche, Beechcroft realizes that his mind has far more potential than he ever gave it credit for. As his new power blossoms, the peace and quiet Beechcroft so desperately craves may end up being the last thing he'll ever want.

I'm eager to believe that the episode's new agey book *The Mind and the Matter* is directly related to the burgeoning transcendental meditation movement in the early 1960s. The idea behind *The Mind and the Matter* is that through concentration we can unlock untapped potential where, with just our mind, we can move the immovable. Transcendental meditation is also about discovering the quiet power of the mind, accessed through thoughtful concentration, but that unfortunately doesn't translate to levitating objects or changing the fabric of reality with our brain!

"The Mind and the Matter" is a warning about why we should be wary of what we wish for. Beechcroft wants to control the world, molding it into his image, but his carelessness backfires as he realizes a world filled with people just like him quickly becomes a difficult, and stale, place to live. Our lives are balanced thanks to the differences we can share with others. How can we be individuals if we aren't exposed to people unlike ourselves? Rod Serling frequently used *The Twilight Zone* to break down the walls that humans create to separate themselves from the invented fear of "the other".

A running joke for the 21st century is that we live in the worst possible timeline, a reference culled from Dan Harmon's 2009 sitcom *Community*. If multiverses are real, we exist in the one no one wants to live in. But Serling's closing narration here gives us cynics who believe that a little bit of optimism. He says, "Mr. Archibald Beechcroft, a child of the 20th century, who has found out through trial and error—and mostly error—that with all its faults, it may well be that this is the best of all possible worlds. People notwithstanding, it has much to offer." As he so eloquently put it, this still can be the best possible timeline, even if it is filled with a bunch of assholes.

Zone Fact

This episode would serve as one of the inspirations for Isaac Ezban's The Similars, *which also features a world where everyone is identical.*

"Will the Real Martian Please Stand Up?"
Episode 28
Original Airdate: May 26, 1961

Directed by Montgomery Pittman
Written by Rod Serling

"Incident on a small island, to be believed or disbelieved. However, if a sour-faced dandy named Ross or a big, good-natured counterman who handles a spatula as if he'd been born with one in his mouth—if either of these two entities walk onto your premises, you'd better hold their hands—all three of them—or check the color of their eyes—all three of them. The gentlemen in question might try to pull you in—to The Twilight Zone."

During a snowstorm, two state troopers (John Archer, Morgan Jones) investigate the report of a UFO crash, where they discover footprints that lead them to a roadside diner. As the officers question the passengers of a cross-country bus waiting for the storm to subside, they make the revelation that there were only supposed to be six passengers on the bus. If that's true, then why are there seven accounted for? Was it merely a miscount from the driver (William Kendis), or is it a visitor from the stars who may not be interested in coming in peace?

    I don't need to tell you what happens in "Will the Real Martian Please Stand Up?" for you to already know the twist. Even if you've never watched the episode, cultural osmosis has likely given away the secret to Barney Phillips' three-eyed short order cook, or the third arm hidden under John Hoyt's overcoat. This story is as ubiquitous with the series as Serling, in part because it's so simple and compact. He's written an Agatha Christie story strained through the lens of Atomic Age Americana, with a setup straight out of a novel like *Ten Little Indians*. Just rather than people getting picked off one by one at a lavish English estate, it's seven passengers in a roadside diner when there should have only been six.

    This episode is a great companion piece to "The Monsters Are Due on Maple Street" (S1E22). Serling showed us in the first season how quick we are to turn on each other, especially under the shadow of night with no authority in sight. So what would happen if we were faced with the same threat, just now under crackling fluorescents with a police escort? Would we act the same way, or would we be able to see our civility breaking apart and stop it before we lose our humanity? The diners at the Hi-Way Cafe fare better than the men and women of Maple Street when it comes to holding the moral high ground, but Serling reminds us at the episode's end that it doesn't really matter. We'll all be dead soon anyways!

Zone Fact

For a time period when being self-referential wasn't in vogue, Rod Serling drops a number of sci-fi references like name dropping Ray Bradbury or quoting "Take me to your leader!" which was coined in a 1953 New Yorker comic.

"The Obsolete Man"
Episode 29
Original Airdate: June 2, 1961

Directed by Elliot Silverstein
Written by Rod Serling

"This is not a new world, it is simply an extension of what began in the old one. It has patterned itself after every dictator who has ever planted the ripping imprint of a boot on the pages of history since the beginning of time. It has refinements, technological advances, and a more sophisticated approach to the destruction of human freedom. But like every one of the super-states that preceded it, it has one iron rule: logic is an enemy and truth is a menace."

Romney Wordsworth (Burgess Meredith) has been deemed obsolete by a Chancellor (Fritz Weaver) in a totalitarian regime, where his occupation as a librarian is worthless in a post-truth world. Though the state may have deemed Wordsworth the worker obsolete, that doesn't mean Wordsworth the man is. Rather, in death he may have found his greatest confidence of all—the knowledge that comes from being a martyr.

The only kindness Wordsworth is given by the Chancellor is a choice in how he is to die, so he chooses a public execution and keeps the method of his death a secret. Wordsworth may be at peace with his impending doom, but what the Chancellor doesn't know is that he has plans for his name to live on long after he's gone.

This is most likely your librarian's favorite episode of *The Twilight Zone,* as it counts a librarian as a sort-of revolutionary folk hero who takes on the establishment in the name of culture, literature and freedom. That is, of course, if you still have a librarian. The career hasn't exactly been made obsolete like it has for Mr. Woodsworth, but libraries aren't exactly the same kinds of institutions as they were 60 years ago. Today, libraries offer a different kind of rare gift as the only places we can exist in peace, without being harassed or advertised to.

No fault of its own, but this episode would have resonated much more 60 years ago than today. We may feel freer than ever before, but

Jacob Trussell

it comes at the cost of those in power getting morbidly creative in how they keep their heels on our necks. Serling could wrap his head around mid-century autocrats like Adolf Hitler and Josef Stalin, but he never would have predicted the techno-war on truth that we see today from the likes of Russian President Vladimir Putin and Donald J. Trump. Try and imagine how this episode would play out if, rather than discussing the need for books and knowledge, it was about facts and truth. What may have been preposterous in the 1960s is now the grim reality of 2020.

We get a glimpse of this in a bit of Serling's closing narration that was cut for broadcast: "He was obsolete. But so is the State, the entity he worshiped. Any state, entity or ideology becomes obsolete when it stockpiles the wrong weapons; when it captures territories, but not minds; when it enslaves millions, but convinces nobody. When it is naked, yet puts on armor and calls it faith, while in the Eyes of God it has no faith at all. Any state, any entity, any ideology which fails to recognize the worth, the dignity, the rights of Man... that state is obsolete."

Zone Fact

Hip hop duo Run The Jewels would sample the opening narration on the track "Thieves! (Screamed The Ghost)" from their album
Run The Jewels 3.

The Twilight Zone

SEASON THREE

SEPTEMBER 15, 1961 – JUNE 1, 1962

"Two"
Episode 1
Original Airdate: September 15, 1961

Directed by Montgomery Pittman
Written by Montgomery Pittman

> *"This is a jungle, a monument built by nature honoring disuse, commemorating a few years of nature being left to its own devices. But it's another kind of jungle, the kind that comes in the aftermath of man's battles against himself. Hardly an important battle, not a Gettysburg, or a Marne, or an Iwo Jima; more like one insignificant corner patch in the crazy quilt of combat."*

Two soldiers (Charles Bronson, Elizabeth Montgomery) on opposing sides of a war meet in the deserted ruins of a bombed-out city, in the wake of what appears to be a nuclear explosion. Distrust fuels their encounter, but despite a lack of communication, their need for connection drives them together. Will the specter of what they were fighting for come back to haunt them, or will they be able to put aside the wars of other men and do what their generals never could—make peace?

Your appreciation for this romance-tinged episode will be gauged on how you feel about Charles Bronson. For me, a huge fan of the indictment on toxic masculinity that is *Death Wish* (1974), I find it thrilling to see a young Bronson working in Serling's space. He's the perfect archetypal male soldier for writer/director Montgomery Pittman to base his metaphors around—which in this episode's case is about seeing the soldier for the army, the people for the war. It can be so easy to just view armies in binary terms—good against evil—that we can forget that there are real humans underneath those helmets. Pittman is asking you to consider the innocent people on both sides of a global conflict, the ones forced to fight wars for governments who do not value their lives.

We believe that the woman is wary of the man because of his political affiliation, but I think that's too easy of a read. She's wary, not because he's the enemy, but because he's a man. If *The Twilight Zone* has made us aware of anything, it's that when dudes are left with nothing but time on their hands, they tend to go crazy. While I believe the intention of her pulling a gun on him is to show distrust between soldiers, a modern reading sees a woman protecting herself from potential assault, a feeling I'm sure any female viewer would pick up on.

Zone Fact

This is an early role for Elizabeth Montgomery, who would go on to make a splash as Samantha in the popular sitcom Bewitched, which co-starred fellow Twilight Zone actor Dick York!

"The Arrival"
Episode 2
Original Airdate: September 22, 1961

Directed by Boris Sagal
Written by Rod Serling

"Picture of a man with an Achilles' heel, a mystery that landed in his life and then turned into a heavy weight, dragged across the years to ultimately take the form of an illusion. Now, that's the clinical answer that they put on the tag as they take him away. But if you choose to think that the explanation has to do with an airborne Flying Dutchman, a ghost ship on a fog-enshrouded night on a flight that never ends, then you're doing your business in an old stand in the Twilight Zone."

A mysterious plane has just landed in Buffalo, New York. Outwardly, there appears to be nothing wrong with it, but when the airport crew go to deplane the luggage, they are shocked to find not only an empty cargo hold, but no one on board. Unsure of how to proceed, FAA Inspector Grant Sheckly (Harold J. Stone) is called in to investigate, but as the night unfolds, their memories of the plane landing become unreliable. As they look for a valid explanation, the Inspector wonders if questioning the very nature of reality is what will provide them with the answer to this impossible problem.

Serling used *The Twilight Zone* to demystify psychoanalysis. But more importantly, I find that he also used it as a way to reassure men that there is no weakness in admitting you suffer from depression or anxiety. Mental health issues are afflictions not unlike war, waged without our permission. The anguish that Sheckley feels about his unsolved case speaks to the power of guilt—an anxiety that burrows into your brain and stays there if you don't let it go. Twenty years is a long time for Sheckley to hold on to that pain, so it's no wonder that it would manifest itself in such a monumental way.

The psycho-supernatural element of "The Arrival" is unnerving because it forces the audience to question how we think about our reality. Is it something that exists just because the world collectively imagines it to exist? If that's so, then what would happen if we suddenly realized that reality was just a figment of our imagination, a

Jacob Trussell

byproduct of the power of suggestion? Would we flicker out of existence like a snuffed candle the moment we became self-aware?

I find questions of existence like this to be frightening, because it makes you realize how many unknowns are out there in the world. The thematic message on mental health at the core of "The Arrival" is important to remember, but the episode stays with you because it takes us to an outer edge of *The Twilight Zone* that the show never really visits again.

Zone Fact

Sheckley's experiment where he puts his arm into the plane's propeller would prove morbidly coincidental as this episode's director, Boris Sagal, would tragically die after walking into a helicopter rotor blade.

"The Shelter"
Episode 3
Original Airdate: September 29, 1961

Directed by Lamont Johnson
Written by Rod Serling

"For the human race to survive, we have to remain civilized."

It's Dr. Bill Stockton's (Larry Gates) birthday and the neighborhood has come out to celebrate. The merriment is interrupted, and panic sets in, when they hear that an unidentified aircraft—potentially carrying nuclear weapons—is heading towards the United States. However, Bill Stockton has been preparing for the worst, toiling away nights and weekends building a modest bomb shelter in his basement. His family retreats to its safety, but are soon met with desperation, fear and anger from neighbors who vie for a spot in his bunker. He pleads with them that there's no more room, that the supplies he has can only sustain one family, but it does nothing to assuage their distress. As the planes draw near, and tensions boil over, the true mettle of every person whom Stockton once called a friend will become known, warts and all.

During times of peace, we masquerade in the idea of togetherness, the notion that we are strongest when our communities become one. What this episode illustrates is how quickly conflict will not only divide us, but blind us to our present realities. Stockton shoulders a lot of the blame for the central conflict, but it's actually his panicky neighbors that drove the wedge between them. Their collective fear allowed them to become irrational, not understanding that it would be impossible for the entire community to fit in the bunker and still maintain the safety it's meant to provide.

The doctor—in this moment—doesn't have the luxury of being selfless. Doing so will only further endanger his family. As *Gremlins 2: The New Batch* (1990) so eloquently put it, the Stocktons are merely enacting the age-old drama of self-preservation. You can't blame them for it, because if the shoe was on the other foot, those neighbors banging down his door would be the first ones barricading themselves in.

The aftermath of the false alarm is like the lights being turned on for a grimy dive bar's last call. You get to see how ugly everyone has become. As they discuss rebuilding their relationships to what they were before this moment, one of the neighbors says, "That was a million years ago. A million years ago." Nothing is more relatable in the present moment than the fact that what was normal before a national emergency, will suddenly become incredibly alien after. In this new world—once our own emergencies pass—we'll know who showed compassion and strength, and who exploited and fear mongered. And we will not forget.

Zone Fact

The episode was inspired by how in vogue at-home bomb shelters became following the Berlin Crisis of 1961 that resulted in the construction of the Berlin Wall.

"The Passersby"
Episode 4
Original Airdate: October 6, 1961

Directed by Eliot Silverstein
Written by Rod Serling

> *"This road is the afterwards of the Civil War. It began at Fort Sumter, South Carolina, and ended at a place called Appomattox. It's littered with the residue of broken battles and shattered dreams."*

Walking down a humble dirt road, an army sergeant (James Gregory) stops to rest at the house of Lavinia Godwin (Joanne Linville), a young Southern woman awaiting the return of her husband at the end of the Civil War. Her fury for the North knows no bounds, especially when facing the prospect that she'll likely never see her husband again. The sergeant and the woman pass time by watching the soldiers slowly parade down the road, all on their own paths towards home. *Are* they going home, or are these soldiers on a course to a more permanent resting place? A place where everyone goes, regardless of what side you fight on.

A colleague of mine pointed out that there is a romanticization of the Civil War in *The Twilight Zone*, and I agree. This romanticization was prevalent throughout the United States in the early 20th century, because antebellum stories like *Gone with the Wind* (1939) were peaking in popularity decades later. I believe it's also due to the prevalence of westerns, which generally took place in the social aftermath of both the American and Spanish Civil Wars. I have to imagine that, because of Rod Serling's approach to social and civil justice, the Civil War romanticization stops there and doesn't spread to yearning for a time "when America was great."

There is a lot that we can understand about humanity by looking at the complex emotions of the losers of war. Lavinia is blinded by rage for her supposed dead husband, but Serling probes deeper, asking us to consider what Lavinia's husband's killer brought home to his family. That person may have physically survived, but with the trauma that accompanies combat, he may be mentally still on the battlefield. You don't need to receive a Purple Heart to have deep scars from war.

Jacob Trussell

Zone Fact

James Gregory's belt buckle is upside down throughout the episode. Initially a goof, Gregory made the case that it's symbolic of his character being in the afterlife.

"A Game of Pool"
Episode 5
Original Airdate: October 13, 1961

Directed by Buzz Kulik
Written by George Clayton Johnson

"Jesse Cardiff, pool shark, the best on Randolph Street, who will soon learn that trying to be the best at anything carries its own special risks."

Jesse Cardiff (Jack Klugman) is an everyday pool shark who thinks his natural talent is overshadowed by 'Fats' Brown (Jonathan Winters), a legendary player whose picture adorns his neighborhood billiard parlor's walls. Jesse wishes he had the chance to best Fats, wanting his name to live in history as the greatest player there ever was. No sooner do those words leave his lips than Fats appears, ready to accept his challenge. But is Jesse ready for the weight that comes with being number one?

Rod Serling loved having a resident company of actors that he could pull his everyman and everywoman from, but none were more spectacular at being ordinary than Jack Klugman. He's not the easygoing type like Dick York, who you can see yourself identifying with—rather, Klugman plays characters you're afraid you may relate to. The real everyman with a nobody face that blends into a crowd. It's in this perceived weakness that Klugman's characters can thrive as their societal anonymity gives them the courage to fail and fail again. You don't sweat taking risks when you're unafraid of losing face. After all, can you really save a face that never existed?

There's no doubt that George Clayton Johnson was inspired by the popularity of *The Hustler* (1961), a novel turned film starring Paul Newman as the titular pool shark who bites off more than he can chew, when faced with the skills of an equally talented player in Jackie Gleason. Hell, Jonathan Winters—also a comedian playing against type—feels like a smooth-around-the-edges version of Gleason's character who is *also* named Fats.

The battle between Fats and Cardiff, the intellectual and the philistine, is one that is familiar in *The Twilight Zone* as the show routinely juxtaposes the salt of the earth with those who think they're above it. The trap laid in the episode's twist speaks to a common refrain in the series—be careful what you wish for, especially if it involves power. You may not enjoy being the top dog forever.

Zone Fact

George Clayton Johnson's original ending had Jesse lose to Fats. This would be restored when the episode was remade for the 1985 revival.

"The Mirror"
Episode 6
Original Airdate: October 20, 1961

Directed by Don Medford
Written by Rod Serling

> *"Ramos Clemente, a would-be god in dungarees, strangled by an illusion, that will-o'-the-wisp mirage that dangles from the sky in front of the eyes of all ambitious men, all tyrants—and any resemblance to tyrants living or dead is hardly coincidental, whether it be here or in The Twilight Zone."*

Budding dictator Ramos Clemente (Peter Falk) has successfully overthrown a Central American government, installing himself as the head of state with four of his trusted aides by his side. Upon evicting the original regime's leader, General De Cruz (Will Kuluva), Clemente is told that the mirror hanging in his office can reveal the faces of any would-be assassin. Growing more powerful, and sparking a string of mass executions, Clemente begins to see his four trusted confidants in the mirror. Are these men his killers, or is there another face in the mirror he hasn't accounted for: his own?

Let's get this out of the way; even if the episode is in black and white, it doesn't excuse Peter Falk playing Clemente in brownface. It should bother you that his skin was darkened to play the Fidel Castro proxy, just like it should bother you seeing Italian-American Al Pacino play the famously Cuban Tony Montana in *Scarface*. There may have been an historical precedent for actors doing this in the 1960s, but that doesn't make it any less wrong. Only two actors in the episode are of Latin American descent, when it could have been the entire cast. Falk is a great actor in everything from *Columbo* to *The Princess Bride* (1987), but there were actors of color in the 1960s who could have played this character without having to darken a white man's skin. Thankfully, there's more representation of people of color in Hollywood now than ever before so hopefully something like this would never happen again, but it's still jarring to see in the 21st century.

The gross legacy of racial brownface overshadows the major themes of the episode, which directly question the insecurities of nationalism and dictatorship. Clemente's mirror is a stand-in for the paranoia of a deteriorating autocrat, struggling and flailing to keep their head above water, even if it means drowning those around them. The point is that everyone is an assassin to a political figure who has severed all friendships. If you only make enemies, no one will be left to have your back.

The political commentary of this episode is complex and compelling, but it's incredibly hard to shake the racist legacy of darkening Falk's skin. It's why I find this line that Clemente says more than a little ironic, "How can you strip off one color and put on another?" How can you indeed.

Zone Fact

This episode premiered six months after the failed Bay of Pigs Invasion, a US-funded military operation meant to oust dictator Fidel Castro, the inspiration for Ramos Clemente.

"The Grave"
Episode 7
Original Airdate: October 27, 1961

Directed by Montgomery Pittman
Written by Montgomery Pittman

> *"We've had the traditional shoot-out on the street and the badman will soon be dead. But some men of legend and folktale have been known to continue having their way even after death. The outlaw and killer Pinto Sykes was such a person, and shortly we'll see how he introduces the town and a man named Conny Miller, in particular, to the Twilight Zone."*

Outlaw Pinto Sykes (Dick Geary) is six feet under after encountering a posse hellbent on driving him out of their town. Their success comes at the cost of gunslinger Conny Miller (Lee Marvin) who'd been on the man's trail for weeks. He's not so much mad that he lost the bounty, than he is that Sykes' last words were to call him a coward. The deadman threatened that if the bounty hunter ever visits his tombstone, he'd reach out of the grave and drag him to hell. Taking this posthumous bet seriously, Miller vows to plant a dagger in the fresh soil of Syke's grave. Miller doesn't believe in ghosts or superstition, but as he'll soon find out, maybe he should.

In this fun, spooky episode, the major thing that gets under famed-tough guy Lee Marvin's (*The Dirty Dozen*) skin is toxic masculinity. This is a term that's often misinterpreted, but all toxic masculinity describes is the limitations that society, and men, have put on themselves. It's why men are made to feel weak or "less of a man" for showing emotional vulnerabilities.

Marvin's Miller voices this social construct with the bit of dialogue, "Grow up and act like men, or move to some place that men can protect you." He uses that language as both a cudgel and a smoke screen for his personal insecurities about Sykes's threat. What drives Miller into that graveyard is the toxic masculine urge that he has to prove himself, even if it's to a dead man.

"The Grave," like many *Twilight Zone* episodes before it, illustrates how we're more afraid of what we *don't* know than what we *do*. The fear that we create in our minds can slowly kill us, no

Jacob Trussell

matter how strong we think we are, but that doesn't mean fear is solely an invention of the mind. We can't discount those gut feelings that tell us there is more to the world than we've thought to conceive.

Zone Fact

This is the first appearance of James Best, who would appear in two more episodes as well as cult-classic The Killer Shrews! Even funner fact, he would go on to write a horror movie called Death Mask that he starred in alongside 80s Scream Queen Linnea Quigley!

"It's a Good Life"
Episode 8
Original Airdate: November 3, 1961

Directed by James Sheldon
Written by Rod Serling (from a short story by Jerome Bixby)

"This particular monster can read minds, you see. He knows every thought, he can feel every emotion. Oh yes, I did forget something, didn't I? I forgot to introduce you to the monster. This is the monster. His name is Anthony Fremont. He's six-years-old, with a cute little-boy face and blue, guileless eyes. But when those eyes look at you, you'd better start thinking happy thoughts, because the mind behind them is absolutely in charge. This is the Twilight Zone."

Peaksville, Ohio, is a town alone in an empty America. That's because six-year-old Anthony Fremont (Billy Mumy) has wished it so, sequestering Peaksville to a world all of its own. Anthony has psychic powers so great that he can rule the world with a tiny fist, forcing everyone around him to "think happy thoughts" or else they'll be wished into the cornfield—a netherworld where he sends anyone or anything he doesn't like. His family and neighbors fear him as he creates unspeakable abominations, but is there any reprieve for their hopelessness? Or will they be forever subject to the very unnatural whims of an extraordinary little boy?

Another of *Twilight Zone*'s most famous episodes, this story about an evil kid with God-like psychic powers has been lampooned (like on *The Simpsons*) and emulated (like in 2019's *Brightburn*) for so long that you bring with it a certain amount of expectations—namely that this kid is evil as fuck. But your expectations can't prepare you for *just* how truly abominable this kid is. I mean, he flagrantly kills a dog! I can only imagine that this 21st century no-no was slightly more acceptable four years after the release of *Old Yeller*, the end all, be all dead dog movie.

In the opening scene, we're told that Anthony has turned a gopher into a multi-headed monstrosity, but we never actually see it. Serling smartly leaves most of his powers off screen, causing his disturbing wishes to become even more graphic. Our imaginations work overtime, filling in the grotesque blanks, like whatever the hell he did to his family's livestock. When he turns a houseguest into a jack-in-the-box, we only see the bobbing of his head and a shadow cast on the wall, but it's all we need to infer what the horrified onlookers are witnessing. Like Tobe Hooper's *The Texas Chain Saw Massacre* (1974), "It's a Good Life" is a supreme example of scaring an audience by showing them as little as possible.

There's two ways to read this episode's underlying metaphors. On one hand, it's about the anxiety of raising children, the worry that your kid could become a monster no matter how loving you are. But in the episode's oppressive hopelessness I find a metaphor for nuclear anxiety. The residents of Peaksville live in a world of put-upon smiles, even though the fear of death is constant.

"It's a Good Life" is most unnerving in that we're given no resolution. As far as we know, Anthony will just keep an iron grip on this family, this community, this world. Serling would later expand this episode in an unproduced screenplay that showed Anthony's reign of terror coming to a satisfying conclusion, but here we're left with nothing but despair. The testament to a great bad character is if you want to strangle them through the screen. I can only assume that you, like me, wanted to murder this kid throughout.

Zone Fact

In the original short story, the boy is only three years-old rather than the six-year-old Billy Mumy.

An Unofficial Journey Into The Twilight Zone

"Deaths-Head Revisited"
Episode 9
Original Airdate: November 10, 1961

Directed by Don Medford
Written by Rod Serling

> *"This is not hatred. This is retribution. This is not revenge. This is justice. But this is only the beginning, Captain. Only the beginning. Your final judgment will come from God."*

Almost two decades after the Second World War, a Nazi Commander (Oscar Beregi, Jr.) hiding his true identity revisits Dachau, the concentration camp where he wielded sadistic control over its Jewish prisoners. As he gleefully reflects on his time as commandant, he's approached by Becker (Joseph Schildkraut), a former prisoner of the camp that Lutze now believes is the groundskeeper. What Lutze doesn't remember, is that he personally tortured and killed Becker 17 years before, and it's now the camp's turn to bring karmic justice for every soul lost during The Holocaust.

While Hollywood tackled The Holocaust only a few short years after the war ended, "Deaths-Head Revisited" is one of the earliest television shows to confront the subject in any substantial way. Between *The Stranger*, the first American film to deal with The Holocaust, and *Judgment at Nuremberg*, which was released the same year as this episode, it's difficult to not draw correlations between their shared themes of retribution.

These unfortunate victims return to hold their own Nuremberg trial, but one where the desire for revenge can be doled out by their own two hands. "Deaths-Head Revisited" is the kind of "justice from beyond the grave" narrative you can ruefully relish in, reminiscent of the supernatural revenge tales of EC Comics *Tales from the Crypt* or *The Vault of Horror*, where evil doers always get a taste of their own medicine.

The lingering question of "Deaths-Head Revisited" is how can a person expect forgiveness from someone that they've marginalized, or even murdered? Their victims may have the capacity for forgiveness, but someone like a Nazi officer—or a racist police officer—should not expect leniency. Lutze says he deserves atonement because he was just following orders, but when you don't balk at war crimes, or any crime against humanity, you become complicit. The Nazi captains weren't prisoners in their government, they were the gaolers. And they deserve the kind of punishment that sadly only exists in *The Twilight Zone*.

Zone Fact

The title is a play on words of Evelyn Waugh's novel Brideshead Revisited.

"The Midnight Sun"
Episode 10
Original Airdate: November 17, 1961

Directed by Anton Leader
Written by Rod Serling

"The poles of fear, the extremes of how the Earth might conceivably be doomed. Minor exercise in the care and feeding of a nightmare, respectfully submitted by all the thermometer-watchers in The Twilight Zone."

Norma (Lois Nettleton) is an artist who lives in a Manhattan apartment, in a world doomed to never ending daylight. As their Earth moves closer to the sun, temperatures across the globe skyrocket, causing the oceans to dry up and water to become a rare commodity. More and more people begin to lose their minds as riots break out, and looters take to the streets making the city increasingly unsafe. All Norma can do is paint landscapes of screaming, burning suns and scorched cityscapes, while she and her neighbor Mrs. Bronson (Betty Garde) struggle to survive against robbers besieging their building. As they resign into their hopelessness, they wonder if this midnight sun will ever set.

The mean streak of desperation coursing through "The Midnight Sun" is similar, if not completely steeped, in modern film and television's popular apocalypse tropes. You can see it in Rod Serling's world building, as he populates his bizarro-version of New York City with dangerous marauders scavenging the streets for food and supplies. Survival is the only reason why the unnamed intruder (Tom Reese) breaks into Norma's apartment. He pleads with her that he's a good man, but ultimately he's not above forcing his way into a stranger's home to steal her last precious drops of water.

When he realizes the consequences of his actions, guilt pours out of him. He's remorseful that he's become like an animal, eschewing his own ethics to survive one more day. It's not just him either, even the elderly Mrs. Bronson isn't above stealing Norma's groceries in desperation. But this isn't something we can outwardly judge them for. Under the circumstances, who is to say that we wouldn't be doing the same?

Jacob Trussell

Zone Fact

Director Tony Leader instructed the heat to be turned up on-set to give the actors a true sense of what their characters were experiencing.

An Unofficial Journey Into The Twilight Zone

"Still Valley"
Episode 11
Original Airdate: November 24, 1961

Directed by James Sheldon
Written by Rod Serling (from a short story by Manly Wade Wellman)

"The time is 1863, the place the state of Virginia. The event is a mass blood-letting known as the Civil War, a tragic moment in time when a nation was split into two fragments, each fragment deeming itself a nation."

Two Confederate soldiers on the last leg of the Civil War are tasked with scouting a potential new Union outpost. After one of his soldiers refuses to accompany him, Sergeant Joseph Paradine (Gary Merrill) goes to reconnoiter on his own. In the small outpost, he finds the Yanks, but it is as if they were frozen in time. He discovers that an old man, Teague (Vaughn Taylor), has used a book of witchcraft to enchant the entire valley. Is it all in the name of peace, a means to end the war, or is something far darker happening in Still Valley that goes beyond the confines of man?

If you weren't sure how Rod Serling felt about the Confederacy during the Civil War, intimating that they'd resort to conjuring Satan should be a major clue that he wasn't hip to their brand of bigotry! The contrast between the God-fearing men of "Still Valley"' and their turn to Satanism reminds me of modern day Bible thumping Senators who outwardly call themselves Christian while going against the very principles that make up the religion. You can't hold the moral high ground when you are swimming in mercilessness!

The witchcraft described at the core of this episode is derived from the idea of the Seventh Son, an ancient folkloric story where insurmountable powers are given to the seventh son of a man, who is the seventh son of another seventh son. The number seven has heavy connotations in superstition and religion—like our seven-day calendar or the seven deadly sins—but used in this episode it's a means to an end, a way to add a second layer to the mystery over Teague's magical abilities.

Jacob Trussell

The Civil War stories that were prevalent on mid-century television like *The Twilight Zone* always seem to take the perspective of the Confederacy. Our first understandable instinct is to feel that these stories are trying to make us sympathize with these prejudiced characters. But I don't think sympathy is what Serling means to evoke here. It looks more like pity, the type that comes from watching characters reflect on their actions, wondering if the intolerant convictions they stood for were worth it.

These complex emotions don't readily come from the side of the victor whose beliefs are cemented through triumph in war. Taking the perspective of the losing side of the Civil War can then be contrasted in Serling's focus on the United States during World War II. He can show that even when you win in war, the emotions are the same, because there *are* no winning sides. In war, everyone is a loser.

Zone fact

Manly Wade Wellman, who's short story is the basis for the episode, would also see his work featured on Light's Out, Night Gallery, and the 1988 genre anthology series Monsters!

An Unofficial Journey Into The Twilight Zone

"The Jungle"
Episode 12
Original Airdate: December 1, 1961

Directed by William F. Claxton
Written by Charles Beaumont

> *"Some superstitions, kept alive by the long night of ignorance, have their own special power."*

Alan Richards (John Dehner) works for a company building a hydroelectric dam in Africa, much to the ire of the native residents. Richards's wife Doris (Emily McLaughlin) returns from the trip with artifacts given to her by a shaman hoping to convince her husband to cease construction and stop further damage to the land. Angered by her indulgence in the supernatural, Alan tells Doris to get rid of the objects, but it's too late. They've already started a chain reaction of events—like the startling discovery of a dead goat in front of his apartment door—that will show Richards what havoc curses can truly wrought.

This episode may share tonal similarities to film producer Val Lewton's expressionistic tales of black magic, but I look at "The Jungle" as an early example of ecological horror, a subgenre about Mother Nature fighting back against the environmentally unfriendly. Alan Richards and his corporation destroyed land for its resources, and in the process unearthed something nightmarish. Eco-horror also speaks to arguments against industrialization, like in Barry Levinson's *The Bay* where illegal waste dumping causes mutated parasites to attack a lakeshore town.

There's also a modern argument to be made that "The Jungle" is a slight commentary on gentrification and cultural appropriation. The curse is a punishment for the injustices of a white man co-opting land from people of color, chopping up habitats and taking pieces of their lives like souvenirs from a vacation. An unsubtle, if not unintentional, visual metaphor that speaks to cultural appropriation and commoditization comes late in the episode as Alan is pursued by an unseen force. He stops and stares into the window of a party store and sees his reflection overlaid on a jungle warrior costume. It's the

Jacob Trussell

cosmos laughing at him, as if to say, "You wanted the land, now you get everything that comes with it."

A question that we never get answered is: who was the vagrant (Jay Adler) that Alan bribed to walk with him prior to his death? Did he just disappear, or was it Alan who was spirited away to some in-between place where the jungle forces could finally reach him? It's likely just one of the many plot holes in *The Twilight Zone,* but it's still fun imagining the possibilities that exist outside the frame of Beaumont's scenes.

Zone Fact

Though uncredited, the lion featured in this episode, Zamba, also appeared in The Addams Family and William Castle's 13 Ghosts.

"Once Upon a Time"
Episode 13
Original Airdate: December 15, 1961

Directed by Norman Z. McLeod
Written by Richard Matheson

"Mr. Mulligan, a rather dour critic of his times, is shortly to discover the import of that old phrase, 'Out of the frying pan, into the fire—said fire burning brightly at all times—in The Twilight Zone."

Woodrow Mulligan (Buster Keaton) is a guy that lives one day at a time as a janitor for a local professor. While he may live in the present moment, he's not entirely thrilled about it. Who would be, when the national surplus is high, prices are skyrocketing, and he's surrounded by a world that is moving on without him? All of that is set to change when Mulligan accidentally hops forward seventy years in time, thanks to a hi-tech hat. Will he be able to get home after the time-hat breaks, or is he fated to be stuck in the noisy, raucous world of the early 1960s forever?

    The first thing that you'll find striking about "Once Upon a Time" is its high concept. The episode begins as if we were watching a silent movie, with interstitial title cards and old-timey organ music, but that's not why it's a high concept. We're not just watching the stylisms of a silent movie, Mulligan lives in a silent *world*. It's why the contrast when he travels forward in time is so fantastic. Just as he is blasted by sound, we are as well when the audio mixing in the transitory moment gets cranked to 11.

    Stylistic concepts aside, the fact is even at sixty-four, there is no better physical comic actor than Buster Keaton. *The Twilight Zone* doesn't stand in the way of The Great Stone Face doing what he does best. Mulligan even feels like an extension of the trampish characters from Keaton's heyday, but when seen at an older age, it strikes a more somber tone. It's sad to see that his character truly went nowhere in life, staying a straight up slacker cruising by from womb to tomb. It makes you ask yourself, when you have no plans for the future, what are you going to do when the future finally arrives? Clearly in Mulligan's case it means going *even further* into the future.

Jacob Trussell

This episode is another cautionary tale for what happens when you wish for things to "go back to the way they were." The modern scientist Rollo (Stanley Adams) wants to travel to a romanticized 1800s without considering what he gains to lose from life without the comforts of the 20th century. That being said, this is just surface level intellectualism on what is otherwise a purely comedic episode. It's a joy to watch Buster Keaton, in the twilight of his career, still have all the moves that made him a superstar decades before.

Zone Fact

A Hollywood Golden Age director, Norman Z. McLeod (Topper) came out of semi-retirement for the chance to work with Buster Keaton.

"Five Characters in Search of an Exit"
Episode 14
Original Airdate: December 22, 1961

Directed by Lamont Johnson
Written by Rod Serling (from a short story by Marvin Petal)

"Five improbable entities stuck together into a pit of darkness. No logic, no reason, no explanation; just a prolonged nightmare in which fear, loneliness, and the unexplainable walk hand in hand through the shadows."

A clown (Murray Matheson), a tramp (Kelton Garwood), a bagpipe player (Clark Allen), a ballet dancer (Susan Harrison) and an Army Major (William Windom) find themselves trapped in a giant cylinder, unable to see anything beyond the sky above them. They muse over where they are and how they came to be there, but none of them can remember *who* they are—the only clue being the clothes on their backs. Unable to admit defeat, the Major rouses the group to escape, but will it lead to their salvation, or will the five characters finally discover that they are living in a nightmare?

Deriving its title from Luigi Pirandello's absurdist play *Six Characters in Search of an Author*, this episode is best remembered for it's anxiety riddled finale that likely left audiences scratching their heads, unaware that they just watched a holiday special.

There are two ways you can look at this highly strange, cerebral episode. In one reading, you have the idea that this is Rod Serling metaphorically showing the fear and trauma that prisoners of war felt, the hopelessness and the despair of knowing that there is no way out of their own personal hell. It's an idea Serling would explore in an earlier radio play, *The Air is Free*, about two men trapped at the bottom of a mineshaft looking to the sky above.

On the other hand, the episode premiered on December 22, 1961, and with closing shots showing a Red Cross bell-ringer collecting donations, it's clear to modern audiences that this is a sad quick Christmas episode. It strikes a far bleaker tone than the touching "Night of the Meek," but even if the twist ending makes your stomach sink, Rod Serling's closing narration acts as a balm:

Jacob Trussell

"But this added hopeful note: perhaps they are unloved only for the moment. In the arms of children, there can be nothing but love."

Zone Fact

J.J. Abrams put an homage to Five Characters in a Twilight Zone-themed episode of Felicity with original series director Lamont Johnson.

"A Quality of Mercy"
Episode 15
Original Airdate: December 29, 1961

Directed by Buzz Kulik
Written by Rod Serling (from an idea by Sam Rolfe)

"If they are the enemy, they will be destroyed."

In the twilight hours of World War II, when soldiers in the Pacific Theatre have long grown weary of the never-ending violence, Second Lieutenant Katell (Dean Stockwell) arrives to squash the remnants of the occupying Japanese forces. His squad tries to reason with him, saying how it's pointless now, but the Lieutenant balks at their pleas to show mercy. In a flash, the Lieutenant finds himself not only three years in the past, but in the body of a Japanese soldier whose commander uses the same vitriolic language he just spit at his own men. Will he recognize the hypocrisy of his moral superiority, or will he learn a different kind of lesson on mercy that can only come from the muggy depths of *The Twilight Zone*?

"A Quality of Mercy" is about a baby-faced Dean Stockwell who learns that it doesn't pay to be a compassionless, racist warmonger when he literally takes a supernatural walk in the opposing side's shoes. Being transformed into a Japanese soldier forces him to see the enemy not as an idea, but as real, flesh and blood people with misgivings and complex emotions. He confronts his own enmity when he realizes that his hate will only beget more hate. If he can't show mercy, he is no better than the Japanese Captain he demonizes. Bloodlust doesn't lead to victory; it leads to moral corruption.

This episode's setting makes me curious what *The Twilight Zone* would have looked like if Serling had been stationed in the European Theatre, rather than the Pacific. We see how much he uses his experience in the Philippines and its landscapes to inform his World War II set stories, but how would he have been inspired by the architecture and the long, dark history of European countries? Would his war stories be peppered with more gothic motifs? Would he have run across more of the supernatural mysticisms that were rumored to have been practiced by certain sects of Nazis?

Jacob Trussell

We'll never know, but if he had, I have a feeling it'd look *a lot* like the 1983 Michael Mann film *The Keep*, based off of F. Paul Wilson's novel of the same name, about a group of Nazis who unleash an evil force from a fort in the Carpathian Mountains that can only be stopped by a Jewish family.

Zone Fact

Dean Stockwell was originally cast in "The Purple Testament," which also features premonitions in the Pacific Theatre.

"Nothing in the Dark"
Episode 16
Original Airdate: January 5, 1962

Directed by Lamont Johnson
Written by George Clayton Johnson

"An old woman living in a nightmare, an old woman who has fought a thousand battles with death and always won. Now she's faced with a grim decision—whether or not to open a door. And in some strange and frightening way she knows that this seemingly ordinary door leads to The Twilight Zone."

Wanda Dunn (Gladys Cooper) is an agoraphobic elderly woman that believes Death is waiting for her on the other side of her front door. When she hears the sounds of a scuffle outside, and the moans of a dying policeman (Robert Redford) on her stoop, she becomes frightened. She doesn't want to let him in, afraid it's secretly Death coming to take her, but reluctantly she agrees. Little does she know how right she is, and with the looming realization that her home is to be taken away from her, perhaps Death is finally visiting.

The casting of Robert Redford in this role is inspired, in part because of how handsome he is. We are scared of death, because it's something we can't completely conceive. No one can understand what happens after we die, which is why it's also something that shouldn't *really* worry us. What will happen will happen, whether we like it or not, and you can either view it as an adventure or as a crippling crutch. And by casting the representation of death as a nice hot dude, it becomes writer George Clayon Johnson's way of saying that the end of life isn't something that should be feared. Especially if death looks anything like a youthful Robert Redford!

That doesn't mean there isn't still a sad sinister reality that the episode pokes at. Maybe the afterlife is just like our world, but it's photographic negative, where everything is the same, but isn't. This concept I find reminiscent of the finale of Damon Lindelof's *The Leftovers,* a show that looks at what could happen to society after a Rapture-like event. It's bleak, spooky, and owes a large debt of gratitude to *The Twilight Zone.*

Jacob Trussell

Fun Fact

This episode was shot for Season Two but held until Season Three, along with the episode The Grave

"One More Pallbearer"
Episode 17
Original Airdate: January 12th, 1962

Directed by Lamont Johnson
Written by Rod Serling

> *"Mr. Paul Radin, a dealer in fantasy, who sits in the rubble of his own making and imagines that he's the last man on Earth, doomed to a perdition of unutterable loneliness because a practical joke has turned into a nightmare. Mr. Paul Radin, pallbearer at a funeral that he manufactured himself in the Twilight Zone."*

Eccentric millionaire Paul Radin (Joseph Wiseman) invites three people from his past—a colonel, a reverend and a teacher—to his well-fortified bomb shelter. Each person humiliated him in some form, from being court martialed in the military to being belittled in school. What they don't know is that Radin has rigged the shelter to be an elaborate prank. He wants to frighten the trio with a nuclear scare, complete with video projections and rumbling walls, as vengeance for the mortification he felt all those years ago. Will they fall for his bait, or do they see through his ruse to the person that he really is?

Paul Radin unearthing past memories of unimpressed guests reminds me of the classic show *This is Your Life*. Filmed live and broadcast across the world, the talk show's host would ambush an unexpecting celebrity and take them through various, oftentimes embarrassing events from their past life. Just this time, the person doing the ambushing is also the person strolling down memory lane, and rather than evoking sympathy, it just makes us hate the guy even more. Paul Radin is undoubtedly *awful*, and it doesn't take you long to realize that—especially when he speaks in hyperboles about how his guests "destroyed" his life. He sees himself as the abused, despite his extreme cruelties, like driving a woman to suicide and refusing orders that caused massive casualties of war.

Colonel Hawthorne (Joseph Wiseman), Reverend Hughes (Trevor Bardette), and Mrs. Langsford (Katherine Squire) each represent a different anxious memory that's vexed Radin for years. Without showing sympathy to Radin, he is the embodiment of how we can't help but carry anxieties with us through life. We're all guilty of dwelling on that embarrassing thing we did 20 years ago, even if it's entirely inconsequential today. For Radin, anxiety has dictated his entire life, to the extent that he's concocted an apocalyptic fantasy in the hopes to, what? Get over it? Mental health doesn't care how many years it's been, how much money, success, or power you hold, it can only be treated through compassionate understanding—not by trapping folks in a bunker and threatening them with radiation poisoning.

Radin thinks he's entitled to forgiveness because he's fantasized himself as the victim, which becomes his own undoing. He believes in his fantasy so much that he even tricks himself into thinking that the fake nuclear attack has actually occurred. He becomes the victim exactly where he's always been: in his own mind.

Zone Fact

Later in 1962, Joseph Wiseman would gain global recognition as the titular James Bond villain Dr. No.

"Dead Man's Shoes"
Episode 18
Original Airdate: January 19, 1962

Directed by Montgomery Pittman
Written by Charles Beaumont

"Nathan Edward Bledsoe, of the Bowery Bledsoes, a man once, a specter now. One of those myriad modern-day ghosts that haunt the reeking nights of the city in search of a flop, a handout, a glass of forgetfulness. Nate doesn't know it but his search is about to end, because those shiny new shoes are going to carry him right into the capital of The Twilight Zone."

A homeless man, Nathan Edward Bledsoe (Warren Stevens), steals the shoes off of a dead body he finds dumped in a back alley. The shoes belong to Dane, a mob boss whose personality begins to infect Bledsoe's own until he loses sight of where he begins and Dane ends. As the Mafioso takes control, Nate starts down a road of revenge that leads directly to Dagget (Richard Devon), the man who originally placed the hit on Dane. Disturbed by the return of a man he knows to be dead, Dagget soon wises up, dooming Bledsoe to relive the demise of the original owner of those ill-fated kicks.

At first glance, this episode seems to be a cut and dry supernatural drama of a man being slowly possessed by something he believes he wants. In this case, the man is homeless and what he wants is simple: a life, of any kind. Lucky or not for him, the life he stumbles into comes with money and, more importantly, power. He spent his life on the streets as a pushover, but that all changes now that he's got the body and soul of a tough talking gangster.

This body-swapping narrative device gets to one of *The Twilight Zone*'s favorite themes: how power can corrupt. How could any writer post-World War II not be entranced by the complexities that came with those authoritarian leaders drunk on power, like Adolph Hitler? Stories like "Dead Man's Shoes" impress upon the viewer the ramifications that come if you flex your control through undue force. If you lose your humanity, you're likely to lose your life as well.

This episode can also be seen as a thinly-veiled critique on alcoholism. Nate becomes someone else when he puts on the pair of shoes, yes, but we first get our hints at this new personality when he starts drinking. And once he starts he doesn't stop, even threatening to break a woman's arm if she doesn't make him a cocktail. His inability to restrain himself is what it means to be an alcoholic. It's like a cosmically stupid version of Robert Louis Stevenson's *The Strange Case of Dr. Jekyll and Mr. Hyde*. Except rather than being a suave, dangerous lothario, Edward Hyde just has no impulse control and can't stop crying.

Zone Fact

This episode was revised as Dead Woman's Shoes for the 1985 revival series, directed by Peter Medak (The Changeling)

An Unofficial Journey Into The Twilight Zone

"The Hunt"
Episode 19
Original Airdate: January 26, 1962

Directed by Harold Schuster
Written by Earl Hamner, Jr.

"A man would walk into hell with both eyes open. But even the devil can't fool a dog."

Hyder Simpson (Arthur Hunnicutt) and his trusty hound Rip go out on a hunt for some raccoons. As Rip chases a critter into a pond, the old man dives in after him, only to awaken with Rip out of the pond and dry as a bone, unsure of what happened to them. As they walk home, Hyder comes across two men digging a hole on his land. When he raises his rifle to get them off his property, he touchingly realizes they are burying a dog. He's so taken by their own grief, he doesn't realize that no one can see or hear him. He's even more alarmed when he finds his wife dressed in mourning, about to attend a funeral: his own.

"The Hunt" is *The Twilight Zone* at its sweetest, the kind of episode with a strong loud moral for a seven-year-old watching it for the first time: if someone ever tells you to get rid of your dog, you may be dealing with the devil!

This is the second of three instances where *The Twilight Zone* uses a dead dog as a plot device. My theory is that audiences at the time were desensitized to it in the wake of the hit film adaptation of *Ol' Yeller* in 1957. Granted, where it's mean spirited in "It's a Good Life," it is a vital part of the story in "The Hunt." The dog's name is even Rip. Get it? R. I. P? Where a dead dog in a modern story is a surefire way to have your audience turn on you, Rip had to die so he could save Hyder's soul. It's writer Earl Hamner Jr.'s way of saying that a dog is man's best friend until the very end, and even long after that.

This episode is also a way to illustrate that the afterlife—heaven, whatever you want to call it—is what you make of it. There are no hifalutin angels with harps and classical music being played on wispy clouds because that's not Mr. Simpson's style. He's not the pearly

Jacob Trussell

gates type, more of a humble wooden fence kind of guy. Even the denizens of the other world aren't like what you expect in a fairy tale. These angels don't have wings, they look just like any good ol' boy with a tattered pair of overalls. Satan isn't completely red with horns and a pointy tale. No, he's merely a man who doesn't like dogs. And honestly, that seems about right.

Zone Fact

Debut episode from writer Earl Hamner Jr. who would later create the generational hit The Waltons

"Showdown with Rance McGrew"
Episode 20
Original Airdate: February 2, 1962

Directed by Christian Nyby
Written by Rod Serling (from an idea by Frederic Louis Fox)

> *"Some 100-odd years ago, a motley collection of tough mustaches galloped across the West and left behind a raft of legends and legerdemains, and it seems a reasonable conjecture that if there are any television sets up in cowboy heaven and any of these rough-and-wooly nail-eaters could see with what careless abandon their names and exploits are being bandied about, they're very likely turning over in their graves—or worse, getting out of them."*

Award-winning actor Rance McGrew (Larry Blyden) is one of the most famous cowboys on television, who just so happens to be an egotistical diva on set. He thinks he's the only one who knows what it means to be a cowboy, even if he is utterly incompetent as one. He can't keep a hold of his gun or his whiskey—quite literally, as a barkeep slides a glass right by his hand and off the counter. McGrew gets a taste of what it means to be a cowboy when reality bleeds into his on-air persona and he's visited by the real Jesse James (Arch Johnson), who has more than a few notes on how his cowboy compatriots have been portrayed in modern television.

Another one of the few purely comedic episodes of *The Twilight Zone*, it's also meant to be an unsubtle satire on the westerns that proliferated mid-century Hollywood. Serling's critique is that these characters had become so glamorized and embellished that they lacked any historical accuracy. Jesse James needles McGrew about his ridiculous feats, like jumping 800 feet onto the back of a horse or shooting a man in a duel by ricocheting bullets, to point out that the real people he knew had been transformed into Saturday matinee superheroes. It's no wonder that correlations are drawn between the popularity of westerns and the modern comic book film. Both are used as thin metaphors for society while mostly being populace fun of good triumphing over evil. Makes you really wonder if Rod Serling would be a fan of the Marvel Cinematic Universe! Based on this episode: I'm thinking not so much.

Jacob Trussell

With all of the satire on Hollywood tropes I can't help but be reminded of Quentin Tarantino's *Once Upon a Time in Hollywood* (2019). In the film, we also get a behind the scenes look at the making of a western TV show, *Bounty Law*, featuring aging star Rick Dalton (Leo DiCaprio). The show-within-a-movie was based on the Steve McQueen series *Wanted: Dead or Alive*, which ran concurrently with the first three seasons of *The Twilight Zone*. Rick Dalton doesn't whine as much as Rance McGrew, but you can clearly see the similarities in ego to these men who feel empowered by their characters' heroism. The actors have a kind of empty courage that is built up by the role they play, but when really pressed, they snap like a twig under pressure.

Zone Fact

There is no movie called The Gunfight at Red Rock that Rance McGrew mentions to Jesse James when propositioned with a duel. There were two westerns that this title could be an amalgamation of, The Gunfight at the O.K. Corral and Escape from Red Rock, both released in 1957.

"Kick the Can"
Episode 21
Original Airdate: February 9, 1962

Directed by Lamont Johnson
Written by George Clayton Johnson

"Sunnyvale Rest, a dying place for ancient people, who have forgotten the fragile magic of youth. A dying place for those who have forgotten that childhood, maturity and old age are curiously intertwined and not separate. A dying place for those who have grown too stiff in their thinking"

Disheartened Charles Whitley (Ernest Truex) is moved to a retirement community by his son (Barry Truex), where he witnesses the staff treat the elderly retirees like they are helpless children. This is ironic as Charles believes he's discovered the secret to the fountain of youth—rediscovering your inner child. Starting to act the part of a kid, such as playing hide and seek after lights out and sneaking into the night for a round of his favorite childhood game 'kick the can,' his increasingly erratic behavior concerns the staff and Charles' best friend Ben (Russell Collins). But is he losing his marbles, or has he really found a way to live forever?

If there is one universal truth we can derive from "Kick the Can," it's that retirement communities have always been dreadful. It comes down to their simple realities. These people don't deserve to be treated like children, just because they need help in their old age. The staff castigating them for things like sneaking out at night deny the retirees the dignity and respect every adult deserves—not to mention the thrill of feeling alive. This speaks to another theme in the episode that just because you're old, or lead a serious life, doesn't mean you still can't engage in the vernal experience of feeling young.

I find the final melancholy moments as the retirees-turned-children vanish into the surrounding woods to be wistfully optimistic. Serling visualizes in these last frames how much we gain from transitioning into the great beyond. It's not something to be frightened of, on the contrary we should be looking forward to it. Why? Because we'll have back what we've always wanted: the freedom of being a kid again.

Jacob Trussell

Zone Fact

Charles Whitley's son is played by actor Ernest Truex's real son Barry Truex

"A Piano in the House"
Episode 22
Original Airdate: February 16, 1962

Directed by David Greene
Written by Earl Hamner, Jr.

"Mr. Fitzgerald Fortune, theater critic and cynic at large, on his way to a birthday party. If he knew what is in store for him he probably wouldn't go, because before this evening is over that cranky old piano is going to play "Those Piano Roll Blues" with some effects that could happen only in The Twilight Zone."

Fitzgerald Fortune (Barry Morse) is a drama critic of some renown, but not a lot of love. He's wicked and savage, which is proven when he buys a player piano for his wife, Esther (Joan Hackett) even though she expressed interest in learning how to play the instrument herself. When he purchases the piano, he's pleasantly surprised to learn that it has the power to reveal the innermost truth of whoever is listening to its song. He decides to use it for his own terrible means at a birthday party he is hosting in Esther's honor. Will he relish in the delight of humiliating his friends by forcing them to share their secrets, or will he find that the universe has ways of biting you in the ass?

What I find striking in this episode is its lack of metaphor. With the exception of where the piano's power comes from, and why a song can only affect one person at a time, there's not much in terms of mystery. Everything that Fortune subjects his guests to all have a very clear motive, like his jealousy towards Marge's (Muriel Landers) joie de vivre or the envy he feels for the inherent talents of playwright Gregory Walker (Don Durant). The secrets revealed aren't really surprising to the audience either. We all have fantasies that we keep tucked away in our minds, those deep desires that are so dear we dare not share.

That being said, if you ever weaponize a player piano that opens the listener's inner soul, be ready for the world to see something you may not want. That's the "taste of your own medicine" comeuppance Fortune receives in the finale. We discover his big secret is that he's just like every other bully in the world; nothing more than a frightened child.

Jacob Trussell

Zone Fact

The butler Cryil Delevanti is a genre vet appearing in four Twilight Zone episodes, the film Soylent Green, and other supernatural anthologies like One Step Beyond and Night Gallery.

"The Last Rites of Jeff Myrtlebank"
Episode 23
Original Airdate: February 23, 1962

Directed by Montgomery Pittman
Written by Montgomery Pittman

"Time, the mid-twenties. Place, the Midwest, the southernmost section of the Midwest. We were just witnessing a funeral, a funeral that didn't come off exactly as planned, due to a slight fallout from The Twilight Zone."

In a rural southern town, young Jeff Myrtlebank (James Best) has died. That is, until he rises from his casket in the middle of his wake wondering what the hell is going on! The townspeople are more than a little alarmed by the revenant of the man they once knew, but this undead Jeff doesn't act like the real life one they were about to bury. For one, this Jeff isn't lazy or shiftless; he works hard and is friendly to everyone, something which couldn't be said about the man when he was alive. And there are more than just personality changes happening to Jeff, especially once he plucks a bushel of roses only to watch them wither and die in his hands. Has the devil really grabbed hold of his soul, or is there something more unexplainable that brought Jeff Myrtlebank back from the grave?

What is there to do when a deadman comes back to life? Distrust them, of course! That's exactly what the townspeople in this episode do when they claim Jeff is possessed by a "Haint," an old southern word used to describe evil spirits. Haint—haunt—you get it! Jeff is way too much of a good ol' boy to be possessed by something evil, especially when portrayed by the lovably goofy James Best. If only the doctors of the town had heard of a little thing called Lazarus Syndrome, a term taken from the Biblical story of Lazarus who was revived by Christ days after death. The term wasn't introduced until over 20 years after this episode, so I can only surmise that this was inspired by tales of premature burial famously written by Edgar Allen Poe.

The town fears Jeff because they think he's different since he came back, like his soul has been possessed by something dark. This is where I sense a well-hidden allegory about soldiers returning from World War II, or any war for that matter. The atrocities that they witnessed changed them, and their families now don't know how to communicate their concerns. There's even an argument to be made that the episode's themes are a precursor to the ill treatment soldiers faced coming home after the Vietnam War. That specific experience would go on to inspire the *Rambo* series and pretty much every military thriller paperback novel published between the end of that war, and the beginning of the next.

I appreciate the episode's final supernatural twist as Jeff's beau Comfort (Sherry Jackson) watches him light a pipe with nothing but his mind. I don't think it speaks to any kind of malevolence with his resurrection; rather this is an anachronism in the midst of the episode's reality. We shouldn't let our lives be dictated by superstition, but we also cannot be so close-minded to believe that scientific fact can explain all of the world's unknowns.

Zone Fact

It's a family affair! Shirley Jackson (not the author behind The Haunting of Hill House) is Montogomery Pittman's stepdaughter. Producer Buck Houghton's son James also appears in this episode!

An Unofficial Journey Into The Twilight Zone

"To Serve Man"
Episode 24
Original Airdate: March 2, 1962

Directed by Richard L. Bare
Written by Rod Serling (from a short story by Damon Knight)

"Or more simply stated, the evolution of man. The cycle of going from dust to desert. The metamorphosis from being the ruler of a planet to an ingredient in someone's soup."

Imprisoned by an unseen jailer, Michael Chambers (Lloyd Bochner) recounts the last few weeks of his life when a race of aliens named the Kanamits landed on Earth. They brought with them new kinds of medicine, agriculture and security that changed the entire world for the better. High on the gifts from the aliens, Earthlings are shepherded off to the Kanamits home planet where they're promised a way of life full of bliss and tranquility, but the United States and other global superpowers remain cautious. They assemble a team of linguists to translate the aliens' mysterious texts in an effort to discern their true intentions coming to Earth. Is it really for peace, or do the words that adorn their book "To Serve Man" have more than one connotation?

You probably know all of the twists and turns in "To Serve Man," as the ending has become as synonymous with the show as the eerie title music and Rod Serling's narration. Knowing how the episode ends though doesn't ruin any fun leading up to that horrifying—and hilarious—revelation. As you wonder why the Kanamits are brazenly carrying around a cookbook like they are The Barefoot Contessa ready to make bruschetta for your next yacht party, it dawns on you how deeply, *deeply* silly this episode really is. It's what makes "To Serve Man" unique, despite having a plot resembling Swiss cheese, meaning there's a *ton* of holes.

The biggest leap in logic is how well the United States handled this alien invasion. It's impossible to imagine 21st century Americans *not* being locked and loaded, ready to fire on the first E.T. they see. If the Kanamits came today, with modern American gun culture, this episode likely would have played much differently. More so, if the Coronavirus pandemic is any indication, we'd actually be *terrible* at

Jacob Trussell

coming together to face a visible threat like invaders from another planet. That being said, after centuries of war and destruction, I doubt extraterrestrials would want any part of Earth's unending dramas.

You can find an in-depth dive into "To Serve Man" in the chapter *If You Only Watch One Episode*!

Zone Fact

The head Kanamit is portrayed by Richard Kiel, who is best known as the metal-mouthed Jaws in the James Bond series.

"The Fugitive"
Episode 25
Original Airdate: March 9, 1962

Directed by Richard L. Bare
Written by Charles Beaumont

"It's been said that science fiction and fantasy are two different things: science fiction, the improbable made possible; fantasy, the impossible made probable. What would you have if you put these two different things together? Well, you'd have an old man named Ben who knows a lot of tricks most people don't know and a little girl named Jenny who loves hi—and a journey into the heart of the Twilight Zone."

Old Ben (J. Pat O'Malley) is a man beloved by the neighborhood children, especially young Jenny (Susan Gordon), an orphan living with her cruel Aunt Agnes (Nancy Kulp). Old Ben has let the neighborhood kids in on a little secret of his: he has magical powers, like shapeshifting and telepathy. What Ben doesn't realize is that there are two men in hot pursuit of him who seem to know this secret and will stop at nothing to take Ben into custody. But have they come to harm him, or help him?

"The Fugitive" is a dated, sentimental episode, but don't let the sap fool you! Charles Beaumont's trademark darkness is all over the script as he hints at many subversive and controversial themes for the early 1960s, like child abuse and pedophilia. Understandably, society has always been wary of men being kind to children, which is exactly how people react to Ben having a relationship with the neighborhood kids. The audience can see he means no harm, but we are still generally more suspicious of him than, say, the young woman's Aunt who is clearly psychologically and verbally abusing Jenny. Since that kind of abuse is happening out of public sight, it isn't as easy to point a finger to. Even though we are relieved to see Jenny escape from under the abusive thumb of her Aunt, I find it more than a little gross that it's insinuated she will become the Queen to Ben's King when they are back on his home planet. Sure, the old man is actually a young man in disguise, but she's still 13 and that's a major red flag in my book!

Jacob Trussell

I'd be remiss not to highlight the similarities between the men who are searching for Ben and the conspiracy theory surrounding men in black. The general consensus is that men in black are government officials sent to investigate and quash paranormal and extraterrestrial phenomena, à la *The X-Files*. But the other theory—one that speaks to this episode—is that they are actually aliens themselves. The former representation would of course be adapted into the popular *Men in Black* series starring Will Smith and Tommy Lee Jones, while the latter is perhaps best seen in The Observer characters in J.J. Abrams' *Fringe*.

Zone Fact

Cruel Aunt Agnes is played by Nancy Kulp who would co-star one year later in The Beverly Hillbillies as shrewd secretary Mrs. Hathway.

"Little Girl Lost"
Episode 26
Original Airdate: March 16, 1962

Directed by Paul Stewart
Written by Richard Matheson

"Missing: one frightened little girl. Name: Bettina Miller. Description: six years of age, average height and build, light brown hair, quite pretty. Last seen being tucked in bed by her mother a few hours ago. Last heard: 'ay, there's the rub,' as Hamlet put it. For Bettina Miller can be heard quite clearly, despite the rather curious fact that she can't be seen at all. Present location? Let's say for the moment... in the Twilight Zone."

Chris (Robert Sampson) and Ruth Miller (Sarah Marshall) are awakened by the cries of their daughter Tina (Tracy Stratford) in the middle of the night. As Ruth goes to comfort her, she's distressed to find her bed empty, little Tina nowhere to be found in her room. Panicked, she and Chris search the house only to realize their daughter's voice is coming from *inside* the walls. Calling their physicist friend Bill (Charles Aidman) for help, they learn she's fallen into an interdimensional rift and the doorway to the other side is quickly closing. Will they be able to find her in the other dimension, or will Tina be lost forever?

If there is one episode of *The Twilight Zone* that I have seen the most, it is "Little Girl Lost." Before getting hip to the darkness of Charles Beaumont, Richard Matheson was my all-time favorite *Twilight Zone* scribe, and this episode is essentially the reason. "Little Girl Lost" may not encapsulate every quality that makes *The Twilight Zone* a great show, but it does perfectly exemplify a tenant of the series that may be the most important to me: the ability to take us beyond the edge of our imagination.

Richard Matheson takes bits and pieces of interdimensional theory and intercuts them with an immediacy that the show so rarely had. It almost feels like it takes place in real time, like you have been startled awake as well, asked to search for the little girl missing somewhere in the spaces in-between her house. The theories that Bill tells Chris and Ruth are still concepts that are wildly popular today.

Jacob Trussell

Just ask any teenager about the multiverse and watch their face light up!

This idea of a house being a doorway into another world would be copied in one form or another for the next half century. The most obvious was Tobe Hooper's *Poltergeist*, especially in the way the paranormal investigators experiment with a literal doorway to the other side. In the film, a young family fights against an existential horror as they search for their daughter lost somewhere in their supernatural suburban home. I mean, that's this episode in a nutshell, right? Like the forces pursuing Carol Anne in the Steven Spielberg produced film, "Little Girl Lost" also has a growling monster stalking Tina. That specific idea would be embellished in the Eldritch location at the center of Mark Z. Danielweski's tome *House of Leaves*. "Little Girl Lost" is a simple, unnerving episode that is unlike anything that came before it.

Zone Fact

Lampooned in a 1995 episode of The Simpsons, "Homer" would prove to be an historic moment in CG animation on television.

"Person, or Persons Unknown"
Episode 27
Original Airdate: March 23, 1962

Directed by John Brahm
Written by Charles Beaumont

> *"Cameo of a man who has just lost his most valuable possession. He doesn't know about the loss yet. In fact, he doesn't even know about the possession. Because, like most people, David Gurney has never really thought about the matter of his identity. But he's going to be thinking a great deal about it from now on, because that is what he's lost."*

David Gurney (Richard Long) wakes up in bed with a heavy hangover, after a raucous party the night before. When he tries to rouse his wife, he's shocked that she doesn't recognize him. Not only that, but all of his clothes and possessions are missing from his closet too. Thinking she's putting him on—or at worst, stoned!—he leaves for work where his coworkers have no idea who he is either. As he tries contacting more and more people he knows, the fewer and fewer actually remember him. Is he really David Gurney? Or has the man lost more than just his identity?

Narratively slim, but with a quick pace, Charles Beaumont has written a story that has no excess fat on it. No scenes feel unnecessary, nor any monologues or bits of dialogue feel extemporaneous. It's a crisp, clear-cut story about a man who has been plunged into a nightmare. The episode's briskness though, makes it so not much is said in a short amount of time, forcing us to wonder if we've missed Beaumont's point entirely. Clearly we are meant to assume that Gurney is suffering from some kind of psychosis, but we are never given any clues as to what may have spurred it. *The Twilight Zone* doesn't always show its hand, but we are usually left with a wisp of an answer to a few of our questions. In "Person, or Persons Unknown" we're left with none. No sign posts up ahead, guiding us to the episode's underlying meaning.

I also wonder if that wasn't Beaumont's point all along, to inspire a transference between the character and the audience. The frustration Gurney is experiencing is mimicked in our own frustration watching. We desperately want answers, just like Gurney is desperately searching for a cause to his identity crisis. When none come, we feel cheated, much like Gurney feels when he stares at the picture of him and his wife and sees only himself.

We're pushed even further into "what the fuck's going on" territory in the episode's final beat. Gurney wakes up to find everyone remembers him again, but now he doesn't recognize the people he once knew. For a character who's frustration we identify with, it's a cosmically unfair fate that burrows under our own skin. This is one *Twilight Zone* world I hope *no one* ever gets stuck in!

Zone Fact

This is an early instance of a television couple sharing a bed. It was considered taboo, so through the mid-1960s, most slept in separate beds.

"The Little People"
Episode 28
Original Airdate: March 30, 1962

Directed by William F. Claxton
Written by Rod Serling

> *"The case of navigator Peter Craig, a victim of a delusion. In this case, the dream dies a little harder than the man."*

When their spaceship malfunctions, co-captains William Fletcher (Claude Akins) and Peter Craig (Joe Maross) are forced to land in a canyon of a rocky barren planet. Scouting for water as they make needed repairs, Craig finds a tiny, but civilized, race of people that he begins communicating with through mathematics. Fletcher watches in horror as Craig, who the tiny race views as a god, grows ruthless and megalomaniacal with the power he suddenly wields. Is Craig prepared for the consequences that come with being a god, or are their larger machinations at work to topple this tiny dictator?

Another famous episode of *The Twilight Zone* best remembered for its fantastic twist ending, what this story exemplifies is Rod Serling's constant fascination with the egos of men, especially when put under immense stress. It's an idea that he would have become familiar with during his stint in the army, seeing first-hand what happened to tough men under the constant strain of combat. Serling understood that what happened to them was more complex and couldn't be explained away as just snapping under pressure. A man didn't have to curl up into a ball and shut down to have a nervous breakdown. On the contrary, their ingrained toxic masculinity would force them to cling to whatever semblance of control they could find. For Craig, he finds it in the colony of little people where he wields power with an authoritarian zeal. He doesn't care about being a benevolent leader, rather being a god to them becomes his form of self-preservation, a way of holding on to sanity which ironically makes him go insane. His ultimate undoing comes when *he* begins to see himself as a god, and you should *never* trust a leader who believes that.

The influence of "The Little People" on other media stretches through the years, like an outstanding episode of *The Simpson*'s

Jacob Trussell

"Treehouse of Horrors," where we get up close and personal with a tiny civilization that deifies Lisa and Bart. In "The Sandkings," the premiere episode of the 1995 revival of *The Outer Limits*, a man deems himself god to a race of insectoid creatures who also have a knack for constructing idols and effigies in their leader's image. Let's just say it didn't end great for him either! This particular story was based on a sci-fi novella from future *Game of Thrones* author George R. R. Martin.

Zone Fact

Episode director William F. Claxton would go on to direct the infamous giant killer rabbits B-movie Night of the Lepus.

An Unofficial Journey Into The Twilight Zone

"Four O'Clock"
Episode 29
Original Airdate: April 6, 1962

Directed by Lamont Johnson
Written by Rod Serling (from a short story by Price Day)

"That's Oliver Crangle, a dealer in petulance and poison. He's rather arbitrarily chosen four o'clock as his personal Götterdämmerung, and we are about to watch the metamorphosis of a twisted fanatic, poisoned by the gangrene of prejudice, to the status of an avenging angel, upright and omniscient, dedicated and fearsome. Whatever your clocks say, it's four o'clock, and wherever you are it happens to be the Twilight Zone."

Oliver Crangle (Theodore Bikel) is a man best described by the word his pet parrot Pete keeps squawking: nut! He's the kind of guy who fantasizes about the evils of the world, taking detailed notes on the perceived wrongdoings of his neighbors to turn over to the feds at a moment's notice. Oliver doesn't need to wait for the FBI to contact him though, he already spends his days and nights on the phone haranguing government agencies with his theories on the global network of thieves, murderers and Communists threatening to overtake our great country. His plan to rid the world of this wickedness is simple: through sheer willpower of the mind, he'll shrink every evil doer down to two feet tall. What Oliver Crangle doesn't realize is that he shouldn't be throwing so many stones in his own glass house, and he may come to regret it when the shards of his wishes come crashing down around him.

If there is one thing that you can gain from binge watching every episode of *The Twilight Zone* it's that McCarthyism—both past and present—is the *absolute worst*. Even worse than those in power that still use McCarthy-era tactics today are the snoops in every community that don't mind their own damn business. The everyday folks who will dial 911 because they saw someone who didn't look like themselves out for a jog or birdwatching in a park. That's Oliver Crangle in a nutshell, pun intended.

Crangle is the same brand of lunatic that we'd see crop up decades later in Alex Jones and his InfoWars ilk, the type that profit on peddling conspiracy theories and misinformation about school

Jacob Trussell

shootings and vaccinations killing you. We see a glimpse at this as he tries to sow distrust for the local doctor, calling him a vile murderer because he lost one patient. This fury provides him with a false sense of moral superiority, but most importantly he believes it gives his life purpose.

His idiocy is perfectly illustrated in his solution to the world's problems. Does world peace really come from being too short to ride a rollercoaster or see over the edge of a bar? All it does is highlight how childish his rationalizations are for his actions. You may think that the world's evils will be solved by shrinking people down to 48 inches high, but don't be so quick to make that wish. After all, how do you know you are not evil yourself?

Zone Fact

Götterdämmerung means "Twilight of the Gods" in reference to the final section in Richard Wagner's opera The Ring Cycle.

"Hocus-Pocus and Frisby"
Episode 30
Original Airdate: April 13, 1962

Directed by Lamont Johnson
Written by Rod Serling (from a short story by Frederic Louis Fox)

"The reluctant gentleman with the sizable mouth is Mr. Frisby. He has all the drive of a broken camshaft and the aggressive vinegar of a corpse. As you've no doubt gathered, his big stock in trade is the tall tale."

If ever a man was more long winded, it was Mr. Somerset Frisby (Andy Devine), the proprietor of the general store in tiny Pitchville Flats. Mr. Frisby loves telling stories, some based in fact, others not so much, but it doesn't matter either way to those who come to hear his tales and listen to his vibrating harmonica. They just find Mr. Frisby to be endlessly amusing. After a night of entertaining his customers, something happens to Mr. Frisby that no one will believe, despite for once it being entirely true! He's abducted by aliens who mistake him for being Earth's one true genius. Does Frisby have the heart to tell them they have the wrong man, or is he going to have to get a little musically creative to wiggle his way back to Earth?

No matter what age you are you probably recognize the voice of Andy Devine, or someone imitating his trademark warbly timbre best realized in Friar Tuck from Disney's *Robin Hood*. Devine's voice transports me immediately back to childhood, which is why I find it perfectly suited for spinning long winded yarns intent on drawing you in. But the modern world really has no place for the kind of whoppers that Frisby doles out, as they'd never hold up against the 21st century fact checking you get in the palm of your hand! What doesn't get lost to time however, is his boisterous exuberance and our love for being fast and free with facts. People will always want to make little embellishments about their life, whether they're friends with a celeb, or have traveled the world.

What this lighthearted and fun episode *really* has going for it is the stellar makeup design from series artist William Tuttle. If the aliens' reptilian faces look even remotely familiar, it's because Tuttle was also the designer of the grotesque doctors and nurses in "Eye of

Jacob Trussell

the Beholder." Those designs look remarkably similar to these aliens in the way the skin wraps around their faces. Tuttle would go on to win four awards from the Academy of Science Fiction, Fantasy & Horror for his work on *Logan's Run* (written by George Clayton Jones, a key writer on *The Twilight Zone*) as well as Mel Brooks' *Young Frankenstein*.

Zone Fact

This is from a story by Frederick Louis Fox, who also came up with the story for "Showdown with Rance McGrew" (S3E20)

"The Trade-Ins"
Episode 31
Original Airdate: April 20, 1962

Directed by Elliot Silverstein
Written by Rod Serling

> *"Mr. and Mrs. John Holt, aging people who slowly and with trembling fingers turn the last pages of a book of life and hope against logic and the preordained that some magic printing press will add to this book another limited edition."*

John Holt (Joseph Schildkraut) is suffering the ineluctable decline towards death that every man experiences, but with his wife Marie (Alma Platt), he plans to do something about it. Rather than seeing a doctor just to learn what he already knows, he sets his sights towards new technology to grant him access to the fountain of youth, or in this case brand new youthful bodies. It does come with a price that is double the $5,000 the couple currently has saved. To ensure they can both grow young together, John sets out to make up the difference through any means necessary. Will young bodies be enough to fix all of their problems, or will it just inspire new ones for the old couple?

The only time in your life when you want to grow old is when you're a kid. Beyond that, we'll do everything in our power to counteract the inevitability of age. For us regular folk, that means having a keen eye on diet and exercise, and generally fighting against the urge to throw yourself around like you are a toddler. For the irregular couple at the center of this episode, their way to extend life is by swapping their dying bodies out for brand new models. For the low, low price of $10,000 they can be filled with youthful vitality and, as they make vague mention of in the opening scenes, an increased sex drive. Old folks gotta get it too!

This episode instantly reminded me of two very different films. The first is called *The Disincarnates* (1988) by Nobuhiko Ôbayashi, director of the 1977 cult classic *House*. Based on a novel by Taichi Yamada, the film follows a man who befriends an elderly couple who look remarkably like his own parents yet seem to have found a way to arrest the aging process. The other film is 2005's *The Skeleton Key*, which has a similar theme integrated into a major plot point that'll remain unsullied (because it's a doozy!)

The difference between "The Trade-Ins" and the two I just mentioned is that the Holts aren't as sinister as the couples in *The Disincarnates* and *The Skeleton Key*. Rather we feel the same sympathy that card shark Farraday (Ted Marcuse) feels towards John when he concedes his hand in poker to him. We want them to get these new bodies, but we also don't want them to sacrifice their well-being. Because no matter how much your body ages, it's perhaps most important to stay young where it matters the most: at heart.

Zone Fact

Elliot Silverstein would direct four episodes of both The Twilight Zone and its genre anthology successor Tales from the Crypt.

"The Gift"
Episode 32
Original Airdate: April 27, 1962

Directed by Allen H. Miner
Written by Rod Serling

"The place is Mexico, just across the Texas border, a mountain village held back in time by its remoteness and suddenly intruded upon by the 20th century. And this is Pedro, nine years old, a lonely, rootless little boy, who will soon make the acquaintance of a traveler from a distant place. We are at present 40 miles from the Rio Grande, but any place and all places can be The Twilight Zone."

Across the Texas-Mexico border lies a small pueblo where the local sheriff runs across a crashed UFO. A humanoid alien (Geoffrey Horne) emerges from the craft and before the sheriff can shoot it dead, the creature kills his deputy. Later that evening, after the sheriff brings the alien body back to the village, the humanoid returns to life. Calling himself Mr. Williams, he tells the doctor (Nico Minardos) who operated on him that he didn't mean to kill the officer, that he came in peace, but it fell on the deaf ears of a scared cop. Pedro (Edmund Vargas), a young boy who works in a bar and dreams of the stars, befriends Mr. Williams, who gives him a present for the town. Will Pedro be able to present it, or will the villages fear and distrust ruin what could potentially save them all?

To find the moral center of this episode you just have to look at the conversation between the blind Igancio (Vladimir Sokoloff) and barkeep Manolo (Cliff Osmond). When questioning why Manolo should pay Pedro kindness after he houses and employs him, the barkeep asks, "Did you ever see him smile?" to which the blind man replies, "Why would he smile, the boy? What is there to delight him? His poverty? Why should he smile? Perhaps on some occasion, some festive location, rather than handing him a broom or a tray, extend him a hand."

When a stranger asks for help, people will either get suspicious or ask what's in it for them. We aren't readily open to supporting our most vulnerable, so even if an alien brought a cure for cancer, do we really deserve that reward? The village destroyed what could have saved millions because they were controlled by their fear and prejudice. They ironically become the very evil that they so fear, and in turn damn the rest of the world because they couldn't see beyond their own noses.

On a morose note for a somber episode, I find that this a very realistic representation as to what we'd do to aliens if disclosure happened on a local level. You could take this same story and plop it across the border into Bible belt Texas and you'd be met with the same distrust, the same desire to kill what they can't conceive of. The cops originally shot Williams because they were frightened, not because they were threatened. We can't lose our rational humanity just because we are faced with an indescribable force. It may be a natural, territorial response, but it's also animalistic and compassionless, which is Serling's ultimate point.

Zone Fact

Serling adapted this episode from an unused script about a young orphan who befriends an injured alien and helps him get back to his own homeplanet. Sound familiar? That's because it's essentially the plot of Steven Spielberg's E.T.: The Extra-Terrestrial, just 20 years ahead of time.

"The Dummy"
Episode 33
Original Airdate: May 4, 1962

Directed by Abner Biberman
Written by Rod Serling (from a short story by Lee Polk)

"You're watching a ventriloquist named Jerry Etherson, a voice-thrower par excellence. His alter ego, sitting atop his lap, is a brash stick of kindling with the sobriquet 'Willie.' In a moment, Mr. Etherson and his knotty-pine partner will be booked in one of the out-of-the-way bistros, that small, dark, intimate place known as The Twilight Zone."

Jerry Etherson (Cliff Robertson) is a popular ventriloquist who has an act with his dummy Willie. An alcoholic, he breaks his sobriety after a strange incident where Jerry swears Willie bit his hand, leaving behind a visible mark. Concerned for his client, Jerry's agent Frank (Frank Sutton) begs him to see a psychiatrist as he believes his drinking problems are exacerbated by the unnerving bond he shares with Willie. Eschewing his advice, Jerry dumps his old dummy for a new model, hoping that it'll help him manage his nerves, but it only inflames what was already agitated. Now Jerry believes Willie is actually alive. Is he spiraling into mania, or has the dummy always been more than just another block of wood?

Based on a story by producer Lee Polk, you can trace the inspiration behind "The Dummy" back to the 1929, pre-code Hollywood musical *The Great Gabbo*, which itself was based on a story by Ben Hecht called "The Rival Dummy." Before the film ratings system as we know today was implemented, pre-code pictures were able to get away with showing a lot more of the dark, complex side of the world. In *Gabbo*'s case, the film focused on a man who's dwindling sanity is seen through the eyes of his ventriloquist dummy Otto. *Gabbo* may not hint at anything supernatural, but one thing is for certain: both Otto and Willie are creepy as fuck.

The legacy of "The Dummy" can be seen most masterfully in William Goldman's novel turned film *Magic* (1978). Directed by Richard Attenborough, with a captivating performance by Anthony Hopkins (and co-starring regular *Twilight Zone* actor Burgess

Meredith!), *Magic* has everything that makes this episode so terrifying—namely, a psychologically traumatized ventriloquist and a spooky ass dummy.

The episode's psychology is personified in the final moments as Jerry begins to hear Willie's voice pounding in his head. He may have been able to physically get rid of the doll, but mentally he is still in there with him. His agent is right, he needs help, but because toxic masculinity urges men not to seek treatment for psycho-emotional issues, Jerry has a complete breakdown. This is beautifully represented by George T. Clemens's cinematography, as the camera's Dutch angles move fluidly to mimic the feeling of losing control. I can't help but be impressed by the way the camera moves in these shots, especially during a time when TV wasn't known for its visually arresting, cinematic images.

So, is Willie real? Yes and no. Jerry thinks he's real, but the dummy seems to understand he's just an invention of his mind: "You breathed life into me." As we see in the final unnerving twist though, maybe imagination doesn't even begin to explain the connection this ventriloquist has with his right-hand man.

Zone Fact

Boomers will remember Cliff Robertson for his Oscar winning performance in Flowers for Algernon, but for millennials he'll always be Uncle Ben in Sami Raimi's Spider-Man series.

An Unofficial Journey Into The Twilight Zone

"Young Man's Fancy"
Episode 34
Original Airdate: May 11, 1962

Directed by John Brahm
Written by Richard Matheson

"The house of the late Mrs. Henrietta Walker is, you see, a house which belongs almost entirely to the past, a house which, like Mrs. Walker's clock here, has ceased to recognize the passage of time. Only one element is missing now, one remaining item in the estate of the late Mrs. Walker: her son, Alex, 34 years of age and, up till 20 minutes ago, the so-called perennial bachelor."

After decades of waiting, Virginia Lane (Phyllis Thaxter) has finally made Alex Walker (Alex Nicol) her husband. Now that they are married, Alex can sell his deceased mother Henrietta's (Helen Brown) home, who passed away only a short year before. Virginia is relieved to finally begin their new life together, but Alex has difficulty giving up the house and its strong memories. Is he simply processing his bereavement, or has Henrietta's jealousy towards Virginia grown powerful enough to blur the lines between life and death?

Mommy issues are on the menu for this foray into *The Twilight Zone*. The newlywed Alex waxes nostalgic for his dead mama by becoming transfixed on the pieces of his past that still exist in his childhood home, like mooning over grandfather clocks and transistor radios. Virginia pushes him to get over her death, but even if the matriarch's constant presence overshadowed their relationship for so long, you can't put such a time limit on grief.

The connection Alex had with his mother was strengthened through adversity after his father walked out on them, and while Virginia wants to have a similarly strong bond to her husband, she *can't* fill the void left by a deceased parent. And because she can't, she becomes spiteful. When Alex innocently questions why his mother kept so many childhood mementos, Virginia dismissively says that it's because she wanted to infantilize him. If the shoe was on the other foot, would she say the same about her own mother? Holding on to childhood keepsakes seems like Parenting 101 to me!

Jacob Trussell

It's understandable that Alex is having a hard time letting go, but that doesn't exonerate his own selfishness. Sure, Virginia is being unconscionable in her callousness, but Alex also needs to act like an adult and confront his grief rather than shutting down at the first pushback. This ultimately becomes his own undoing as he damns himself to a life—if that's what you can call it—of skirting responsibility just so he can hide behind the apron of his dead mother.

Zone Fact

Actor Alex Nicol would make his directorial debut with the American International Picture's horror classic The Screaming Skull.

"I Sing the Body Electric"
Episode 35
Original Airdate: May 18, 1962

Directed by William F. Claxton and James Sheldon
Written by Ray Bradbury

"A fable? Most assuredly. But who's to say at some distant moment there might be an assembly line producing a gentle product in the form of a grandmother whose stock in trade is love. Fable, sure, but who's to say?"

After the tragic death of his mother, Mr. Rogers (David White) and his three children attempt to move forward with their life. To help them along, the father takes his family to Facsimile Ltd., a factory where they can purchase a robotic assistant to take care of the house and home. Despite helping select their new grandma (Josephine Hutchinson), the eldest daughter Anne (Veronica Cartwright) refuses to treat her like family. After she saves Anne from being hit by a truck, the Rogers' come to realize how human—and indestructible— their electronic granny is, but what becomes of a robot once their work is complete?

    This is the sole episode of *The Twilight Zone* written by titan of science fiction Ray Bradbury, best known for *Fahrenheit 451* and *The Martian Chronicles*. Bradbury borrows this episode's title, "I Sing The Body Electric," from the Walt Whitman poem of the same name. In the poem, Whitman intimates that the body and the soul are intertwined, the body not dictating the worth of what's under the skin.

    Bradbury uses this idea to make the argument that robots not only can have a personality but could one day emote and feel just as deeply as you or me. By taking a more tender approach to theorizing what the future of our technology could be, it acts as a counterpoint to the robot uprising stories that have become so popular since the advent of personal computers and the release of *Terminator 2: Judgment Day* (1991). I find "I Sing the Body Electric" to be a direct elaboration on the Season Two episode "The Lateness of the Hour" (S2E8) where a young woman grows to hate her robot servants because they can't replace the touch and affectations of humans. Bradbury says not so fast, we're the ones who built the machines so

Jacob Trussell

why can't we ensure they reflect our ethical values too? In the future, we shouldn't discount a robot's potential for compassion.

Zone Fact

This is the first time the series would use the modern pronunciation for the word robot.

"Cavender Is Coming"
Episode 36
Original Airdate: May 25, 1962

Directed by Christian Nyby
Written by Rod Serling

"Submitted for your approval, the case of one Miss Agnes Grep, put on Earth with two left feet, an overabundance of thumbs and a propensity for falling down manholes."

Agnes Grep (Carol Burnett) is the klutz to end all klutzes, which makes her guardian angel Harmon Cavendar's (Jesse White) job all the more difficult. If he's to earn those wings he so desperately wants, he'll have to swallow his pride and guide this hopeless woman to a better life. Just because Harmon and the rest of heaven believe they have a clear understanding of what makes a "wonderful life," doesn't mean they know what makes a fulfilled life for Ms. Grep.

Who doesn't know the phrase "Every time a bell rings, an angel gets his wings" from the film *It's A Wonderful Life*? In the film the angel in question, Clarence, earns his stripes by guiding George Bailey back from the brink of suicide. Angels were never depicted as having wings in the Bible though, so I wonder then if this phrase was invented to bridge the gap between the big book and what has historically been depicted in religious art. It's as if a precocious child asked a Sunday school teacher why angels don't have wings in the Bible, so the flustered teacher tells them it's because angels have to *earn* their wings through service, like they are receiving commendations from serving in the military.

I say this because it's exactly how Serling plays it in the episode. Cavendar's boss acts like an army general, his wings like war medals he proudly displays. He even tells Cavender he's part of the Third Celestial Unit, which sounds a hell of a lot like a militarized heaven. Just, you know, not as serious as the name implies.

The easy read on "Cavender is Coming" is that money doesn't buy happiness, but it's also about living a life not dictated by others à la "Mr. Bevis" (S1E33). Society and religion don't have to be the motivating factors for the decisions you make. Even if there's a god

Jacob Trussell

out there, guiding every step, live your life like there's not. You shouldn't wait for an invisible entity in the sky to tell you to live your life to the fullest, and on your own terms.

Zone Fact

This episode was originally intended to be a backdoor pilot for a TV show featuring the Cavender character which is why this is the only episode of the series to feature a laugh track.

"The Changing of the Guard"
Episode 37
Original Airdate: June 1, 1962

Directed by Robert Ellis Miller
Written by Rod Serling

"Professor Ellis Fowler, a gentle, bookish guide to the young, who is about to discover that life still has certain surprises, and that the campus of the Rock Spring School for Boys lies on a direct path to another institution, commonly referred to as The Twilight Zone."

Ellis Fowler (Donald Pleasance) is an aging literature professor at an all boys school where he's taught for over five decades. He's told by the school's headmaster that he's being forced into retirement, causing him to reflect on his past and the sinking feeling that it was all meaningless. He's afraid that nothing he taught his students has affected any one of their lives. As he contemplates suicide, he is visited by past students—ageless since he last saw them—who express how much his teaching meant to them. Are they ghosts, or figments of his mind set to bring him back from the brink of death?

"The Changing of the Guard" is like a mix of *It's A Wonderful Life* and *A Christmas Carol*, just rather than watching someone who's suicidal or miserly reflect on their mistakes, it's about showing a man all of the good he never knew he did. His old worldliness may have not connected with his students, but his dedication helped these boys become the men they were before dying during the Second World War. The classical literature he taught didn't vibrate with modernity but trapped in their antiquated purple prose are lessons that are still relevant today, and because Fowler passionately believed in them, his students did too. If only more teachers were like him—a hardass with a heart of gold who was just terrible at giving compliments, like his semesters end creed: "It is rare young men that in 51 years of teaching I have ever encountered such a class of dunderheads. But nice dunderheads, and potentially fine young men that will make their marks and leave their marks."

Despite the uplifting message at its core, the premise of a suicidal teacher is incredibly dark. Fowler's willingness to die reminds me of harakiri, the honor of death in Japanese culture. Fowler would rather kill himself then be seen as superfluous. His depression is relatable, especially as millions across the world find themselves out of a job. A collective sense of displacement, coupled with feelings of inadequacy, make for a potent, and sometimes deadly, combination.

Zone Fact

Star Donald Pleasance would receive worldwide recognition in John Carpenter's Halloween as Sam Loomis, the doctor hunting down Michael Myers.

The Twilight Zone

SEASON FOUR

JANUARY 3, 1963 – MAY 23, 1963

"In His Image"
Episode 1
Original Airdate: January 3, 1963

Directed by Perry Lafferty
Written by Charles Beaumont

> *"What you have just witnessed could be the end of a particularly terrifying nightmare. It isn't—it's the beginning. Although Alan Talbot doesn't know it, he's about to enter a strange new world, too incredible to be real, too real to be a dream. It's called The Twilight Zone."*

Alan Talbot (George Grizzard) has just murdered a homeless woman, but he doesn't seem to remember that he did. More so, with the exception of his fiancée Jessica (Gail Kobe), everything he does remember has completely changed. The school he teaches at is gone, the house he lives in has a different occupant, and even the grave for his parents has disappeared, replaced with a tombstone for someone named Walter Ryder. As troubling thoughts continue to push Alan to kill, he uncovers the identity of Mr. Ryder and realizes the nightmare he thought he was in is *much* worse.

The New York City subway system is a wild and unexpected circus where, like Alan Talbot, you'll contemplate murder at least once or twice a ride. The thing that New Yorkers understand is you don't *actually* kill the straphangers that fail to respect personal space, but Talbot never got that memo in this cold open that strikes a decidedly more sinister tone than you may expect from *The Twilight Zone*.

"In His Image" is hard science fiction, but Charles Beaumont packages it inside a horror story. Talbot being beckoned to kill by his inner self reminds me of shows like *Dexter,* that offer a glimpse into the impulses behind a serial killer. It even has the same unnerving juxtaposition between his normal family life and his murderous dark passenger. His fiancée even fits the bill of the archetypal paramour for the vulnerable psycho in movies like *Maniac* (1980) or *Manhunter* (1986). She's reserved, a little lonely, and that blinds her to the fact that the man she loves is a lunatic. Since we watch Alan fight his urges from Jessica's perspective, we develop sympathy for the character similar to her own.

Jacob Trussell

In the finale, Beaumont let's Walter triumph over his creation without a second thought. In a modern context though, you may be waiting for one final gotcha moment that never comes. Shows like *Black Mirror* and their deep cynicism have conditioned audiences to want an ending that reflects how unfair the real world is. Nowadays there would be a fake-out in the final few seconds and we'd realize it was Alan all along, not Walter, who was defeated. Simply put, we just don't believe in happy endings anymore.

Zone Fact

This is the second episode featuring George Grizzard, after Season One's "The Chaser."

"The Thirty-Fathom Grave"
Episode 2
Original Airdate: January 10, 1963

Directed by Perry Lafferty
Written by Rod Serling

"Small naval engagement, the month of April, 1963. Not to be found in any historical annals. Look for this one filed under 'H' for haunting in The Twilight Zone."

A Navy ship on the Guadalcanal picks up a mysterious sound on their sonar. The crew is alarmed to learn that the source of the metallic noise is a submarine deep below them, where no ship has sunk for over 20 years. A diver sent to investigate the sound is shocked to hear someone—or something—knocking in on the sub's hull. Captain Beecham (Simon Oakland) believes this is proof that there are survivors on the ship, but a Petty Officer fears it's a phantom sent to remind him of a terrible secret he's kept for decades.

"The Thirty-Fathom Grave" is about unseen fears that linger just below the surface—of the ocean, or the self—but the payoff completely depends on what kind of fears you're looking for. As a kid of the mid-90s, I loved horror movies set on spooky ghost ships like *Deep Rising* or *Virus,* so my gut reaction was that this episode is proto-aquatic horror. Even the opening scenes tease some kind of supernatural menace deep below. Regretfully, Cthulhu doesn't emerge from the titular grave and the episode is more related to David Twohy's *Below* (2003) which juxtaposes the supernatural with the psychological traumas of war.

Serling uses curt, cringey dialogue about mental health to make an overall point on compassion. Chief Bell (Mike Kellin), the sole survivor of the sunken cruiser, is on the edge of a nervous breakdown when Captain Beecham calls him a child over his behavior. Toxic masculinity makes him question Bell's strength, even though a man's mettle has nothing to do with how the mind processes stress. This is traditional masculinity bending to break under the weight of shame men feel when facing a mental health crisis.

Beecham's first act language was purposefully coarse so that it

Jacob Trussell

could then be contrasted in his thoughtful speech to Bell, once he realized his fear was the product of guilt he held over the sunken sub. He finally understands what's happening to his crewman, so rather than berating him again, he offers empathy. This is a way for Serling to show how you don't have to be an Oxford trained psychologist or use language from the DSM-5 to support a friend experiencing a nervous breakdown. You can simply be a colleague that says, "I'm here for you."

Zone Fact

The Incredible Hulk himself Bill Bixby appears in this episode!

"Valley of the Shadow"
Episode 3
Original Airdate: January 17, 1963

Directed by Perry Lafferty
Written by Charles Beaumont

"You've seen them. Little towns, tucked away far from the main roads. You've seen them, but have you thought about them? What do the people in these places do? Why do they stay? Philip Redfield never thought about them. If his dog hadn't gone after that cat, he would have driven through Peaceful Valley and put it out of his mind forever. But he can't do that now, because whether he knows it or not his friend's shortcut has led him right into the capital of The Twilight Zone."

Phillip Redfield (Ed Nelson) is a reporter driving across the country with his trusty pooch Rollie. After getting lost, he stops at a small town called Peaceful Valley to ask for directions, and maybe get a bite to eat. As he reorients himself, he's stunned to see Rollie vanish before his eyes after chasing a house cat, but no one else seems to notice. Determined to get to the bottom of this, Redfield meets with the Valley's city council who have no intentions of revealing their long held secrets, and will stop at nothing to keep their town safe.

What do you think of when you imagine the setup to a hillbilly slasher movie like *The Hills Have Eyes*? Do the main characters take a shortcut or make a wrong turn and wind up lost? Maybe they meet a shifty gas station attendant who offers an ominous warning, but is secretly in cahoots with the bad guys? If so, then you may find a lot of familiarities in the setup to "Valley of the Shadows." There may not be any mutant rednecks, and one-hundredth of the gore, but the major elements of the slasher subgenre are on display here.

It's all in Rod Serling's opening monologue about the urban fear of small town evils. *"You've seen them, but have you thought about them?"* He phrases it in the first person to speak for all city folk, distancing us from those spooky little communities off the sides of interstates. How do I know they were spooky? Because I was born in one! Just rather than populating his town with literal monsters, we're given figurative monsters empowered by alien technology.

Jacob Trussell

I mentioned there was 100th of the gore of a slasher movie because there *is* some blood in this episode, and it's way more than I expected. Attempting to escape, Phillip stabs one of the town governors. I was expecting some vanilla violence that immediately cuts away, but not here. The blood pools around the wound, oozing droplets that press through his shirt long enough for us to really process what we're watching. Don't expect any grindhouse geysers, but there is more realistic blood here than you'd expect to see on 1960s television!

Zone Fact

Features a cameo from James Doohan, three years before becoming famous as Scotty in Star Trek.

"He's Alive"
Episode 4
Original Airdate: January 24, 1963

Directed by Stuart Rosenberg
Written by Rod Serling

"Used to be people laugh at him. But now he gets a crowd. And few people are laughing"

Peter Vollmer (Dennis Hopper) is a young man who fancies himself the leader of a budding group of Neo-Nazis. Despite the fire and fury of what he preaches, Vollmer isn't connecting with his audience, and is being outwardly mocked by anyone he confronts with his beliefs. This is further complicated by his close relationship with Ernst (Ludwig Donath), a Jewish man who's become a father figure to him. One night Vollmer is visited by a short man shrouded in shadow with a thick German accent and a funny little mustache who coaches Vollmer on how to be a powerful orator and leader. Will Vollmer listen to his conscience, or will this mysterious man send him down a path to hell?

The shining achievement of *The Twilight Zone*'s foray into hour-long stories is, unfortunately, the episodes will bum you out the most. This is because "He's Alive" is a stark reminder of just how little we've come in addressing fascism, prejudice and hate in this country. Dennis Hopper's Peter Vollmer, his round face the shape of a budding Donald Trump, is a pair of khakis and tiki torch away from being the image of white supremacy in the 21st century.

It's maddening today to think that nationalist groups like Vollmer's were springing up so early after World War II. We look back at that era in the United States as a time when we were, for lack of a better word, united against the threat to freedom that the Nazi party stood for. The rose-colored glasses we've worn for the past 60 years have made us forget that hatemongers have *always* existed, even when we had a unified enemy.

Luckily, modern white supremacists aren't being coached by the spirit of Adolph Hitler. Playing the role of a hate speech and debate coach to Vollmer, he teaches him that the greatest tool at his disposal is victimhood. "They are not the minority: we are!" he screeches. Victimhood is the bread and butter for white supremacists, especially in movies like *The Believers*, *Apt Pupil*, and *American History X*. Broken homes are the primordial soup that white nationalism feeds on, offering fellowship for those desperately craving a sense of belonging.

Embracing victimhood is what forces Vollmer to create a false-martyr. By murdering one of his own, he gives the party an "other" to rally against. But as we know from the rest of this series, "the other" is nothing but a straw man for hate to knock down. Vollmer is even unwilling to see the contradiction between his beliefs and his close friendship with Ernst. He doesn't realize where his convictions are leading him, so he buries his gut instincts deep underneath the path he chooses to walk. His undoing comes from his fear of admitting that he made the wrong choice.

Zone Fact

The hate mail Rod Serling received from "He's Alive" reached into the thousands. Coincidentally, he also considers it one of the most important episodes of the series.

"Mute"
Episode 5
Original Airdate: January 31, 1963

Directed by Stuart Rosenberg
Written by Richard Matheson

"The main character of these final scenes is Ilse, the daughter of Professor and Mrs. Nielsen, age two. At the moment she lies sleeping in her crib, unaware of the singular drama in which she is to be involved. Ten years from this moment, Ilse Nielsen is to know the desolating terror of living simultaneously in the world and in The Twilight Zone."

Sheriff Harry Wheeler (Frank Overton) and wife Cora (Barbara Baxley) adopt a young mute girl named Ilse (Ann Jillian) after her parents die in a house fire. As the couple believes that Ilse doesn't speak because of neglect, Cora begins caring for her like a mother—the young girl becoming a proxy for her own daughter who died years before. When their attempts to contact her relatives are in vain, thanks to Cora intercepting and burning any communication, they enroll Ilse in school hoping she'll learn to speak. What the Wheelers don't know is that Ilse can communicate telepathically, and it will take a special teacher (Irene Dailey) to get the young girl to come out of her silent shell.

I know what you may be thinking at the beginning of "Mute." A group of people pledge to dedicate their lives to the practice of telepathy, only for their house to tragically burn down leaving a young girl behind. Is this a budding *Firestarter* (1984) escaped from Stephen King's The Institution? Yes, and no.

Yes, this is a story about a young girl with strong powers of Extra Sensory Perception, but she's not lighting things on fire or causing chaos. She really just misses her parents, and feels conflicted having to live with a suffocating new stepmother and stepfather. And can you blame her? After years of homeschooling and psychic communication, who wants to sit in a classroom and have to speak up using *your words*! Ugh!

Remarkably for the young girl, her teacher Miss Frank shares her same gift of psychic communication. It's in this student-teacher relationship that I'm immediately reminded of Helen Keller's story in

The Miracle Worker, which was at the height of its fame after the film was released in 1962. Call it parallel thinking or unconscious inspiration but the similarities between these stories about teachers helping mute young women communicate are striking.

It feels like a pulled punch to end "Mute" on such a sentimental note after setting up that Ilse would leave this family that, in no small way, manipulated her into staying. But for all its schmaltz, there's a dark thread in how Miss Frank attempts to relate to Ilse's powers. The way Miss Frank describes her childhood and how she was forced to become a medium to contact the dead feels like a thinly-veiled reference to child abuse. Even the way she phrases what happened to her insinuates as much, "My father did the same thing. He pushed his sickness on to me." You don't have to be a child psychologist to read between the lines in that statement.

Zone Fact

Oscar Beregi, who plays Ilse's Godfather, starred in Season Three's Deaths-Head Revisited.

"Death Ship"
Episode 6
Original Airdate: February 7, 1963

Directed by Don Medford
Written by Richard Matheson

"Picture of the crew of the spaceship E-89: Captain Ross, Lieutenant Mason, Lieutenant Carter. Three men who have just reached a place which is as far from home as they will ever be. Three men who in a matter of minutes will be plunged into the darkest nightmare reaches of The Twilight Zone."

Three astronauts—Capt. Paul Ross (Jack Klugman), Lt. Ted Mason (Ross Martin) and Lt. Mike Carter (Fred Beir)—are scouting for habitable planets after Earth has become untenable due to overpopulation. Seeing what could be a signal from a planet, they land only to discover the crashed remains of their own ship, their lifeless corpses scattered inside. Disturbed by this, two of the men attempt to persuade their captain to take off immediately, but he refuses for fear that leaving now will seal their fate. As the men have visions of life back on Earth, will they be able to leave, or was their fate sealed the moment they saw that signal from space?

Richard Matheson gets so much presciently right in his science fiction stories. Here, we have a group of astronauts on a survival mission because in the future, naturally, we Earthlings have destroyed the fine ecosystem of our planet. We can infer that with global overpopulation comes climate change, war, famine and all the normal things you expect from a science fiction end-of-days narrative. This set-up only serves as a sobering reminder that our own world is suffering from overpopulation, climate change, and war with no end—or plans to fix it—in sight. Let's hope our future doesn't entail jumping ship from our home planet, but with the rise of privatized space travel from companies like SpaceX, only time will tell.

Despite the episode being about astronauts on an alien planet, "Death Ship" acts more as a ghost story like *The Others* (2001), where—spoilers!—the protagonists don't realize they're actually the spirits. As the time loop in the finale indicates, the men are destined

Jacob Trussell

to experience the same day, the same mission, again and again, like a residual haunting. It's an unexpected, if not all together unsettling and sad, end to this dour Matheson story.

Zone Fact

The spaceship model used was a leftover from the sci-fi classic Forbidden Planet, a prop that was reused extensively on the series.

"Jess-Belle"
Episode 7
Original Airdate: February 14, 1963

Directed by Buzz Kulik
Written by Earl Hamner, Jr.

"The Twilight Zone has existed in many lands, in many times. It has its roots in history, in something that happened long, long ago and got told about and handed down from one generation of folk to the other. In the telling the story gets added to and embroidered on, so that what might have happened in the time of the Druids is told as if it took place yesterday in the Blue Ridge Mountains. Such stories are best told by an elderly grandfather on a cold winter's night by the fireside in the southern hills of The Twilight Zone."

Jess-Belle (Anne Francis) is envious that Ellwyn Glover (Laura Devon) is engaged to marry her ex-beau Billy-Ben Turner (James Best). She goes to visit Granny Hart (Jeanette Nolan) in the hope that she'll cast a love spell making Billy-Ben forget everything about his bride-to-be. The only problem is that every spell comes with a cost, and for Jess-Belle it's the low price of her eternal soul. Cursed to transform into a leopard every night, she prowls the small hamlet until she's shot by a hunting party. Her death may have broken the spell, but it doesn't mean the curse of Jess-Belle is gone. On the contrary, it may have made her more powerful than before.

Even before we learn that Granny Hart is a witch, we know she is. It's what you expect from backwoodsy horror like this. On the whole, "Jess-Belle" has a tonality similar to Stan Winston's *Pumpkinhead*, both sharing a mythology rooted in old-world magic and mysticism. They both bewitch an eerie feeling of not knowing the true cost of what you are paying for. In *Pumpkinhead*, a father doesn't fully realize the extent to which hell will come to Earth when he begs revenge for his murdered son. In this episode, Jess-Belle learns that something is always lost when making deals with the darkside.

The representation of witches in Jess-Belle is far more interested in their feminist legacy than the crone-esque stereotypes found in *Macbeth*. I'm reminded of films like *The Craft*, or shows like *The*

Chilling Adventures of Sabrina and *Charmed* when Granny Hart emphasizes the independence and strength Jess-Belle will feel from her powers. This episode is also steeped in werewolf mythology. To protect others from her nightly transformation, Jess-Belle pleads with her mother to lock her up, no matter how much she begs to be let out—a cliché in so many modern lycanthrope stories.

It's a shame that we don't have more female werewolves (outside of Wes Craven's campy *Cursed*) because there is a wealth of stories that could be mined from the idea. This element does help identify the last clear inspiration for *Jess-Belle*, Jacques Tourneur's *Cat People*. Retrospectively seen as a feminist and queer horror film, *Cat People* follows Irina (Simone Simon) who fears that she will transform into a leopard when sexually aroused, forcing her to keep everyone in her life at a distance. Much like Jess-Belle, jealousy begins to take hold of Irina's life, turning her world upside down. The only difference between Tourneur's film and this episode is that *The Twilight Zone* had the balls to turn their female protagonist into a cat right in front of our eyes. Who needs to leave stuff up to your imagination!

Zone fact

Jeanette Nolan and her husband John McIntire both appeared on the series as characters selling love spells. He played Professor Daemon in Season One's "The Chaser."

"Miniature"
Episode 8
Original Airdate: February 21, 1963

Directed by Walter Grauman
Written by Charles Beaumont

"To the average person, a museum is a place of knowledge, a place of beauty and truth and wonder. Some people come to study, others to contemplate, others to look for the sheer joy of looking. Charley Parkes has his own reasons."

Charly Parkes (Robert Duvall) is a mousey man in his twenties who lives at home with his mother (Pert Kelton). He visits a museum daily where he can breathlessly watch miniatures in an ornate, sprawling dollhouse come to life. While he's told that the dolls do not move on their own, Charly returns again and again to view their private lives, even falling in love with one trapped in an abusive marriage. Charly's family is concerned that these delusions are disrupting his life, but can they be sure what he sees is *really* all in his head?

Anchored by a moving turn from a young Robert Duvall, who etches heartache into every scene, "Miniature" is one of the few hour-long stories from *The Twilight Zone* that stands the test of time partially because it's the only episode in the series with identifiable queer subtext.

Charly Parkes is a nebbish man who lives with an overbearing mother, who attempts to dictate every aspect of his life like he is still a child, even though he's well into his twenties. Parkes has a clear disinterest in women, but he falls passionately for the *idea* of a woman—specifically one that's behind glass, immaculately dressed, bleeding with feminine energy, and *literally* a doll. Her life becomes his entertainment, like a daytime television soap opera that he stops everything to watch. He sees himself in the lady of the dollhouse because he too feels trapped by what society dictates for him, her in a loveless marriage and him immobilized by a world he doesn't fit into. Through watching this dollhouse, it gives him some semblance of belonging. He can't see himself reflected in anything in his real life, but he can see himself in these dolls.

Jacob Trussell

    I have to make the argument that Charly's compulsion to visit the dollhouse is remarkably similar to our own penchant for binge watching. The urge he has to get back every day to the museum to catch up on the comings and goings of these dolls is not unlike our own urges that draw us back to the couch every night to binge watch new favorites and old classics. At least it's easier to spend hours on end in the comforts of your own home than any stuffy museum!

Zone Fact

Due to a lawsuit regarding potential plagiarism of a script submitted to the show, this is the only hour-long episode that was not included in original syndication packages. When it finally reached syndication in 1984, the scenes featuring the doll house had been colorized.

"Printer's Devil"
Episode 9
Original Airdate: February 28, 1963

Directed by Ralph Senensky
Written by Charles Beaumont

"Try to imagine his thoughts in your mind"

Editor of *The Courier*, Douglas Winter (Robert Sterling) is on the verge of losing it all as a big newspaper moves into his small town. Contemplating suicide, Winter meets Mr. Smith (Burgess Meredith), a strange little copywriter who just so happens to be looking for a job. Enchanted, Winter hires him on the spot and Mr. Smith, armed with an archaic printing press, begins writing headlines that predict future scandals and tragedies. When his headlines target Winter's girlfriend Jackie (Pat Crowley), will the editor threaten his paper's success and confront Smith over his power of actualizing scoops?

Burgess Meredith racked up some of the greatest *Twilight Zone* characters ever, simply by being in some of the most memorable episodes of the series, but he was at his absolute best as the infernal Mr. Smith. The major difference between Meredith's previous appearances and his performance in "Printer's Devil" is that he finally gets to play a villain. And not just any villain, he gets to relish in being the ultimate evil! You can draw a clear line from this performance to his highly campy Penguin in Adam West's *Batman*, cigar chomping and all!

The wicked humor of Meredith's impish devil is what makes this the blackest comedy the series would produce. The headline proclaiming that the mayor of the town is bigamist is so outlandish for the 1960s that you can't help but laugh. The devil has hilariously good timing when Mr. Smith writes that the rival newspaper would burn down the moment *after* they threaten to buy out the small press. You have to hand it to him, Satan knows how to land his punchlines.

I also need to point out how *fearsome* they made the printing press appear. It's got the same strange angry energy of the laundry-folding machine at the center of Tobe Hooper's *The Mangler*, adapted from the Stephen King short story of the same name.

Jacob Trussell

Zone Fact

The episode's title is derived from an historical term that meant a person, usually a young boy, who would serve as a level below apprentice for print media.

"No Time Like the Past"
Episode 10
Original Airdate: March 7, 1963

Directed by Justus Addiss
Written by Rod Serling

> *"You must remember, the face of your enemy is not devoid of compassion."*

Paul Driscoll (Dana Andrews) is a man who wants to change the past to save the future. With the help of his colleague Harvey (Robert F. Simon), he uses time travel in an effort to alter the course of history, such as visiting Hiroshima before the bomb dropped, Germany prior to World War II, and the Lusitania moments before it sank. Demoralized after countless attempts to change the future, Driscoll decides to live the remainder of his life in the past, but he quickly finds out that the knowledge of things to come will only haunt him.

Since this episode originally aired, movies and shows have asked the question numerous times, "Would you go back in time and assassinate Hitler?" It's a riff on the time travel dilemma called the Grandfather Paradox, which begs the question what would happen if you prevented your own birth, by traveling back in time and murdering your grandparents? In the Hitler Paradox, the argument is what would happen to the world if you did assassinate Hitler? You may be able to prevent World War II and the Holocaust, but modern history is dictated by the effects of that war, so what butterfly effect would the assassination cause? More so, by killing Hitler wouldn't you also be affecting the very reason you went back in time in the first place?

These aren't questions that are central to "No Time Like The Past," but they are something Paul Driscoll should have kept in mind before becoming a seasoned time traveler. He may say that he's staying hands off on altering history when he settles in the past, but that doesn't call into question what he's already changed by his trips through time. When the Gestapo discover his abandoned rifle in a German hotel, could the knowledge of an American assassination attempt have pulled the country into the war sooner, causing untold casualties?

Jacob Trussell

Many *Twilight Zone* scholars cite Martin Sloan in Season One's "Walking Distance" as the character Serling wrote himself into the most, but if there was any character that carried his moral center more, it is Paul Driscoll. It's evident in Driscoll trying to save the people of Hiroshima before he attempts meddling elsewhere in time. Even though the McCarran-Walter Act of 1952 allowed first generation Japanese-Americans to become naturalized citizens—a show of unity between the countries as they rebuilt their culture after the war—I can only imagine it would've still been incredibly subversive to show on television such sympathy for a country that was our enemy only two decades before.

Regardless of the country's quickness to repair relations, it should be noted that it would take over 20 more years before the United States apologized for Japanese-Americans internment camps during the war, a blight on our country's history that should not be soon forgotten.

Zone fact

Dana Andrews was the star of the horror classic Curse of the Demon from future Twilight Zone director Jacques Tourneur!

"The Parallel"
Episode 11
Original Airdate: March 14, 1963

Directed by Alan Crosland, Jr.
Written by Rod Serling

"We'll be a step closer to filing a claim on another piece of sky"

Test pilot Major Robert Gaines (Steve Forrest) orbits the Earth in an experimental spaceship. During flight, he sees a blinding white light before blacking out and awakening in a hospital with no recollection of how he landed. An uneasy feeling begins to creep into Gaines, as he notices inconsistencies in the world he returned to, like how his daughter is certain the man who came back isn't her father. Is he experiencing some kind of trauma, or has Gaines slipped through a fissure in space and time?

Something younger audiences shouldn't forget when watching *The Twilight Zone* is that the series aired six years *before* we landed on the moon. All of these episodes about astronauts and space travel were born from the excitement and anticipation around the Space Race, the metaphorical competition between the United States and the Soviet Union which—if we're calling a spade a spade—was nothing more than a dick measuring contest. There were scientists who surely were solely interested in exploring the undiscovered regions of our universe, but for many it was just about beating the enemy in a brand new way.

The competition did give immediacy to Serling's ideas about the future of space travel, the global fantasy that this was the beginning of our expansion to life on other planets. Since the sky wasn't the limit anymore, our imaginations could run wild with the possibilities of life to, and from, outer space. "The Parallel" doesn't feature space aliens, but it does feel reminiscent of the classic tropes of alien abduction, from missing time to memory loss. Even all of Gaines' mechanical equipment and radio signals malfunction, much like how car radios and engines suddenly stop in encounter stories. It's these elements that give the entire episode a tone not unlike *The X-Files*, specifically Season One's "Space," wherein an astronaut is tormented

Jacob Trussell

by nightmares of a ghostly apparition he witnessed on a spacewalk. Creator of *The X-Files*, Chris Carter, has said that *The Twilight Zone* was a major influence on his series.

Unfortunately though, this episode is a great example of why Season Four's experiment in hour-long stories didn't always work in the series' favor. The concept of an astronaut returning to Earth that he doesn't recognize is stupendous, but it spins its wheels for 20 minutes, dragging out a second act reveal that the audience has already guessed. It's a shame; if it had been the typical 25 minute length, it would have given the episode the shot of urgency it desperately needed.

Zone Fact

Initially it was explicit that Gaines discovered he was in a parallel dimension after sleeping with his wife. Due to strict censorship over sexual situations at the time, this detail was changed.

An Unofficial Journey Into The Twilight Zone

"I Dream of Genie"
Episode 12
Original Airdate: March 21, 1963

Directed by Robert Gist
Written by John Furia, Jr.

"Meet Mr. George P. Hanley, a man life treats without deference, honor or success. Waiters serve his soup cold. Elevator operators close doors in his face. Mothers never bother to wait up for the daughters he dates."

George Hanley (Howard Morris) is a textbook pushover who would make Mr. Bevis look like Fabio. Searching for a gift for a coworker's birthday, a shopkeep swindles the unsuspecting Hanley into purchasing an ornate lamp. Humiliated at work by his belittling colleagues, Hanley takes the lamp home and inadvertently awakens a genie (Jack Albertson) from inside. This genie—who looks less like Kazaam and more like an everyday guy from Brooklyn—grants him one wish, but advises him to sleep on it first. Hanley dreams about what he would do with a beautiful wife, fortune and power, but will any of these desires satisfy this self-described jerk?

Rod Serling would be the first to tell you that many episodes of *The Twilight Zone* were lousy, and perhaps none more so than "I Dream of Genie," a story that lacks any creative spark the series is known for. Frankly, the most creative thing about the episode is its title, which beat the wildly popular television show *I Dream of Jeannie* to the puny punch by two years.

They *really* emphasize the dream aspect of the episode's title, as everything that happens to Hanely is just something he dreamt, a gimmick that deprives the episode of any stakes. He's dodging a bullet rather than learning a lesson about why greed, power and beauty will lead to a hollow existence. Hanley really should have been taught a lesson, especially since the episode features extremely outdated sexism.

It's not just Hanley that needs to be taught a lesson, but episode writer John Furia Jr. too.

The office environment he's written oozes misogyny, specifically surrounding office secretary Ann Larson (Patricia Barry) who the men of the office pine for. After being gifted a negligee from one man, Larson says, "This shows you my appreciation, *and* that I can't even count over 30 yet!" Yikes. This is a sexist stereotype on women's intelligence that just makes your whole body cringe 60 years later.

We're as disgusted as Hanley is by his coworkers' behaviors, but not for the same reasons. He's put off by how cloying the men are to Ann while we're skeeved about the rampant misogyny, a feeling extended into a dream sequence where Hanley marries a movie star. The punchline of this segment is that he meets a young starlet who comes onto him with a fake accent, but it's also insinuated that the woman is underage, and Hanley is more than ok with that. The whole exchange is uncomfortable now, but let's be real. It should have been uncomfortable then too.

Zone Fact

This is the actor James Millhollin's third appearance on The Twilight Zone after The After Hours and Mr. Dingle, the Strong

"The New Exhibit"
Episode 13
Original Airdate: April 4, 1963

Directed by John Brahm
Written by Charles Beaumont

"Leave me to my friends, please!"

Martin (Martin Balsam) is the tour guide for a serial killer wax museum on the verge of bankruptcy. Distressed at the news, Martin convinces his former boss Mr. Ferguson (Will Kuluva) into letting him continue caring for the wax murderers in his temperature-controlled cellar. The stress of their upkeep strains Martins' marriage, which is compounded when he discovers his wife (Maggie Mahoney) dead at the feet of the Jack the Ripper sculpture. Do the figures have a life of their own, or has Martin's obsession pushed his mind to the breaking point?

Credited to Charles Beaumont, but ghost written by Jerry Sohl, "The New Exhibit" fails to capture the characteristics that gave Beaumont's stories vitality. The episode isn't pedestrian by any means, but it lacks that cosmic sense of scale that comes with his narratives. The idea is that there is something far greater guiding our actions, and that it may be more sinister than we know.

There is a supernatural element to Sohl's incredibly contained story, but the horror is far more *Psycho* than *House of Wax*. We don't buy for a minute that anyone but Martin killed his wife, brother-in-law and ex-boss, even if his psychosis hints that the figures are alive. Losing his job caused his mind to spiral because his identity was tied to those wax figures, so Martin clings to the supernatural as a coping mechanism for what his psychosis has wrought.

Even the twist feels projected the moment we connect the dots as to what's happening to Martin. Naturally his obsession will transform him, quite literally, like the twist in "The Dummy" (S3E33). Martin becomes what he cared for the most—a serial killer. Let's hope that doesn't become the same fate of our favorite true crime podcast hosts who have dedicated their life to preserving the memory of the worst people imaginable!

Jacob Trussell

Zone Fact

Director John Brahms previously made The Lodger (1944) which also featured Jack the Ripper.

"Of Late I Think of Cliffordville"
Episode 14
Original Airdate: April 11, 1963

Directed by David Lowell Rich
Written by Rod Serling (from the short story "Blind Alley" by Malcom Jameson)

"Mr. William J. Feathersmith, tycoon, who tried the track one more time and found it muddier than he remembered, proving with at least a degree of conclusiveness that nice guys don't always finish last"

What do you give a man who has everything? A deal with the devil, of course! Mr. Feathersmith (Albert Salmi) is a ruthless businessman that will destroy anyone he considers competition, just for the fun of it. After a night of drinking, Feathersmith discloses how unsatisfied his life has become to a janitor named Hecate (Wright King), who happens to be from his own hometown. Drunkenly leaving his office, he stumbles to the 13th floor and meets Ms. Devlin (Julie Newmar), a woman who offers him the chance to remake his fortune by traveling back in time. In his haste, and greed, Feathersmith doesn't read the fine print of Ms. Devlin's contract, and he'll soon find the good fortune he has in the present doesn't extend to the past.

If you were looking for an episode that makes the least subtle stories in the series seem like *Inception*-level psychological thrillers, look no further than "Of Late I Think of Cliffordville." Another in a long line of tales about men being blinded by their nostalgia to the realities of the past, the episode's obviousness is the one thing it has going for it. I mean, Mr. Hecate? Ms. Devlin? It's fun that there is no pretense to who these characters are, especially once Ms. Devlin sprouts horns. Rod Serling was never trying to be sly with his glaring allusions to witchcraft and magic here.

Naturally, deals with the devil come with millions of strings attached, all of which aren't apparent to the shrewd Feathersmith until it's too late. Once the air has been knocked out of him, cinematographer Robert Pittack's Dutch angles effectively convey his deteriorating emotional state as he regresses into the sniveling child he always was.

Jacob Trussell

Time traveling in this episode isn't born from any scientific theory, rather Ms. Devlin's satanic skills. But the final button will be extremely familiar to anyone hip on Robert Zemeckis' *Back to the Future*. Just like how Biff (Thomas F. Wilson) goes from bullying boss to groveling groundskeeper once Marty (Michael J. Fox) returns from the past, we see that Feathersmith and Hecate have switched roles from multi-millionaire to custodian, practically overnight.

Zone Fact

Julie Newmar was best known as Cat Woman on the campy 1960s Batman starring Adam West.

"The Incredible World of Mr. Horace Ford"
Episode 15
Original Airdate: April 18, 1963

Directed by Abner Biberman
Written by Reginald Rose

"Mr. Horace Ford, who has a preoccupation with another time, a time of childhood, a time of growing up, a time of street games, stickball and hide-'n-go-seek. He has a reluctance to check out a mirror and see the nature of his image: proof positive that the time he dwells in has already passed him by."

Horace Ford (Pat Hingle) is a man with the heart of a child, despite his friends urging him to grow up. Reflecting on his beloved childhood neighborhood, he revisits his old street to find that literally nothing has changed. Even the same gang of kids that he remembers still stalks the sidewalks, hooking Horace's interest until he returns night after night. Dismayed by her husband's erratic behavior, Laura Ford (Nan Martin) reaches out to his coworkers in an effort to snap Horace back into reality, but are his nightly retreats to the past threatening to entrap him there forever?

If "Kick The Can" was the rosy version of waxing nostalgic on our youth, then "The Incredible World of Mr. Horace Ford" is the chilling assertion that it's dangerous to dwell on a past that was *never* all it's cracked up to be. Unconsciously we push out the bad memories of growing up, skewing our perception of those years to romanticize our childhood. Your heart aches as you watch Horace fantasize about the street he lived on, only to see it was a rundown skid row, speckled with tenement houses and crawling with crime.

We're never given a clear reason as to *how* Horace is experiencing these echoes from his past, but we do learn why. In the finale we watch a young Horace be robbed by the gang of hoodlums he's been seeing in his present. This event effectively froze his maturity in time. He dedicated his life to creating intricate children's toys because the event forever infantilized him.

In a lack of subtlety that works in *The Twilight Zone*'s favor, Horace's supervisor Mr. Judson (Vaughn Taylor) tells him "I want you to see a psychiatrist. I think you're approaching a nervous breakdown." before Horace voices his reproach, "There's nothing wrong with me!" Calmly, Judson replies, "That may be. But if there is, it's nothing to be ashamed of." This is the first time the show plainly says there is nothing wrong with seeking help for mental health issues. There still exists a stigma about men seeking counseling, but if we want to destigmatize that, we need to approach the subject like Mr. Judson does with Horace: with compassion.

Zone Fact

The writer of this episode, Reginald Rose, is also the author of 12 Angry Men, which premiered on Playhouse 90, Rod Serling's old stomping grounds.

"On Thursday We Leave for Home"
Episode 16
Original Airdate: May 2, 1963

Directed by Buzz Kulik
Written by Rod Serling

"This is William Benteen, who officiates on a disintegrating outpost in space. The people are a remnant society who left the Earth looking for a Millennium, a place without war, without jeopardy, without fear, and what they found was a lonely, barren place whose only industry was survival."

In 1991, an expedition sending families into space lands on an uninhabitable planet. Realizing their fate too late, they became marooned on the craggy rock, scorched by its double suns. Thirty years later, they have survived by maintaining a close commune ruled by the kind—if not condescending—hand of Captain William Benteen (James Whitmore). As they fantasize about Earth, regaling the children who were born on the planet with stories of the night sky, a U.S. spaceship finally arrives to rescue the lost colony. The community is overjoyed, but Benteen's concern for their safety begins to twist into a possessive last grasp for power. He maintains that they are a family, and will never be apart again, but is he their true leader, or is this the final gasp of a dying dictator?

If it's been 30 years since interstellar settlers landed on the dead planet, that makes the date 2021. Is it safe to say these settlers were lucky to be off planet for the disaster that was 2016-2020? Absolutely! We don't get a lot of information about what Rod Serling's 2021 looks like, but he did get *very* close to predicting how digital screens would be used in modern schools. When asked about what's changed, Colonel Sloan (Tim O'Connor) tells them they now have devices that bring visual representations of geography directly to the student's desk. Sure he may not have said the word "tablet," but it does sound extremely similar to the ways teachers use media to enhance a students learning experience.

Prescient storytelling aside, what's most engaging in this episode is how Captain Benteen, as Colonel Sloane remarks, fashions himself to be a god amongst the settlers. But his version of being a benevolent presence quickly turns into being unquestioningly possessive, like a partner you need to get a restraining order on—so I don't think a dictator adequately describes what he's become. He acts far more like a modern day cult leader in the way he patronizes the other colonists, robbing them of their individuality, and dismissing their concerns as if they were children. Even the idea of how cults live is mentioned from the Colonel when he questions Benteen, "After living their lives in a compound, they'll return to Earth *just* to walk back into one?" Like all cult leaders, his convictions become his undoing, damning himself as Serling eloquently puts it in his closing monologue, "William Benteen, once a god, now a population of one."

Zone Fact

Despite being the 16th episode aired, this was the last one shot for Season Four.

"Passage on the Lady Anne"
Episode 17
Original Airdate: May 9, 1963

Directed by Lamont Johnson
Written by Charles Beaumont

"Portrait of a honeymoon couple getting ready for a journey—with a difference. These newlyweds have been married for six years, and they're not taking this honeymoon to start their life but rather to save it, or so Eileen Ransome thinks. She doesn't know why she insisted on a ship for this voyage, except that it would give them some time and she'd never been on one before—certainly never one like the Lady Anne."

Alan (Lee Philips) and Marie Ransome (Joyce Van Patten) embark on a second honeymoon, hoping to revitalize their marriage on a steamer trip to London. As they've made this decision last minute, their choices of ships are limited, and they settle on the Lady Anne. Before they depart, they're urged by the other passengers not to board, even being bribed $10,000. Rebuffing their pleas, the couple is further surprised to find that they are the youngest couple on board, and that their fellow passengers refer to the ship as if it were alive. As their marriage continues to strain, a sinister fog clouds the deck, and it becomes clear that something other than a London port may be the final destination of The Lady Anne.

Based on his short story "Song for a Lady," this is the final episode that Charles Beaumont penned himself. His name would be attributed to other episodes in Season Five, but because of the advanced stage of his illness, he was unable to write the episodes himself. It's heartbreaking how young Beaumont was at his death, as his health began declining when he was only 34. His friends at the time believed it was caused by alcoholism, but it also may have been a combination of early onset Alzheimer's, Pick's Disease or Spinal Meningitis he had as a child. As tragic as it is, it seems fitting that Beaumont succumbed to an illness beyond comprehension. So many of his stories took us to the edges of our imagination, to places where we couldn't conceive what we were witnessing. It ties all his work together, even in an unnaturally tenderhearted episode like "Passage on the Lady Anne."

Jacob Trussell

The characters aren't sinister, but there is an air of unease that permeates throughout the ship, leaving us on the edge of our seat waiting for the other shoe to drop. Unfortunately, the drop never really comes, but Beaumont leaves us with so many unknowns about the Lady Anne that I want to believe it's more complex than just the passengers going to heaven. If this ship is alive, perhaps they are passing over to some other great beyond, one that's more than a mere after-life.

Zone Fact

The actors who play married couple Toby and Millie McKenzie who go on to appear together the following year in My Fair Lady (1964)

"The Bard"
Episode 18
Original Airdate: May 23, 1963

Directed by David Butler
Written by Rod Serling

"You've just witnessed opportunity, if not knocking, at least scratching plaintively on a closed door. Mr. Julius Moomer, a would-be writer who, if talent came 25 cents a pound, would be worth less than car fare. But, in a moment, Mr. Moomer, through the offices of some black magic, is about to embark on a brand-new career. And although he may never get a writing credit on The Twilight Zone, he's to become an integral character in it."

Julius K. Moomer (Jack Weston) desperately wants to be a Hollywood screenwriter. The only problem is his story ideas are garbage! With his chances at success dwindling, Julius stumbles upon a book of black magic spells that allows him to conjure anything he desires. Through accidental luck, Moomer calls forth the spirit of William Shakespeare (John Williams), who he immediately exploits for his own advantage as a ghostwriter. But Shakespeare's style is no match for the parlance of the 1960s, and no sooner does the playwright turn in a draft than the producers begin cutting it to pieces. The question is, what will the world's greatest author do when he discovers he's been rewritten?

    The final episode of Season Four finds Rod Serling writing his best impression of a sitcom. The whole of the episode can essentially be summarized as "Shakespeare would *never* be able to sell a script in modern Hollywood!" That's it. That's the episode. Don't get me wrong, the gimmick is fantastic. I'd love to see an episodic series where black magic assists a Hollywood screenwriter by reincarnating different famous writers to write spec scripts. Its easy, but fun humor that's perfectly suited for, you guessed it, situation comedy. "The Bard," and Season Four, just don't feel like the series we know and love. This is *The Twilight Zone,* but just barely.

    Be that as it may, there are still things to admire in "The Bard," namely all of the intellectual humor Serling sneaks in. For example,

Julius starts naming famous writing partners after he strikes his deal with Shakespeare, "Gilbert and Sullivan! Lerner and Loewe! Rimsky and Korsakov!" I admit, this flew completely over my head and, if it wasn't for my wife, I would have had no idea that there was a Russian composer named Nikolai Rimsky-Korsakov, and the joke is that he believes it's two different people. Rimsky-Korakov's name would have been better known in the 1960s, but it's still a joke that requires you to have some knowledge of classical music, otherwise it's just going to zoom right past you, like it did me.

The episode's greatest joke comes from a cameo by Burt Reynolds doing his best Marlon Brando impression as young hotshot actor Rocky Rhodes. As he mulls over his motivations for walking through a door, Reynolds becomes a hilarious burn on the method acting technique used frequently by young actors on shows like *The Twilight Zone*. When Rocky confronts Shakespeare about what he has against Stanislavski, Shakespeare exclaims, "You!" and clocks five fingers into his jaw, sending the actor flying. I can only imagine how many screenwriters during the Golden Age of Hollywood wished they'd have been able to do the same for every James Dean wannabe that walked into a casting office.

Zone Fact

Jack Weston's second appearance on the show after appearing as vile neighbor Charlie Farnsworth in the Season One classic "The Monsters are Due on Maple Street."

The Twilight Zone

SEASON FIVE

SEPTEMBER 27, 1963 – JUNE 19, 1964

"In Praise of Pip"
Episode 1
Original Airdate: September 27, 1963

Directed by Joseph M. Newman
Written by Rod Serling

"I dreamed instead of did. I wished and hoped instead of tried!"

Pip, the only son to small time booker Max Philips (Jack Klugman), is fighting in South Vietnam. Meanwhile, Max is caught in the middle of a struggle between an acquaintance and his bookie. When Max receives word from the army that his son has been injured in combat, and will die unless he receives an emergency surgery, he lashes out at his bookie, murdering him and his hired goon. Inconsolable, he wanders the streets until he comes across a young boy who looks exactly like his son did when he was 10. Has Pip miraculously found a way to speak with his father one last time?

When "In Praise of Pip" premiered, we were still two years away from President Lyndon Johnson sending Marines to Da Nang, beginning the chain reaction that resulted in the Vietnam War. It would become a conflict that defined the next generation, wreaking new-found psychological havoc unseen in World War II or Korea. Rod Serling saw the writing on the wall about the senselessness of the war, explicitly writing it into Max's character in a prescient, if unsubtle, snippet of dialogue, "He's in South Vietnam. There isn't even supposed to be a war going on there." Serling used the series as a way to presuppose a future, so that his audience could reflect on their present. But this future wasn't decades away; it was tomorrow. The Vietnam War took so many young men like Pip away from fathers like Max, and this episode was just the beginning of that tragic realization for many Americans.

Through Jack Klugman's everyman, Rod Serling was able to paint remarkably complex portraits of the archetypal deadbeat. Even though he was a con, and a shill, who made Pip's life a living hell growing up, Klugman makes us ache for Max as he confesses how much he loved his son. Serling connects us emotionally to Max, without saying he deserves our pity. He's just another guy who's filled

Jacob Trussell

with regret with no one to blame, but himself. The only way for Max to atone and mend the bruises he caused is to sacrifice his own life to save Pip's. Everything he experienced with 10-year-old Pip may have been a hallucination from massive blood loss after the fight, but he still died believing he saved his son. There is no hard evidence for a soul, but in this moment, Max was finally able to rest his.

Zone Fact

This is the second earliest instance of the Vietnam War being mentioned on television. The first was on the show Route 66, which had a Vietnam veteran character debut six months before this episode aired.

An Unofficial Journey Into The Twilight Zone

"Steel"
Episode 2
Original Airdate: October 4, 1963

Directed by Don Weis
Written by Richard Matheson

> *"They called me 'Steel' Kelly, on account of me never being knocked down."*

It's 1974 and professional boxers have been replaced with androids, maintained by human coaches and promoters. Manager "Steel" Kelly (Lee Marvin) and his partner Pole (Joe Mantell) have a fighter named "Battling Maxo," an outdated model on its last legs. In one last ditch effort to put themselves back on the map, Kelly has bought his way into a match where, win or lose, they'll come away with some cash. Their plans are dashed when Battling Maxo short circuits and is unable to compete. With no money to make the repairs, Kelly realizes he must live up to his old namesake in the ring, just this time against a literal man of steel.

The blue-collar fear at the heart of Richard Matheson's "Steel" is the inevitably that our jobs will be replaced by machines. In some ways, this is simply a reinterpretation of folk legends like John Henry and Paul Bunyan, both about men facing the tide of automation. John Henry's legend tells of a steel-driving competition against a steam engine that he wins, even though the stress causes his heart to give out. In Paul Bunyan's tall tale, best seen in a 1958 Disney short, the monolithic lumberjack competes against a steam-powered chainsaw, but where Henry succeeds, Bunyan fails—but only by a small margin.

Man's stamina will never be able to match the tirelessness of a machine—something both stories concede—but humans do have one advantage over our robo-counterparts: our iron will to succeed. Steel Kelly may have lost the match, but because he refused to quit, in his heart he still wins. His opponent may have beaten him to a bloody pulp, but he survived, and they got paid. Against the real thing, he proved he was a man of steel. Machines can outlast us, but they'll never match the triumphant nature of the human spirit.

Jacob Trussell

The pathos behind Matheson's words have made this episode memorable, but the striking makeup design cements it. If you look closely you'll see a clear detachment in Maxo's face, like the robot's skin is peeling away from his chromium skull. This is an early example of the Uncanny Valley, the unnerving sensation we have when seeing an artificial human that looks *so* real but clearly isn't, such as the very real humanoid android named Sophia, or CGI creations like Tom Hanks in Robert Zemeckis' *The Polar Express* (2004). The robo-boxers are just life-like enough that it could be the actor's actual face, until we see the shadows move behind its sunken eyes and we realize how wrong we were.

Zone Fact

This story would be lampooned in the Futurama episode "Raging Bender."

"Nightmare at 20,000 Feet"
Episode 3
Original Airdate: October 11, 1963

Directed by Richard Donner
Written by Richard Matheson

"I know I had a mental breakdown. I know I had it in an airplane. I know it looks to you as if the same thing is happening again, but it isn't. I'm sure, it isn't."

Bob Wilson (William Shatner) is discharged from a psychiatric ward after suffering a nervous breakdown during a flight six months earlier. To prove he's conquered his fears, Bob and his wife Julia (Christine White) decide to fly home, but his confidence is tested when he sees *something* on the wing of the plane. No one believes him, but he's certain it's a gremlin—the fabled monsters of war that cause malfunctions in allied tanks and planes. Forced to take matters into his own hands, Bob arms himself with a pistol lifted off a sleeping sky marshal and aims to take down both the monster and his phobia.

This is arguably the most famous episode of the entire series, but *why* is it so famous? Is it because the line "there's something on the wing" has become synonymous with fears of flying? Is it the evocative title that instills terror in four short words? Maybe it is the creature itself, a big gilly-suit fur monster with the moves of a gymnast? It could simply be William Shatner's performance, years away from his tenure as Captain Kirk in *Star Trek*, but still with his trademark hammy panache that is an art form unto itself.

Yet it may also be writer Richard Matheson's candor about mental health and how it factors into the episode. Framing the story about a fear of flying allows audiences to have an easier time processing the psychological subtext than if it were about PTSD or depression. Matheson leaves no room for misinterpretation about what is causing Bob Wilson's manic episode, as we're plainly told that he spent time in a sanitarium. It's because of this admission that Bob becomes an unreliable narrator for the audience. The gremlin on the wing is real to Bob, but we're forced to constantly remind ourselves that it's not.

Jacob Trussell

Or is it? The button on the episode, like so many before it, makes us question everything we just watched. Did Bob's anxieties bring this creature into existence, giving him a physical representation of his fears to defeat, or was there really a creature on the wing? After all, we see the damage that *something* left behind. Was it human error, like improperly installed parts, or is it something more? That's the question you walk away with, and why "Nightmare at 20,000 Feet" has lingered in our collective unconscious for over 60 years.

Zone Fact

The actor who played the Gremlin, Nick Cravat, was in a circus act with famed actor Burt Lancaster.

"A Kind of a Stopwatch"
Episode 4
Original Airdate: October 18, 1963

Directed by John Rich
Written by Rod Serling (from a story by Michael D. Rosenthal)

> *"Submitted for your approval or at least your analysis: one Patrick Thomas McNulty, who, at age 41, is the biggest bore on Earth. He holds a 10-year record for the most meaningless words spewed out during a coffee break. And it's very likely that, as of this moment, he would have gone through life in precisely this manner, a dull, argumentative bigmouth who sets back the art of conversation a thousand years. I say he very likely would have except for something that will soon happen to him, something that will considerably alter his existence—and ours."*

Patrick Thomas McNulty (Richard Erdman) is a pitchman constantly looking for the big idea that will cement his name in history. Unfortunately, every idea he has fails to capture the attention of his boss, partly because the underwear company he works for isn't interested in revolutionizing the manufacturing industry. Fed up with the never-ending stream of McNulty's unsolicited pitches, his boss fires him, sending him slinking to the local bar to drown his sadness.

As he's getting liquored up, McNulty is approached by a drunk who gives him a pocket watch with the unique ability to stop time. McNulty tries to sell the concept to his former boss who is only incredulous to the notion of a magic watch. Bitter by his dismissal, McNulty realizes there are far more lucrative ways to use the watch than selling it. What he doesn't remember is that easy money is never really easy.

There are a lot of horrifying things that happen in *The Twilight Zone*, from nuclear war to killer robots and psychopathic children, but few are as horrifying as the fate of Patrick McNulty. Put yourself in his shoes and imagine the profound loneliness he faces, surrounded by people frozen in motionless action. Life is all around him, but he can't participate. He can only watch, deafened by their silence. It's almost mythological in the severity and irony of his eternal punishment. He wanted to be remembered for something, but through his greed for notoriety, he's fated to be forgotten. Not through the passage of time, but the stagnation of it.

McNulty's boorish behavior is what ultimately dooms him, but his internal struggle should be familiar for anyone who wants to make something of themselves. When McNulty pitches an idea for a saloon-style entrance to his neighborhood bar he says, "I can look at those two swinging doors and say, I did that!" That's the aspirations of any creative type in a nutshell.

We want something that we can be remembered for and can call our own. By having people still read your words, watch your films, admire your paintings, laugh at your jokes, you achieve immortality. You extend your life long after your death. But just remember, if you ever do get a magic stopwatch, make sure you get a protective case for it. Otherwise, you may have all the time in the world to become a master horologist.

Zone Fact

Richard Erdman would later go on to find fame as Leonard in Dan Harmon's sitcom Community.

"The Last Night of a Jockey"
Episode 5
Original Airdate: October 25, 1963

Directed by Joseph M. Newman
Written by Rod Serling

> *"Unfortunately for Mr. Grady, he learned too late that you don't measure size with a ruler, you don't figure height with a yardstick, and you never judge a man by how tall he looks in a mirror."*

Grady (Mickey Rooney) is a jockey caught in a scandal. He's received a permanent ban on racing after being accused of using performance enhancing drugs on his horses, sending him into a spiral of depression and alcoholism. Mad at the world as much as he is himself, Grady is visited by his alter-ego—a mirror image of himself that resides in his mind's eye and is everything that Grady is not. After arguing about where his life went wrong, Grady's alter-ego gives him one wish, which he immediately uses to grow taller—the only thing that he has ever truly wanted. But sometimes what we want isn't what we need, and for Grady, this growth spurt may have come at just the wrong time.

Mickey Rooney was one of the biggest stars of the early 20th century, best known for starring with Judy Garland in "Let's put on a show!" and musicals like *Babes in Arms*. He'd become typecast in these wholesome roles throughout his life, but Rod Serling gave him the rare opportunities to stretch his dramatic skills like in "The Comedian," a 1956 episode of *Playhouse 90* where Rooney starred as a brash TV comic. His "Aw shucks!" legacy is what makes his dramatic turns so thrilling, because we hadn't seen Rooney be so ugly before. Grady is sweaty and unshaven, draining bottles of booze and looking on the verge of collapse at any moment. It's from this ugliness that the episode's supernatural element emerges.

Serling refers to Grady's double as his alter-ego, a clear Freudian reference to the Id, Ego, and Superego. In simple terms, the Id is the Devil on your shoulder, the Superego is the angel, and your rational is the Ego. Grady isn't the rational one though. His double may be the Superego, but he has given himself almost entirely to the Id, forcing his alter-ego to emerge.

Jacob Trussell

Grady faces self-destruction if he keeps feeding the desires of the Id, like his ravenous wish to be tall. This is a part of Grady that's manifested directly from Serling's own experience as a man of 5'4, only two inches taller than Rooney himself. Emasculating men because they aren't tall or big enough is one of the oldest, and simplest representations of ingrained toxic masculinity. Unless a person like Grady can look inwardly at where their anger comes from, they will only grow more resentful at what they can't change. Using Grady as a proxy, Serling questions his own bitterness in "Last Night of the Jockey," leaving the impression that a man's worth isn't measured in feet and inches, but character.

Zone Fact

Serling wrote this role specifically with Mickey Rooney in mind.

An Unofficial Journey Into The Twilight Zone

"Living Doll"
Episode 6
Original Airdate: November 1, 1963

Directed by Richard C. Sarafian
Written by Charles Beaumont

"I'm Talky Tina, and I think I could kill you."

Annabelle Streator (Mary LaRoche) buys a wind-up doll for her daughter Christie (Tracy Stratford) named Talky Tina, much to the ire of her new husband Erich (Telly Savalas). Since he is unable to give Annabelle children of his own, he views the new doll as a mockery against him, and takes his insecurities out on Christie. When Erich examines the doll, Tina opens her eyes and stares at him saying, "I'm Talky Tina, and I don't think I like you." Startled by the ambiguous warning, Erich is plunged into paranoia, convinced that the doll is really alive. Is Talky Tina planning to kill him, or will Erich's personal demons take care of that for her?

When you think of *The Twilight Zone*, it's hard not to see Talky Tina's beady eyes promising death in Telly Savalas' hands. Credited to Charles Beaumont, and ghostwritten by Jerry Sohl, "Living Doll" is the progenitor for essentially every major killer doll movie to come, from *Child's Play* (1988) and *Dolly Dearest* (1991) to *Annabelle* (2014). Sixty years later, Talky Tina is still as creepy as ever. What's so remarkable about this episode is how the doll is the projection of a neglected, frightened young girl, unloved by her brutish stepfather. Tina speaks and acts on Christie's behalf saying the things she could never say herself, like "I hate you!"

Another perspective is that Erich is projecting his own anxieties about being a father onto Tina. It's instantly clear to the viewer that he should have never gotten married if he didn't want to be a stepdad, but that doesn't take into consideration the societal expectations we had around marriage at the time. It's so easy to be single, and successful in the 21st century, but that wasn't the case 60 years ago. If you wanted to be taken seriously at a job, you had to have a family. Why do you think we've never had a bachelor President? Tina is Erich's way to channel his self-loathing for being forced into the role of father-figure and, exacerbated by his emotional issues, it's what ultimately kills him.

If Erich dies at the end of this episode, Annabelle will likely collect life insurance, giving her and Christie the means to start a better life for themselves. It's incredibly easy to view Tina as the villain of the episode, but in a way she's the hero, liberating a family from an abusive man!

Zone Fact

Call it coincidence or call it fate, but the wife's name Annabelle would become synonymous for killer dolls in the 21st century through the Blumhouse franchise Annabelle.

"The Old Man in the Cave"
Episode 7
Original Airdate: November 8, 1963

Directed by Alan Crosland, Jr.
Written by Rod Serling (from the short story "The Old Man" by Henry Slesar")

"What you're looking at is a legacy that man left to himself. A decade previous he pushed his buttons and a nightmarish moment later woke up to find that he had set the clock back a thousand years."

By 1974 the apocalypse had already come and gone, leaving the United States a barren wasteland filled with primitive communities trying to survive in deserted cities. One community, led by the kind-hearted Mr. Goldsmith (John Anderson), receives guidance from a figure they refer to as the old man in the cave. After discovering a ration of canned foods they hope to eat, the old man tells them it's contaminated with radiation. At the same time, a group of cocksure soldiers arrive, led by French (James Coburn), promising to unite the scattered communities into a new America. French quickly turns the town against Goldsmith, mocking the mysterious man. Despite Goldsmith's protestations, French begins a crusade to reveal the truth behind him, but the reality of the cave may be far more than any of them bargained for.

    Like the rest of the world after the United States dropped nuclear warheads on the Japanese, Rod Serling was disturbed by the apocalyptic implications that the Atomic Bomb represented. In an instant, our world could be decimated, setting society back centuries and changing the very fabric of what life is. The bomb wouldn't just wipe out our cities, but destroy our humanity, forcing us to rely on our most base instincts for survival—even if it means killing another person over scraps of food, like wild dogs distrustful of anyone not part of their pack. This is what I call the "monsters of men" theme that is so common in modern apocalypse narratives, especially zombie fiction like *The Walking Dead*.

    As Serling says in his closing narration, this is just what *could* happen, rather than what *will* happen. We have fail-safes to prevent nuclear war, but what Serling means is that he trusts we'll retain faith in something bigger than ourselves, something that we can hook our hopes of survival on. It could be a spiritual figure, or it could be a super-massive computer that this group of survivors has based their decisions on.

"The Old Man in the Cave" may have originally been read as the survivors dying because they lost faith in God, but today it's less about religious faith, and more man's penchant for willful ignorance. Even when presented with the truth, the survivors don't want to face the fact that the person they believed in isn't even a person at all. They lose their life because they refuse to acknowledge uncomfortable truths. Today, we have movements of people that believe "facts" from social media, rather than testimony from public health officials. They choose to have faith in their convictions, rather than face the queasy realities of life. You're bound to suffocate in the apocalypse if you leave your head buried in the sand.

Zone Fact

Another short story from Henry Slesar would be adapted into "The Self-Improvement of Salvadore Ross" (S5E16)

"Uncle Simon"
Episode 8
Original Airdate: November 15, 1963

Directed by Don Siegel
Written by Rod Serling

"Dramatis personae: Mr. Simon Polk, a gentleman who has lived out his life in a gleeful rage; and the young lady who's just beat the hasty retreat is Mr. Polk's niece, Barbara. She has lived her life as if during each ensuing hour she had a dentist appointment."

For the last 25 years, Barbara (Constance Ford) has cared for her Uncle Simon (Cedric Hardwicke), a miserly, despicable inventor who takes pleasure in wielding pain. He belittles and degrades Barbara, hoping to spark any reaction he can from her. Barbara has formed a thick skin however, causing Simon to push harder, not knowing that his behavior has caused his niece to close herself off from the world. When Simon attempts to strike Barbara after she peers into his lab one night, she pushes him down the stairs, leaving him to die. Wanting the last word, Simon swears that if she wants her inheritance, she'll have to dote on a robot Simon has crafted to act just like him. But is the creation even worse than the creator?

The Twilight Zone is the central inspiration for Charlie Brooker's show *Black Mirror*, and no *Zone* episode feels more at home in that bleak series than "Uncle Simon." This is because the episode is built on *Black Mirror*'s foundation of unbearable tragedy. Barbara is abused by Simon, who views conversations as if they were battles meant to be fought and won. He takes blithe amusement from needling Barbara as if insults were the only way he felt comfortable communicating. When she eventually kills him, his death is cosmic comeuppance—a shock of violence birthed from the only language he understood, resentment.

We feel relief for Barbara once Simon dies, because we know she's been under his abusive thumb for years. But that joy is punched out of us when we discover what she must do to earn her inheritance. The cost of her new life amounts to caring for her abuser, even if he now looks like Robby the Robot. Like the conclusion to "Time

Jacob Trussell

Enough at Last," this is Serling at some of his most mean-spirited, dooming a victim to care for her tormentor lest she risks losing her own livelihood.

The story's twist is where Serling veers into EC Comics territory in the vein of *Tales from the Crypt*. In the "Father's Day" segment of the film *Creepshow*, George Romero and Stephen King's ode to the comic series, a daughter kills her verbally abusive father only for him to rise again on Father's Day in search of his annual cake. Not only is this similar to Simon's constant demands for hot chocolate, but the bitter torment he wielded is the same. The typical moral you walk away with from an EC comic, and a Serling story, is that hate begets more hate. But that moral doesn't sit well with Barbara's story. She did hate her Uncle, but it was a justified emotion. When you push someone to their limits, it's hard to villainize them once they finally push back.

Zone Fact

Directed by Don Siegel, genius behind the original Invasion of the Body Snatchers!

"Probe 7, Over and Out"
Episode 9
Original Airdate: November 29, 1963

Directed by Ted Post
Written by Rod Serling

> *"Colonel Cook has been set adrift in an ocean of space in a metal lifeboat that has been scorched and destroyed and will never fly again. He survived the crash but his ordeal is yet to begin. Now he must give battle to loneliness. Now Colonel Cook must meet the unknown."*

After crashing on a far distant planet, astronaut Adam Cook (Richard Basehart) learns his home world is on the precipice of global nuclear war. With no chance for rescue, General Larrabee (Harold Gould) comforts Cook to the reality that he'll be marooned for life on this unknown rock. Dismayed, but determined, Cook explores the planet's surface looking for some semblance of life. As he uncovers strange drawings etched into the ground, he's swiftly knocked unconscious by a woman (Antoinette Bower) who speaks an alien tongue. Stranded together, and cautious of each other, they must learn to communicate in order to survive in this strange new world. A world that may be closer to home than imaginable.

Where Rod Serling was revolutionary in his approach to racial representation in the 1960s, he needed a lot of work when it came to female representation. He knew it too, even mentioning how Vera Miles called him out on his poorly scripted females in an interstitial he shot ahead of Season One's "Mirror Image."

His lack of nuance is flagrant in two-handers like "Probe 7, Over and Out" and "Two" (S3E1). The female characters in these episodes are given plenty of screen time, but it rubs the modern viewer the wrong way that he renders them both essentially mute. In "Two," Elizabeth Montgomery plays a foreign soldier who doesn't speak Charles Bronson's language. Rather than trying to communicate, she simply remains tightlipped. For "Probe 7," we're never given a good reason why Eve can't adequately communicate outside of her being from another planet. What this inadvertently does is force the viewer to see these women through the male gaze, rather than as individuals—a sentiment that'd cut deep a staunch individualist like Rod Serling.

Jacob Trussell

Even worse, Cook talks to Eve as if she were a simple-minded child, and not an intelligent woman who just is on the other side of a language barrier. Rod Serling isn't a misogynist, but this episode points towards his implicit bias. Much like racism, these are ingrained biases that every person is guilty of having sometime in their life. It's not your fault that you have implicit biases, but it is your duty to do something about it. Rod Serling may not have intended to demean these two female characters, but that's what happens when you just let men do the talking.

Zone Fact

Most of Eve's language is merely English but spoken backwards.

"The 7th Is Made Up of Phantoms"
Episode 10
Original Airdate: December 6, 1963
Directed by Alan Crosland, Jr.
Written by Rod Serling

> *"June 25th 1964—or, if you prefer, June 25th 1876. The cast of characters in order of their appearance: a patrol of General Custer's cavalry and a patrol of National Guardsmen on a maneuver. Past and present are about to collide head-on, as they are wont to do in a very special bivouac area known as...The Twilight Zone."*

On the 88th anniversary of the Battle of Little Bighorn, a group of National Guardsmen is conducting military exercises near the site of the famous massacre between Native American tribes and the United States. Three of the soldiers, Sgt. William Connors (Ron Foster), Pvt. Michael McCluskey (Randy Boone), Cpl. Richard Langsford (Warren Oates) are given orders leading them along the same path that General Custer took when he made his last stand. On route, they begin hearing strange sounds and seeing the impossible, like villages of abandoned tipis. When they report this eerie phenomenon, their Captain remains skeptical, forcing them to search for an answer in the unknowns of time and space.

What most modern viewers will likely question in "The Seventh Is Made Up of Phantoms" is the allure of the Battle of the Little Bighorn, also referred to as Custer's Last Stand, and in Native American history, the Battle of the Greasy Grass. It occurred in 1876 as the result of the U.S. attempting to strip land from Native Americans, who fervently defended what was rightfully theirs. Seeing a memorial to the white men who took native lives, erected on that very land is a stark reminder of the brutal legacy of bigotry in the United States.

This is why I think it's a carefully made point that the show cast Greg Morris as one of the National Guardsmen. The raison d'etre isn't merely casting a Black actor, it's that he's playing a General giving direct orders to white guardsmen in a time when Black people couldn't sit at the front of a public bus. Serling is pointing a finger towards progress saying, "Look where we came from, and look where we are now." That said, it would have been a more powerful allusion to this nation's bloody history if the actor had been Native American.

We see at the episode's end that Connors, McCluskey and Langsfords names have all been magically etched into the statue commemorating a battle they never fought. It's ironic that it only took a short jaunt to *The Twilight Zone* to get these soldiers honored, while it'd take decades before the Native American lives lost during that skirmish would get their own tribute.

Zone Fact

Warren Oates had previously appeared as a cameo in Season One's "The Purple Testament"

"A Short Drink from a Certain Fountain"
Episode 11
Original Airdate: December 13, 1963

Directed by Bernard Girard
Written by Rod Serling (from a story by Lou Holz)

"Picture of an aging man who leads his life, as Thoreau said, 'in quiet desperation.'"

Harmon Gordon (Patrick O'Neal) is a 70-year-old man utterly devoted to his wife Flora (Ruta Lee) who is almost 50 years his junior. Harmon attempts to keep up with his wife's bouncy, abrasive energy and lavish lifestyle, but she finds his age irritating, using threats of divorce to cut him to the core. On the verge of giving up on life, Harmon pleads with his brother, Dr. Raymond Gordon (Walter Brooke), to inject him with a de-aging serum he's been testing on animals.

Nowhere near ready for human trials, Harmon persuades Raymond once he confesses his suicidal thoughts. When the serum shows signs of success, Raymond quickly realizes that Harmon may have shed more years than he bargained for.

From the first moment I saw Harmon and Flora together my immediate thought was why don't these two just get a divorce? She's clearly unhappy with him, and he is understandably pained by how unhappy he makes her but they can't break it off because divorce, while not unheard of, was still highly frowned upon in the early 1960s. More so, because Harmon is so deeply in love he stays with her despite being unhappy. Flora on the other hand sticks out the marriage because she is deeply in love with Harmon's wealth. It's mutually beneficial, mutual destruction which makes for a complex, but torpid, love affair.

I find the underlying metaphor of this episode is revealed when Harmon mentions that, at his age, he doesn't care whether he lives or dies anymore. This ambivalence to life is an existential feeling that would have been familiar to war veterans in the 1960s. The survivor's guilt they likely felt, forced them to consider why they deserved to live when so many of their friends unjustly died. Like Harmon trying to return to his youth, the soldiers of the Second World War just

Jacob Trussell

wanted to turn back time to a point in their lives before the horrors of combat changed them. For the Greatest Generation, finding a fountain of youth wasn't about cosmetic transformations, it was about getting back to a time before their innocence was lost.

Zone Fact
One of four "lost episodes" that wasn't included in the original syndication packages sold to local television stations.

"Ninety Years Without Slumbering"
Episode 12
Original Airdate: December 20, 1963

Directed by Roger Kay
Written by Richard De Roy (from a story by George Clayton Johnson, credited as Johnson Smith)

"Each man measures his time; some with hope, some with joy, some with fear. But Sam Forstmann measures his allotted time with a grandfather's clock, a unique mechanism whose pendulum swings between life and death, a very special clock that keeps a special kind of time
—in The Twilight Zone."

Sam Forstmann's (Ed Wynn) hobby is to constantly care for a grandfather clock that's been in his family for years. Recently this has become more of an obsession, as Forstmann eschews everything in his life to ensure the clock is consistently, and precisely, wound. This is because he believes that if the clock stops ticking even for a second, his heart will stop beating. His family attempts to get him psychiatric help, but Forstmann implores the doctor that his fears are justified. But once his eyes have been opened to the reality of his mental condition, will Forstmann ever be able to close them again?

Ed Wynn returns to *The Twilight Zone* in an episode that, on first appearance, seems to touch on the emotional toll Alzheimer's places on a person and their family. But I don't necessarily believe Forstmann has dementia, rather I think he's suffering from an undiagnosed obsessive-compulsive disorder that causes him to fixate on the grandfather clock. Forstmann will make up any reason to maintain his neurotic routine, but like many people with OCD, he's quickly angered when the compulsion is pointed out to him. His irritation is a mix of embarrassment at something out of his control, and desperation because to him his compulsion is a life or death situation.

Once Forstmann decides to stop winding the clock, a ghostly apparition appears to him. This isn't a spirit here to help him pass to the other side, rather it's a psychic manifestation of his OCD. It's why the apparition puts up a fight when Forstmann mentions therapy.

Jacob Trussell

"I don't trust psychiatrists" the apparition yells, a common refrain from any mid-century American. Forstmann's reply can be seen as the episode's mission statement, "That's because you're from another generation!"

I find the point of this episode is to demystify psychotherapy in a decade when it was still misunderstood. The reason Forstmann is able to overcome his problems is because therapy made him aware of them. The moment that he realizes how much he needs the clock is the moment that he can finally set himself free. "Nine Years Without Slumbering" wants the audience to understand that they can set themselves free from their emotional problems too, just so long as they face them. Preferably under the supervision of a trained professional.

Zone Fact

The mustachioed clock mover is none other than Mr. Whipple himself, Dick Wilson, long before he'd become Charmin's go-to guy to sling their toilet paper.

An Unofficial Journey Into The Twilight Zone

"Ring-a-Ding Girl"
Episode 13
Original Airdate: December 27, 1963

Directed by Alan Crosland, Jr.
Written by Earl Hamner, Jr.

"We are all travelers. The trip starts in a place called birth, and ends in that lonely town called death. And that's the end of the journey, unless you happen to exist for a few hours, like Bunny Blake, in the misty regions of The Twilight Zone."

Bunny Blake (Maggie McNamara) is a world-famous actress who receives a mysterious ring from a group of fans in her hometown. The ring shows her the faces of people she grew up with, all beckoning her to return home. Unable to resist, Bunny leaves Hollywood immediately, but is gripped by mysterious seizures whenever she stares into the ring. Poor health won't stop the pugnacious Bunny from enjoying her one-day trip home though, and she decides to restage her Las Vegas one-woman show for the whole town—even if it means interrupting the city-wide picnic the community holds every year. But are the premonitions Bunny sees in her ring merely the psychological manifestations of an exhausted actress, or are they triggering real warnings?

"Ring-A-Ding Girl" is one of the most obscure episodes of the series, not only because it's a bait-and-switch—the episode isn't about a psychic mood ring at all!—but you're left in the dark on what's really going on until the final few seconds.

For most of the runtime, I'm left wondering what Earl Hamner Jr. is attempting to say by submitting us to the irritating whims of Bunny Blake. She jetsets back into town and, rather than going to visit friends and family, she expects *them* to drop everything to make time for *her*. As we see when she visits her old school, people in Bunny's hometown don't take kindly to her egocentric behavior, and the janitor tells her as much, despite it going in one ear and out the other. Her willful ignorance is frustrating for the audience because we don't know what we are supposed to ascertain from this. Is the episode just to shine a light on how selfish Hollywood celebrities can

Jacob Trussell

be, especially ones that seem to have forgotten they came from Nowheresville, USA?

That is, until the final moment when we realize that Bunny returned not only to make amends, but save her town. Celebrities are always looking for ways to give back to the community, but rather than Bunny signing a check or opening a school, she uses supernatural means to save her friends and family from a fiery plane crash that she herself wouldn't survive.

At the episode's end, a radio announcer describes how Bunny was reported being seen around town, prior to the crash. This phenomena reminds me immensely of doppelgänger mythology. There have been reports throughout the centuries of people seeing family members or friends places that they absolutely could not have been, like walking in the front door when they're known to be in another city. Doppelgänger sightings are frequently viewed as harbingers of tragedy, so for Bunny, her return effectively foreshadows her death.

But is the Bunny we follow really her, or is it her doppelgänger? We aren't sure, but I'd gather that Earl Hamner Jr., similar to an avant garde artist like David Lynch, isn't really sure either. So let's chalk it up to her being some moralistic-doppelgänger, subconscious-spirit celebrity and call it a day on a very strange, but very fascinating trip into *The Twilight Zone*.

Zone fact

The term ring-a-ding originated in the 18th century and means a thing of superb or excellent quality.

"You Drive"
Episode 14
Original Airdate: January 3, 1964

Directed by John Brahm
Written by Earl Hamner, Jr.

"Oliver Pope, hit-and-run driver, just arrived at a crossroad in his life, and he's chosen the wrong turn. The hit occurred in the world he knows, but the run will lead him straight into —The Twilight Zone."

Oliver Pope (Edward Andrews) is driving home from work, but his mind is elsewhere. Not paying attention to the road, Pope turns his car and hits a young paperboy cycling through his route. In a panic, Pope hits the gas and flies away, barely stopping to see if the boy was hurt. Arriving home to his wife Lilian (Helen), Pope tries to play it cool, but breaks down and calls the hospital where the young boy has died. Distraught, but unsure what to do, Pope keeps quiet and believes he may have gotten away with it—especially when his friend Pete (Kevin Hagen) is accused of the crime. But something isn't right with the car. It seems to be operating all on its own, flashing its lights and radio, banging down its hood, and even stalling out at the scene of the hit-and-run. Are these the normal malfunctions of a damaged car, or is there some thing forcing Pope to confess the murder?

    I think we can all agree on one thing: guilt will eat you up inside. If you ever get into a traffic accident, or God forbid hit someone with a car, you're much better off just dealing with the consequences in the moment, rather than making things worse for you by fleeing. Oliver's conscience makes him initially hesitate, but fear is stronger than doing what is right.

    Amidst the supernatural elements birthed from Oliver's remorse, Earl Hamner Jr. finely interweaves real plausibility as to what's happening with Oliver's car. His flashing headlights and phantom radio could mean that the vehicle has gained sentience, or it could just be a short circuit caused by the accident. Which, if so, could be worse for Oliver than a car possessed by the memory of a murder, because it would be hard evidence tying him to the crime.

    This fine line between the physical and the metaphysical is *The*

Jacob Trussell

Twilight Zone's sweet spot. We can take the reasonable explanation that it's just a damaged car brought to life by Oliver's guilt ridden-mind, or we can help ourselves to the yummy, otherworldly explanation that Earl Hamner Jr. presents us. This is a possessed car calling for justice from beyond the grave.

Zone Fact

The title is taken from "U-Drives," an old Hertz Rental Car ad campaign lampooned later by comedy duo Abbott and Costello.

"The Long Morrow"
Episode 15
Original Airdate: January 10, 1964

Directed by Robert Florey
Written by Rod Serling

> *"This is not a hospital, not a morgue, not a mausoleum, not an undertaker's parlor of the future. What it is is the belly of a spaceship. It is en route to another planetary system, an incredible distance from the Earth. This is the crux of our story—a flight into space. It is also the story of the things that might happen to human beings who take a step beyond, unable to anticipate everything that might await them out there..."*

Commander Douglas Stansfield (Robert Lansing) is tasked with an impossible mission; he is to be the sole occupant of a spacecraft traveling lightyears away to a whole new universe. The astronaut is ecstatic, but he must go into suspended animation, because even though his ship is the fastest ever made, it will still take him 40 years to travel there and back. During his voyage, he takes solace in the memories of a love affair he developed with his colleague Sandra Horn (Mariette Hartley). Sandra promises to greet him on his return, when she will be 70, and he will have aged only a few weeks. Will the loneliness of space prove too much for Commander Stansfield, or will his profound love stand the test of time?

The Twilight Zone has had romantic episodes in past seasons, like "Two" and "The Trade-ins," but no episode is more powerful—or as obviously romantic—than "The Long Morrow." Robert Lansing and Mariette Hartley have a lived-in chemistry that leaps off of the screen, especially in the emotional farewell that Stansfield has with Horn once he returns from his 40 year-long intergalactic sojourn.

The lovelorn tragedy feels magnetized by a line from General Walters (Ed Binn): "His loneliness must have been something brand new in human experience." I can't stop dwelling on what that must have felt like for Stansfield. It's unknowable, the emotional and mental torture he put himself through in the hopes that, when he returns an old man, he can be with Sandra for the twilight years of their life.

Jacob Trussell

All of Stansfield's if-onlys makes the O'Henry-esque twist ending even more of a knife in the heart. If only he had communications, if only he had stayed in the chamber, if only he had known what Sandra would do. But if you've ever been in and out of love, you know that what-ifs will only fill you with regret. You can see it in Lansing's resigned face as he fights back tears on seeing Sandra's young face. That resignation is what makes Walters tell him "It may be the one distinction of my entire life, that I knew you... that I knew a man who put such a premium on love." The resilience Stansfield shows is inspiring, even if it destroys him inside.

Zone Fact

Ed Binns was first seen in the Season One classic "I Shot An Arrow Into The Sky."

"The Self-Improvement of Salvadore Ross"
Episode 16
Original Airdate: January 17, 1964

Directed by Don Siegel
Written by Jerry McNeely (from a short story by Henry Slesar)

"The Salvadore Ross program for self-improvement. The all-in-one, sure-fire success course that lets you lick the bully, learn the language, dance the tango and anything else you want to do. Or think you want to do."

Despite her better judgment, Leah Maitland (Gail Kobe) is in love with Salvadore Ross (Don Gordon), an abusive man who wants to own Leah's life, not share in it. Leah tries to escape the relationship, but he won't let go, even when Leah's father forcibly tells him to. After breaking his hand in an argument, Sal discovers that he can transfer aspects of his body—like age, health, emotions—to anyone else. He first switches his broken hand for a respiratory infection, then makes a mint on selling his youth, only to make it back by buying it off an unassuming elevator operator. Soon, Sal makes his way back to Leah, now flush with cash, in hopes to woo her back. Even though Leah falls back under his spell, her father plans to make sure that Sal always remembers what happens to those who lack compassion.

Temper expectations all ye who watch this episode! If you read the description on Netflix, it says that it's about a man who can change his physical characteristics with others, which to me echoes the plot of George Clayton Johnson's "The Four of Us Are Dying" (S1E13). But that's not so much the case with Sal, as he can only change age and ailments, like swapping a broken hand for a cold.

It's a neat gimmick, especially considering how steely Sal is to the sick man when he asks for his chest cold back, but the character figures out the supernatural racket a little too fast. Before he even gets over the sniffles, he's already selling his youth for a million dollars. How did he figure this out so fast? It's a plot hole that doesn't need to be filled—considering the pace of the series—but it doesn't give the episode a real sturdy foundation to build a story around.

The emotional core of the episode is also shaky. Even though he says the money and power is all for Leah, Sal's selfish actions and language show that he doesn't love her, he just wants to possess her. Earl Hamner Jr. adds further complexity to this relationship by letting us see two sides of Leah, both the headstrong, independent woman she is, and a glimpse at the side Sal manipulates to lure her back. Much like Harmon Gordon in "A Short Drink from a Certain Fountain" (S5E11), Leah is subconsciously drawn to this abusive love affair like a moth to a flame. Someone needs to extinguish it, and that somebody is Leah's dad.

Personally, I find Sal eerily reminiscent of greedy sociopaths like Donald Trump. Much like how Trump said that he likes people who were not prisoners of war, Sal considers Leah's father to be a failure because he is a disabled war veteran relying on his daughter for help. Sal can't even come up with a good response when Mr. Maitland asks, "Will you be a good husband to her?" Sal's inevitable demise is so satisfying because we see him caught in his own deadly game, by a father protecting his daughter. Imagine how many dads out there would jump at the chance to dole out comeuppance to sociopathic real estate developers of 1980s New York City!

Zone Fact

Another Henry Slesar short would be adapted into "Examination Day" for the 1985 revival of The Twilight Zone.

"Number 12 Looks Just Like You"
Episode 17
Original Airdate: January 24, 1964

Directed by Aber Biberman
Written by Charles Beaumont and John Tomerlin

> *"Given the chance, what young girl wouldn't happily exchange a plain face for a lovely one? What girl could refuse the opportunity to be beautiful? For want of a better estimate, let's call it the year 2000. At any rate, imagine a time in the future where science has developed the means of giving everyone the face and body he dreams of. It may not happen tomorrow, but it happens now, in The Twilight Zone."*

In the year 2000, at the age of 19, everyone on Earth must undergo what is called "The Transformation." This process alters your body to resemble one of a set of models, unifying the way everyone looks across the world. On the eve of Marilyn Cuberle's (Collin Wilcox) transformation, she shows hesitation to the transformation, asking if there is any way to postpone the procedure until she feels more ready. The lookalikes she speaks to urge her to go through with the process, claiming that she will be happier once it's completed. Will Marilyn succumb to the fate of her father, who also didn't want to conform to society, or will the inevitability of The Transformation finally catch up to her?

Adapted from a short story by series stalwart Charles Beaumont, this episode is a thematic cousin to "Eye of the Beholder" (S2E6), where a woman who's gone through intensive cosmetic surgery is revealed to be conventionally gorgeous. The surface level lesson is that beauty is a construct that changes from person to person since it's—as the saying goes—in the eye of the beholder. What happens then to a society where *everyone* has the same eye? That's the dystopia at the heart of Beaumont's story. While "Beholder" had an undercurrent about prejudice, the main goal in "Number 12" is to reinforce the importance of individuality. Our differences and imperfections are what make us who we are. If we take those things away, we risk losing what makes us unique.

Plastic surgery didn't really gain traction until the 1970s, so this

Jacob Trussell

episode can be viewed as a cautionary tale looking into a future that, in many ways, has come true. For the right price, you can now make your face and body look however you want. Serling and Beaumont likely never dreamed we would actually see body modifications like we're shown in this episode, but if you look at modern stories about "Real Life" Barbie and Ken dolls, they weren't *too* far off the mark.

Cosmetic surgery isn't just normal now—for certain professions it's practically expected—and I think Serling could see that on the horizon. He mentions in his closing narration, "Portrait of a young lady in love—with herself. Improbable? Perhaps. But in an age of plastic surgery, bodybuilding and an infinity of cosmetics, let us hesitate to say impossible. These, and other strange blessings, may be waiting in the future, which, after all, is The Twilight Zone."

Zone Fact

Charlie Brooker said in an interview that this episode influenced the Black Mirror's Fifteen Million Merits, starring Daniel Kaluuya.

"Black Leather Jackets"
Episode 18
Original Airdate: January 31, 1964

Directed by Joseph M. Newman
Written by Earl Hamner, Jr.

"Three strangers arrive in a small town; three men in black leather jackets in an empty, rented house. We'll call them Steve, and Scott and Fred, but their names are not important; their mission is, as three men on motorcycles lead us into the Twilight Zone."

A small community grows wary of three outsiders who have moved into a new house on their block. They aren't concerned that their new neighbors have no furniture, or don't seem to speak, they're suspicious because of their black leather jackets and motorcycles! This trio of men are more than hoodlums, they are psychic aliens from another planet. Their orders are to exterminate the human race, because Earth has been intergalactically identified as a planet filled with hate. As the aliens await further instructions, the youngest of them falls for a local girl, threatening to put their entire invasion at risk. Could their love be the one thing that saves the world?

Is "Black Leather Jackets" just a pastiche of Marlon Brando's infamous film *The Wild One*? Undoubtedly yes. In that film, Brando plays Johnny Strabler, the leader of a biker gang who take over a small town after they are detained following an accident. The film is famous for Brando's oft-quoted line of dialogue about rebellion, "What've ya got?", but also for igniting a wave of other outlaw biker movies inspired by the Hollister Riot of 1947.

Rather than joining in the Conservative handwringing over the rise in biker culture, writer Earl Hamner, Jr. chose to lampoon the mass hysteria by making his bikers exactly what the old guard feared: creatures from another planet. This is another example of *The Twilight Zone*'s theme of "othering." The prejudice and fear the town has towards the black leather jacket boys is unfounded, born not out of provocation, but from their inner fear of outsiders. Our quickness to distrust someone who doesn't look like ourselves is an animalistic instinct we have to fight against, not make excuses for.

Jacob Trussell

It's interesting how biker culture, like everything else in *The Twilight Zone*, was a direct response to World War II. When soldiers returned to civilian life they began to miss the exhilaration of combat, so driving motorcycles became a thrill seeking activity. Hamner, Jr. was drafted into the Army so he perhaps saw something of himself in these bikers which allowed his story to come from a place of compassion, rather than contempt, for this burgeoning counterculture.

Zone Fact

The inspiration for this episode can be felt in other films and television series' that play with the idea of otherworldly bikers, from the Japanese film by Tetsuro Takeuchi Wild Zero to the animated 1990s cartoon Biker Mice from Mars!

"Night Call"
Episode 19
Original Airdate: February 7, 1964

Directed by Jacques Tourneur
Written by Richard Matheson

"According to the Bible, God created the Heavens and the Earth. It is man's prerogative—and woman's—to create their own particular and private Hell. Case in point, Miss Elva Keene, who in every sense has made her own bed and now must lie in it, sadder, but wiser, by dint of a rather painful lesson in responsibility, transmitted from the Twilight Zone."

Miss Elva Keene (Gladys Cooper) has been receiving a series of increasingly unsettling phone calls. Because the calls are just static, Elva and her housekeeper (Nora Marlowe) believe that it's simply a faulty connection. That is until Elva begins hearing a man's voice on the other end of the line asking, "Hello? Where are you?" When she replies, there's no answer. Becoming increasingly disturbed, Elva learns that the phone company has traced the calls to a fallen line in a cemetery. The line rests on a gravestone that is set to flood Elva with haunting memories she long thought lost.

As much as I love "Night Call," the conceit would have to be drastically changed in the 21st century. "Night *Robocall*" anyone? With our phone's getting spammed by scam artists and telemarketers 24/7, how could we ever discern what is the ghost of a long dead lover trying to make contact, and some phone bank trying to give me an all-expense paid vacation in exchange for my social security number?! We couldn't, but in the antiquated days when phones were fewer and farther between, unexpected calls could bring a pang of anxiety like they do in Elva. See, it's not just a millennial thing to get stressed over a random unwarranted phone call! That anxiety is only made more palpable when the voice on the other end of the line seems to have come from the bowels of hell.

The real star of "Night Call" is the creative team which features two titans of horror, series writer Richard Matheson and Jacques Tourneur, director of horror classics like *Cat People* and *Night of the*

Demon. Tourneur's usage of shadow and light is legendary, inspiring generations of horror filmmakers, from Steven Spielberg to James Wan and his *Insidious* series. The one two punch of his steady hand, and Matheson's dark melancholy, are perfectly attuned for an episode dealing in classic themes of the show like aging and death. While the old woman isn't sure who the calls are coming from at the beginning, death hangs over each like a dark cloud. It could be a ghost, or the grim reaper itself, but we're sure it's someone attempting to make contact from the beyond.

This chilling story is one of quiet sadness as Elva resigns herself to the facts of her past. It leaves you with a wistful pit in your stomach with the knowledge that you too one day will be that woman, reflecting back on your life. Let's hope it's not with the same regrets.

Zone Fact

Richard Matheson's original short story ended far differently, with the voice Elva hears not being from her late fiancé, but from something more inhuman that tells her, "Hello, Mrs. Keene. I'll be right over."

An Unofficial Journey Into The Twilight Zone

"From Agnes – With Love"
Episode 20
Original Airdate: February 14, 1964

Directed by Richard Donner
Written by Bernard C. Schoenfeld

> *"James Elwood: master programmer. In charge of Mark 502-741, commonly known as Agnes, the world's most advanced electronic computer. Machines are made by men for man's benefit and progress, but when man ceases to control the products of his ingenuity and imagination he not only risks losing the benefit, but he takes a long and unpredictable step into ... The Twilight Zone."*

Nerdy programmer James Elwood (Wally Cox) is the new replacement for an overworked operator of the massive supercomputer Mark 502-741, otherwise known as Agnes. Elwood uses the boosted confidence from this promotion to finally ask out Millie, a coworker he's developed a crush on. What he doesn't realize is that Agnes has developed a crush on Elwood, and she plans to drive a wedge between him and Millie. Will Elwood choose flesh and blood, or be charmed by the chromium and metal of a supercomputer with one hell of a jealous streak?

In A.I. stories, computers typically become sentient almost by accident. In science's quest to perfect a digital human mind, we accidentally unlock a will to live far more powerful than our own. If we believe Agnes wasn't sentient before, then she sprung to life because of Elwood's affections towards Millie. His feelings were so strong that they imprinted on Agnes, allowing this hyper intelligent computer to grow a burning, envious heart.

Look at the indignation Agnes expresses after Elwood friendzones her. "That's just like a mother!" he says to the computer after she offers more dating tips, only for her to reply when his back is turned "MOTHER!?" Ah, if only the scariest A.I. imaginable were jealous room-sized computers, rather than a nuclear weaponized neural network!

There's plenty of subtext to pick through in any episode of *The Twilight Zone*, but don't ruin the fun of "From Agnes—With Love" by overthinking it. When the episode originally aired, it was a silly look at what computers may bring to our life, but now it plays simply as an amusing reflection on what could have been. If tech continued down that path, our modern dating apps may have looked a lot more like Agnes! She doesn't play matchmaker, but she is still a computer program offering dating advice to help Elwood win Millie's affection. It's a far cry from what apps like Tinder or Grindr ever intended to do, but it's still an interesting retro-futuristic peek at what could have been, if computers were still the size of a studio apartment.

Zone Fact

The lead in this episode, Wally Cox, may be best remembered as the voice of Underdog, as well as his close personal friendship with Marlon Brando, who retained his ashes upon Cox's death.

"Spur of the Moment"
Episode 21
Original Airdate: February 21, 1964

Directed by Elliot Silverstein
Written by Richard Matheson

"You know the expression, "Go chase yourself"? Wells that's what I've been doing ... chasing myself."

Anne Henderson (Diana Hyland) is a person split in two. Confronted by a crazed woman dressed in black, she quickly races away, narrowly making it back home to tell her parents and fiancé Robert (Robert J. Hogan) what happened. As they leave to go find this mysterious woman, Anne's old flame David (Roger Davis) turns up unannounced. Despite her silence, David declares his love for Anne once more, before her father sends him away. Twenty-five years later, having forgotten that fateful day, Anne is now bitter and in a loveless marriage to an alcoholic. What decision did she make almost three decades before that led her here, and does it have to do with the lingering haunted memory of that mysterious screaming woman?

Despite Season Five being full of straight up bangers, it still manages to have some of the most obscure episodes of the entire series. Case in point: "Spur of the Moment," a strange little story about future anxieties, past regrets, and the oppressive power of young love. When I was a teen, getting a girlfriend was more important to me than anything—over college or even leaving my small, one-light town. I couldn't see beyond my immediate years, nor could I truly fathom how much of my life I had yet to live. But you can't explain that concept to a teen, because they won't listen; they need to make mistakes when they're young to truly appreciate what they have when they're older. Luckily, not all of our youthful mistakes have such dire consequences as they do for Anne Henderson.

Anne becomes her own self-fulfilling prophecy, a specter haunting her own past, destined to always fail to warn her younger self about the future. It's a great twist that Anne's life was ruined by following her heart, rather than by marrying a man likely chosen for her. You can't exactly blame Anne for marrying David, because in the moment, wouldn't you have done the same? By following her heart, she was able to make a claim on her own individuality, which is what makes this twist so tragic. The one choice she makes for herself turns out to be the worst choice of her life. I have this funny feeling that Richard Matheson wrote this episode with his own daughters in mind, as some gentle paternal ribbing on what may happen if they don't follow his dating advice!

Zone Fact

This episode was later referenced in Gilmore Girls as the character of Lorelai voices her anxiety over getting married.

"An Occurrence at Owl Creek Bridge"
Episode 22
Original Airdate: February 28, 1964

Directed by Robert Enrico
Written by Robert Enrico (from a story by Ambrose Bierce)

> *"This is the stuff of fantasy, the thread of imagination... the ingredients of The Twilight Zone"*

Peyton Farquhar (Roger Jacquet), a Confederate sympathizer during The Civil War is caught attempting to burn down a Union controlled bridge. For his crimes, he has been sentenced to death by hanging on the very overpass he attempted to destroy. As they bind his hands and feet, and slip a noose around his neck, he dreams of his family and the life he will be forced to leave behind. As he falls, waiting for the snap of his neck, the rope breaks and he plummets deep into the water below him. He frees himself, dodging Union bullets, and escapes into the nearby forest to get back to his family. Has Farquhar successfully escaped, or is this nothing more than the fantasy of a dying man?

As Serling tells us in the snippet of narration he gives at the episode's end, "An Occurrence at Owl Creek Bridge" literally *is* the ingredients of *The Twilight Zone*. We know that Serling was greatly influenced by his time spent in the war, but the series had numerous literary influences as well. You can see the show draw inspiration from H.P. Lovecraft to H.G. Wells, so undoubtedly Serling was a fan of Ambrose Bierce's work as one of the most influential horror and weird fiction authors of the late 19th century.

Perhaps what also drew Serling to Bierce, was that they were both veterans-turned-writers, with Bierce having served as a First Lieutenant in the Union Army during The Civil War. Both men brought their own experiences of combat to their writing, with "Occurrence" having a strong anti-war subtext. There are no heroics like you'd see in books or films, about brave and cunning soldiers trapped behind enemy lines. There are no superheroes—there's just bullet-riddled bodies and men hanging from the ends of ropes. Bierce gives us the hard truths of war, but fed to us with the sweetness of genre storytelling.

Jacob Trussell

The episode itself is visually breathtaking, and a welcome departure from the film quality we've come to expect over the last four seasons. The cinematography is crisp and has a striking use of composition and slow motion photography that helps the forest come to life, like serenely watching a spider weave a web over a quiet folksy song. It's also memorable for its lack of sound, focusing more on diegetic noises of the forest as a way to immerse us into the story. We feel just as full of wonder as Farquahar is to the lushness of the natural world, which he sees as if for the first time. "An Occurrence at Owl Creek Bridge" is a wholly unique vision of a different type of terror on the outer rim of *The Twilight Zone*.

Zone Fact:

Not only did this short film win an award at Cannes for best short subject film, but it also won best short film at that year's Academy Awards.

"Queen of the Nile"
Episode 23
Original Airdate: March 6, 1964

Directed by John Brahm
Written by Charles Beaumont

"Everyone knows Pamela Morris, the beautiful and eternally young movie star. Or does she have another name, even more famous, an Egyptian name from centuries past? It's best not to be too curious, lest you wind up like Jordan Herrick, a pile of dust and old clothing discarded in the endless eternity of The Twilight Zone."

Jordan Herrick (Lee Phillips) is a newspaperman writing a column on movie star Pamela Morris (Anne Blyth) who lives with her elderly mother Viola (Ceila Lovsky) in a palatial estate adorned with Egyptian iconography. Over the course of his visit, Jordan becomes charmed by Pamela, who invites his advances much to the worry of her mother. When the mother claims that Pamela is much older than she says she is, Jordan starts looking into Pamela's past to uncover the secret of her ageless beauty. What Jordan doesn't know is that he may not like the process for how Pamela has tapped into the fountain of youth.

In 1961, the exhibit Tutankhamen Treasures toured the globe for six straight years, sparking an immense interest in ancient Egypt and its artifacts, mythology, and lore. It was only inevitable that a genre television show like *The Twilight Zone* would mine the depths of this modern fascination with the dead.

This episode is credited to Charles Beaumont, but due to his illness he only helped develop the story with Jerry Sohl, who would ghostwrite the teleplay. Despite this, "Queen of the Nile" is still teeming with Beaumont's genius, especially for adapting ancient evils to modern society, like he did in "The Jungle." Classic Beaumont hinges on the oppressive, practically Lovecraftian terror his characters exert over others. Don't expect tentacle monsters, but the reverence that Lovecraft's protagonists have for his cosmic aberrations is mirrored in elderly Viola's mythic fear of Pamela. In turn, it's how the audience is meant to view her, with a mix of anxiety and anguish.

Jacob Trussell

Personified by the score, the fear Pamela wields feels almost too big for one single person. As we come to find out, she isn't exactly a person anymore. More than immortal, Pamela acts like a vampire, or even a succubus. With the scarab, she uses it to suck the life force out of her suitors, before placing it onto herself to, for lack of a better term, ingest it. Pamela is cold, ruthless, and combined with her immortality, she becomes wildly formidable. Her powers are made even worse by how much she relishes in them, like when she arrogantly spells out her queen status for Herrick as he succumbs to the poison.

The events of the episode are foreshadowed in the opening moments, as we see the shady glances Viola casts at Pamela, immediately putting the audience on guard for both of these characters. But despite the foreshadowing, nothing in the strangely dark episode would prepare us for *easily* the most metal image from any episode of The Twilight Zone. As Herrick succumbs to Pamela's poison, we watch as his body ages rapidly until it's nothing but a skeleton. As the music swells, his skull slowly begins to separate, cracking into three pieces. It's unexpected, gnarly, and could easily be the cover art for a Scandinavian black metal band.

Zone Fact

The scarab that Pamela Morris wears was a symbol of immortality in ancient Egyptian culture.

An Unofficial Journey Into The Twilight Zone

"What's in the Box"
Episode 24
Original Airdate: March 13, 1964

Directed by Richard L. Bare
Written by Martin M. Goldsmith

> *"Portrait of a TV fan. Name: Joe Britt. Occupation: cab driver. Tonight, Mr. Britt is going to watch "a really big show," something special for the cabbie who's seen everything."*

Joe and Phyllis Britt (William Demarest, Joan Blondell) live in a loveless marriage in modern, 1960s New York City. After returning from a long shift driving his taxi, Joe gets hit with philandering accusations from Phyllis, and he vents his steam directly at the television repairman. Annoyed at this, the repairman "fixes" the set before leaving him with a knowing smile. Joe discovers that his TV now only picks up one station—one that broadcasts visions of his past and present, and offering deadly predictions for his future. When he confides in Phyllis with what he's been seeing, she consults a physician who believes it's stemmed from her husband's obsession with television. Are these simply the delusions of an overactive imagination, or has a mischievous repairman created a domino effect that'll lead directly to tragedy?

 Stop me if you've heard this one before: "If you sit too close to that TV, you'll ruin your eyes!" or "Television will rot your brain!" If you're a product of the late 1980s like I am, these are familiar refrains thrown out by parents and politicians on why we should be wary of spending too much time getting sucked into the boob tube. Similar to what's still happening today with the internet and smartphones, doctors and physicians of the '60s began to theorize the psychological ramifications of too much TV, a decade after there was a set in every home.

 Without a lick of irony, Dr. Saltman (Herbert Lytton) asks Phyllis, "Is your husband a TV addict?" He explains that people can have delusions due to our over stimulated modern culture. But there's a big difference between daydreaming about your favorite show and the straight up hallucinations Joe experiences. This isn't *just* an

Jacob Trussell

overactive imagination, but a plot that intellectual audiences of the 1960s would have found just as cheesy as if we saw a show today about a YouTube channel that could predict the future.

The clue to this being a pointed bit of satire is that Dr. Saltman confesses to Phyllis that this isn't his diagnosis, but rather he's just parroting something he read. There are questions about morality and guilt at the center of this episode, but it's mostly a darkly humorous razzing from writer Martin Goldsmith and Rod Serling about the kind of manufactured hysteria over the industry they found a home in.

Zone Fact

The TV repairman that acts as the inciting incident for the episode is none other than the voice of Winnie the Pooh!

An Unofficial Journey Into The Twilight Zone

"The Masks"
Episode 25
Original Airdate: March 20, 1964

Directed by Ida Lupino
Written by Rod Serling

"Mr. Jason Foster, a tired ancient who on this particular Mardi Gras evening will leave the Earth. But before departing, he has some things to do, some services to perform, some debts to pay—and some justice to mete out."

Jason Foster (Robert Keith) is a wealthy, dying man who believes that at midnight he will inevitably pass away. His admission comes on the eve of his daughter and her family visiting him—a detestable group of shitheels who salivate at the prospect of finally earning Jason's hefty inheritance. However, if they are going to get that money, they will have to play a little game on the night of Mardi Gras: they must wear grotesque masks of his choosing until the clock chimes 12 o'clock. Jason, donning his own Red Death mask, sees through his family's selfish, sociopathic ways, and he intends to make sure everyone else does as well.

Ida Lupino, who made her *Twilight Zone* debut in "The Sixteen Millimeter Shrine" (S1E4), returns to the show, but this time behind the lens. Lupino would become the first and only female director on the series until Martha Coolidge (*Valley Girl*) and Shelley Levinson (*Violet*) would direct segments of the 1985 revival. She may have been the first female director in series history, but this was no big break for Lupino. She had been working consistently behind the lens since the late 1940s, becoming the first female film noir director with 1950's *Never Fear,* before going on to have a healthy career shooting TV shows like *The Donna Reed Show, Have Gun - Will Travel*, and *Alfred Hitchcock Presents.* Luckily for us, Lupino was chosen to direct one of the all-time great episodes of *The Twilight Zone.*

In cadence with Season Five's lack of subtext, "The Masks" doesn't beat around the bush as to what they are trying to say about this family's greed and lack of compassion. They don't really need the masks to show their true faces, as they are as ugly on the outside

Jacob Trussell

as they are on the inside. The ugliness of their personality shines bright as we see their clear distaste and annoyance at their dying grandfather. They just want their money without having to do any of the emotional heavy-lifting.

Even though the ending feels forecast from the very beginning, it still doesn't rob the episode of its devilishly delicious conclusion as the dysfunctional family finds their interior selves matching their exteriors as their faces now reflect the masks. Even schadenfreude can be found in *The Twilight Zone*.

Zone Fact

This would be Robert Keith's final performance.

"I Am the Night—Color Me Black"
Episode 26
Original Airdate: March 27, 1964

Directed by Abner Biberman
Written by Rod Serling

> *"A sickness known as hate. Not a virus, not a microbe, not a germ—but a sickness nonetheless, highly contagious, deadly in its effects. Don't look for it in the Twilight Zone—look for it in a mirror. Look for it before the light goes out altogether."*

Sheriff Koch (Michael Constantine) can't sleep, because his conscience is troubled by a looming execution. The remorseless accused murderer, Jagger (Terry Becker) claims he killed a "cross burner" in self-defense, to save the life of a Black man who was about to be lynched. The entire town, from Koch's deputy (George Lindsey) to his wife (Eve McVeagh), takes a sick interest in the coming hanging, showing cruel excitement at the prospect of watching someone die. A reporter (Paul Fix) inquiring about Jagger accuses the Sheriff's department of fabricating the reports and damning the murderer, just so Koch could ensure his re-election. On the morning of the execution the sun doesn't rise, and a dark shadow is cast over the town. The darkness spreads, not only across the town, but anywhere in the world that hate exists.

It's disheartening that arguably the most important episode of *The Twilight Zone* is overlooked when considering the best of the series. I have the sneaking suspicion that it's purposefully been forgotten, because the themes in "I Am the Night" are uncomfortably relevant, especially today. I'm certain Rod Serling's message about hate and white supremacy turned off many a bigoted viewer when the episode initially aired in 1964.

That's of course *if* the bigots of the world were smart enough to comprehend the damning narrative about a man accused of murdering a "cross burner." But execution shouldn't make us salivate; it should make us sick to our stomachs. That loathsome feeling is what separates us from the wolves, a point Jagger makes to the reporter Mr. Colby. The difference between the town's zeal and Jagger's murder is that Jagger didn't enjoy killing, he just did what he had to do to save an innocent man's life. The town, though, wants to feel ok about their own barbarity, so they goad Jagger to admit that he relished in the murder, coaxed by a Black reverend (Ivan Dixon) walking his own tightrope as a prominent Black man in a clearly racist community.

When Mr. Colby confronts Sheriff Koch and his Deputy about the falsified arrest reports, I was reminded of the injustices surrounding Breonna Taylor's murder. Just like how Koch left out key facts that would have proven what Jagger did was in self-defense, the Louisville Metro police department reported nothing that happened the night Taylor was shot. This episode is a stark reminder that corruption and law enforcement have been intertwined for generations.

Another strong moment comes from a line Mr. Colby gives when he visits Jagger in jail: "You can't go around dispensing people's lives because they offend you." Watching someone about to be lynched isn't something you're *offended* by, it's something that should horrify you. We're talking about human suffering here, not some bad joke. Using the word "offended" is an attempt to minimize something monstrous to being merely trivial. Keep an ear out, because you'll hear the word continue to be weaponized today by the kind of people who want to spew hate without so much as a challenge.

Rod Serling punches you in the gut with his ending narration. The horror we just witnessed is worse than anything we'll find in *The Twilight Zone*. These kinds of atrocities only exist in our world, and the heartbreaking reality is that over six decades later, nothing has changed. We have to wonder, will it ever? I look outside my New York apartment and see protests marching through the streets for Black lives just as 60 years before in the Civil Rights Movement. Maybe this time will be different. Maybe this time we'll finally see permanent, lasting societal change. Or maybe we'll look back at these words and frown. Let's hope not.

Zone Fact
The episode was written in direct response to JFK's assassination just a few short months earlier. The event is even referenced on the news radio in the final moment.

"Sounds and Silences"
Episode 27
Original Airdate: April 3, 1964

Directed by Richard Donner
Written by Rod Serling

> *"This is Roswell G. Flemington...a noisy man, one of a breed who substitutes volume for substance, sound for significance, and shouting to cover up the readily apparent phenomenon that he is nothing more than an overweight and aging perennial Sea Scout whose noise-making is in inverse ratio to his competence and to his character."*

Ex-Navy serviceman Roswell G. Flemington (John McGiver) owns a toy model company that he leads like a warship. Roswell originally joined the Navy to escape his tyrannical mother who silenced him throughout childhood, so as an act of rebellion, he now lives his life to the fullest—and the loudest—dismissing anyone who balks at this quirk. After finally pushing his wife away, his world is turned upside down when he's assaulted by incredible noises coming from the smallest of sources, where squeaky shoes sound like screeching violins and leaky faucets go off like Gatling guns. Is his condition due to psychological stress from unresolved past and present trauma? Or is this cosmic karma just long overdue retribution?

John McGiver plays a man who seems to be bursting at the seams with energy, but awash with nerves. He isn't acting like the archetypal nervous Nellie, instead funneling those shaky emotions through his need to be unforgivingly loud. He stomps when he should walk, slams instead of closes, shouts when he should speak, and rather than music he blares the sounds of guns and explosions to remind him of the Navy. This insistence causes rifts in every facet of his life, and ultimately what leads to his quasi-supernatural affliction.

What happens to him seems otherworldly, even though it's really not. Roswell explains as much when he confesses to his wife, that his penchant for raucousness is spurned from a borderline abusive relationship with his mother. She even denied her kids cookies because they crunch too loudly, instead favoring a chewier, and far quieter dessert like brownies.

His mommy issues are the source of the psychosomatic episode he has with his hearing, but I think his emotions could be exacerbated by his own lack of willingness to talk about past traumas. Like every man subject to toxic masculinity, he'd rather suffer in silence with pride than show a side of him he might consider weak—because society has told him it's a weakness.

That's why his wife seems surprised when she learns about why he is the way he is. It's quietly sad that she is just now learning this integral aspect of his personality. He's been carrying this burden for so long, and if he had felt more comfortable being open with his wife, he may not be on the precipice of exploding. "Sounds and Silences" speaks once again to Serling's overall point with the series: discuss your mental health issues or risk your world rocking and swaying like the bow of a warship.

Zone Fact

Was not part of the original syndication package for the series as it was the subject of a plagiarism lawsuit when it first aired.

"Caesar and Me"
Episode 28
Original Airdate: April 10, 1964

Directed by Robert Butler
Written by Adele T. Strassfield

> *"A lethal dummy in the shape of a man. But everybody knows dummies can't talk—unless, of course, they learn their vocabulary in The Twilight Zone."*

Jonathan West (Jackie Cooper) is an Irish immigrant and ventriloquist, who has an act with no legs to stand on. Facing dwindling audiences with his dummy Caesar, Jonathan begins looking for a legitimate job, only for Caesar to suddenly grow a mind—and mouth—of his own. Trying to keep his secret from a nosy young neighbor (Suzanne Cupito), the dummy urges Jonathan to make ends meet by becoming a crook. Is Caesar really alive, or has desperation changed Jonathan from the inside out?

This is the only *Twilight Zone* episode that goes all in on the living dummy trope. "Caesar and Me" makes no bones about whether the dummy is real or just a figment of Jonathan West's imagination. Unlike Willie in "The Dummy" who just tortured Cliff Robertson's mind, we get to see Caesar plainly walk on screen. This is a living and breathing block of wood. But that isn't to say that Caesar's will to live didn't come from Jonathan's psyche. The dummy's awakening acts as the kick in the pants Jonathan needs to try and make something for himself in life, even if that means becoming a small-time criminal to match Caesar's hoodlum persona.

Before he decides to rob a delicatessen, Jonathan tries to think of another way to make money, but Caesar yells at him to drop the "Irish Shanty" act because this is America. He's forced into a life of crime because, as an immigrant, he can't find legitimate work. Why? Because prejudice, duh! It's not the thematic through line of the episode, but in the 21st century it's hard not to see correlations with the struggles immigrants still face in this country today. This is compounded by America's penchant for racism, as immigrants today don't have the fair skin of this Irish ventriloquist. The episode would be even more provocative and poignant if we reimagine Jonathan as a modern immigrant escaping a war-torn country, only to be met with hostility when trying to rebuild their life in the United States.

Zone Fact

This is the only episode written by a woman, Adele T. Strassfield, who would go on to write episodes of Gilligan's Island and Insight, a religious-themed anthology show.

"The Jeopardy Room"
Episode 29
Original Airdate: April 17, 1964

Directed by Richard Donner
Written by Rod Serling

"His name is Major Ivan Kuchenko. He has, if events go according to certain plans, perhaps three or four more hours of living. But an ignorance shared by both himself and his executioner, is of the fact that both of them have taken the first step into The Twilight Zone."

Major Ivan Kuchenko (Martin Landau) is an ex-KGB agent attempting to defect from the Soviet Union, by passing through an unnamed neutral country. He is found by Commissar Vassiloff (John van Dreelen), who plans to assassinate him, but not before playing a little game. Rather than just simply shooting Kuchenko, Vassiloff wants him to suffer. Upon waking in a strange hotel room, Kuchenko plays a tape left for him of Vassiloff explaining that the room is rigged to explode, but he can save himself by finding the booby trap before three hours are up. Will Kuchenko find the bomb in time, or is Vassiloff destined to become a player in his own game?

Perhaps the biggest takeaway from "The Jeopardy Room" is how un-*Twilight Zone* it feels. It's very well-written by Serling, immaculately directed by all-time great Richard Donner, and it features strong performances from Martin Landau and John van Dreelen. But for all of this class and talent, it lacks the one thing that really brings the series together: the fantastical signpost that tells us we're in *The Twilight Zone*. There's no dystopian future, horny computers, blood hungry machines, or even a little bit of magical realism; this is just a pure psychological thriller, a game of cat-and-mouse like Serling spells out in the opening narration. This verisimilitude is why "The Jeopardy Room" is a highlight of Season Five, even if it's overshadowed by the slight, if not undeniable, influence this episode has over a film that feels as far removed from *The Twilight Zone* as you can imagine: *Saw*.

In the film franchise *Saw*, a serial killer named Jigsaw kidnaps people and locks them in a room where they must play an elaborate game of life and death communicated to them through a tape recorder. To win they must submit themselves to the gory, violent puzzles of a booby-trapped room. If they survive, they're free to go.

Here Kuchenko is drugged, and when he wakes, he too finds a tape recording telling him that Vassiloff wants to play a game. He has rigged the room to blow, and if Kuchenko is able to solve the puzzle, he'll be allowed to leave with his life. So let's go over that again. Both have a killer saying "I'd like to play a game" before telling their victims via tape that they have a time limit to escape. While there are no elaborate traps on display like in *Saw*, the tenants of what made James Wan and Leigh Whannel's splatter franchise such a monumental success are all here. Except in *Saw*, the villain wants to teach his victims a lesson about the value of life. In *The Twilight Zone*, it's basically to remind you of how evil the Soviet Union was.

Zone Fact

One of many episodes directed by Richard Donner, who would later direct the 1970s Superman, which provided the template for the modern superhero movie.

"Stopover in a Quiet Town"
Episode 30
Original Airdate: April 24, 1964

Directed by Ron Winston
Written by Earl Hamner, Jr.

"I'm gonna tell them I'm tired of their creepy little town! And I'll pay anyone anything they want to get us on the next bus, train or plane."

After a night of heavy partying, married couple Bob and Millie Frazier (Barry Nelson, Nancy Malone) wake up in a strange house in an unfamiliar neighborhood. As they try and find anyone who can tell them where they are, they begin to notice peculiarities around them, like phony phones and fake squirrels. Their desperation grows when they realize the one train out of town just circles back around to stop where they started. Did they die and this is their purgatory, or is this small town smaller than they think?

"Stopover in a Quiet Town" has a plot that feels influenced by multiple past episodes of the series, like the disorienting isolation of "Where is Everybody?" or the fatalistic dread of "Five Characters in Search of an Exit." This episode though is a far more entertaining watch that's a teensy bit more compelling, thanks to the very realistic dynamics between our two leads.

Bob and Millie have found themselves in a strange place, but that doesn't change the reality of their relationship issues. In a way, this supernatural occurrence acts as a therapeutic couple's retreat where they are able to work out their problems without the stresses of the real world. The couple become closer through this shared experience, so in a way, despite the horrifying ending, it's moderately happy! They may be stuck as the playthings of an enormous child, but at least their relationship has never been stronger!

I find that the twist is intentionally meant to dupe the keen eye of the original fans of *The Twilight Zone*. As I mentioned, we've seen episodes just like this before, so certainly they would have guessed what the wife eventually theorizes—that they died in a car accident. The only rational explanation as to why they have no memory is that they are stuck in a kind of purgatory.

Jacob Trussell

But nope! Earl Hamner, Jr. pulls the rug from under us and treats us to a giant alien the spitting image of a human child. Just like you wouldn't try to explain reason to an ant, the kid doesn't attempt to explain what's happening to these adults-turned-toys. This is Hamner, Jr.'s expression of how truly insignificant we are in this vast cosmos. We are just a microscopic particle in the grand scheme of life. Let's just hope we never end up in the toy aisle of an intergalactic department store.

Zone Fact

Proving just how far reaching the series' influence was, this episode plot was loosely adapted for the Pokémon episode, "Abra and the Psychic Showdown."

"The Encounter"
Episode 31
Original Airdate: May 1, 1964

Directed by Robert Butler
Written by Martin M. Goldsmith

"Two men in an attic, locked in mortal embrace. Their common bond, and their common enemy: guilt. A disease all too prevalent amongst men both in and out of The Twilight Zone."

Fenton (Neville Brand), a veteran, discovers in his attic a samurai sword he brought home from the war. But no matter what Fenton tries to do, the sword keeps finding its way back into his possession. Etched on the blade in Japanese are the words, "This sword will avenge me." Enter Arthur Takamori (George Takei), a Japanese-American looking for work. His visit causes friction, as Fenton tells Arthur that the sword belonged to a Japanese soldier he killed. Realizing they've become trapped in the attic together, Arthur is drawn to the sword, feeling compelled to reap the vengeance engraved in its steel. As both men share secrets over beer, tensions crescendo to a deadly confrontation that began in the past and has now boiled over into the future.

The Twilight Zone is both known, and not known, for its subtlety. Where others are slyer in their intentions, episodes like "The Shelter," "I Am The Night—Color Me Black," and "The Encounter" have no qualms with putting their critique of bigotry and fear front and center. Here, Serling and writer Martin M. Goldsmith use themes of dogmatism and intolerance to highlight the grudges that Americans held against the Japanese following World War II.

"The Encounter" also emphasizes the complexity of being Japanese-American post-World War II. Both Arthur and George Takei have traumatic pasts tied to the war. For Arthur, it's because he watched his own father assist Japanese forces bombing Pearl Harbor, but for Takei it's because his family was sent to American internment camps. Takei's life is intrinsically entwined with the war, so the vividly real emotions he brings to Arthur put us right in his shoes.

Much like the weaponized usage of the word "offended" in "I

Am The Night—Color Me Black," Fenton telling Arthur that he's "too darn sensitive" to his racial epithets feels *so* relevant today. How many times have you heard political talking heads parrot out the word "snowflake" when someone gets upset by racist jokes or cultural stereotypes? That you aren't allowed to feel that way, because you're "too sensitive." When Fenton says this to Arthur, he may as well have said "Why can't you take a joke! It's not all about skin color!" But it has everything to do with Arthur's race. By trying to deflect, Fenton attempts to erase part of his identity. It's why terms like "I don't see color" are problematic. It's a phrase that diminishes the lived-in history of a non-white person. It's a term that let's someone off the hook for their own implicit biases, but allies can't afford to be color blind. They have to be aware that when your skin color isn't the standard people historically were told to aspire to, your race becomes central to your identity.

After being called "boy," Arthur demands to be called by his name, but eventually relents and gives a half-hearted apology for becoming angry. This is the insidiousness of ingrained racism. You don't have to be kneeling on a Black man's neck to be a bigot. You can call someone a boy, or use callous language like Fenton toasting Arthur with "Banzai!" It's not the uncompromised violence, but the subtle derision that continues the tide of racism.

Zone Fact

The racial overtones of the episode made it so controversial that it was never sold into syndication packages with the rest of the series.

"Mr. Garrity and the Graves"
Episode 32
Original Airdate: May 8, 1964

Directed by Ted Post
Written by Rod Serling (from a story by Mike Korologos)

"And Mr. Garrity, if one can believe him, is a resurrecter of the dead—which, on the face of it, certainly sounds like the bull is off the nickel. But to the scoffers amongst you, and you ladies and gentlemen from Missouri, don't laugh this one off entirely, at least until you've seen a sample of Mr. Garrity's wares, and an example of his services."

Mr. Garrity (John Dehner) rides into Happiness, Arizona, offering the townsfolk something beyond their wildest dreams; he promises to resurrect every person buried in the town cemetery, whether they like it or not! At first optimistic to the idea of their loved ones returning, the town soon grows wary once Mr. Garrity reminds them that the dead may have died holding more than a few grudges. Seeing evidence of his godlike powers, the town quickly coughs up every nickel and dime they have to quell the coming zombie apocalypse. But is Mr. Garrity nothing but a charlatan, or does he wield cosmic powers unlike he ever thought possible?

The back half of the final season of *The Twilight Zone* is full of emotionally hard-hitting episodes, like "The Encounter" and "I Am The Night—Color Me Black," but that doesn't mean that the series concluded on a dour note. Case in point: "Mr. Garrity and the Graves." This is a fun, darkly humorous episode from Rod Serling that feels like he's pulling inspiration from his top three writers. It has Earl Hamner Jr.'s worldbuilding, Richard Matheson's inventiveness and Charles Beaumont's trademark malaise packed together in the palatable way that Rod Serling delivered all of his moral social messaging. Hamner's world building gives unique characteristics to the ensemble cast, Matheson's inventiveness births the episode's gimmick of Garrity blackmailing the town by raising their abusive wives and philandering husbands from the grave, while Beaumont's brand of eeriness perpetuates the episode's general mood. But Serling isn't worrying about parables or allegories, he just wants to tell a rip-roaring barnburner of an episode about a two-bit con man who has more power than he gave himself credit for.

"Mr. Garrity and the Graves" is obviously meant to be funny, but Serling wrote the town's fears as being very much real. They are terrified of their loved one's coming back, and when you combine that with the shocker ending that feels plucked from *Night of the Living Dead*, you're left with a weird pit in your stomach. As if maybe you shouldn't have laughed so much at these peoples soon-to-be-realized misfortune.

Zone Fact

Based on a true 1873 account of a mysterious man who promised to resurrect the dead in Alta, Utah.

An Unofficial Journey Into The Twilight Zone

"The Brain Center at Whipple's"
Episode 33
Original Airdate: May 15, 1964

Directed by Richard Donner
Written by Rod Serling

"There are many bromides applicable here: 'too much of a good thing,' 'tiger by the tail,' 'as you sow so shall you reap.' The point is that, too often, Man becomes clever instead of becoming wise; he becomes inventive and not thoughtful; and sometimes, as in the case of Mr. Whipple, he can create himself right out of existence."

Mr. Whipple (Richard Deacon) is a man who likes to be on the cutting edge, especially when it comes to running his late father's manufacturing company. His focus is on mechanization, and he prides himself on the efficiency his machines bring the factory. Whipple looks for every opportunity to automate, regardless of the human toll, firing linemen and foremen with decades of experience—all in the name of cost cutting and penny pinching. Surrounded by machines and computerization, Mr. Whipple doesn't realize that he is dangerously close to becoming a victim of his own progress.

Since technological automation began, we have asked the same question, "What does this mean for the jobs of countless Americans?" Capitalism dictates that to make money, you have to work more, while cutting costs, so by the very nature of the industry, progress is always set to leave people in the lurch. Think about what happened almost 40 years ago, when automation advanced the automotive industry and countless families lost their jobs. Serling could see the writing on the wall and it's what makes "The Brain Center at Whipple's" so morose. If progress is inevitable, we need to tackle this shift head on with training programs, so that people can work alongside the machines that inevitably replace them. Our society has to find a way to counteract the greed of capitalism somehow, otherwise people—and their jobs—won't survive.

If you want to imagine what Whipple's factory would be churning out in modern times, just look towards the 2019 *Twilight Zone* revival where throughout each episode the Whipple logo is emblazoned on everything from spaceships to televisions. As we've seen in the 60 years since it aired, Whipple's robots haven't *completely* taken our jobs, but the unease at the possibility still lingers heavy in every union office across the country.

Zone Fact

Richard Deacon went to the same Binghamton New York high school as Rod Serling!

"Come Wander with Me"
Episode 34
Original Airdate: May 22, 1964

Directed by Richard Donner
Written by Anthony Wilson

"Mr. Floyd Burney, a gentleman songster in search of song, is about to answer the age-old question of whether a man can be in two places at the same time. As far as his folk song is concerned, we can assure Mr. Burney he'll find everything he's looking for, although the lyrics may not be all to his liking."

Floyd Burney (Gary Crosby) is a rockabilly traveling around the south looking for a song that'll make him a bigger star than he already is. Stopping off at a local music store turned recording studio, Floyd hears the beautiful sound of a woman (Bonnie Beecher) singing a mournful tune that he instantly knows he has to have. As he sets up his recording equipment, he doesn't see the ominous signs around him that this song is more than just music. It's his own life, and he's fated to live—and die—as the lead singer of its tragic final notes.

This episode reminds me of a scene in Dennis Hopper's counterculture classic *Easy Rider*. In the film, Hopper and Peter Fonda's characters pick up alcoholic George Hanson, played by Jack Nicholson. The trio bond over the road, but after ducking out on some small town rednecks looking for a fight, George is murdered in his sleep by a posse of good ol' boys. While we don't typically use the word lynch when it comes to the ritualistic murder of a white man, that's ostensibly still what it was. If these bigots were bold enough to do this to numerous Black men, they wouldn't have balked at doling out their evil justice to any person they "other," even Caucasian hippies. So, as the Rayford Brothers begin to hunt down Floyd, I instantly wondered how more potent the themes of this episode would have been if he was played by a young Black man rather than this white rockabilly.

This image also spoke to another underlying theme of the episode: the ravenous appropriation of cultural music by white musicians. This is most clearly seen in how white musicians appropriated blues music that rose out of African American communities, to twist it into rock and roll. Floyd doesn't care where the song came from, who it belongs to, or even what it means—he just knows he needs it. What's bitingly ironic is that because of his blind ambition, he doesn't recognize the dirge is about him.

This was the final episode of *The Twilight Zone* filmed, but it wasn't the series finale, which I think is a bullet that the show dodged. Not that this isn't a fine episode, it just doesn't have that "Oomph!" you expect from the series. It's confounding and frustrating to watch Floyd make mistake after mistake (like those accidental murders!), but the biggest of all was the writers letting us know Floyd dies in the beginning. If that had been the twist, rather than the set-up, we would have been more invested in Floyd's arc over this long twenty-five minutes.

Zone Fact

Television debut of Bonnie Beecher, the supposed inspiration for Bob Dylan's song 'Girl from the North Country,, which would later be adapted into a Broadway musical.

"The Fear"
Episode 35
Original Airdate: May 29, 1964

Directed by Ted Post
Written by Rod Serling

"The major ingredient for any recipe for fear is the unknown."

Highway Trooper Robert Franklin (Peter Mark Richman) is called to the remote home of Charlotte Scott (Hazel Court) who has been experiencing unnerving phenomena like flashing lights and strange noises. As Robert and Charlotte share hot and cold flirtatious banter, Robert decides to stay the night after his car is destroyed by something with fingerprints the size of truck tires. The next morning, discovering a gigantic footprint, they realize the mysterious presence must be gargantuan. Will they come face to face with their threat, or can looks be deceiving?

There's no question that Chris Carter, creator of *The X-Files*, was inspired by *The Twilight Zone* for his show about monsters, UFOs, and the uncharted regions of the human mind. As I rewatched the series, I was eagerly looking for a *Zone* episode that reminded me of Carter's show. What I wasn't expecting was the episode I'd find would actually be reminiscent of the stranger, funnier episodes of *The X-Files* like "Jose Chung from Outer Space" and "Clyde Bruckman's Final Repose."

The setup to "The Fear" is simple and familiar to my fellow X-Philes out there. A cop shows up to a remote cabin, because there are mysterious occurrences happening in the surrounding woods. Serling sets a brooding tone at first, but once it's revealed what's causing the disturbances, he gleefully leans into B-movie shenanigans. Even the inflatable monster that Robert shoots at the end is the spitting image of Phil Tucker's 1953 classic *Robot Monster*. I'm sure sci-fi aficionados of 1963 balked at this schlocky aesthetic, but from the 21st century lens there is something stupidly-fun about this conclusion.

That doesn't mean this popcorn episode is without substance. There's something generally inspiriting about Robert's optimism towards the small aliens, wishing them luck that the next planet they find, they'll be the giants, like a comedic companion to "The Invaders" (S2E15). As Charlotte points out, the next aliens that visit Earth could be giants themselves.

The commentary on fear is why I find the episode pairs well with "I Am The Night—Color Me Black," and its stark statements on hate. As Rod Serling says in his closing narration, fear is relative, and it depends on "who can look down and who must look up." Fear is dictated by those afraid, just like hate is dictated by those filled with it. These two emotions go hand in hand, but we can break this cycle if—like Trooper Rob—we can have a shred of optimism that there is good somewhere out there, not just in *The Twilight Zone*.

Zone Fact

Lead actor Peter Mark Richman would appear in another famous genre franchise, Friday the 13th Part VIII: Jason Takes Manhattan!

"The Bewitchin' Pool"
Episode 36
Original Airdate: June 19, 1964

Directed by Joseph M. Newman
Written by Earl Hamner, Jr.

"For this pool has a secret exit that leads to a never-neverland, a place designed for junior citizens who need a long voyage away from reality, into the bottomless regions of The Twilight Zone."

Gloria (Dee Hartford) and Gil (Tod Andrews) Sherwood probably shouldn't have had kids, but here they are with two: Sport (Mary Badham) and Jeb (Jeffrey Byron). What their parents don't know, is that Sport and Jeb have found a secret hideaway at the bottom of their pool that takes them to a magical oasis looked over by Aunt T. (Georgia Simmons), a kindly grandmother who cares for a group of children who've become lost or alone. She understands that they still have parents that love them, so she urges them to return home, while telling Sport that they will never be able to return to her if they do. But when the siblings are told that their parents are getting a divorce, the kids realize that only one place that will ever feel like home again is with Aunt T.

The final episode of *The Twilight Zone* tries its damndest to end on a saccharine note. Don't get me wrong, it certainly does—albeit a downbeat one—but you may forget that the episode begins very similarly to Season Three's "Little Girl Lost." It's eerie as you watch the parent's despair over witnessing a physical impossibility of their children disappearing in broad daylight. This episode showcases just how adept Earl Hamner, Jr. is at blending salt of the earth naturalism with fully realized supernaturalism.

Even if it starts on a sinister note, the episode is genuinely heartwarming, mainly rooted by Sport (played by Mary Badham, best known as Scout in 1962's *To Kill A Mockingbird*) and Georgia Simmons as Aunt T, who is basically peak white southern grandma stereotype. Like everything that's too sweet, this episode is likely to give you a toothache.

A modern-day cautionary tale for the fantasy of the nuclear

Jacob Trussell

family, some of the luster of "The Bewitchin' Pool" is lost in a lack of subtext. This episode is painfully clear in its intentions to be a morality tale meant to shock the bickering parents watching from home. The mother and father are *cartoonishly* terrible. Even the worst parents *should* know not to say resentful things like "we only stayed together because of you!"

For every cautionary tale there is a lesson, and Rod Serling makes no qualms about what the lesson is here. He says in his gutting closing narration: "But who can say how real the fantasy world of lonely children can become? For Jeb and Sport Sharewood, the need for love turned fantasy into reality; they found a secret place—in The Twilight Zone." The moral to me though is a little bit more direct: if it takes your children veritably dying for you to realize how much you love them, then *maybe you shouldn't have kids*.

Zone Fact

Mary Badham's voice had to be dubbed for all of her outdoor scenes by famed voice actress June Foray.

If You Watch Only One Episode

When I originally set out to write this chapter, I had in mind "Little Girl Lost" (S3E26), my personal favorite that captures the interdimensional ethos that Rod Serling describes in every opening narration. It's one of the few stories that really delivers on that feeling of traveling through another dimension of sight, sound and mind. That cosmic spirit though is merely one piece of *The Twilight Zone* puzzle. If you only have time for one episode, you should come away with a total sense of why this series was so influential and important.

The Twilight Zone is a show that teaches us about the complexities of human nature through the themes and concepts of genre storytelling, from horror to science fiction and beyond. These are modern parables with oft-times bleak twist endings that aim to shock and enlighten us, while not shying away from being pure, undeniable entertainment. If you want one episode that can epitomize all of that—and is unequivocally one of the greatest of the series—then you have to watch "To Serve Man" (S3E24).

In 1962, we learned there was life beyond our galaxy. When the Kanamits first arrived, they came with tidings of peace and prosperity. They were greeted with cautious optimism by the United Nations, grateful for these gifts, but wary of what the aliens' intentions might be. In order to uncover any ill-intentions the Kanamits may be harboring, the government conscripts codebreakers Patty (Susan Cummings) and Michael Chambers (Lloyd Bochner) to decipher a mysterious book they had left behind. As the globe reaps the benefits of the aliens' generosity and Earthlings pack into ships that ferry them to their home planet, Patty finishes her translation and makes a startling discovery. The Kanamits didn't come to our planet to save us, but to harvest us.

When "To Serve Man" first aired, audiences were already familiar with First Contact stories like *The Day the Earth Stood Still*

Jacob Trussell

(1951), but *The Twilight Zone* has the unique knack for taking well-worn ideas and looking at them from new angles. Instead of focusing on how a group of scientists, teachers, or even average Joes would react to aliens landing, "To Serve Man" expands its scope to a global team of linguists, government and military officials wanting to understand why the Kanamits came. By placing the story in modern times, we get to have an idea of what our politicians would do, right here and right now, when faced with the existential threat of not being alone in the universe.

Turns out, politicians would react like they always do, hemming and hawing over what actions the world should take while decidedly not taking any action at all.

That ironic contradiction is the clue to the gallows humor at the heart of this episode. We have such reverence for this thought-provoking show that we can completely forget *The Twilight Zone* was frequently hilarious, either in stand-alone episodes like "Cavender is Coming" (S3E36) or as moments of levity in white-knuckled narratives like "It's a Good Life" (S3E8). More often than not the humor was strictly satirical, lampooning American ideals or our government's own ineptitudes. A perfect example is early in the episode when the Secretary General asks the Kanamits if they are willing to be interrogated immediately, as there are delegates present from "most of the important countries." It shouldn't come as a surprise that the extreme spectrum of American patriotism would cause politicians to designate certain countries as less important than others but hey! At least he didn't call them shitholes.

The satire of "To Serve Man" acts as a 25-minute set up to a ruefully funny punchline. The Kanamits text being a cookbook is horrifying, but it's also *hysterical* by catching us in an "Oh, duh!" moment. We were so busy with how the characters perceived the phrase that we overlooked a *very obvious* alternative reading.

Once we're in on the joke and rewatch the episode, certain actions become even sillier. We now get why the Kanamits were so fervent about pushing Michael Chambers to eat—you've gotta fatten up your herd somehow! As the Russian ambassador waits to board the ship to the Kanamits planet, he acts like a spoiled child at a circus, chewing on a bag of peanuts and elbowing his way through the line citing "Diplomatic privileges." Serling's satirization illustrates the consequences of a politician's juvenility by making him hilariously unaware that he's about to become somebody's stew.

It's ridiculous that the Kanamits brought a cookbook to their in-person meeting with the world leaders. Is this just one big interplanetary trip to the grocery store for them? If they brought it by mistake, then it becomes even funnier! It's ludicrous in the best ways that this highly intelligent species, preparing to long-con the planet, brought the wrong file to an important meeting. How do you make that big of a mistake when you all share the same consciousness!? Some people may consider that a plot hole, but I find it is Rod Serling's way of pointing to the humor underneath the episode's skepticism towards these galactic saviors.

The ending is incredibly funny, but it doesn't make it any less gruesome. The reality of who the Kanamits are speak to the bleak pessimism that courses through so many Rod Serling stories. Unknowingly, we've traded human lives for peace on Earth, but was it worth it? We're forced to ask ourselves; would we really trade unimaginable suffering for a taste of the progress we've built dreams on? The world has already sent thousands to the slaughter by the time Patty deciphers the book, but would this revelation change anyone's minds or would the truth become politicized, dividing Kanamit skeptics from believers?

If 2020 is any indication, then that's a resounding yes.

If that happened, then the only winners *are* the Kanamits. They get to keep their homo sapien cash crop while we continue to bicker and in-fight. Only in *The Twilight Zone* should we have listened to our Soviet Union counterparts and remained wary over what kind of quid these aliens would ask in return for their quo.

The 2019 revival of *Twilight Zone* gave us the opportunity to understand the Kanamits a little better in the quasi-sequel "You Might Also Like," written and directed by Osgood Perkins (*The Blackcoat's Daughter, Gretel and Hansel*). Set in a dystopic, consumerist society we follow Mrs. Janet Warren (Gretchen Mol) as she grows increasingly worried about a series of blackouts she's having. On the day she is to pick up a nebulous, highly sought after "egg," she begins to have second thoughts, fearing the "egg" may be connected to her missing time. Determined to find out what's happening to her, Janet discovers she's being abducted nightly by a group of bulbous headed aliens: the Kanamits. Unfortunately, in "You Might Also Like" the Kanamits are treated more as a plot device than a straight continuation of "To Serve Man," even if there is a vague implication by the Queen Kanamit that the world of the episode isn't Earth, but the Kanamit home planet itself. Maybe this is what happens to everyone waiting to be devoured, or it's all just another short grift from these spaceward swindlers.

"A Small Talent for War," an episode of *The New Twilight Zone,* feels like the perfect companion piece to these dual Kanamit episodes. In it, an alien ambassador (John Glover) tells the United Nations that humanity hasn't lived up to the potential they saw millennia ago, so they have no choice but to eradicate us. World leaders beg for a single day to try and prove their intergalactic worth and, miraculously, they create unity. Unfortunately, that is the exact opposite of what the aliens wanted from us; we were meant to prove ourselves as warriors, not reveal ourselves as peacemakers. The alien leader is endlessly amused that for a world claiming to be forged in the fire of combat, all we subconsciously want is harmony. It's an ironic twist worthy of "To Serve Man," but with a dash of critical commentary on the United States combative nationalism at the height of Reagan-era politics during the run of the 1985 revival.

"To Serve Man" is required viewing because it also illustrates how widely influential *The Twilight Zone* is. You just have to look at modern pop culture to find endless in-jokes and references to the series, and "To Serve Man" specifically. The title, twist ending, and the line "It's a cookbook!" are practically necessary in any TV show that features stories about cannibalism, from *Supernatural* and *Angel*, to *Futurama* and *Millennium*.

As a child of the early '90s, I was first introduced to this episode through *The Simpsons* annual Halloween special "Treehouse of Horror." Each year the animated series would put together an anthology riffing on everything ooky and spooky, from George Romero-esque zombies taking over Springfield to James Earl Jones reading Edgar Allen Poe's *The Raven*, with Bart replacing the baleful bird.

In the segment "Hungry are the Damned," the Simpson's are abducted by tentacular aliens Kang and Kodos. As they jettison the family to their home on Rigel IV to attend a massive feast in their honor, the Simpsons are urged to gorge themselves on food, much to the suspicion of Lisa who finds a book titled "How To Cook Humans." Dismayed, she shows it to her family, questioning the aliens' true intentions for abducting them. The aliens blow dust from the cover to reveal the title actually reads, "How to Cook *for* Humans". Unconvinced, Lisa blows back more dust to reveal, "How to Cook *Forty* Humans" before the full title is revealed as "How to Cook *for* Forty Humans." Kang and Kodos show they meant no harm, but the damage is already done and the Simpsons are uncermoniously beamed home as the aliens zoom away.

It's a perfectly crafted parody that Rod Serling likely would have loved, especially considering *The Simpson*'s would go on to send up even more episodes of the original series, from "Nightmare at 5 1/2 Feet" (based on "Nightmare at 20,0000 Feet"*)* and "The Genesis Tub" (based on "The Little People*")* to "Bart's Nightmare," based on "It's a Good Life,*"* which features an opening narration in the same familiar baritone of Rod Serling. The man himself would be immortalized by the show in the opening credits of the 24th installment of "Treehouse of Horror," designed by film director Guillermo del Toro.

The influence of "To Serve Man" goes beyond parody. Denis Villeneuve, screenwriter Eric Heisserer and author Ted Chiang never explicitly stated that their 2016 film *Arrival* was inspired by this episode, but it feels impossible not to view these two different works of fiction as indelibly interconnected. *Arrival*, just like "To Serve Man", frames a First Contact story around a team of linguists trying to decipher an alien language to determine the true nature behind this life-changing encounter. Unlike the humanoid Kanamits, the squid-like Heptapods are eight-legged creatures who communicate through what can only be described as symbology. Using cloudy black ink, they can create intricately defined circles that act as complete sentences. The linguists, headed by Dr. Louise Banks (Amy Adams) and Ian Donnelly (Jeremy Renner) work to translate the heptapods language by developing simple vocabulary so they can ask complex questions like, "What is your purpose for coming to Earth?" They are pressured by the US government to work fast as the Heptapods, like the Kanamits, have visited nations across the globe who are all working to be the first to lick the code, as Patty would say. You wouldn't be wrong in assuming *Arrival* would end on a similar pessimistic note as "To Serve Man" but it subverts your expectations by giving you an optimistic—if melancholy—resolution. Louise receives the Heptapods gift of prophetic foresight, but the world was at the brink of losing it all.

Arrival offers a more realistic portrayal of how the world would react to First Contact, but it also gives us more nuanced look into how a team of terrestrial code breakers could have unlocked an alien language. This is often cited as one of the many plot holes in "To Serve Man" and is the crux to Marc Scott Zicree's criticism of the episode in his book *The Twilight Zone Companion*.

If Patty had no Rosetta Stone to work off of, then how did her team even begin translating their language? They likely took similar steps to what we see in *Arrival*, discerning patterns and redundancies that appear in every language, be it human or animal, and applying it to these aliens' words. Those patterns that Louise uses to decipher the Heptapods language are meant to indicate that language is analogous, regardless of its origins. If we are to believe that the Kanamits didn't assist Patty in the translation, we can only assume she was able to devise a vocabulary from noticing these consistent similarities.

Another plot hole commonly cited is the likelihood the Kanamits had a word with the same double meaning as the English word 'Serve,' a leap in logic we admittedly have to take to give the twist ending its cynical punch. The original short story from Damon Knight offers some clarity to this—it's one big coincidence—but I find the dual meaning speaks more towards the episode's underlying humor. Originally the book was meant to read as "To Assist Mankind," but the Kanamits unintentionally used a word that has multiple English definitions. It's cosmic irony to the highest degree.

Despite the humor, the horrifying finale illuminates the serious question at the heart of this famous episode: what are we willing to give up in our pursuit of peace on Earth? Are we willing to sacrifice human lives? We may not be sending people to factory farms on far distant planets, but what's *really* different between that and sending young adults to fight in wars? They both are about forfeiting human life on the off chance we'll achieve peace. Unlike soldiers though, the Earthlings headed to the Kanamit planet don't know they're being sent to die. Masking this morbid curiosity inside of satirical genre entertainment is why *The Twilight Zone* has persevered over all these years and why, if you only watch one episode, you have to make it "To Serve Man."

AFTER YOU WATCH

You've made it through all 73 ½ hours of *The Twilight Zone*, but your journey into the mind of Rod Serling is far from over! Across the next six decades his seminal series would see resurgences and revivals on both the small and big screen that brought the show to new, younger audiences all across the world. These continuations of Serling's mythos is simple proof of *The Twilight Zone*'s timeless relevance. We'll always have use for a show that can take us to faraway worlds as a way to enlighten our own terrestrial existence.

Welcome to the Night Gallery

The best place to start this next chapter of your binge watch is with the show's original successor, *Night Gallery*. Another genre anthology series, *Night Gallery* aired more on the side of literary weird fiction than *The Twilight Zone*'s social allegories, featuring a number of adaptations of celebrated horror and fantasy authors from H.P. Lovecraft to Margaret St. Clair. Notably absent from the series was the artistic style of *The Twilight Zone*, swapping moody art direction and impressionistic cinematography for creaky sets and very little visual appeal.

Each episode was also now an hour long, split in two so that you were essentially watching back-to-back stories the length of a typical *Twilight Zone*. The episodes would be broken up even more in the last two seasons through blackout sketches—short comic skits with a visual gag, like "Junior" where a beleaguered father (Wally Cox) is roused from bed by his young son crying for water. It's only when he hands him the glass that we realize his "son" is actually Frankenstein's Monster, neck bolts and all. It's a bit cringey, but these segments have a "gaudy Halloween decoration" quality that I find endearing, like in "An Act of

Chivalry," where a polite skeleton removes way more than his hat when a woman gets on a crowded elevator. Rod Serling though hated these lowbrow inclusions saying, "I thought they distorted the thread of what we were trying to do on *Night Gallery*."

It does pale in comparison to his earlier work, but there are still great stories in *Night Gallery,* they're just fewer and further between. Serling explores moral ambiguity of the future in "Class of 99," when a professor (Vincent Price) quizzes his students on different ethical conflicts, some of which come with deadly consequences. Luckily for the students, they're all secretly robots! Exploring similar themes to *The Twilight Zone*'s "Eye of the Beholder" (S2E6), "The Different Ones" follows a father looking to save his disfigured son from a pending execution. Sanctuary comes when the son enters a kind of foreign exchange program with a far distant planet where he's surprised to find people who look just like him. In passing he meets the man he's switching with, who looks normal by Earth standards, but is filled with the same self-loathing the son carries from being an outcast all his life. Luckily now their looks will get them quite far on their new home planets.

"Fright Night" essentially works as a riff on *The Amityville Horror* seven years before that film would be released. A couple move into a new house and are immediately besieged by malevolent spirits set to possess and terrorize them. The secret of the haunting is kept locked away inside a steamer trunk that was not to be removed from the house. Naturally, the moment the couple moves in, they haul the trunk out unlocking a psychedelic supernatural manifestation. Serling's adaptations of "Cool Air" and "Pickman's Model" do an effective job at mimicking a specific kind of Lovecraftian horror that's not your typical cosmic tentacle monster imagery. Ironically "Cool Air" is quite stuffy, despite a satisfyingly gruesome ending, while "Pickman's Model" fares better if only for the giant rat monster at the episode's end. The make-up here would garner *Night Gallery* one of its few Emmy nominations, the second of which was a writing nod for "They're Tearing Down Tim Riley's Bar," a classic Serling yarn about a burnt-out businessman trying in vain to cling to the past.

If you are looking for *Night Gallery* at it's spookiest you could check out "A Fear of Spiders," where a tarantula the size of a dog terrorizes an arachnophobic. A malevolent doll that is so horrifying it's practically comical is at the center of "The Doll," an adaptation of an

Algernon Blackwood story about a Victorian-era British colonist who is gifted the cursed object after returning from India. In his first Rod Serling venture since *Playhouse 90*'s "The Velvet Alley," Leslie Nielsen stars in "A Question of Fear" as an adventurer who places a $10,000 bet that he can last one night in a haunted house. Turns out, the specters of war are far more frightening than your average poltergeist. Stephen King has referred to "The Caterpillar" as the most chilling episode of the series, and he's right. Who isn't completely horrified by the thought of an earwig burrowing into your eardrum and leaving behind a nest of eggs? All of us; we're all horrified.

The series did, however, have occasional dips into territory so bizarre that it became comical. "Brenda" follows a budding 12 year-old sociopath who becomes emotionally attached to a real-life monster that she traps in a pit at her family's beach house. "Nature of the Enemy" gives us an answer to a question we never thought to ask: "If the moon is made of cheese, wouldn't that attract space mice?" A mortician gets an offer he can't refuse in "The Funeral," when a vampire wishes to stage his own wake and a cadre of creatures come to pay their last respects. Most inventive of all is "Professor Peabody's Last Lecture," starring Carl Reiner as the titular teacher who accidentally summons The Great Old Ones while schooling his class on the ins and outs of the Cthulhu Mythos. Not only is it a treat to hear those unpronounceable names spoken aloud, but it's also one of the earliest representations of Lovecraft's work on television.

Much like *The Twilight Zone,* the best part about *Night Gallery* was Serling himself. Surrounding by a cavern of ghoulish and gorgeous paintings, his opening narration has the same kind of panache you'd expect in the *Zone*, but now injected with a trifle more impish, self-deprecating humor like this opening bit from an early episode: "For those of you who've never met me, you might call me the under-nourished Alfred Hitchcock."

The third season of *Night Gallery* would be padded out with episodes of a completely separate series called *The Sixth Sense*, an *X-Files*-esque show about a team of paranormal investigators, before being summarily cancelled in 1973. Following his death, Serling's work would lie dormant until *The Twilight Zone* was revived as a feature film from Steven Spielberg, who got a big career break when Serling fought for him to direct the pilot of *Night Gallery*.

Jacob Trussell

Entering The New Twilight Zone

The importance of *Twilight Zone: The Movie* (1983) is mainly being a marker on the roadmap of the show's second life. In the 20 years following its cancellation, the series grew in popularity, which led to enough interest to warrant a feature film. As producer, Spielberg brought together some of the most fiercely original voices in genre filmmaking at the time, passionate about bringing classic episodes and brand new stories to life. But due to on-set negligence—and a profound lack of compassion that Serling likely would have been abhorrent to—actor Vic Morrow and two children were accidentally killed while filming an action sequence in John Landis' opening segment.

The ensuing fallout from the tragedy cast a black cloud over the entire film, with endings being rewritten and Spielberg almost walking away from the project entirely. Initially, he was set to film a second original story about a bully pursued by real life monsters on Halloween night, before turning his eyes towards a remake of "The Monsters are Due on Maple Street." He ultimately chose George Clayton Johnson's modest (and controversy-free) story "Kick the Can."

It's my personal belief that the movie should not have continued filming, let alone been released, because it's impossible to extrapolate the malfeasance on that set with what we're seeing on screen. The only positive to come from the film was seeing the uncompromised visions of Joe Dante (*Gremlins*) and George Miller (*Mad Max*) in their big budget remakes of "It's a Good Life" and "Nightmare at 20,000 Feet." What this film ultimately did was show the inherent profitability of the series, leading directly to network executives green lighting the first television revival of *The Twilight Zone* in 1985.

Prior to 1985, there had been plenty of shows that riffed on Serling's work. During the run of the original series, CBS produced the Roald Dahl-led *Way Out*, sometimes referred to as *Dahl's House of Horrors* as a companion piece to *The Twilight Zone*'s Friday night timeslot. In the final year of the original run, *The Outer Limits* premiered with chilling, fourth-wall breaking narration almost as iconic as Serling's own, "There is nothing wrong with your television. Do not attempt to adjust the picture."

The dramatic genre anthology format waned after *Night Gallery* and there was a dearth of inventive shows through the early 1980s, most lasting only one season like William Castle's *Ghost Story* or the James Coburn-hosted *Darkroom*. The only series that showed a modicum of popularity was in the UK with ITV's *Tales of the Unexpected*. Unconnected to the Quinn Martin series of the same name, this *Tales* was yet another attempt at bringing Roald Dahl's weird fiction to life—and it worked. The show ran for a staggering nine seasons.

Stateside, the style began to have a resurgence in 1983 with HBO's *The Hitchhiker*—a sleazier take on genre anthologies—and George Romero's *Tales from the Darkside*. Effectively an extension of his E.C. Comics film *Creepshow*, the series had a modest budget with an all-star cast that made it one of the first anthology series since *Night Gallery* to run multiple seasons. That is until 1985 with the debut of two shows: Steven Spielberg's *Amazing Stories* and *The New Twilight Zone*.

Where *Amazing Stories* was more family-friendly, similar to Amblin Entertainment's other productions, *The New Twilight Zone* attempted to capture the essence that made the original series enduring. Due to the minor success of the ill-fated feature film, CBS executives had confidence that this revival could prove successful.

They were both right and wrong.

The New Twilight Zone assembled a sharp team of emerging horror and science fiction writers and directors to give the new show a serious sense of style. In place of the famous opening music was a new theme composed by The Grateful Dead and Merl Saunders that sampled Marius Constant's iconic guitar riffs, next to strange diegetic sounds that gave the foreboding—if not a little cheesy—opening credits its creepy atmosphere. In place of Serling's on-screen presence was an off-screen narrator voiced by Charles Aidman, who appeared in two episodes of the original series, "And When the Sky Was Opened" and "Little Girl Lost."

The revival started with a strong one-two punch with "Shatterday" and "A Little Peace and Quiet," both directed by master of horror Wes Craven, a year after *A Nightmare on Elm Street* was released. "Shatterday," adapted from a Harlan Ellison short story, stars Bruce Willis as a man having increasingly panicked conversations with someone claiming to be himself, after accidentally calling his home phone. Worse yet, his alternate has his life together, while his own slowly begins to fall apart. Ellison, a wildly influential genre author in his own right, was hired as a creative consultant for

Jacob Trussell

the series and contributed scripts for three episodes, not including the infamous "Nackles," a Krampus-esque Christmas story about an abusive husband that CBS rejected for being *considerably* unjolly.

Where "Shatterday" sets a brooding, melancholic tone for the '80s revival, "A Little Peace and Quiet" captures a bit more of the original's magical realism. In it, an exasperated housewife (Melinda Dillon) finds a necklace that allows her to stop time whenever she yells at her family to "Shut up!" She's thrilled by this newfound power, as it gives her a much-needed break from her children and equally childish husband. One night after taking a quiet bath, she hears on the radio that a nuclear missile strike is imminent. With the family huddled together waiting for the blast, she yells "Shut up!" one final time. As a dead calm sets into the night, she wanders into a busy city street, frozen in motion, while a cruise missile hovers in place above. She's stuck in limbo, and we're left to wonder what happens next—two stomach-sinking qualities that are perfectly attuned for *The Twilight Zone*.

The show found a tentpole creative voice in Rockne S. O'Bannon who, as writer, story editor, and consultant would contribute to 27 of the series 65 episodes. His first script "Wordplay" is one of the most accomplished stories of the revival. With his child in the hospital, a man slowly loses the ability to communicate as everyone around him begins speaking in gibberish. It's a clever concept bolstered by a strong performance from Robert Klein that is genuinely imaginative, with a weird quality similar to an original series episode like "Person, or Persons Unknown" (S3E27).

O'Bannon also wrote an adaptation of "The After Hours," swapping the Macy's style department store for a posh mall, as well as "The Shadow Man," where a bullied boy takes advantage of the monster under his bed. That episode was directed by Joe Dante, his second trip to *The Twilight Zone* after contributing to the feature film. In one of his final stories "Personal Demons," about an author pursued by invisible creatures, O'Bannon gives the central character (Martin Balsam) his own name, so when the end credits roll and reveal him to be the episode's writer it gives it a sly, meta twist.

Over the first two seasons there's no shortage of incredibly fun episodes, like "Chameleon" which finds Terry O'Quinn attempting to reason with a nuclear-armed intelligent lifeform brought to Earth after a spacewalk. Piper Laurie and Andre Gower regret picking up Roberts Blossom in "The Burning Man," but he's nothing compared to the ancient evil that awaits them in this adaptation of a Ray Bradbury story. The '80s Spielberg vibe is alive and well in "Monsters!" about a young boy (Oliver Robins, *Poltergeist*) who believes his neighbor is actually a vampire. Charles Beaumont's "Shadow Play" is revisited in an update that offers more chilling details to the false realities of Adam Grant (Peter Coyote). And if you're craving the Lovecraftian twists of Serling's latter work, "The Beacon" and "Need to Know" are great representations of Americana folk horror about tiny insular communities harboring terrible secrets. Bonus points to the latter episode for co-starring future Academy Award winner Frances McDormand!

The New Twilight Zone brought back original series writers alongside new titans of the genre. "Gramma," Harlan Ellison's adaptation of a Stephen King short story, is an atmospheric campfire tale about a young boy who has become deathly afraid of his grandmother, believing she's turned into a witch. Bradford May's slick cinematography makes "Gramma" look and feel like an incredibly dark episode of Spielberg's *Amazing Stories*. Richard Matheson was pulled back into the *Zone* with his short story turned script "Button, Button" where a desperate couple are faced with a moral dilemma when given the option of receiving $200,000 by pressing a button that will kill someone. Matheson's story would later be adapted by Richard Kelly (*Donnie Darko*) as *The Box*, starring Frank Langella, Cameron Diaz and James Marsden. Kelly plows through Matheson's ambiguity by making the purveyors of his box omniscient extraterrestrials. Despite a profound lack of subtlety—that feels very on-brand for *Twilight Zone*—Matheson's core story still manages to get under your skin.

The revival also understood the macabre streak of fun the original series had, like the monster mash of "The Elevator" where a pair of brothers run across the genetic mutations responsible for their father's disappearance. With "A Small Talent for War," an omnipresent alien (John Glover) grants Earthlings 24 hours to prove themselves worthy of being part of the universe or face total annihilation. When the nations of the world come together and prove peace is possible, the alien laughs in their faces. They didn't want

Earth to find peace, they wanted humans to prove themselves as warriors, and we just failed miserably.

Unfortunately, the series was the victim of poor scheduling and the first few episodes were shifted from a late-night timeslot to earlier in the evening when more families were likely watching. It goes without saying that the cerebral series didn't do well with parents of younger kids who may have just been sitting down to dinner as the show premiered. How do you explain the implications of a nuclear missile crisis in Reagan-era America to a five-year-old?

You don't. You just change the channel.

Fortunately, the show did find a small cult following that allowed it to extend into a third season, produced strictly for syndication purposes. The new narrator Robin Ward couldn't top the forlorn gravel of Aidman, and though the fresh writing staff was talented, including future *Babylon 5* creator J. Michael Straczynsk, it became a more general genre show without the ingenious flare the moniker calls for. Of course there are highlights, like "Something in the Walls," an eerie spin on the short story "The Yellow Wallpaper," and "Special Service" which served as inspiration for the Jim Carrey film *The Truman Show*. Harlan Ellison would take the series out in style with "Crazy as a Soup Sandwich," a campy fantasy about a hoodlum in debt to a demon. What stands out in this episode is its visual flair and mash-up of genres, presaging both the hard-boiled, comic book aesthetic of Tim Burton's *Batman* (1989) and the blending of occult and noir in *Cast a Deadly Spell* (1991).

Ultimately the final year of the 1980s would mark the end of this important era for *The Twilight Zone*. It was the decade where the show truly returned to prominence and introduced a whole new generation to the infinite potentials of Serling's opus.

The Lost Classics

Five years after the first revival ended, a television movie was produced called *Rod Serling's Lost Classics*, hosted by James Earl Jones who had appeared in *The Man* (1972), one of Serling's final projects. *Lost Classics* compiled two unproduced scripts that Carol Serling reportedly found stashed away in a garage at the bottom of a trunk, which frankly sounds like a great setup to an episode of *The Twilight Zone*.

The first story "The Theatre" was fleshed out by Richard Matheson and follows Melissa Sanders (Amy Irving) who can't fully commit to her fiancé-doctor James (Gary Cole). After he misses yet another dinner date, Melissa takes herself to the movies for a late-night screening of *Bringing Up Baby,* but instead of the classic Cary Grant and Katharine Hepburn comedy, she's treated to visions of herself. At first she just sees her immediate past, like James apologizing in a clown costume, but when she returns the following night the screen shows premonitions of a future that isn't too bright for Ms. Sanders. It certainly strikes the right tone, but the story lacks the spark that made *The Twilight Zone* feel alive.

The second story, "Where the Dead Are" is stronger, but it isn't *The Twilight Zone.* It may begin and end with Serling-style narration, but what was found in that trunk was likely an unused script for *Night Gallery*. It's rooted more firmly in horror and is evocative of the same gothic melodramas that cropped up on the '70s show. A young surgeon (Patrick Bergin) travels to a shady seaside town in search of answers to a mysterious corpse, only to get wrapped up with a local doctor (Jack Palance) and the town's dark past. Palance's Dr. Wheaton developed a serum that could bring the dead back to life, but once he revived the entire town, they turned on him, cutting off his legs and forcing him to make the serum forever. The story is a hodgepodge of different, albeit interesting motifs that you'd find in H.P. Lovecraft's oeuvre from "The Shadow Over Innsmouth" to "Herbert West: Re-Animator." But like the adaptations on *Night Gallery*, it's stiff and stodgy, even if the idea of a seaside town filled with slowly deteriorating reanimated corpses is decidedly rad. There's nothing offensively bad in this sweeps week TV special, but there's not a whole lot to recommend. File this trip into *The Twilight Zone* under C for "Completists Only."

Twilight Zone in the New Millennium

In 2002, when the United States was still eclipsed in the twilight zone of September 11th, the series was revived yet again. The platform Serling created to tell meaningful stories contextualized to current events was the soapbox that Paramount Pictures' network UPN hoped would help audiences process the nation's collective trauma.

Jacob Trussell

Unfortunately, this revival is hindered by uninspiring stories and uninventive visuals to create a flat, unpleasurable experience. Certain stories, like "Evergreen" and "Homecoming," act more like adult-oriented episodes of *Are You Afraid of the Dark* than anything Serling invented. If you were the right age to appreciate Nickelodeon's mid-90s genre anthology, this criticism isn't necessarily a bad thing.

There are highlights that strike the tonality that we're expecting like "Mr. Motivation," an underdog story in the vein of "Penny for Your Thoughts" (S2E16) where a burnt-out office worker is given a possessed bobblehead (voiced by sportscaster Pat O'Brien) that helps him fight back against his aggro boss (Christopher McDonald). There's a compelling picture of helicopter parenting in "It's Still a Good Life," a sequel to the original "It's a Good Life" (S3E8), which finds Anthony Fremont the father of his own budding psychic-demigod. There are other remakes and elaborations on classic episodes, but by bringing back original cast members Billy Mumy and Cloris Leachman, a direct tether is created to Serling's original masterpiece.

In "Memphis," an unlucky man with terminal brain cancer is hit by a car and wakes up in civil rights-era Georgia, the day before Martin Luther King Jr.'s assassination. It's a fine episode made memorable by Eriq La Salle, who is given auteur reigns to write, direct and star. "The Collection" is a killer toy riff with pop star Jessica Simpson as a psych student babysitting a troubled girl with a massive doll collection. Naturally, those Barbies are going to wreak some havoc! Like Talky Tina, they only give the impression of movement, even though it's implied that they run around off-screen. These budget constraints encapsulate a quality the series could never overcome; it doesn't look or feel stylistically advantageous. There is an introspective twist in "The Collection," but it gets lost under a blanket of mediocrity. The same can be said for "Sunrise" where a group of college students believe they snuffed out the sun after accidentally knocking over an ancient relic, or "The Placebo Effect" where a man's (Jeffrey Combs, *Re-Animator*) hypochondria begins manifesting itself in deadly, ridiculous ways.

The second revival's stylistic shortcomings were used in its favor for "How Much Do You Love Your Kid" about a woman forced into a reality competition by a slimy TV host (Wayne Knight, *Seinfeld*) after her son is kidnapped. The host forces the mom to find clues and solve riddles before time runs out to save her son, not to mention win a hefty cash prize. The episode is a clever lampoon of the reality television craze of the early 2000s, but it fundamentally lacks the classic show's tone and perspective. Unfortunately, this is a sentiment that extends into the third revival of *The Twilight Zone* that premiered in 2019.

Twilight Zone Returns

"Social Thriller" is how Jordan Peele describes his 2017 Academy Award winning film *Get Out*, an epithet I'm sure Rod Serling would have *loved* because it could easily be prescribed to his own work. Executives at CBS must have thought so as well, because there was no clearer choice than Peele to take over Serling's role in a modern iteration of the *Twilight Zone*.

Despite his own auteur status, Peele isn't attempting to give the show his singular voice like Serling did. Instead he assembled a team of fresh creatives to give each episode it's own unique flavor, not to mention finally injecting the show with a shot of diversity behind the camera with directors like Ana Lily Amirpour, J.D. Dillard, and Cristina Choe helming multiple episodes.

With this revolving door of different creators each week, the show unfortunately is more inconsistent than before. While an episode like "Replay" can make a poignant, if on the nose, statement on race, other episodes like "Not All Men" or "Point of Origin" let their obviousness hang on their sleeves, preaching to the choir about misogyny and immigration. This is a whole new level of conspicuousness apart from the shows typical unsubtly. A standout is "Six Degrees of Freedom" where a group of astronauts are forced to make an emergency launch to escape an impending nuclear attack. The gimmicky ending aside, it's a character driven episode buoyed by strong performances from DeWanda Wise, Jessica Williams, and Jefferson White with an urgency similar to an original series episode like "People Are Alike All Over" (S1E25).

The first two revivals directly adapted classics like "The After Hours" and "Eye of the Beholder," but not here. Instead Peele and company have taken general conceits and imagery from past episodes and created wholly new stories around them like "Nightmare at 30,000 Feet" which switches the gremlin on the wing of a plane with a true crime podcast detailing the disappearance of the flight Adam Scott is on.

"A Traveler" riffs on the premise of "Will The Real Martian Please Stand Up?" (S2E28) while "The Wunderkind" uses "It's a Good Life" as a launching pad to remind us why children shouldn't be in politics. Easter eggs to the original series are baked into each episode, like the Whipple Company from "The Brain Center at Whipple's" (S5E33) emblazoned on flight suits or the devilish mystic seer in yet another roadside diner. The Season One finale "Blurryman" takes this idea to the max by making the original series central to the plot about a writer on the *Twilight Zone* revival finding herself written into an episode of the *Twilight Zone* revival. She runs from the titular figure—who is actually Rod Serling—through a back lot of vacant sets, an idea taken from the original inspiration for the *Twilight Zone* pilot.

An issue I have with the 2019 series is the same issue that Rod Serling took with the fourth season of the original show: hour-long episodes of *The Twilight Zone* just don't work as well as the half-hour format. The 25-minute length of the first three seasons didn't leave us much time to find the holes invariably in each plot, but in the 45 minute format we can feel the stories stretch their narrative devices thin. The longer episodes of this revival drag out in a format more fitting of *Black Mirror* than *The Twilight Zone*.

The second season better understood the power of the half-hour and cut some episodes closer to the 25-minute sweet spot like "A Small Town." Evocative of the original series, Tananarive Due and Steven Barnes' tale about a handyman repairing his withering town through the help of a magical diorama of its main street captures that sad, sweet quality of classic episodes like "I Sing the Body Electric" (S3E35).

Even though most of this season still runs long, it does a better job of embodying the tenants of both the original and even the '85 revival. In "The Who of You," a depressed bachelor (Jimmi Simpson) begins having telepathic conversations with the woman of his dreams, who may be luring him into a trap to escape her own nightmare. "You May Also Like" marks the return of the alien race the Kanamits from "To Serve Man" (S3E24) in a story about a mother's fracturing reality in a dystopian society.

The best episodes though feel more recycled from the creator's

An Unofficial Journey Into The Twilight Zone

unrealized projects than anything written specifically for the series. In "8" directors Justin Benson and Aaron Moorhead (*Spring*), with writer Glen Morgan (*The X-Files*), give us a very spooky look at the inevitable octopus uprising. It's top-notch speculative fiction that's perfectly suited for a different anthology show. The same can be said for Tayarisha Poe's (*Selah and the Spades*) "Among the Untrodden," an ingenious and haunting coming of age story about a young woman developing psychokinetic powers. Poe's voice rings strong and loud, but it just isn't echoed in *The Twilight Zone*. This season features stronger storytelling than the first, but as a whole it fails to capture the powerful simplicity behind Serling's parables.

If you crunch the numbers, since 1985 we've had a revival of the series effectively every 15 years, which means regardless of the moderate success of the most recent redux, we'll likely see another iteration in the 2030s and then again in the 2050s with the shows 100th anniversary. The staying power of what Rod Serling created means that regardless of how a new version is received, it won't be a death knell for the show. It's a perpetual machine now, forever living beyond the confines of a half-hour of television.

The Twilight Zone is out there. It exists in the blank spaces between each word, the vast expanse of the natural world, and the farthest corners of our mind. To find it, all we have to do is look. And maybe grab the remote.

Films from the Fifth Dimension

Since 1983, attempts at bringing the series back to the big screen have failed to materialize. At one point, actor Leonardo DiCaprio was set to produce a version that would see updates of classic episodes akin to the first film. There have been several quasi-official adaptations of individual episodes, as well as tangential Serling stories fleshed out into feature length films. In the late '90s a pair of his teleplays were adapted for television, *In The Presence of Mine Enemies* (originally premiered on *Playhouse 90*) and *A Town Has Turned to Dust* (also *Playhouse 90*). The latter film, directed by arthouse filmmaker Rob Nilsson, was given a sci-fi makeover swapping the setting from a bordertown at the turn of the century to a dystopic industrial wasteland in the aftermath of a nuclear war.

Prior to the most recent revival, directors Matt Reeves (*Cloverfield*) and Joseph Kosinski (*Tron: Legacy*) had both been attached to helm a new adaptation of the series that's subsequently been sent to development hell. Assuredly, out there in the ether, another *Twilight Zone* film is being written. Will it ever be released is another question entirely.

Whether directly or indirectly, Serling's work has served as inspiration for innumerable movies over the last six decades. Because the series was so ahead of its time, there's an argument to be made that you could point to any genre film since 1964 and find traces of *The Twilight Zone*, from the social satire at the heart of *Robocop* to the magical realism of *Last Action Hero*. These are films that, on paper, you wouldn't connect to the show, but when you look closer and see the criticisms against corporations or a simple story about a lonely child escaping into a fantasy word, you recognize shades of classics like "The Brain Center at Whipples" or "The Bewitchin' Pool."

Until we see another official *Twilight Zone* film, all we have are movies like these, both past and present, that were influenced or inspired by the series. These films—including related work from some of the series best screenwriters—will help deepen your appreciation of Rod Serling and enhance your experience binging his original classic!

The Intruder (1962)

Based on a novel by Charles Beaumont and directed by legendary cult filmmaker Roger Corman, *The Intruder* is about a slick stranger (William Shatner) who stokes a small town's racial animus towards the desegregation of a high school. Alongside his writing duties, Beaumont also appears in the film with fellow *Twilight Zone* writer George Clayton Johnson and Shatner, whose chilling performance feels like an elaboration on the character he played in Serling's teleplay "A Town Has Turned to Dust." This is also an important film as it was one of the first to deal directly with racism amidst the desegregation of schools in the south.

Logan's Run (1976)

From the novel written by George Clayton Johnson, this film bears a remarkable similarity to the rejected pilot for *The Twilight Zone*, "The Happy Place," as both follow a society who euthanize its population at a specific age. In the pilot it was 60, but Johnson cuts that number in half, offering even more immediacy for its young protagonists.

Planet of the Apes (1978)

One of the most popular science fiction movies of all time also has one of the most iconic images in all of motion picture history, and that's thanks to the ingenious mind of Rod Serling who thought, "They'll never guess this all takes place on Earth!"

Altered States (1981)

From Rod Serling's *Playhouse 90* contemporary Paddy Chayefsky, *Altered States* follows a scientist who uses psychotropic drugs and sensory deprivation tanks to find the origin of human existence. Chayefsky's ideas are way, *way* out there, but it's director Ken Russell's (*The Devils*) unflinching aesthetic that makes the film a must-see.

Poltergeist (1982)

About a family searching for their lost daughter in a netherworld that exists in their suburban house, *Poltergeist* is the be-all-end-all haunted house movie. This collision of grind-arthouse director Tobe Hooper and genre powerhouse Steven Spielberg is a direct elaboration of Richard Matheson's "Little Girl Lost" (S3E26).

The Brother from Another Planet (1984)

John Sayles (*The Howling*) directs Joe Morton (*Terminator 2*) as the titular alien, pursued by men in black, who crashes on Earth and finds brotherhood in 1980s Harlem. The allegory on immigration and race would have been right in Rod Serling's wheelhouse.

The Fly (1986)

David Cronenberg's remake of the classic B-film acts in a similar fashion to "The Long Morrow" (S5E15), which poses a complex, moving love story against the backdrop of hard science fiction. Except in Cronenberg's case, his sci-fi is a bit more of an ooey gooey monster mash.

Alien Nation (1988)

A social allegory on immigration and bigotry in the 1980s, this film from *The New Twilight Zone* writer Rockne S. O'Bannon sees cop James Caan team up with alien Mandy Patinkin to take down intergalactic drug lord Terrence Stamp. It's by the numbers, but with a social relevance at home in the *Zone*.

They Live (1988)

This sci-fi actioner from John Carpenter finds "Rowdy" Roddy Piper and Keith David fighting back against a covert alien invasion with the help of some enhanced sunglasses. It's a biting black comedy and political satire that feels like a discarded plot from the 1985 revival.

Brain Dead (1990)

In the late 1980s, producer Julie Corman tasked her production interns to scour rejected scripts from the last few decades. The script they chose, about a neurologist slowly losing his mind, was written by Charles Beaumont. What's remarkable is that, if it had been produced when it was initially written, *Brain Dead* would have proven wildly influential for future psychological thrillers from *Gothika* (2003) to *Shutter Island* (2010.)

12 Monkeys (1995)

Based on the influential short film *La Jetée* (1962), Terry Gilliam's *12 Monkeys* tells the story of a prisoner from a dystopian society who's sent back in time to stop a deadly virus from decimating the world, only to get tangled in his own chronology. It's the same kind of timey-wimey, apocalyptic fear that pulsated through Serling's nuclear conscious writing.

Cube (1997)

When a group of people wake up in an enclosed cube, they are forced to move through a series of elaborate booby-trapped rooms in the hope of finding an exit. Canadian director Vincenzo Natali's film offers the kind of existential crisis we crave from episodes like "Five Characters in Search of an Exit" (S3E14).

Pleasantville (1998)

Leaning towards the more saccharine side of the *Zone* sandbox, this sweet film finds a diehard fan of classic television sucked into a monochrome world to help the town bring color to their life. It's a meditation on intolerance in small communities while swimming in the same nostalgic pool as classic *Zone* episodes like "Walking Distance" (S1E5).

The Truman Show (1998)

Rumored to have been inspired directly by "Surprise Service" from the 1985 series, this film finds Jim Carrey slowly coming to terms with the fact that his entire life has been played before a live television audience.

Final Destination (2000)

Glen Morgan recycled an unused script for *The X-Files* into this film about a group of teens who narrowly escape a fatal plane crash, only to find death coming for them around every corner. The setup to the film is remarkably similar to the ending of the original series episode "Twenty-Two."

Donnie Darko (2001)

It would take an entirely separate book to properly make the full comparison, but the similarities between Richard Kelly's debut film about a young boy plagued with horrifying visions, and Season Five's "Ring-a-Ding Girl" (S5E13) are too uncanny to discount!

The Man from Earth (2007)

On the eve of his retirement, a man brings together his friends and reveals his great secret: he's been alive for 14,000 years, and holds the key to many of life's mysteries. This is the final, posthumous script from Jerome Bixby, writer of the original short story for "It's a Good Life."

The Box (2009)

Going above and beyond *The New Twilight Zone*'s adaptation of Richard Matheson's short story "Button, Button," this film finds Frank Langella and his mysterious box as part of a larger alien conspiracy. While not successful in its initial release, the film has found a cult following for its brazen artistic choices taken by director Richard Kelly.

Moon (2009)
A miner (Sam Rockwell) stationed on a distant planet has his world turned upside down when he uncovers a shuttle with a copycat version of himself. Director Duncan Jones has created a captivating, existential sci-fi story that calls to mind some of Serling and Matheson's best space-set allegories.

Kill List (2011)
Like the greatest Charles Beaumont story that he never wrote, this film from Ben Wheatley is a creeping slow burn about a hit man tasked with one final job that sets the stage for a diversion straight into folk horror. This is the brutal brush with bleakness that we'd expect from the occult writing of Beaumont.

Real Steel (2011)
If you wanted to see what a Hollywood version of Richard Matheson's classic "Steel" (S5E2) would look, then here you go! Not especially memorable by any means, the film still ties together fun, emotional storytelling with a magnetic lead performance from the ever-reliable Hugh Jackman.

The One I Love (2014)
A young couple trying to rekindle their romance take a retreat to an opulent estate, where they meet identical versions of themselves who seem to have a vested interest in keeping them apart. The inventive twists from writer Justin Lader and director Charlie McDowell would have felt right at home on the original series' more romantically-tinged episodes.

The Similars (2015)
This low budget riff on one of the classic series' most famous episodes finds a group of travelers stuck in a bus station during a storm on their way to Mexico City. One by one, their faces slowly begin to transform until they look identical to each other. Is this being

caused by the unnatural, torrential storm raging outside, or is it because of a young boy and his divine illness?

Arrival (2016)

Denis Villeneueve (*Blade Runner 2049*) didn't expressly direct a remake of "To Serve Man," but this film about a team of linguists looking to translate an alien language takes the general conceit of the classic episode and makes it alarmingly realistic. It was rightfully nominated for numerous Academy Awards, including Best Picture, Director, and Adapted Screenplay.

Colossal (2016)

From Mexican filmmaker Nacho Vigalondo, alcoholic Anne Hathaway finds her subconscious connected to a gigantic alien anytime she visits a local playground. Like Serling did in the early 1960s, this film uses alcoholism as a way to make a comment on the need to take ownership for your mental health, especially now that it's acceptable to speak about our shared struggles.

Get Out (2017)

Jordan Peele's triumphant debut about a centuries old conspiracy involving hypnotism and brain transplants revolves around a Black man (Daniel Kaluuya) visiting his white girlfriend's wealthy family at their palatial, secluded estate. What I wouldn't give to hear Serling's thoughts on this one.

Sorry to Bother You (2018)

Set in a dystopic capitalist society, a Black man (Lakeith Stanfield) climbs the ranks of a call center when he adopts the voice of a white man (David Cross), only to uncover a vast conspiracy to control the masses through genetic mutation. Again, what I wouldn't give to be a fly on the wall of the afterlife while Serling watches this.

The Vast of Night (2020)

The most recent film on this list is also the most faithful adaptation of a *Twilight Zone* script that never was. A radio DJ and a switchboard operator stumble upon a mysterious sound beamed across their small Nevada town that points towards a government

Jacob Trussell

cover up and the possible existence of UFOs. Writer/director Andrew Patterson manages to capture the mysterious fun of the original series, while also tipping his hat to Serling's own life. Played by Jake Horowitz, DJ Everett Sloan—itself a reference to the actor who appeared in *Patterns* and "The Fever" (S1E17)—feels like a proxy for a young Rod Serling, smooth talking and smart with a charm that excites every woman he meets.

Appendix

The following is a list of books and biographies that I've used as reference for this guide and will provide invaluable insight as you further explore *The Twilight Zone*.

Books

The Twilight Zone Companion
By Marc Scott Zicree

Serling: The Rise and Twilight of Television's Last Angry Man
By Gordon F. Sander

Rod Serling: His Life, Work, and Imagination
By Nicholas Parisi

As I Knew Him: My Father, Rod Serling
By Anne Serling

The Twilight Zone and Philosophy: A Dangerous Dimension to Visit
Edited by Heather L Rivera and Alexander E. Hooke

Dimensions Behind the Twilight Zone
By Stewart T. Stanyard

Visions from The Twilight Zone
By Arlen Schumer

The Twilight Zone: Unlocking the Door to a Television Classic
By Martin Grams Jr.

Websites, Blogs, Related Articles

The Rod Serling Memorial Foundation
RodSerling.com

The Twilight Zone Archives
TwilightZone.org

The Twilight Zone Vortex
http://twilightzonevortex.blogspot.com/

"The Twilight Zone Marathon: A History of a Holiday Tradition"
https://www.denofgeek.com/tv/the-twilight-zone-marathon-a-history-of-a-holiday-tradition/

"KTLA's 'Twilight' Tradition ... and Other Southland Marathons"
https://www.latimes.com/archives/la-xpm-1991-06-30-tv-2174-story.html

"Netflix Finds Plenty of Binging, but Little Guilt"
https://money.cnn.com/2013/12/13/technology/netflix-binge/index.html

Documentaries and Podcasts

Rod Serling: Submitted for Your Approval
American Masters | PBS

Remembering Rod Serling
Fathom Events | A 60th Anniversary Celebration

The Twilight Zone Podcast
http://thetwilightzonepodcast.com/

The Fifth Dimension: A Twilight Zone Podcast
https://consequenceofsound.net/thefifthdimension/

About the Author

Jacob Trussell is a writer and actor based in New York City. His editorial work has been featured on the BBC, Rue Morgue magazine, Film School Rejects and One Perfect Shot. As an actor, he's worked in New York and regional theatre, as well as appearing in short films and commercials. For updates on new work, scary movies, and pictures of his cat, follow Jacob on Twitter @JE_TRUSSELL.

Other Riverdale Avenue Books You Might Like

The Binge Watcher's Guide to Doctor Who:
A History of the Doctor Who and the First Female Doctor
By Mackenzie Flohr

The Binge Watcher's Guide to the Films of Harry Potter
An Unauthorized Guide
By Cecilia Tan

The Binge Watcher's Guide to The Handmaid's Tale
An Unofficial Companion
By Jamie K. Schmidt

The Binge Watcher's Guide to Riverdale:
An Unofficial Companion
By Melissa Ford Lucken

The Binge Watcher's Guide to The Black Mirror:
An Unofficial Companion
By Marc T. Polite

CPSIA information can be obtained
at www.ICGtesting.com
Printed in the USA
BVHW042323250821
615174BV00007B/142

9 781626 015845